Caroline Harvey is the pseud... Trollope, the award-winning... highly acclaimed contempor... *Village Affair*, *A Passionate Man*, *The Rector's Wife*, *The Men and the Girls*, *A Spanish Lover*, *The Best of Friends* and *Next of Kin*, are all published under the Black Swan imprint. As Caroline Harvey she has written several historical novels including *Legacy of Love*, *A Second Legacy*, *Parson Harding's Daughter*, *The Steps of the Sun*, *Leaves from the Valley* and *The Brass Dolphin*, which are all published by Corgi Books.

She was born and lives in Gloucestershire where she now lives with her husband, the playwright Ian Curteis. Joanna Trollope was appointed OBE in the 1996 Queen's Birthday Honours List.

Also by Caroline Harvey

A SECOND LEGACY
PARSON HARDING'S DAUGHTER
THE STEPS OF THE SUN
LEAVES FROM THE VALLEY
THE BRASS DOLPHIN

and published by Corgi Books

By Joanna Trollope

THE CHOIR
A VILLAGE AFFAIR
A PASSIONATE MAN
THE RECTOR'S WIFE
THE MEN AND THE GIRLS
A SPANISH LOVER
THE BEST OF FRIENDS
NEXT OF KIN

and published by Black Swan

LEGACY
OF LOVE

Caroline Harvey

CORGI BOOKS

LEGACY OF LOVE
A CORGI BOOK : 0 552 13872 X

Charlotte and *Alexandra* first published in Great Britain in 1980 by
Sundial Publications Limited; *Cara* first published in Great Britain in
1983 by Octopus Books Limited

This edition first published in Great Britain by Octopus Books Limited

PRINTING HISTORY
Octopus edition published 1983
Corgi edition published 1992
Corgi edition reprinted 1995
Corgi edition reprinted 1997
Corgi edition reprinted 1998

This book is set in 10/11pt Sabon by
Falcon Typographic Art Ltd, Fife, Scotland

Corgi Books are published by Transworld Publishers Ltd,
61–63 Uxbridge Road, London W5 5SA,
in Australia by Transworld Publishers (Australia) Pty Ltd,
15–25 Helles Avenue, Moorebank, NSW 2170
and in New Zealand by Transworld Publishers (NZ) Ltd,
3 William Pickering Drive, Albany, Auckland.

Printed and bound in Great Britain by
Cox & Wyman Ltd, Reading, Berkshire.

Contents

Charlotte

NOTE

The British Resident in Kabul in 1841 was Sir Alexander Burnes, murdered by Afghan rebels in November of that year. Therefore the substitution of Alexander Bewick as Resident is entirely fictitious.

CHAPTER ONE

'Praise the Lord!' Charlotte said, 'George is coming tomorrow,' and she threw the letter so that it whirled about the room like a seagull and then came to rest in the log basket.

Mamma affected not to notice. She was eating toast – indeed we were all three eating toast – and the morning sun was slanting into our little parlour and shining on the Bristolware teapot and the posy of primroses and the butter on a green glass plate.

Charlotte leaned forward.

'Tomorrow, Mamma! He wants to take us to ride in the Park. And he is bringing a friend whom he declares you will find irreproachable.'

Mamma glanced at the log basket. I knew she was in a dilemma. Like me, she could never resist Charlotte's high spirits and unlike me, she could never wholly trust her only nephew, our cousin George. I suppose she had to be careful, over-careful perhaps, bringing us up alone, a widow, in Richmond, where everybody peered and pried and respectability was nearer to godliness than cleanliness.

'I am not sure,' she said.

Charlotte drummed with her fingers on the table. Mamma said, 'I do not like you to go out with George. The last time there was talk. He makes you behave so foolishly.'

'That was my fault!' I said hastily. 'My hat blew into the pond! Someone had to rescue it—'

Mamma looked at me levelly.

'It was a new hat,' I said lamely.

'Charlotte was wearing a new habit, as I recall. She came home wet to the waist and draggled with weed. It was not an episode to inspire confidence in George.'

9

Mamma went back to her toast. I glanced quickly at Charlotte and saw, to my relief, that she was smiling and easy. She gave me a laughing look, and left her chair to stand by the window and swing the wooden acorn that ended the cord of Mamma's painted sun blind.

It was a pretty room, our parlour. It was prettier than the drawing-room because it had an eastern window and a southern window and the sun poured in all day until after dinner, to such an extent that the wallpaper, a flowery stripe of lettuce green on white, was faded to beige on two walls where the light struck it. The floor was of polished boards, the colour of cider, and in the middle was an Eastern rug my father had brought home from his travels, and our little round table stood in the centre of it. Mamma had hung up white curtains fringed with green, and put all her pretty Chelsea plates above the picture rail. There was a little rosewood sideboard to carry our silver candlesticks, and a wine cooler inlaid with shells made of walnut wood, and above the mantelshelf hung a picture our Mamma had recently done of our young Queen – only twenty and so small and neat – which Charlotte and I had framed in our own embroidery. You could tell which Charlotte's stitches were, half as many and twice as large as mine, but somehow twice as vigorous and important as well.

'You will send a note back to George,' Mamma said, laying down her knife with precision, 'and tell him that he and his friend are most welcome to dine with us tomorrow. But there will be no riding.'

Charlotte swung round and the wooden acorn flew about wildly and cracked against the window.

'Please, Mamma!'

'Charlotte, you are not a child, you are a young woman now. You cannot be wilful and careless of opinion any longer. Quite apart from that, it is hardly kind to plague me.'

Charlotte came and knelt by her chair. The sun caught her hair, her curious beautiful dark red hair, the colour

10

of a cornelian, and made it glow like wine. She put her hands on Mamma's arm.

'I do try not to be wilful. I try harder than you know. And I love our life here, our quiet little life, just you and me and Emily. I don't mean to plague you. But I do sometimes long for something wild and free and – and dangerous. Surely to ride with George and an irreproachable friend is not so very dreadful a way to appease that longing?'

Mamma bent and kissed her forehead, and then shook off her hands.

'No riding, Charlotte.'

She rose and moved round the table to the door. She was wearing her pink morning gown banded with brown velvet across the bodice and round the sleeves, and her cheeks were now as pink as her gown. She said, with her hand on the latch.

'At twenty, Charlotte, you should be ashamed to besiege me so. There is the linen cupboard to be done before summer, and Emily, I should be grateful if you would see to the rent in my cream fichu. At least your stitches are small enough.'

I looked about the room, at everything so small and trim and well cared for. When George ate dinner with us there at our little round table, it always seemed to shrink and become the size of a doll's room, fragile and female like we were. When he laughed in our parlour, you could almost feel the walls bulge and buckle at the impact of the noise, and all the furniture became delicate and miniature, as if it were made of matchsticks. He was the only man who came often, the only real, large man. His father came at Christmas of course, and once a year to wish Mamma, his sister, a happy birthday, but he was a small man, delicate like Mamma, and the house stayed quite stable in his presence.

Charlotte went back to swinging the acorn.

'What shall we *do*, Emily?'

'Do?'

'Yes, do. *Do*. I know today we must do the linen and that wretched fichu, but tomorrow, and the next day? And next year, when I am twenty-one and you nearly twenty? And the year after that? It can't all be linen cupboards.' She turned back to me. 'Can it?'

I leaned over my plate.

'What should you like, Charlotte? Should you like to be a King's mistress?'

She looked horrified, but I knew it was not at the idea. When we were small, nine and ten perhaps, we had been taken to George IV's funeral, and an old woman in the crowd had told us that his stays had measured nearly sixty inches round. Then he had been succeeded by ugly William with his plum-coloured face speckled with blemishes, mulberry and meal, so we had never seen a handsome King. It was not the notion of being a mistress that made Charlotte stare at me, simply the notion of sharing the bed of any being as physically monstrous as the kings we knew. Charlotte leaned forward and put her hands on the table.

'Find me the king, Emily!'

I shut my eyes.

'Where shall he be?'

'Anywhere but Richmond!'

I opened them again. Charlotte was still leaning on her hands and her face was alive with interest. She had a beautiful face, full of life, with brilliant eyes like aquamarines and teeth that were the envy of everyone. I said, 'What about the East?'

'The East? A *black* king?'

'Well, a brown one. Covered in jewels, emeralds, and rubies and pearls. Sitting in a tent in the desert drinking sherbet, with elephants to carry you about and barefoot servants with peacock feathers in their turbans.'

Charlotte clapped her hands.

'Bring him here!'

'No,' I said. 'He would feel foolish in Richmond.'

'Oh,' she said in despair, '*Richmond*.'

Richmond was lovely when the nineteenth century began, there is no denying it. The river so close, that beautiful park, the lovely, graceful new houses with their long windows and balconies and gardens full of acacias. There were probably exciting people there too, people who travelled and went often to London and knew people at Court, but we had nothing to do with them. We knew the Rector and his huge family, the Doctor and his, and a great many widows and daughters like ourselves all contriving to seem to be more prosperous than they really were. We were proud of Mamma because she managed it so much better than most.

Charlotte stretched her arms above her head and the blue cotton of her gown cracked at the strain.

'I am so confined!' she said. 'I am penned in like a goose for Christmas. Look at this hateful sleeve, Emily, even it confines me. What a stupid, heartless fashion to have sleeves so tight at the top that one's blood can hardly struggle down. No wonder my hands are so clumsy. Now if I had my Eastern king I could be in lovely flowing robes and gallop about on a camel and never know what a tight sleeve was.'

'You wouldn't,' I said. 'He'd lock you up in his Zenana and you would not gallop anywhere. You would still be a Christmas goose.'

Charlotte sat down in Mamma's place and ran her finger round the fluted rim of the handleless cup before her.

'Does it not worry you, Emily? Do you really not mind living here always, sewing and painting and gardening and always being so good?'

'I should rather do it all with a husband and children, but I do not mind the sewing and painting in itself.'

'But where do you suppose we shall find husbands?'

I said jokingly, 'Oh Charlotte, what about the Rector's eldest?' expecting that she would smile at me at the ludicrousness of that weedlike youth being a fit husband for anyone, but she didn't. She looked back at me with all seriousness.

'It might come to that.'

'*Charlotte.*'

'Don't Charlotte me, like Mamma. It might. We hardly meet anyone, Emily, anyone at all.'

'George would marry you. I think he's admired you always. Should you hate to marry George?'

'I shouldn't hate it, but quite frankly I should be better amused here at home with you in the long run. George is perfect for short bursts of excitement, but I don't think he could sustain a steady life of it. And I am much fonder of you than I am of George. In fact, if it wasn't for you, Emily, I think I should go mad.'

I blushed with pleasure. I could not help it.

'I will try and persuade Mamma about the riding,' I said.

She reached out the hand that had been playing with the cup, and squeezed mine.

'You have spoilt me, Emily. You are much too kind. I don't think there's a man on earth would be so good to me.'

'I think,' I said, getting up, 'that if half the men on earth knew you were here, they would be fighting like mad things for the privilege of being good to you.'

The cream fichu was mended before George's arrival the next day, and all the hateful linen, as Charlotte called it, was sorted and smoothed. We put daffodils in the drawing-room and the last snowdrops in the parlour and the whole house looked about as unsuitable for a young man's arrival as it possibly could do. We had tried to persuade Mamma to a fillet of beef, but she was convinced that there was something indelicate about red meat, so a pair of chickens were roasting in the kitchen and the air was full of the clove and onion scent of bread sauce.

'I wish we had some wine,' Charlotte said, surveying

the white table, and the green and white flowers, and our spoons and two-pronged forks polished like looking-glass. 'The table looks so – so *ladylike*.'

'There's some port,' I said. We both looked at the decanter and observed the two inches left from Christmas, that remained. Charlotte sighed.

'Poor friend,' she said, 'I doubt he'll come again.'

George was not punctual. He had been asked for two o'clock, and came nearer three, and Mamma was in despair over the chickens. We all fidgeted about the drawing-room, Charlotte banging on the harpsichord until Mamma asked her to stop because of her head, and we ran back and forth to the kitchen while the chickens shrank and the potatoes disintegrated.

'If he were not my brother's son,' Mamma said, 'I should not tolerate such manners. Five more minutes and we shall eat in any case. I cannot afford to waste good food.'

When he marched in at last, of course she was all smiles. She was wearing her flounced lavender gown, and he held her at arm's length and said it was a downright privilege to have such a pretty aunt. He seemed larger than ever, and his hair more riotously curly. He kissed Charlotte with a great deal of enthusiasm and me with rather less, then he spun round and pulled into our little drawing-room a good-looking fair young man who seemed somewhat dismayed at the combination of George's energy and our frailty. He was tall too, but slender and not solid, like George, and he wore uniform.

'A soldier!' Charlotte said in delight.

George laughed and the young man blushed.

'A soldier indeed, fair cousin! Aunt Maria, may I present Captain Hugh Connell? Hugh, these are my pretty cousins, Charlotte and Emily over there, in grey. I'm a lucky dog, ain't I, to have such deuced good-looking relations?'

Captain Hugh Connell turned to Mamma and bowed

so elegantly that she clearly had no fear that he would knock something over.

'Not only good-looking, ma'am, but hospitable.'

This put Mamma in a flutter because of the spoiled chickens. She took him by his scarlet sleeve and began a flurry of explanations, and Charlotte began to scold George for his lateness which he clearly relished. He stood and gazed down at her like a great pleased dog. I just watched them, and I saw Mamma begin to draw Hugh Connell towards the parlour, and as he went he glanced over his shoulder at Charlotte and his eyes had just the same dog-like look in them as George's, but less assured.

In its curious way, the dinner was a success. The chickens were a little dry, but the fish was good, and Mamma had made a plum tart from the bottled fruit of our old tree by the front gate. At the beginning of dinner, when Mamma poured water into Hugh Connell's glass, he showed no surprise, but George jumped up and rushed out of the room shouting for his groom (who was flirting in the kitchen with our little maid) and came back with three bottles of claret.

'Oh!' said Charlotte, and her face lit up. 'Wine!'

Mamma looked at her with the utmost disapproval.

'It was a sensible thought, George,' she said, 'but you know Charlotte and Emily only ever take a little Madeira.'

'Nonsense!' George cried. 'We won't touch a drop unless you all do!'

'Please, Mamma!' Charlotte said. 'We long to try!'

'Just a little,' I pleaded, though I did not much care for it.

'It is most unsuitable,' Mamma said firmly.

Hugh Connell looked at Charlotte, and then he turned to Mamma. 'Perhaps they may try a little mixed with water? I agree entirely that it is too strong on its own, but would you object if I were to dilute a glass for each of them?'

Mamma beamed upon him and consented. He ate two helpings of plum tart and said it was excellent, and he praised the room and said how charming her taste was.

'Is it not too small for you?' Charlotte said. She had picked all the plums out of her tart and left the pastry as she always did and I prayed Mamma would not notice.

'Small?'

'The house always seems to shrink when George comes in and he is eternally breaking something. I wondered if you felt as he clearly does.'

Hugh Connell looked at her gravely.

'I should hate to break anything in so charming a dwelling.'

'Ah!' George said, replete with food and nearly two bottles of his three, 'Hugh ain't a clumsy bear like me. He's had much more polish, moved in much better circles altogether, haven't you, eh?'

Hugh looked at him reprovingly.

'Wider rather than better, I should say.'

Mamma was looking at Charlotte's plate, so I leaned forward and said, 'Wider?' with as much emphasis as I could muster.

'I should be in India,' Hugh Connell said. 'I was posted to the North-West frontier, to Afghanistan, two years ago, but my father was dying and asked me to come home. I had been four years in India. I go back this summer, to Kabul. We are an occupying force.'

'Kabul!' Charlotte breathed.

Mamma asked a little timidly, 'Where is Kabul?'

'In the western Himalayas, my dear aunt. It is the capital of Afghanistan, which is a very turbulent place full of extremely troublesome tribesmen.'

Mamma's eyes strayed again to the uneaten pastry on Charlotte's plate. I said quickly, leaning forward in a pretence of eagerness, 'Then why, if it is so troublesome, do we bother with it?'

Across the table, George and Hugh smiled at each other in male complicity.

'Miss Emily,' Hugh Connell said with careful politeness, 'we must keep Afghanistan neutral. If we do not, the Russians will swoop down from the north through Afghanistan and fall upon India. If we are to safeguard India, we must have Afghanistan as a buffer, we must have an Amir upon the throne in Kabul who is well-disposed towards us.' He waited a moment to see if I had assimilated his information, so I smiled helpfully at him and nodded, and he turned away and said to Charlotte, 'Kabul is a wretched place I am told. The Afghans are a savage and violent people.'

Charlotte smiled at him. 'Wonderful!' she said.

Mamma cleared her throat repressively.

'Charlotte's head is full of romantic notions, I fear,' she said. 'Our life is very quiet, you see, very simple, and Charlotte thinks she craves adventure.'

Charlotte said directly to Hugh Connell, 'I don't think it, I *do*.'

'Charlotte!'

Hugh looked across the table at Charlotte with the same expression, but more confident, that he had worn in the drawing-room.

'I think you would find India very uncomfortable. The Governor General there has his sister with him and I have heard her say that the only place she really cares for is Simla because everywhere else is so unlike England.'

'Then I expect Simla would be the one place I should *not* like.'

'Charlotte!' Mamma said again.

George had noticed the port decanter and had suppressed almost all his disappointment. He scraped his chair back and stood up, just missing knocking the ceiling.

'Now Aunt Maria, I'm to take this pretty pair riding. Don't look governessy at me, aunt, for I've Hugh to keep me in order and I've asked for ponies as quiet as lambs that are used to carry ladies.'

Mamma rose so that she was not at too much of a disadvantage.

'I'm afraid it is out of the question, George. After the last occasion.'

George looked at Charlotte and me and burst out laughing.

'What a scrape, Aunt! Covered in weed like old men of the woods! If Emily will tie her hat on properly we will promise not to go wading, eh?'

'No, George,' Mamma said firmly.

I looked at Charlotte. Her light eyes were fixed on Hugh Connell and full of pleading. He had blushed rosy red once more.

'Forgive me, ma'am,' he said to Mamma, 'but I give you my word no harm shall come to either of them. We cannot be long because it will be dark shortly. Just half an hour.'

Mamma said, 'One should ride in the morning, it is not suitable to ride after dinner.' But her voice was relenting.

Charlotte flew across and kissed her.

'Darling Mamma! Bless you! Half an hour only, I promise you. Come Emily, we must hurry and change.'

She ran out before me and up the narrow staircase, and as I followed her, I heard Mamma say, 'You will look after her, will you not? I do not fear for Emily, she is so sensible, but you will look after Charlotte?' and Hugh Connell replied fervently, 'With my life, ma'am.'

CHAPTER TWO

The rector's wife came next morning accompanied by the two eldest Miss Adams in grey bombazine trimmed with black, and bonnets ornamented with tired black velvet flowers. They were all three gaunt and awkward, and looked as if they lived in some clammy, marshy place, as indeed they did, for the Rectory was as damp as a sponge. They sat down in our drawing-room like a row of grey tombstones amid our daffodils and embroideries.

Mrs Adams unrolled from her shabby muff – 'Dyed rabbit,' Charlotte whispered to me – a parcel carefully wrapped in tissue.

'The Rector's Lenten stole,' she said reverently.

Mamma looked suitably respectful. 'You will observe,' said Mrs Adams, lifting one end of the stole and signalling to her second daughter to do likewise with the opposite end, 'it is quite without ornamentation. I am come to ask, Mrs Brent, if your daughter Emily would accept the honour of embroidering the ends of the stole. It would be, naturally, to the greater glory of God. A gold cross placed centrally at either end, a formal design of leaves and scrolls in gold and violet, that is what is required.'

We all sat awed by the prospect. I had a distinct impression that Charlotte was suppressing something violent because the arm pressed to mine was shaking so.

I said, 'Mrs Adams, I have no experience of *ecclesiastical* embroidery.'

'Perhaps gold primroses would do instead,' Charlotte said, and her voice was tight with restrained laughter. 'You do such pretty primroses. And after all, primroses are appropriate for Lent—'

'Charlotte!' said Mamma. Mrs Adams' presence always made her unsure what to say and anxious for our good behaviour.

Mrs Adams turned her pale cold gaze upon us, and as she did so we heard the familiar bang of the front gate, and then determined footsteps came up the path and someone hammered at the door.

Mamma was instantly apprehensive. She could not leave the room for fear Charlotte might be outrageous and yet she was highly dissatisfied with the way Annie answered the door, smearing her nose with the back of her hand and screwing her apron all about.

'Miss Emily?' Mrs Adams said.

'I should of course be honoured,' I said, 'but I am very doubtful that I am skilled enough.'

Mrs Adams cast her gaze towards the ceiling.

'In the eyes of God—' she began, and then Annie burst into the room without the smallest knock and said, 'It's a gentleman, mum!' with as much amazement as if she had found herself announcing a dinosaur.

Hugh Connell came into the room behind her, still carrying his whip and gloves which she had obviously forgotten to relieve him of. Charlotte sprang up with a cry of pleasure.

'Charlotte!' said Mamma again.

Hugh Connell was looking very handsome. It was a fresh day and his face glowed from riding. He looked at Charlotte with undisguised delight, and then he went over to Mamma and bowed and said that he wished to thank her fervently for the most charming day yesterday and that as he happened to be passing—

'Mrs Adams, this is Captain Hugh Connell, a friend of my nephew George. Captain Connell, Mrs Adams, our Rector's lady, and Miss Adams, and Miss Laetitia Adams.'

They sat like grey rocks and held out their bony hands to him. He did very well, bending over each in turn, so elegant and slender in his uniform.

Miss Laetitia Adams said to him with disapproval, 'We saw you riding yesterday in the Park. With Miss Brent and Miss Emily. You jumped a log,' she added accusingly.

Mamma looked instantly at Charlotte.

'Mamma, I promise *I* did not jump anything. Did I, Emily? Hugh, tell Mamma how decorously I behaved.'

Mrs Adams cleared her throat and brandished the purple stole. Hugh looked at her in some surprise and said to Mamma, 'Indeed she behaved so decorously that I am come to ask if I may take them both riding once more. I have called at the livery stables and both the ponies they rode yesterday are available.'

'Oh, Mamma please—' Charlotte began, her face full of eagerness.

'The matter under discussion,' said Mrs Adams loudly, waving the stole once more, 'is not riding but embroidery.'

Hugh looked thoroughly puzzled.

'Embroidery, ma'am?'

'Emily,' Mamma said. 'Answer Mrs Adams.'

I must have looked as reluctant as I felt for Charlotte said, 'Why cannot Emily do one end only, and someone else the other?'

Mrs Adams ignored her.

'Charlotte,' Mamma said, 'put on your shawl and take Captain Connell out to the garden. The spring flowers are so very pretty.' Then, lest he should think he was being reproved as well as Charlotte, she added, 'And I hope you will stay and dine with us, Captain Connell.'

This was noble of her, for I knew she intended us to eat the scraps of chicken that remained as a fricassee, and one could hardly offer a man a fricassee for the most substantial meal of his day. It seemed only fair to give her time to think over alternatives to this problem in peace, and so when the door had closed behind a jubilant Charlotte and a grateful Hugh, I said to Mrs Adams, 'Even if I did think myself capable ma'am, we are halfway through Lent already—'

'The Rector is nobly resigned to his old stole this present Lent,' Mrs Adams said in the tone of one admiring a great sacrifice.

'Then – then I will try,' I said.

'It is a task that many would regard as an immense – nay, sacred – honour.'

I wanted very much to say that if there was a horde of eager and pious embroideresses that I was depriving by accepting, I should not dream of disappointing them so bitterly. Mrs Adams rolled up the stole again and handed it to Miss Adams, who rose and crossed the room with a stately step and placed the parcel ceremoniously on my lap. I looked at it with distaste.

'I will do my best,' I said.

Mrs Adams seemed to feel that that was the least I could do, for she rose without a further word to me and said to Mamma, 'Riding in itself may be regarded as a healthy occupation if performed moderately. However, to ride without a hat excites comment of the worst kind.'

Mamma went very pink. I said quickly, 'Charlotte's hat blew off in the wind, Mamma. She did not have pins long enough to keep it secure. Captain Connell had to ride some distance to retrieve it.'

I did not add that Charlotte's hat had blown off half a dozen times, and George and Hugh had raced each other to recapture it, nor that when Charlotte's hair came down and flew about, Hugh said that not for the world could she have her hat back. Chasing it was like some Indian sport he knew, called pig-sticking, and the reward of seeing her with her hair down was better than any prize he had gained pig-sticking in India. Charlotte had laughed at him, and snatched her hat back and tied it on her head with her scarf, but she left her hair hanging down her back and the wine-red curls danced about in the wind. We pinned it up again all anyhow at the livery stables and with her hat on properly, Mamma had never noticed how dishevelled it was when we got home.

When Mrs Adams and her daughters had stalked down the path, pausing to remark that they doubted the plum tree would bear heavily this year as it had clearly not been pruned severely enough, Mamma said to me, 'Emily, run and find Charlotte for me.'

I said, 'Oh Mamma, please not more scolding. Nobody saw us but those stuffy Adams'. Charlotte behaved beautifully. She tries so hard to be good and Richmondish. Don't scold again.'

Mamma sat down abruptly in her little spoon-back chair.

'Emily, you are loyal but blind. You must see how

intolerable Charlotte makes life for us here. I build up our reputation brick by brick, slowly and carefully, and then Charlotte goes romping about like a hoyden and destroys everything. It is all very well for her, and for you. You will marry and leave Richmond, but I must stay, and struggle with the ruins of our reputation. Please find her for me.'

I bent and kissed Mamma's forehead and she patted me in an absent way and sighed.

'You are a good girl, Emily. At least you are—'

'Please don't say sensible.'

'Oh,' she said crossly, 'if you only knew how I valued sense. Go and find Charlotte for me, and leave me to worry as to how I shall make a cabbage and two chicken wings into a dinner for a man.'

We kept our shawls hanging in the passage by the garden door, and our bonnets as well. It was such a small house that one often felt the need to run out into the garden, Charlotte most of all. I put my shawl and bonnet on, but I saw Charlotte's bonnet, blond straw with blue ribbons, was still on its peg, so she must have simply thrown on her shawl and gone out bareheaded into the garden. At least nobody could see her, except the six fat Friesian cows in the meadow beyond the fence, and although they would be much interested, being insatiably curious, their opinion would hardly matter.

The garden was just beginning to wake up. The grass was still tawny and rough from the winter, but the daffodils and forsythia were bright against the leafless boughs, and among the tufts on the lawn were blue clumps of hyacinth and crocus. The birds were singing in a hopeful way although the sun was still so pale and weak and the sky was a bleached blue, as if from much washing.

I could not find Charlotte. I went up and down the paths between the hedges which chequered our garden. Charlotte always said the family which planted our garden must have detested one another because they had made the garden full of private nooks to enable them to get away from each other so that it was like an Elizabethan maze. It made lovely sun-traps in summer, full of bees and butterflies, but was rather depressing and forbidding in the winter. I went up and down the hedges until my dress was entirely sodden at the hem, and just when I was wondering what on earth I should say to Mamma, I found them.

They were standing by the garden fence with an absorbed audience of cows. Charlotte had her shawl half over her head so that she looked like a very pretty engraving we had of an Irish peasant girl, and she was gazing up at Hugh with an expression of the deepest interest. He was talking, and gesturing with one hand, while his other hand was in a clenched fist behind his back as if he couldn't trust himself not to seize Charlotte with it.

I trod deliberately upon some sticks.

'Oh Emily!' Charlotte called without the slightest selfconsciousness, 'you cannot imagine what wonderful things Hugh has been telling me of India!'

Hugh looked confused. I said, 'I am so sorry, but Mamma wants you.'

Charlotte looked down at the grass and pushed a twig about with her toe.

'The riding? My hat?'

'I'm afraid so.'

'Those *Adams*,' Charlotte said with venom.

'I *shall* go to your mother,' Hugh said.

We looked at him admiringly. I wished he would smile more often, but smiling or not, he was certainly very good-looking.

'I don't want you to be the whipping boy,' said Charlotte. 'It was my hat and I didn't really try to stop it.'

Hugh looked at her for a moment and said rather thickly that he doubted he could have borne it if she had. Then he bowed to us briefly and went quickly away towards the house.

'Charlotte?'

'Mm.'

'Do you mean to encourage him so much?'

Her face glowed.

'Oh, Emily! He told me such things of India! You cannot believe what things. Elephants and great dusty deserts and rivers as wide as lakes and princes and jewels and palaces of fretted marble and blazing sun and stars at night as big as saucers—'

'And probably snakes and a great many poor, starving, ragged people.'

'Emily,' she said in despair.

I took her arm.

'Be serious, Charlotte. What about Hugh? Not India. *Hugh*.'

'Do you like him, Emily?'

'I think so. I hardly know. I wish he laughed more. But he is very pleasant and polite and kind and Mamma likes him.'

'Exactly,' said Charlotte with relief. 'My feelings exactly.'

'Then you are *not* encouraging him?' I persisted.

'Emily, he may have to do.'

I said, 'Oh Charlotte, think, please think. It is so important.'

She put her arms round me.

'I know it is important. Of course the rest of one's life is important. That is why I cannot spend it in Richmond. Darling Emily, do not look so careworn. Whatever I do, I shall tell you of it and probably take you along too. Now not another word. Be your usual trusting self.'

Then she kissed me and began to hum and I had to be content

During the next week, Hugh dined with us upon four occasions and took us riding twice. Mamma became so used to entertaining him that on the fourth occasion she produced a fillet of beef and an enormous gooseberry

26

pie with as much nonchalance as if she had been feeding young men daily all her life. It was a very successful dinner because Hugh brought Mamma a basket, quite a large basket, entirely filled with the most beautiful freesias. Mamma was so much softened by these that when Hugh proposed taking us riding the next day she smiled benignly upon him and agreed without a murmur.

It rained the next morning so we did not ride. Hugh came early and Charlotte took him into the parlour to sketch him for posterity. She said she would call the drawing *Hero of the Himalayas* because Hugh was going out to Afghanistan. I took up the purple stole and went into the drawing-room with it.

I suppose Mrs Adams had deemed it part of the honour that I should buy the expensive gold thread necessary for the embroidery of the crosses. As they had to be done in satin stitch, they would take a deal of thread. I took up my seat in the window overlooking the front garden, and began to mark out the design with chalk, feeling extremely unChristian at the prospect of both the labour and the expense. When the gate banged, I looked up immediately, glad of any excuse to take my eyes from the purple brocade, and saw that George was coming up the path, and that his man was leading the horses round to the crumbling ruin that had once been our stable.

I went to open the door, for Mamma was in the kitchen with Annie, and I knew they would both be all over flour.

'Are you alone, Emily?' George said.

I nodded and led him into the drawing-room. When the door was closed, I said, 'Charlotte is drawing Hugh and Mamma is making pastry.'

George flung himself into a chair.

'Well, my dear Emily, how does this business go on?'

It was useless to pretend ignorance. I said, as truthfully as I could, 'Oh, I think she likes him well enough.'

George gazed at his boot toes for a moment.

'Emily, he's mad for her. I've known him a year perhaps, ever since he came home from India, and he's such a decorous, self-controlled fellow, and never have I seen him as he is now. Of course,' he added, getting up and going to lean on the mantlepiece, 'it is a bit of a blow to me. If the governor would only come down a trifle more handsomely, I should – But that's neither here nor there.'

'I am sorry, George.'

He smiled at me through the looking-glass above the fire.

'I'll heal, Emily. Charlotte is a habit with me, you know. Hugh asked me last night what sort of chance I thought he had. That's why I'm here. Thought you would know as much as anyone.'

'He means to ask her to marry him?'

George turned round.

'He does.'

'But he has only known her a week!'

'He is absolutely sure. Is Charlotte?'

I began to wander about. It was all going so fast and I felt unsettled.

'She isn't – mad for *him*. She thinks him amiable and kind. Mamma likes him very much.' I stopped. 'Would he take her to India?'

'I imagine so.'

I felt a sudden pain and sat down abruptly on the striped sofa.

'She does chafe at our life here.'

'I know.'

He came to sit by me.

'You see, Emily, Hugh has his pride. He wants Charlotte above everything but he would like her to accept him for reasons of affection, even if not love – yet. He does not want her to accept him for – for other reasons.'

'What other reasons?'

28

'He's deuced wealthy. Perhaps one of the richest men I know.'

My gaze wandered to the freesias.

'His *own* hothouses!'

'That's nothing. There's acres of them. Peaches, nectarines, roses all winter. There's a mansion in Hanover Square and a palace out in Hertfordshire. If Charlotte knew, would that make her better disposed towards him?'

'No. No, I do not think so. She does not mind our lack of money here, only our lack of freedom.'

'Ah,' said George, 'but the one brings the other.'

'Then I suppose it might make a difference. But why is he in the Army? And why in India, why not in one of those smart regiments with tiny waists and huge moustaches?'

'He's a man of honour, Emily dear. He likes to be occupied, he likes the action he sees in India. He says he has all his life when he is too old to ride about in scorching temperatures, to enjoy his money.'

'May I tell Charlotte?'

'Would it help Hugh?'

I considered for a moment.

'I think it would help both of them.'

George got up and stretched.

'Then you had better share a girlish confidence on your pillows tonight.'

Charlotte seemed thoughtful rather than surprised when I told her how rich Hugh was. She was sitting on the edge of our bed braiding her hair for the night, and I was under the covers already with a book, even though Mamma did not like us to read by the light of a single candle.

'Do you love him, Charlotte? Even a little bit?'

'I don't know. I certainly don't love him one hundredth part as much as I love you.'

I was shocked.

'Charlotte! One shouldn't begin to compare the love one feels for a sister with the love one feels for a husband!'

'Why not?' She leaned across the bed. 'And what do you know of the love one feels for a husband in any case?'

I blushed.

'I know nothing. I'm aware of that.'

Charlotte tweaked my copy of *Evelina* out of my hands.

'You read too many novels, Miss Emily Brent.'

'Shall you accept him, Charlotte?'

Charlotte put *Evelina* back into my grasp, and then resumed the plaiting of her hair.

'If I refuse him Emily, contemplate what my life will be. I will try to paint and garden and talk to Mrs Adams and be kind to Mrs Marshall, and every so often I shall break out and distress Mamma immeasurably. On the other hand, if I marry Hugh – and Emily, I know he has not much humour, but he is upright and kind – I shall go to India and see all kinds of astonishing things and meet all kinds of peculiar and fascinating people and I shall not need to break out.'

'Yes,' I said, in a small voice. 'And there might be disease and dirt and discomfort.'

Charlotte finished her braid and climbed into bed. She blew out her candle and lay propped on one elbow, regarding me.

'Should you mind that?'

'I mind? Of course I should mind for you. But why should I mind?'

'Because you would come with me.'

Evelina slithered to the floor. I gazed at Charlotte in a whirlwind of feelings.

'Hugh proposed to me this morning, in the parlour. I said I should think it over and tell him tomorrow. Even if I did not want you for myself, Emily, you would have to come to chaperone me. Hugh has to sail next week, in five days in fact, and there is no possible way Mamma could be persuaded to allow me to be married in five days. So I should have to be married in India, and I could not travel out alone.'

My wits seemed to be flying about like a feather pillow burst in a draught.

I said, 'But – but can he not postpone his passage?'

'No. It has been arranged for months. He offered to, if that was a condition of my marrying him, but I said being married in India was no obstacle at all.' She smiled at me. 'In fact it is a definite advantage.'

'India!'

'Yes, darling Emily. India. I might even be married in camp, for we shall land in Bombay and travel to the north-west. So it might happen in a tent. Imagine!'

Her eyes were glowing with pleasure. I turned over and buried my face in the pillow. Everything suddenly seemed inexpressibly dear, Mamma, the house, the garden, even Annie with her running nose and red hands. But if I succumbed to those affections and stayed with Mamma and the house and garden, how would they all seem without Charlotte? The one road seemed terrifying and brightly coloured, the other beloved and immeasurably drear.

I felt Charlotte's hand on my shoulder.

'If it would kill you to come, Emily, I will refuse him. There will be others.'

I rolled towards her.

'It isn't fair to make me make the choice for you!'

'I have made my choice. But all the same, I had rather be with you than with him. If I have to choose between you, that is.'

I lay and looked at her. Her eyes were glittering with excitement and her dark red hair woven into plaits made her look like a child of twelve. No wonder Hugh wanted her. Even if she was not as charming and fascinating as she was, she was so very beautiful.

31

'You – you accept him, Charlotte.'

She flung her arms around me and kissed me.

'Oh Emily, it will be such an adventure! You will never believe you ever lived in Richmond! Months at sea on an East Indiaman – and we have never done more than go boating on the Thames! – and then Egypt and a chance to see the Pyramids and then overland to Suez and on by sea to Bombay which is set in beautiful countryside, and then a marvellous journey all across upper India to the mountains. The highest mountains in the world!'

Long after she had gone happily to sleep, I lay against her warm back and watched the spring moonlight slip lightly over all the dear, familiar objects in our room; the washstand with its sprigged basin and ewer, the freckled looking-glass, the Staffordshire figures Annie had chipped while dusting them, our pictures, my books, Charlotte's sketch of Mamma in a huge hat picking raspberries, the wallpaper even, with its small pattern of pink and white and green. I could not imagine not seeing them; I had not the knowledge to visualize Indian things instead.

And Mamma? What would Mamma say and feel? She had perhaps another twenty-four hours of tranquillity before her, and then she would know that both daughters were to be gone, and the little house would be still and silent and entirely hers. I did not think she would object to Hugh, he was so eminently suitable and she would be pleased at his being so rich. Even if she did, Charlotte would not heed her, so I very much hoped for her acquiescence.

I lay first on one side and then the other. I tried picturing elephants and deserts and mountains, but I had only ever seen pictures, and they were impressions only, tinged by the artist's view of them. The moonlight slid relentlessly on and came to rest on Papa's portrait in which he wore his Turkish trousers and a funny little flowerpot cap with a tassel.

'It's your fault,' I said to him, as he stared past me quite unmoved at my turmoil. 'It's your fidgets Charlotte has inherited.'

This time next year, I shall be there, I thought. I shall have seen an elephant. And an Indian, lots of Indians. I turned over for the hundredth time and pulled the pillow round my neck. It struck me suddenly that if I were to go to India, perhaps I shouldn't have to finish the Rector's Lenten stole. I must have gone to sleep at last thinking that, because Charlotte said later she woke and found me smiling in my sleep and she was so pleased to think I wanted to go to India as much as she did.

CHAPTER THREE

Looking back I don't think that anything that has since happened in my life, even those incredible things in Afghanistan that were to follow, did I detest as much as that near half year it took us to reach India. Hugh went away the first week in April, with a miniature of Charlotte round his neck and promises, which we knew he would keep, of letters waiting for us in every port and a comfortable welcome in Bombay.

Mamma, at first utterly dismayed at the barbaric plan Charlotte proposed to her, recovered her equilibrium remarkably well. She did not even make any attempt to dissuade me from going too; in fact, she seemed to think it prudent.

'If Charlotte were to go alone, I fear she might run quite wild and that would be an end of her. Hugh does not quite realize how headstrong she is. He will need an ally with good sense to keep her in check.'

Having assigned to me this role of nursemaid and damper of fun, she occupied herself with her own future, and proposed that she should go and live with her brother, himself a widower, and keep house for him. George was gallant about this plan, but clearly doubtful.

'It will cheer the old place up immensely to have my aunt about. It needs a pretty woman. I just hope she knows I'm a grown man now and don't need running after.'

Our passages were booked for the end of May; by early winter we should be in India. Hugh insisted upon our having reserved cabins and seemed to think almost £200 apiece for this privilege a mere trifle. He sent us a respectful person from the upholsterers at the East India Docks, who sat in an obsequious attitude on the edge of a parlour chair and begged to inform us we should need sofas with mattresses, hanging lamps, swing trays, looking-glasses with sliding covers, chests of drawers that came ingeniously in two parts, carpets, linen bags – and that only for the basic furniture for our cabin. He bowed himself out at last with our enormous order in his hand, leaving us with a traveller's handbook which lectured us on what we might need ourselves for the voyage.

'Emily!' Charlotte said. 'Look at this! a dozen pairs of kid gloves. A dozen! and *two* dozen white jean jackets! And here's a Mrs Wise of Saville Row who says she provides "corsets of inestimable utility in a relaxing climate!" At least there's one thing I recognize – it says here one should have a common straw bonnet for walking on the deck.'

I looked at the list uncomfortably. It seemed so wrong for me to spend Hugh's money so lavishly, even if he had plenty of it, and especially upon articles we should only use upon the journey. Charlotte said, her arm round my waist. 'He *wants* you to come. If it were not for you, I should not be able to go. You must think of yourself as wonderfully cheap at the price.'

So I tried to, and steadily worked through our mountainous luggage, feeling that by being some kind of lady's maid, I was at least performing a vicarious service in return for Hugh's generosity. The parlour filled with objects; boat cloaks, telescopes, cards, bottles of raspberry vinegar, boxes of Windsor soap, materials for tapestry and crochet work, drawing things, a case of Cologne water and a bucket on a rope which our handbook recommended for the drawing up of sea water. The handbook also told us we must sew with silver needles otherwise the implements would rust in our damp fingers. It had obviously been compiled by someone with an alarming eye for detail.

We had two cabins, and very comfortable they were. The obsequious upholsterer had done his job excellently and our cabins resembled small complicated sitting-rooms even down to our pillows wearing daytime covers of flowered chintz. We even had a maid of our own, or rather Charlotte did, a black-browed girl called Jane whom Mrs Connell had pressed upon her from her own household, and who pounced upon our luggage and put away our dozens of gloves and jackets in a trice. She was clearly used to grander things than we were.

We were to sail down the coast of Spain and Portugal, and then along the entire length of the Mediterranean to Alexandria. This route, known as the 'overland' route, was very new, and generally involved taking a French boat, a suggestion which appalled Hugh. I think if it had become necessary, he would, in order that Charlotte might see the Pyramids and Pompey's Pillar, have bought his own 2,000-ton steamer to take her the way she wished to go and to avoid the shocking prospect of a French boat. One had to share cabins on most French boats, he said, sometimes with one's maid or a stewardess. We tried to look as horrified as he felt.

He found us an English steamer, however, the SS Pasha, which would take us to Egypt. Then we would look at the antiquities in Alexandria – which every seasoned traveller on the Pasha described as disappointing, in a superior way – rumble on to Cairo, look at the Pyramids and then be loaded into vans and bundled off for sixteen hours over rocks and holes to Suez. At Suez we and

35

all our monumental possessions, which were to follow us from the *Pasha* in a separate van, would be put upon an East Indiaman and taken slowly down the Red Sea and across over 1,500 more miles of sea, Arabian this time, to Bombay.

I could not help wishing that Charlotte's thirst for adventure could have been confined until we reached India. The old-fashioned route round the Cape sounded so peaceful, the same ship, the same cabin, not all this chopping and changing. And if we had been going to Calcutta, we might have left from Suez on a smart new steamer with a spacious saloon seating eighty people. But Bombay was where Sir John Keane, Hugh's commanding officer, had raised his force to go to Afghanistan, and where Hugh had such roots in India as he had anywhere there. When we reached him, he would take us up north, partly by river, partly overland, through places with outlandish names, to join his men in Afghanistan. I should be travelling for a year it seemed, and I did not like the prospect. Charlotte, on the other hand, could hardly wait.

By the time we got to Suez, I was exhausted. The *Pasha* had been quite pleasant but I was dreadfully sea-sick, and Charlotte, who was radiantly well, had to nurse me for days and nights, which she did with angelic good temper. I struggled on shore at Alexandria and was put to bed in the Europe Hotel. Charlotte had wanted to stay at the Orient because she had heard it was run on French principles, but luckily Hugh had thought she was joking, and I lay in a hard wide bed and listened to the palm trees rattling in the hot wind outside and longed for Richmond. We saw Cleopatra's Needle and Pompey's Pillar and the Pasha's palace, which was decorated in a gone-to-seed French style and had gardens full of topiary ships and peacocks. The Egyptians seemed either very fat or very thin, and whatever shape they were, they were all very dirty. They wore striped robes and greasy turbans or little cotton caps and they whined for money all the time, holding out grimy palms.

We travelled to Cairo in sunshine hotter and more threatening than any I had ever known, and put up at Shepheard's Hotel which was far more comfortable than the Europe, but one of our fellow passengers complained it had no facilities for moustachio-dyeing. We went to the Pyramids from Cairo, and I nearly lost Charlotte.

We had all gone in a great van, perhaps twenty of us, lumbering over the dusty, stony plain outside Cairo, while the sun beat down and Egyptians ran crying beside us. I could not deny that Cairo was better than Alexandria, but I could not be in such transports as Charlotte was, and when we reached the Great Pyramid of Cheops, and Charlotte cried, 'I must ride a camel!', I began to feel that Cairo was a very dangerous place, and to understand how Mamma had felt when riding in Richmond Park was proposed.

I said 'No, Charlotte, please don't. They look so disagreeable and you only have a native guide.'

'An English one would be precious little use,' she said, and ran off, *ran* in that heat, towards where the camel men were waiting and gesturing.

They crowded round her, and I felt awkward and anxious and was about to enlist the help of one of the gentlemen of the party, when I saw she had selected her beast with great competence and it was being made to kneel down for her on the sand. Then she climbed on with the greatest agility and when the camel lurched to its feet, back legs first, I almost began screaming, but Charlotte never faltered. She even laughed; I could see her white teeth gleaming through her veil. The camel began to walk forward, led by an Egyptian in a ragged robe of plum and blue, and suddenly Charlotte leaned down, and twitched the leading rope from his hand and lashed the camel with it so that it leaped forward into a dreadful stumbling run.

I did scream then. So did all the ladies in the party,

and the gentlemen too, and the camels that were left behind howled and tugged at their ropes, and the camel men began to jump up and down and shout. Charlotte was being carried away, past the Great Pyramid, down towards the slight hollow where the Sphinx's forehead might just be seen over the rim of the land. Beyond that it was just desert, yellow-brown, quivering-hot, stony desert, and it seemed to go on and on until it melted into the dusty heat-filled sky.

One of the gentlemen, with more presence of mind than any of us, ran over to the camel lines and persuaded, by gesture, a camel man to mount and pursue her. He went past us at the same stumbling, swaying gallop that had carried Charlotte away, shouting hoarsely, and the noise he made caused Charlotte to turn her head for a moment, but she did not raise a hand in acknowledgement.

After what seemed an age he brought her back. She was laughing still, and she had made the camel man laugh too, and when she eventually slid off and handed him a coin, he knelt on the ground in front of her and knocked his forehead on the baked earth.

We had a dreadful ride back to Cairo, for the rest of the party was very much shocked, and I was afraid that if I spoke, my words would be all reproaches. Charlotte hummed under her breath, and threw coins from the back of the van to the Egyptians round the wheels and only when we got back safely to our rooms at Shepheard's, did she say to me, 'I am truly sorry if I frightened you, Emily, but it was the most glorious fun. Do you suppose an elephant will be even better?'

We left next morning for Suez and that was a journey too awful to chronicle. I have never been so thankful for anything as to reach our cabin on the *Dharwar*. It was an old ship, but felt sturdy and reassuring, and as usual Hugh had been before us and we had the best cabins with all our prodigious quantity of furniture in them. We ploughed slowly down the hot, oily Red Sea under the relentless sun, every timber creaking, and then set out to crawl across the glittering wrinkled waste of water to India. Charlotte drew maps, and watched the sky through her telescope, and sketched the other passengers and said to me at least a dozen times a day, 'Oh Emily! Isn't it wonderful? Are you not thankful you came?'

We reached Bombay in November. It looked, apart from some of the Italian coasts and Greek islands we had passed, the most beautiful place we had yet seen. The city, white and dun, jagged with towers and domes, lay along the elbow of a huge hill stretching away to the north, and the bay the land enclosed was bright blue and dotted with boats.

It is very difficult when you have travelled achingly for weeks and months to believe you are at your journey's end. I stepped down the gangplank of the *Dharwar* and tried to realize that I was here, I had come; that this was what I had tried to picture lying in our white-curtained bed in Richmond, with the comforting knowledge of Charlotte next to me and Mamma through the wall. I looked about at the thin dark people in their rags and tatters, and the hard bright light, and the dust and rubbish, and I smelt the acrid, human, spicy, charcoal smell and I said, meaning only to speak to myself, 'This is *India*.'

Charlotte heard me. She turned on the gangplank and her eyes were like blue fire.

'It is, it is, at last. We are here. Isn't it wonderful?'

Hugh was waiting, impeccable in his uniform. He looked at Charlotte in a devouring sort of way, and she laughed and put her arms round his neck and I heard a murmur of disapproval rise from the group of passengers behind me. He held his hand out to me then, the hand that was not holding Charlotte.

'I have to thank you for her safekeeping, Emily.'

'No,' I said truthfully, 'I am afraid it is the other way about,' and then I thought it would not perhaps be suitable to tell him of the camel, so I simply smiled at him, and then he gave me his free arm and led us away among the bundles and boxes and crouching Indians to an open carriage.

He looked deeply preoccupied as he settled us in, but Charlotte did not seem to be noticing, not looking at him even but twisting and turning in her seat and giving little exclamations of interest and pleasure. I tried to indicate Hugh's expression to her, but she just laughed and said, 'Look, oh, do look! The little boy with the monkey!'

So I put my hand on Hugh's sleeve and said loudly, 'What is the matter? Is something troubling you?'

He looked straight past me at Charlotte.

Charlotte turned her head from the monkey and said, 'Oh, Hugh! Are you not well?'

'Perfectly, thank you. But I have some – awkward news. I am much disappointed myself and I cannot quite think how the difficulty is to be overcome.'

Curious dark faces were pressing up round our carriage, seeming to be as eager for Hugh's revelation as we were.

'What difficulty?' Charlotte said.

'I am to proceed directly to Kabul. I had thought we might have a few weeks, here in Bombay, and you might be able to get used to India, and we might be married here, by an English clergyman among English people and now it seems – it seems—'

Charlotte clapped her hands like an excited child.

'Oh, but Hugh that is wonderful! That is just what I had hoped! We can be married as we march, in a tent perhaps!'

He looked thoroughly baffled.

'But – but you do not mind?'

'Mind? How could I mind? Nothing could be more entirely to my taste. I am absolutely delighted.' She leaned forward and put her gloved hand on his knee very briefly. 'You see, there was nothing to worry about, no difficulty. I am ready to go at once and I am – oh Hugh, I shall love to be married in a tent!'

'Shall you?' he said, and his tone was utterly dejected.

She did not seem to notice. She had caught sight of a great scrawny white cow shouldering its way through the crowd beside us and her attention was captured. I saw Hugh give a small sigh and then, as I was about to speak to him as much to soothe my own sudden doubts as his disappointment, he jerked his head up and shouted an order and the carriage moved forward among the people.

Hugh took us to a peculiar one-storey house that we learned to call a bungalow. Charlotte talked all the way, telling him how magnificent the journey had been, how she had enjoyed herself, pointing out remarkable things as we passed them. Hugh leant back, his cap tipped over his eyes, and watched her. I watched them both for a while, and then my eyes were drawn away by what we were passing. We went trotting through mud-paved streets at first, streets baked as hard as brick, and they were lined with simple white houses for the most part, except where there were big new buildings going up that had a distinctly un-Indian air, or where there were high buff-coloured walls shutting in some secret. There were thousands of Indians in these streets, and they had rows of stalls in them piled with watermelons and trays of bright sticky things clotted with flies.

After a while we began to twist up some little hills, and we passed several temples, some most surprisingly and brilliantly painted, and there were trees and gardens and whiffs of a strong spicy scent.

'Oleander,' Hugh said.

The bungalow was very odd, at first glance. Hugh said it was new, and he said that very proudly, but it looked to me most undistinguished and Charlotte said, 'Good heavens, it looks for all the world like a cow house!'

It was very long, and very low, and it had an overhanging thatched roof and almost no walls. Hugh had been lent it by a prosperous businessman for our use and he did not smile when we laughed at it.

'I believe you will be better pleased with the interior.'

We were. We mounted some steps, crossed a huge and shady verandah, and went straight into a vast and elegant drawing-room supported on pillars. There were sofas covered in red silk, and mahogany chests and tables, and the huge windows were shaded with blinds of cream tussore.

'We laughed out of ignorance,' I said to Hugh, but he was not listening. He was watching Charlotte while she walked around the room, lightly touching things and humming.

'Does it please you?' he asked.

She turned towards him and smiled.

'Oh yes,' she said, 'vastly.' But her voice did not sound as it had when she had asked me twelve times a day if I did not think the ship wonderful. She patted a cushion absently, and ran her finger over a curious black Eastern cabinet delicately painted in gold and red and then she came back to us across the intricately patterned rug that almost filled the room from side to side.

'Hugh, when do we leave?'

He looked startled.

'Leave?'

'For Kabul.'

'I think you should rest,' he said, and his voice was disapproving.

'Oh, I don't need to rest. I was never so much exhilarated in my life before.' He seemed baffled. I said quickly. '*I* need to rest.'

Charlotte smiled and put her arm around me.

'You can rest all the way to Afghanistan. In a palanquin. Can't she, Hugh?'

'I had rather not use palanquins,' he said seriously. 'The bearers are so insubordinate and always striking for higher wages. I was simply left on the way to a dinner party last week and the rogues scampered off until I promised to pay them more.'

'A curricle then,' said Charlotte, suppressing a smile, and before he could object to its unsuitability added quickly, 'I am only being silly, Hugh.'

We dined off fried fish and rice and a curious chicken dish Hugh said was called a pilau, and then came some wonderful mangoes and ice, and Hugh had provided champagne. We ate in another huge apartment divided from the drawing-room by a red silk screen, and we were waited on by an absolute tribe of dark, silent servants in white tunics and narrow white trousers and scarlet sashes and bare feet.

When we were lolling on the verandah afterwards in great deep basketwork chairs, with the early evening sun on the slopes of the hillside and shining stretches of sea below us, I suddenly realized that I was comfortable for the first time since leaving home, comfortable and safe. I looked at Charlotte. She was lounging back like me, but she did not look as if she were deeply relaxed in her chair, merely laid lightly across the surface and ready to spring up again. Hugh had, after much persuading that we would be neither sickened nor shocked, lit up a cigar and he was drawing on it slowly, his eyes fixed on Charlotte. I said to myself that I would count to a hundred and then I should say I was very tired and slip away along the verandah to my white-draped bedroom and leave them alone together.

When I had reached fifty, Charlotte said, 'Do I hear a band?'

'Yes. They play each night on the Esplanade. People drive up and down to look at one another.' He paused. 'Should you like to drive?'

'No. Not just to look at *people*. It sounds like Richmond.'

He blew a cloud of blue smoke out which was quickly lost in the blue twilight air.

'Dearest Charlotte, it is not at all like Richmond. It smells most regrettable for one thing on account of the uses the beach is put to, and for another there are savage dogs who attack anyone foolish enough to leave his carriage.'

Charlotte's eyes gleamed with interest.

'Really, Hugh?'

I reached a hundred and stood up. I stretched slowly.

'I seem to be exceedingly sleepy. Would you forgive me if I went to my room?'

Hugh rose at once. I stooped to kiss Charlotte, who squeezed my hand sharply, then I offered him a sisterly cheek. As I walked away down the verandah, I heard the creak of wicker as Hugh resumed his seat, and then Charlotte's clear voice said again, 'Hugh, when do we leave?'

His sigh was audible down the length of the verandah.

'In three days,' he said.

CHAPTER FOUR

I could not believe how much energy Charlotte had. For the next two days Hugh took her riding in the dawn before breakfast – an enormous meal of fried fish and omelettes and rice and preserves – and then she would shop all morning for our expedition north, an expedition I was beginning to dread. Hugh took us to a shop owned by an Indian called Jangerjee Nasserawarijee, and although Charlotte and Hugh bought hams and tins of sardines and blankets and basketwork furniture for our tents, they might easily have added French china and lithographs, gold lace, jewellery, clocks and birdcages, not to mention whole Gruyère cheese. I never saw such a place.

After dinner each afternoon, while I lay on the verandah and thought how comfortable and pleasant it all was,

Charlotte would make Hugh take her riding again, not on the Esplanade, but away into the hills in the dusk. I was sure Mamma would have been horrified, despite their being engaged, but there was nothing I could do.

On the day before we left Charlotte came back highly elated, but Hugh looked displeased. We sat on the verandah in awkward silence. Then Hugh said he must be going and he said good night to Charlotte very stiffly for a man so much in love, and to me more warmly than usual, and left.

'Charlotte, what has happened?' I said.

She was rolling bread into little balls and throwing them to a dear little mongoose that had decided to become our pet. When she wanted to feed him she called out and a silent servant padded from the bungalow and brought bread on a bone china plate on a brass tray.

'Nothing, Emily. It was entirely nothing. I do not understand him. We had the most wonderful ride among some mango groves and it was so beautiful in the sunset and so warm and full of lovely bright birds, except that birds seem very silent here and do not sing like English ones. And then we came upon a temple, partly ruined and covered in great sinewy creepers. There was a tank in the courtyard and an old Brahmin was washing his feet and I wanted to go in but Hugh said no, I mustn't. I said the old man was obviously harmless, and Hugh went red and said it was not that at all. So I asked him what *was* the reason and he would not say, so I simply rode past him, and got off my horse and tied it to a mango and went into the temple on foot. Then I saw that the walls were covered with carvings and when I looked very closely, I saw that they were of naked people all locked together, and writhing about. They were so beautiful, Emily, so full of life and – and love, you couldn't believe their arms were stone arms, they looked so real, holding each other so closely. I wanted to cry and laugh, looking at them, I wanted to look and look but Hugh called me and I went running over to him and begged him to come

45

and see how lovely the embracing people were and he became very angry and said I must mount and he would take me home at once. That was why he was so cross, Emily. That is all. I came at once like a lamb and still he was cross.'

'Did – did you say you were sorry that you had looked at the temple? That you did not realize that the carvings were there?'

Charlotte threw the last bread pellet to the mongoose and looked at me in amazement.

'Of course not,' she said. 'What was wrong with looking at the carvings anyway? They were beautiful and exciting – so tender and passionate. If it had offended the Brahmin to have a white person in his holy place, of course I shouldn't have gone in. But he didn't mind. He smiled at me.'

'Oh,' I said, 'of course,' and I thought how right Charlotte was not to be affected and silly, and how wounded poor Hugh must feel that she had behaved, to his mind, so indelicately.

'It is just as well we are going tomorrow,' Charlotte said, 'because I think Hugh would be so careful where he took me riding now that it would hardly be an adventure any more.'

It was the first week of December when we left Bombay. I looked back at the bungalow with genuine regret, but Charlotte, in a new travelling dress and jacket of fine cream cloth braided in green, with a green bonnet veiled in cream gauze, seemed hardly able to wait to be gone. There were the three of us, our black-browed Jane, who clearly felt Indians were not to be trusted to look after us, Hugh's man, and 180 servants.

'A hundred and eighty!' Charlotte said, looking at the vast cavalcade of dark-skinned men waiting patiently to begin among the horses and camels that were to carry our mountainous luggage.

'For India,' Hugh said severely, 'a hundred and eighty is very modest.'

We had huge white tents like canvas pavilions, one each as bedrooms, and a fourth as a sitting-room, and they had a stencilled frieze of oak leaves around the top of the walls. They and their poles were laid along the sides of the camels' humps, and I wondered, standing there in the hot white light, which mine was, and if I should be able to sleep in anything so insubstantial. We had had a letter from Mamma the day before, enclosing some drawing paper for Charlotte and all the *Pickwick Papers* in a bundle for me, and this had unsettled me dreadfully. Should I be reading *Pickwick Papers* that very night in my queer canvas room?

I was put into a sedan chair, but Charlotte rode. Hugh said that at a place called Nasik we should pick up some elephants and Charlotte looked immediately elated. It seemed a very wearisome first day and I felt quite jogged to pieces. Charlotte rode ahead most of the time, never looking behind her, but Hugh came and rode by me for a while, looking deeply preoccupied until I could bear his troubled expression no longer and asked if there was anything I could do for him.

He said at once, in a sort of outburst, 'I had so much hoped to be married in Bombay.'

'I know,' I said, 'but Charlotte has set her heart upon a tented wedding.'

'It – it is so unsuitable,' Hugh said fretfully. 'It means we must travel like this – unmarried – almost until Delhi, until an army chaplain can be found. It would have been so much easier, so much better in Bombay, with a church and priests and English people in abundance.'

'It does not much matter that you are not married as we march,' I said, 'for there is nobody to shock but me.'

'*I* am shocked,' said Hugh, and he dug his heels into his horse's sides and cantered on to catch up with Charlotte.

*

It was weeks before we reached Delhi. We marched every day, seldom covering more than ten or twelve miles, and even though it was tiring it was much better when we had the elephants, who proved amiable and intelligent. Our white tents became brown with dust, our camel trunks battered with so much heaving on and off, but somehow I did not feel anything like as cross and tired as I expected. It was properly exciting somehow, far more exciting than dusty Egypt or those endless seas, and Hugh had brought along an Indian cook who had been trained by a Frenchman and every night we sat down to delicious, magically produced meals. Hugh seemed to relax a little, once away from Bombay, and he would have had to have been a man of stone indeed to have resisted Charlotte's delight in every day, every new place, every hill we climbed and river we forded.

Sometimes, when we crossed the lands of native princes, we were met by runners who came to say that the Rajah wished to be received by us. Then we would stop and put up the tents and wait, and eventually a great procession would come marching through the brown dust with the Rajah borne on a silver chair and Hugh would make a halting speech of welcome in Hindustani. (Charlotte had picked up a good deal of the language, but Hugh had forbidden her to use her favourite expression, *Jow Jehanum*, because he said, embarrassedly, that it meant 'Go to hell').

Then the prince would be set on the ground and everyone would exchange astonishing compliments about roses blooming in the garden of friendship and nightingales singing in the bowers of affection, and the prince, who was usually very ugly and quite encrusted with jewels, would make all his speeches directly to Charlotte. Then he would produce trays of jewellery and shawls and Hugh would signal for his bearers to do the same, and he told us we must pretend not to have noticed the presents because that was not the custom, and bad manners. It seemed both ungrateful and unnatural to behave so, and after the first time, Charlotte hardly waited until the silver chair had been borne off again before she said, 'Oh, Emily, I longed to see what we had been given! It seemed so absurd to pretend nothing was happening. And then they were all so disappointing, weren't they, those little lumpy pearls so badly set in horrid orange gold, and the emeralds and rubies so dusty-looking.'

'The shawls were lovely,' I said, stroking mine, a huge fine square of white cashmere. 'Wouldn't Mamma love a shawl like this?'

Charlotte's face clouded.

'Yes,' she said fiercely, 'I shall take her back a hundred. When I go back.' She paused. 'If I go back.'

One ruler asked us to his palace to see a nautch. Hugh demurred.

'I think not. They are hardly amusing.'

'What are they?' Charlotte asked, her eyes alight with interest.

Hugh gestured in a vague way.

'Oh – dancing girls. They sing in a dreadful way. It goes on for hours.'

'I should like to go,' Charlotte said.

'You would be most disappointed.'

'Please, Hugh!'

'No,' he said.

Her head went up.

'Yes,' she said.

We went. The Prince seemed very pleased and sat us one on either side of him. There were no other women but two very handsome young men painted and bejewelled like girls, and at the sight of them Hugh seemed to become very uncomfortable and disconcerted. The nautch was indeed very long, and consisted of a troop of richly dressed brown girls dancing and singing and acting scenes out of the lives of Indian gods. One plump little girl came and sang a song directly at Hugh with little meaning smiles and he looked more bothered than

49

ever. When it was over, Charlotte said to him, 'What did she mean? What was she singing?'

'It was nonsense, not worth repeating.'

'Then why did you blush so?'

'Charlotte,' Hugh said with a sort of desperation. 'Please do not persist.'

'But I am interested,' she replied, smiling. 'I won't be shocked.'

He said angrily, 'Very well then. She sang, *I am the body, you are the soul; we may be parted here but let no-one say we shall be separated hereafter.* Are you satisfied now?'

She looked at him very gravely.

'But that is beautiful, Hugh.'

'It is vulgar nonsense.'

She said nothing more, but linked her arm in his to appease him, and of course he melted at once and I let them go on together ahead of me, back to our tents.

We had a very amicable few days after that. Charlotte was charming and docile and Hugh so much in love that he seemed to carry his feelings visibly about with him, like an angel's aura. I left them as much alone together as I could and spent the long, hot, dusty hours jerking onward in my palanquin or rolling about on an elephant if I felt brave enough, scolding myself severely for ever having entertained doubts that either of them could fail to make the other happy. Despite the dust and heat Charlotte seemed to bloom in a way I was sure no girl could do unless her heart was light, and Hugh's rather insipid fair good looks were elevated to golden handsomeness by his happiness.

And then came the episode of the leper child and I was flung back into my sea of doubts. We had pitched camp for the night and the red Indian sun was rolling down into the blue dust of the plain when some of the servants came rushing in to us, rolling their eyes and shouting wildly and cast themselves down at Hugh's feet, grovelling on the rug spread upon the sandy floor of the tent.

'What are they saying?' Charlotte demanded at once. 'Tell me. What is the matter?'

Hugh said something sharply to the men at his feet. To Charlotte he merely said, 'It is nothing. A domestic matter.'

The servants did not move away. They went on wailing and swaying and wringing their hands and Hugh began to shout at them and they took no notice.

Charlotte stood up.

'What *is* it?' she cried. 'Tell me! I demand you tell me!'

Hugh said angrily, 'A leper child has strayed into the camp. They are all terrified. They want to strike camp and move on. I have told them to drive the child out. We are not going on until dawn.'

Charlotte said in horror, 'You can't drive a child away! It isn't an animal, it's a human being! How can you speak so? Tell them to bring the child to me, we will take it with us to Delhi.'

Hugh stood up too. 'No!' he shouted. 'Do not be absurd. You must go nowhere near the child! I forbid it! Of course we shall not take it with us, you do not know this country, you are ridiculous, do not expose your ignorance. There is nothing you can do about leprosy, but it is violently dangerous, you must go nowhere near the child, I forbid it, I forbid you—'

I heard myself gasping, 'Oh don't, Hugh, don't order her—!' but nobody heard me for Charlotte made a sudden plunge for the tent doorway and had slipped through it in a second and then Hugh, shouting, was after her and the servants, wailing still, had streamed after him and I was left alone in the dusk listening to their angry voices echoing among the tents.

They were gone some fifteen minutes and when they came back Charlotte was pale with fury and would not look at Hugh. She crossed quickly to me and sat beside

51

me, taking my hand in hers and gripping it painfully and Hugh came and stood before us and pleaded silently and pitifully for her to look up. She would not. She looked down at the rug and breathed hard and fast.

I said, at last, to Hugh, 'Did you send the child away?'

'Yes,' he said, 'with money. With enough money to feed for a month.'

'Money!' Charlotte spat. 'Money! And who will sell the poor little wretch anything to eat? It will be robbed in minutes and it cannot defend itself with its poor crippled fists. You are a monster of cruelty. A monster.'

Hugh gave a strangled sound that might have been a sob. He fell on his knees before her and tried to take her hands, but she only gripped mine more tightly.

He said, his voice unsteady, 'Beloved – beloved Charlotte, do not be angry with me, I beg you, please – I – know you think me cruel, but if anything should happen to you, if you caught leprosy, I should never forgive myself, I should want to die. Don't hate me, please understand, you are so precious to me, so precious—'

I released my hands from Charlotte's and took hers up by the wrists and guided them to Hugh's face. She resisted me at first and then I felt her arms relax and her hands went forward voluntarily and rested against his cheeks. He turned his head then, with a gasping sigh, and put his lips to her hand and I rose softly and crept out of the tent in the dusk and tried not to think of the leper child limping away alone out there across the vast and empty plain.

Charlotte got her way and was married in a tent outside Delhi. When we had reached Jaipur and she had seen the beautiful peach-coloured palaces she had wanted to be married there, but I saw Hugh had been tried enough so I went to her tent after dinner and persuaded her to be obliging.

'Emily, I am not being deliberately difficult. It is only

the same feeling that I had when Hugh translated that song. Jaipur is so beautiful, so memorable that I thought it would be the most fitting place.'

She was seated on a camp stool in a cream wool wrapper, for the nights were getting cooler, and her hair was down her back in a red mane.

'But Hugh does not see it like that. He wants it to be proper and – and English. I do not think you can ask him to wait about in Jaipur until an English priest can be brought from Delhi.'

Charlotte reached out and picked a white flower off the sprays of jasmine one of the servants had draped over the dressing chest Hugh had bought her in Bombay.

'Emily,' she said, suddenly, 'I think I – I am not sure, it might be such a terrible—' she stopped.

I put my arms around her and smelt the scent of the jasmine and the scent of her hair.

'What, Charlotte, what? Tell me. What is it?'

She twisted round and put her face into my shoulder for a moment. Then she took it away again and gently disengaged herself.

'Nothing, darling Emily. Nothing at all. A silly moment.'

'Are you – doubtful about marrying Hugh?' I persisted.

She rose and picked up her hairbrush.

'No,' she said, 'How could I be? If I wasn't marrying Hugh how could I be living this wonderful life?'

I opened my mouth again and she laid her hand across it.

'Not another word, Emily. We will be married in Delhi.'

The servants made them an altar in the sitting-room tent out of the elephant housings, splendid structures of scarlet and gold, and laid a row of velvet cushions in front. They covered the tent walls with branches of tamarind and trails of jasmine, and we put candles all round and two on the altar.

'If you faint,' I said to Charlotte, 'you must not faint

53

towards the altar because it will come down with a crash,' and she laughed, but Hugh looked very pained.

A pleasant Army chaplain called Mr Grant had come out from Delhi to perform the ceremony and he did not seem at all surprised to be marrying people in a tent.

'Indeed no,' he said. 'When the Governor General went up country three years ago, a lady and gentleman in his party were married in a tent.'

Charlotte looked lovely. She wore a beautiful Kashmiri shawl dress Hugh had given her, so fine that he said it must have taken a year and a half to weave, and the most wonderful pearls that were his wedding present to her, and her hair was coiled up smoothly behind her head like coppery satin. Hugh looked pale and tense but immaculate in his uniform and he held himself at the altar like a ramrod.

When the ceremony was over and Mr Grant said, 'You may kiss the bride,' Hugh took her in his arms and kissed her with such intensity that I had to look away, and as I did so, I saw that Jane, who was standing behind me, had turned away also. Then all the servants rushed in and salaamed and cheered and began to clear away the altar so that they might set up a table for the wedding breakfast. Hugh did not seem to notice. He went on standing in front of where the altar had been, Charlotte tight in his arms, either kissing her or gazing down at her with a most passionate, almost frightening expression. I went out of the tent, after a while, and walked about in the sun, and thought that Charlotte was not my sister first any longer, but Hugh's wife, and in spite of the sun and it's being a wedding day, I felt cold and empty inside and full of foreboding.

I tried to keep away from them for the next few days. I had an instinctive feeling that the frail plant of their marriage would never develop roots unless it were left severely alone for a while. But on the third night after the wedding, when I had expected them both to be asleep some hours, Charlotte came into my tent and sat on the rug on the floor hugging her knees.

'Hugh has gone riding,' she said.

'Riding! But – but, look Charlotte, it is past two in the morning—!'

'I know.'

She began to rock gently backwards and forwards, still clasping her knees.

I said apprehensively, 'You – you haven't quarrelled?'

'Not exactly.'

'Oh – oh *Charlotte*—'

'Don't,' she snapped.

I said nothing but sat on my bed and stared down at her and waited.

'Nothing,' she said carefully, after a while, 'is quite what I expected.'

I felt myself blushing.

'Charlotte, you don't have to – I mean, do you think you should—'

'I don't know, Emily. I really don't know. I keep thinking of those people on the temple walls and the love and excitement that was there, and the beauty they had, and the ease. They were thrilling and calming all at once—' she stopped.

My face was fiery now. I said in a whisper, 'But – but they were just carvings, statues, they weren't real people—'

'Oh yes they were. Carvings *of* real people. They were more real than many people you see, more alive, much more alive.'

'But Charlotte,' I said, 'you have only been married three days, it is all new for both of you, you must give Hugh a chance—'

She rose and stretched and her movements were so full of some disturbing, graceful power that I could not speak but just gazed at her. She stooped then and kissed me and went away to her own tent without another word.

After Delhi, we plodded endlessly across a great flat

plain to a place called Lahore, and Charlotte begged Hugh to let her go into the old native city because it looked so large and fascinating, and Hugh, with his new authority as a husband, was adamant that she should not. He said now that the old ruler of the Punjab, Ranjit Singh, was dead it was not as safe for the English as it used to be. How easily she acquiesced I do not know, for I could seldom go into her tent now that Hugh shared it with her, and have those late-night confidences we had known all our lives. At night now, when they went out of the sitting-room tent together, I would remain behind a while and read the daily ration of *Pickwick* I allowed myself and try not to look across the dark space to their tent, nor to think of the writhing figures Charlotte had told me of on the temple walls.

After Lahore, a long way after, there was Rawalpindi, and there some of our army of servants said they must leave, they were too far away from home. Hugh was not pleased at this, but there was nothing he could do, so he paid them and we were left with a mere eighty.

'It does not matter in the least,' Charlotte said. 'Why do we not just leave half our luggage here?'

'No, dearest. You will be glad of every item in Kabul. Kabul is not like India, there is nothing comfortable to be had.'

Charlotte seemed about to speak, but said nothing. So we hung about outside Rawalpindi while Hugh found a new column of porters and then, at last, we set off for Peshawar.

'Peshawar!' Charlotte said excitedly.

'I fear you may not care for it,' Hugh said. 'It is very different to India, very barbaric.'

But there was no resisting Peshawar. I was prepared to like it in advance because it was only 100 miles east of Kabul and thus of our journey's end; and because we should not have to camp outside the city but might sleep in a house, a real house, belonging to an acquaintance of Hugh's from Bombay, an Indian merchant who came up to Peshawar to trade. But when we saw it that first morning, refreshed by a night's sleep under a solid roof, for we had arrived in darkness, there was no question of our feelings and when Hugh suggested that we should wait indoors in safety while he went and bargained for things we should need in Kabul, we both resisted him strongly.

There was a balcony that ran the length of the front of the house, and we had come on to it and found that we were looking down on to a huge central square below the towering white minarets of a great mosque. The square was packed with people, hundreds upon hundreds, some in turbans, some in white robes, some in billowing pyjamas, some with falcons on their wrists. The square was ringed with what appeared to be some sort of tea shops, open closets with brass urns and a few stools within, and these were thronged with customers. Behind the tea shops rose the three- and four-storied houses fringed with balconies, all the balconies laden with men in white turbans and blue shirts who were smoking some sort of water pipe.

'Oh!' Charlotte cried, and her knuckles gripping the balcony rail were white. 'I must go down there! I must!'

Hugh looked very doubtful. He pointed to odd corners where beggars and cripples crouched.

'Should you really like to?'

'Yes,' we said in chorus. 'Yes!'

It was a memorable morning. We had Hugh for an escort and six of our original bearers so that we were quite fenced about with humanity, but all those colourful and fascinating people were so busy with their own affairs and so varied themselves that two European ladies and a soldier hardly seemed to attract any attention at all. We found a street full of goldsmiths, one of jewellers and coppersmiths, we saw carpet sellers and merchants who sold prayer rugs from Samarkand. There were silks and swords and muskets, huge melons and white Kabul grapes wrapped in cotton wool, precious stones and terrifying curved blades called scimitars. There were piles of walnuts and almonds and apricots, and a street of money changers with gold and silver coins stamped with bulls and elephants piled in shining heaps.

Charlotte seemed almost in a daze, a dream. Her lips were parted and her light brilliant eyes were darting hungrily from sight to sight, from face to face, as if she could not see enough. Only once did she speak, when she turned to Hugh and said, 'Will Kabul be like this?'

'I don't know,' he said.

When we got back to our house, someone was waiting, a tall heavy man with an expression of great kindness that made me like him immediately. He was dressed in the same uniform as Hugh. He and Hugh greeted each other warmly and then he kissed Charlotte's hand, and mine, and said he was come over the mountains to lead us into Kabul. He bowed to Charlotte with a flourish.

'Richard Talbot at your service, ma'am.'

He stayed to dine with us and then we pressed him to remain for the night.

'There are so many rooms!' Charlotte said. 'Even with our army of servants we cannot fill it.'

So he consented, and we went to the upper sitting-room which gave on to the balcony and seated ourselves in curious chairs lacquered dark red and padded in silk. The sky outside was deep hyacinth blue, and from the square rose the hum of voices interspersed with the weird cries of the holy men we had seen that morning with ashes in their beards. A charcoal brazier had been lit in the centre of the room, and there were queer lamps on low tables made of fantastically shaped globes of pierced brass. I felt absolutely happy and secure.

'How long can we stay?' I said to no-one in particular.

Richard Talbot looked at me as if he understood exactly how I felt. He said with great kindness, 'I'm afraid we must go tomorrow.'

My gasp of disappointment was drowned by Charlotte's cry of pleasure. She said, 'Through the Khyber

Pass?' in a voice of happy anticipation, and I shrank among my cushions and felt sick with apprehension.

Richard Talbot leaned towards me and said, 'You mustn't worry, you know, Miss Emily. Our army has been in Kabul almost two years now. We know the ropes. And we pay the tribesmen on the Pass almost £8,000 a year not to molest our caravans. So you will be quite safe, I promise you.'

'How can you be frightened now?' Charlotte asked. 'You've done so much, seen so much. We have nearly been away from home a year—'

'Don't,' I said. I wanted to thank Richard Talbot for his sympathy and reassurance, and to explain to Charlotte that there was something menacing in the notion of Afghanistan that I had not felt at all until now, but I suddenly found my throat was full and I could not trust myself to speak.

I heard Richard say, 'You've been seconded, Hugh. So have I. Keane took our lot back to India since the Afghans were behaving so well. I don't think they will keep up this docility, I don't think Keane should have gone. But he has, leaving only one cavalry regiment and two infantry brigades and we're to hope for the best.'

'Seconded?' Hugh said indignantly. 'To whom?'

'Shah Suja's force.'

Hugh sat up so suddenly that his chair lurched across the polished floor.

He said, 'The hell I have!' and Charlotte laughed.

'Who is Shah Suja?' she said.

'He's a puppet, really,' Richard Talbot said. 'We want him on the throne as Amir of Afghanistan because he has been in our protection for years, and if he is ruler he will be pro-British and keep away the Russians which is the point of all this blood, sweat and tears in the first place. He's quite an impressive fellow really, immensely dignified and there's no doubt about his personal courage, but his ministers are as corrupt as they come and it doesn't look as if his people are exactly warming to him.'

Hugh leaned forward and the lamplight thrust hard shadows up into his face, making him look suddenly much older.

'And you, Dick?'

'I'm on MacNaghten's staff.'

Hugh leaned back again and closed his eyes. Charlotte, who was listening as avidly as a child being told a fairy story, asked who MacNaghten was, but Hugh didn't seem to hear her and it was Richard Talbot who explained that he was the Indian Government's Chief Secretary, really the most important British political adviser in Afghanistan.

'You must be grateful to him,' Richard Talbot added, smiling. 'He issued the directive saying that officers and men might bring their wives into Afghanistan. Lady MacNaghten has come, complete with her cat, and Lady Sale, Fighting Bob's wife, and I sometimes feel she could take on the whole Afghan army unaided.'

I said diffidently, 'Forgive me, but I don't quite understand. Will – will you be fighting on the same side?'

'Absolutely,' Richard Talbot said with quick reassurance. 'I am on the staff of the British political adviser in Afghanistan, the man sent by the Government of India, and that Government has put Shah Suja on the Afghan throne because he is pro-British, and Hugh is on his staff to help guide his decisions in governing Afghanistan and keeping it our ally.'

'So things are very stable, you see,' Hugh said to me. 'Otherwise I should never be allowed to bring you.'

'Shah Suja took MacNaghten's directive really to heart,' said Richard Talbot with relish. 'He's brought in all his harem. You never saw such a caravan. We had to evacuate the Bala Hissar – that's the fortified palace in Kabul – because there simply wasn't room for all of us and all of them. We're in a cantonment outside the city now – it's

60

excellent soil out there. I've grown a magnificent crop of artichokes.'

I suddenly felt more reassured. It didn't seem that a place where this large and kindly young man could devote time to a kitchen garden could be so very terrifying. I didn't mean to say, 'How long shall we stay there?' but the question broke from my subconscious before I knew it was there.

'Ages, I hope!' Charlotte said.

'Until we have got rid of Akbar,' Richard Talbot explained. 'He is the son of the deposed Amir, the man we took the throne from to give it to Shah Suja. He's a fascinating man, an iron disciplinarian, but he's a thorn in our flesh. He's gathering troops in Turkestan I hear, but our commanders say he can be talked out of using them. I doubt it myself. I saw him once, when we first came up here, wonderfully handsome he is, almost as handsome as Bewick—'

Hugh's chair gave another lurch.

He said 'Bewick?' in a tone of horror.

Richard Talbot turned his kindly smile upon him.

'He's assistant British Resident in Kabul. Or rather, since the Resident's death, he is acting Resident himself and glorying in it. Didn't you know?'

'No,' Hugh said shortly. 'I can't think why he wasn't called home years ago.'

Charlotte said, 'Why? What has he done?' and Hugh looked repressively at Richard Talbot as if he shouldn't say too much in reply.

'He's a charming rogue. He's as handsome as the devil and quite as badly behaved. It's amazing the Afghans tolerate him the way he uses their women—'

'Richard,' Hugh said in a warning tone.

I thought of the temple episode and did not look at Charlotte.

'But he's brilliantly clever, there's no doubt of that, and if anyone's going to reason with Akbar, it would be him if MacNaghten will let him, which he won't . . .'

My eyelids were drooping, heavy and helpless. I heard their voices go droning on, Richard's deep one, Charlotte's excited questions, Hugh's tones, anxious and abrupt. Everything began to swim lazily round me, past and present impressions wheeling slowly across my brain, things I had seen that day, last week, last month. A runner had caught up with us as we entered Peshawar and brought a letter from Mamma, and a new book of Charles Lamb's essays, and with this heartaching reminder of the past to contend with too, my head became blurred with Richmond as well as India, and my thoughts were shot through with uneasy images of what was ahead, that great mountain pass and the wild men that haunted it. I must have slept then, for I fell into a dream in which I sat in the garden in Richmond, in one of the little sunny hedged corners and Mamma was nearby reading to me and suddenly there was a savage cry and a man in a turban leaped over the hedge and waved a scimitar at us and Mamma did not seem at all surprised, but only stopped reading to say in a calm voice, 'Oh look Emily. It's Bewick!' Then someone picked me up, and carried me out of the garden and as I was laid on a bed I realized that I was not in Richmond, but Peshawar, and that I was very warm and comfortable, and so I fell into a deep and dreamless sleep until morning.

CHAPTER FIVE

As fate would have it, my coming into Afghanistan was just as much like a dream as my sleepy brain had foretold. I woke that next morning with a fever and aches in every limb, and so I was put on a litter and carried like the Queen of Sheba, and remembered little for days but Charlotte's voice and her cool hands and the endless jogging of my bed. It was quite a severe fever, enough to make me silly and muddled and careless of where I was, always sleepy and confused. My head ached a good deal and my eyes smarted in the sunlight, so the curtains of my swaying bed were kept closed.

The first morning that I awoke clear-headed, the curtains were pulled back by a strange and lovely woman in black peasant robes and silver and turquoise jewellery, and I screamed because I didn't know her, and she laughed and threw off her black veil and revealed herself as Charlotte.

'Emily, I'm so sorry to frighten you, but aren't they lovely? I bargained for them two days ago, from a man with a camel train all roped together with blue and scarlet braids. Hugh was so angry he says I mustn't forget I am a European—'

She looked immensely un-English, it was true. She had plaited her hair in two long thick twists, and she wore a silver band across her brow from which hung discs of turquoise, and more turquoise swung in her ears, and on her wrists, thrust out from her billowing black robes, were bracelets of coral and silver.

I said, 'You look like a princess.'

She laughed again, and said how glad she was I was better and then she clapped her hands and cried, 'But oh Emily! You are better just in time! Look where we are, isn't it wonderful? Can you imagine where we are?'

I peered nervously out of the litter. We were on a rough track, part stones, part ruts of pale mud and to our right hand a great wall of reddish rock soared up to the sky. To our left – and I heard my own gasp as I took it in – the land fell away seemingly for ever, plunging down hundreds of feet to an invisible valley and beyond that rising again in huge blue folds like humped dragons, limitless and bare.

'Are – are we there?' I said hesitantly.

'No. No, not yet. This is the Khyber Pass. Isn't it the most gloriously exciting place you ever saw? Doesn't it make you want to sing for joy? We are nearly at Landi

Kotal so you are better just in time, for that is the highest point of the whole Pass, the same height as Kabul—'

I said, 'Where is Hugh? And Captain Talbot? Where are they?'

Charlotte sighed a little.

'Hugh has gone to find us breakfast. Richard is still asleep. He is exhausted with worry, Emily. The poor man has ridden beside you ever since we left Peshawar.'

It took us almost a day to toil on upward to Landi Kotal. The road clung precariously to the swerving, wheeling hillside and we clung precariously to the road, and I tried not to look down at the twisting folds of bare blue land way below us in the valley nor to notice how often the ponies stumbled on the narrow rocky path. We passed little red villages, windowless inside high red walls with look-out towers on every corner, and sometimes there were camels tethered near and a black tent or two and strange-looking men in long belted coats and turbans who watched us with disconcerting intentness.

Landi Kotal was no more than a straggle of crude houses, built of grey-brown mud, along the track into Afghanistan. It was thronged with people, however, and mule trains and disdainful camels and the high mountain air was thick with jabbering voices and the sound of bells on the woollen reins of the beasts. The mules had wooden pack saddles piled with bundles and they were thin and moulting and their hooves were untended, dry and over long and splitting. The people smelt as powerfully as the animals but they were fascinating to look at with their high cheek bones and proud noses and bold dark eyes. They were all turbaned and all heavily armed.

Hugh was anxious to find us somewhere for the night.

'We must find somewhere for Emily. I am sure her fever has not abated before because she had nowhere proper to rest—'

I said I did not mind. My bones ached, every last nerve and sinew ached, I felt as jumbled up as if I had been tossed in a blanket all day, but I also felt that I could sleep quite well on the stones of the road if they would only let me stop and rest.

'I shall not be long,' Hugh said. 'I will find a house that will at least take Charlotte and Emily in.'

He went off, leaving us with Richard by the side of the packed road, me still in my litter, Charlotte mounted on her pony, Richard at its head. The crowd went swaying past us, hardly casting us a glance, a moving mass of animals and people as hypnotic to watch as water.

'Look!' Charlotte cried suddenly. She pointed along the street, but from our lower level, neither Richard nor I could see what she had seen. We craned upwards, helplessly. Charlotte said, 'Oh, it's terrible! They are beating him with rifle butts! Poor man, what can he have done?'

Richard shrugged.

'Some kind of criminal. I really shouldn't watch. The Afghans are not very delicate in their punishments—'

'Oh, no! Look! Oh, I can't stay here, I can't! Let go of my bridle, Richard, I must go closer, I must—'

'Please do not,' he said, and I cried, 'Oh Charlotte, don't go, not in this crowd!' But she leaned down with an expression of determination and flicked her whip lightly across Richard's wrist. With an exclamation, he let go of the rein, and Charlotte immediately urged her pony forward into the crowd.

I screamed, 'Go with her! Don't let her go alone! Go on! Follow her!'

He didn't hesitate, but nodded at me simply and plunged into the mêlée of humans in Charlotte's wake. The servants were much agitated by this and crowded round my litter full of questions, so I had to assume a calm I did not feel and speak to them as soothingly as I could. When Hugh came back and said he had found a house that would take us in which, if not clean, was at least not as filthy as most, Charlotte and Richard had been gone ten minutes.

'I must follow them.'

I was ashamed of my own cowardice but I said, 'Oh, I am sure Richard is more than competent! He has been here many months you know, he knows the people—' and then the crowd before us parted a little and the pony came in sight, ridden by Charlotte, led by Richard, and at its stirrup a filthy brigand in boots and breeches and a turban. His chest and back were bare and smeared with blood and his savage hawk-nosed face was turned up to Charlotte with an expression no milder than adoration. Richard looked defeated.

I could feel, beside me, the precise moment at which Hugh lost his temper. He began to shout at Charlotte, demanding to know where she had been, what that scoundrel was doing clinging to her habit, how dared she ride off and alarm him so—

'This is no scoundrel,' Charlotte said calmly. 'This is Sayid. He is a Pathan. Richard has very kindly translated for me and I know exactly what was happening. Sayid's brother accused him of seducing his wife, but Sayid assures me that she has pursued him relentlessly for months and that his brother misunderstood the situation entirely. The brother managed to persuade several of his friends that Sayid was guilty and they seized him as he came in here to the bazaar and they beat him and were going to kill him. That was when we arrived, we got there in the nick of time. So I bought him.'

I said in horror, 'But you can't! You can't just *own* him, he *can't* be a slave! How can you trust him? Oh Charlotte it isn't right, it isn't normal—'

'It is out of the question,' Hugh said.

Charlotte gave him a cold, steady blue stare.

'I have saved his life, Hugh and now he will serve me. He told Richard so. I am a foreigner, a feringhi, and a woman, but he says that will make no difference. I am honoured by what he says, Hugh, and I believe him.'

Hugh swung round on Richard.

'Talbot, how could you let this happen? You were

supposed to protect her, not stand by and let her buy up villains as if they were trifles at a fair—'

Richard said, 'I could not stop her. You know that.'

'Then you may tell this ruffian in no uncertain terms that he may be off, at once, if he values the worthless life my wife has so ludicrously bought—'

'No!' Charlotte said sharply. 'Sayid stays. He will protect me from now on, should I need it. And Hugh, you forget something. After the leper child you owe me a human life.'

Hugh opened his mouth but no sound came. He punched his fist into his open hand and then he swung around so that his back was to us. Richard looked embarrassed. Charlotte, on the other hand, remained perfectly collected, and bent down to say something, smiling, and gesturing towards me, to Sayid, and he came and knelt by the litter and grinned up at me with dazzling white teeth in his dark face. He smelt strongly, like a goat, like wet leather, and his hands and nails were lined and edged with black, like ink.

'You see, Emily, Sayid will protect you too. Of course I trust him. I shall learn Pushtu and he will learn English.' She dismounted and came over and leant into the litter and put her arms round me. Her clothes smelt spicy and strange, the black cloth rough on my neck and cheeks. 'Don't worry, Emily. You are absolutely safe.'

'But Hugh,' I persisted. '*Hugh*.'

Her face clouded.

'It will be better in Kabul,' she said. 'He has nothing to think about but me at the moment. Richard said the army organizes races and cricket matches and costume balls and concerts and amateur theatricals—'

'Oh!' I said crossly and whipped my curtains across in her face. 'After all your wild adventures, won't you find it *dull*?'

The next day we jolted down the other side of the Khyber Pass and camped in a huge flat plain ringed all about with mountains, vast, towering, snow-capped mountains, larger than I ever saw, rearing up into the blue sky. There was a river rushing past, wide and shallow and studded with boulders, and its water looked clear and cold. There were fields around us, little square fields marked out with low stone walls, but around these, and stretching and folding away and away to those astonishing peaks, was the green and purple land, empty, huge and quiet. I pointed to the mountains.

'The Hindu Kush,' Hugh said. His face looked tired and pinched. 'The western range of the Himalayas.'

'Wasn't it worth it?' Charlotte said to me, her face illumined with delight. 'Isn't it like paradise?'

Hugh came over to me, bringing a cup of pale, greenish tea. He stooped to set it beside me and I saw his hands were not at all steady.

He said in a low voice, 'I am most anxious that Charlotte does not ride into Kabul in that absurd fancy dress because we shall be there before long. Will you persuade her for me? She laughs at me when I protest.'

I looked across at Charlotte who was breaking off pieces of bread and tossing them at Sayid. He was leaping like a gazelle and spearing them on one of his awful blades before they hit the ground.

'Of course, Hugh. Hugh – is – is that man safe?'

'Perfectly,' Richard Talbot said across Hugh's snort of despair. 'He mightn't be in anyone else's hands but he would lay down his life for Charlotte and anyone she cared for.'

'Afghans,' Hugh announced angrily, 'are violent and treacherous. Pathans are an extreme form of them. She – she will not listen to me.'

Richard put his hand on Hugh's arm, but Hugh shook it off.

'Don't waste your breath, Richard, I've wasted enough of mine since we left Peshawar. Emily, do what you can for me. I can just visualize Lady MacNaghten and Lady

Sale's reaction as I ride into the Cantonment accompanied by Charlotte in that ridiculous costume.'

He walked away and began to shout at the servants.

Richard stooped and laid a bunch of wild flowers in my lap. They were like giant harebells in shape, some blue-white, some deep purplish-blue like midsummer lavender. I looked down at them for a long time in silence and thought what they meant and then Richard said in a voice that was not quite relaxed, 'We will go through the Kabul Gorge today. You never saw anything so dramatic, it must be thousands of feet deep and in places not a hundred wide. And the river roars at the bottom of it. It was terrifying for some of the sepoys when we came up from India.'

I said, 'Thank you for my flowers,' and Richard coloured a little.

'I'll give you roses in Kabul. They were magnificent last summer.'

'I am – so glad you are with us. Not just because I am a coward, you know, that isn't the strongest reason—'

He went down on his knees beside me.

'I should not care if it were,' he said, 'It would satisfy me absolutely – for the moment that is. I – I was demented with worry when you were ill.'

He put his hand out and laid it on mine, on the blue flowers on my lap, and I did not take my hand away but let it lie there under his large, warm touch and we did not speak for a while. And then I thought he might be going to say something that I wanted him to say very much but that I did not want him to say yet, so I drew my hand away slowly and said, 'Do you think things are very – difficult between Charlotte and Hugh?'

He removed his own hand with visible reluctance.

'Yes,' he said.

I waited, pleating the cloth of my gown.

'I see both their points of view, Emily. There isn't a shadow of doubt that Charlotte is wonderful at this kind of thing, she's so resourceful and brave and energetic. She'll be riding as well as any crack cavalryman soon and I'm sure she'd be a splendid shot.' He paused. 'Was she like this in England?'

I said cautiously, 'There was never a chance to be anything but conventional in England.'

'And that's how Hugh first saw her.'

'But he knew she was different even then. She wasn't – suitable in Richmond if you know what I mean. He fell in love with her because she was so uncommon, not because she was ordinary.'

'Perhaps he didn't bargain for quite such extraordinariness.'

I felt suddenly very miserable in spite of Richard's comforting presence and being recovered and the glorious morning. Charlotte and Sayid were still playing at bread and daggers, and Hugh was striding up and down as the mules were loaded, shouting.

'She must change her clothes, though,' Richard said. 'The Kabulis will think Hugh has an Afghan mistress.'

'Charlotte wouldn't mind that.'

'The Afghans would, Emily. That's one of the reasons Alexander Bewick is always getting himself into such scrapes. He holds the wildest parties and has hordes of Afghan women there, and their menfolk get extremely indignant. They don't like to see a feringhi with their women.'

'Are they very beautiful?' I said, conscious of my limp sickroom hair all over my shoulders.

Richard looked at me keenly.

'I don't think so, but plenty do. There are lots of flowery poems about Afghan beauties, all large eyes and pouting mouths, but they are too dark and heavy to my taste.'

'Oh,' I said, and I nearly added, 'Good,' but stopped myself just in time. Then Hugh shouted that we must go onward, and Richard moved away to his pony and the procession set off again with Charlotte at its head and Sayid running at her stirrup.

It took two days of persuading to prise Charlotte out of her black robes. Only when I was nearly in tears and forced to say untruthfully that it was *I* who would feel so awkward, not Hugh, did she relent and vanish behind a boulder with Jane. When she re-appeared she looked quite subdued, dressed once more in her green and cream habit, and she mounted her horse in silence and rode away in front of us, her head very high.

Kabul itself looked rather a disappointment as we neared it, a sprawl of low mud houses, unrelieved by domes or minarets, but it appeared that on this occasion at least, we were not going to enter it. The British Cantonment, built when Shah Suja filled the citadel with his harem, was a scattering of small stone houses and forts on the eastern edge of the city. It looked to me a very poor choice of site because not only did the ground seem swampy and low, but the mountains reared up sheer behind it and I could imagine, gazing up at the little village clinging to the rocks directly above it, a whole lot of screaming Sayids launching themselves down on us with knives between their teeth.

We were met by Sir William and Lady MacNaghten. He was extraordinary looking with thick black eyebrows and moustache and little round spectacles, but they were most kind to us and very welcoming, and Hugh whispered that it was a great honour that they should take the trouble. I thought privately that it was probably on Richard's account that they had, because Sir William greeted him with real warmth, but I also thought they must be pleased they had bothered when they saw Charlotte, so beautiful and so delighted to be there. She stood beside Hugh in her green-feathered riding hat and turned her lovely smile from Sir William to his wife, and I saw Hugh look down at her with just the hungry adoring look he had always worn in England and at first in Bombay, and which seemed to have vanished as we travelled north. She was being the perfect wife, just then, beautiful, well dressed, grateful and charming. The only thing that spoiled the picture was Sayid, standing as close to her as he dared in his filthy robes, but Hugh luckily had not noticed him, and no-one else would have dared tell him to step back.

The MacNaghtens led us through the Cantonment to our quarters. It was a tidy, symmetrical place, very clearly built by an army for an army, with straight empty lanes running between mud walls behind which were either small houses with flat roofs and courtyards, or rows of barrack rooms as uniform and functional as stalls for horses. It was dull to look at, being built entirely of pale brown mud and pale brown stones and, on account of being new and for practical purposes only, devoid of trees or creepers or any kind of green thing. Its only beauty was the backdrop of those alarming but magnificent mountains and the clear, pure mountain air which triumphed even over the dust we kicked up as we rode along.

Our quarters turned out to be really a little house, whitewashed and quite blank on the outside walls – 'Like the villages on the Pass!' Charlotte exclaimed in pleasure – but revealing a courtyard inside on to which all the rooms opened. They were small and dark, all of them, despite the sun in the courtyard, and one could only get from one to another by walking outside and then in again next door. A flight of white steps led up on to the roof, and some washing was blowing up there and there were empty stone pots out of which bright flowers should have been spilling.

'There now,' said Hugh with satisfaction. 'Aren't you glad I made you bring all our things from India? If I hadn't you would have had not so much as a stick of European furniture.'

'I shouldn't mind,' Charlotte said. 'I should live like the Afghans do.'

Lady MacNaghten looked shocked and said that was not at all desirable. The Afghans only had rugs and cushions really, no proper furniture at all.

'I think that would be much better,' Charlotte said. 'Think how much time we waste in England looking after furniture. If we only had rugs we could just bang the dust out every so often. Nothing to polish at all. Where can I keep my ponies?'

Lady MacNaghten said that most of the horses were kept in the cavalry lines.

'Oh, but I should like mine at hand!' Charlotte said. 'Then I can simply ride on impulse. When I am reasonably accurate shooting from a standing position, Sayid is going to teach me to shoot at full gallop and I'm sure that will need a deal of practice.'

All eyes swung to Sayid who was still shadowing Charlotte closely. I saw Hugh's colour rise and he said angrily that Sayid was a Pathan who had attached himself to us on the Khyber Pass, but who was about to return to his village.

'He most certainly is not,' said Charlotte, and she actually put out her own white hand and grasped Sayid's grimy one.

I said, '*Charlotte!*' I could not help myself.

Lady MacNaghten looked both horrified and disgusted and her husband, in a kind attempt to cover up an awkward moment, said that they would be delighted to help us over any difficulties about settling in, and then he took his wife's arm and steered her towards the rutted lane outside the courtyard.

'But my dear, she *touched* him,' I heard Lady Mac-Naghten say as she went. 'She actually *touched* him.'

There was a sort of explosion when they had gone. Hugh said something in a most furious voice, and then he lunged forward and there was a scuffle and Sayid went rolling in the dust. He was swearing – at least it sounded like the most savage language imaginable – and Hugh and Charlotte were shouting at each other, and then Charlotte tried to help Sayid up and I think Hugh might have hit her too if Richard had not plunged in and prevented it. Sayid scrambled up, knife in hand, howling with fury, but when Charlotte, very white and shaking, went over to him and took the knife from him, he surrendered it as good as gold and stopped yelling at once.

'That was intolerable,' Charlotte said to Hugh. Her voice was low but her eyes were blazing like jewels. 'Intolerable.'

Hugh was panting and a lock of hair had fallen across his pale forehead. He freed himself from Richard's grasp and said loudly, 'I will not have it. I will not have that savage around. He has no idea how to behave.'

Charlotte took a deep breath.

'*You* are the one with no idea how to behave,' she said and then she came to me and took my arm. 'Come Emily, and we shall see about setting up the rooms. We must make one comfortable for you because you look worn out.'

We crossed the courtyard slowly, Charlotte almost carrying me, and went into the first of the rooms. As we crossed the stone threshold from sunlight to no light, I looked back and saw that Hugh was where we had left him, standing by the well in the centre, and that his head and shoulders had drooped suddenly, as if in utter dejection.

CHAPTER SIX

Within a few weeks, we were thoroughly settled in – and thoroughly isolated. Assisted by Sayid, Charlotte plundered the bazaar in Kabul and came home with carpets and quilts patterned in russet and black and ochre, Chinese jars, pierced brass lamps to swing from the black beams of the ceilings and strange marvellous chests and stools stained dull red and finished with greenish brass. The beaten earth floors and rough white walls vanished under rugs and hangings, my camp bed, now dear and familiar, was whisked away and replaced by a bedstead of black carved wood with huge claw feet, piled high with cushions, and my clothes disappeared into boxes with ornate clasps and hinges from which they emerged smelling of sandalwood. The dull imported English china we had bought in Bombay gave way to blue and white Chinese porcelain patterned with pagodas and willow trees and almond blossom, and in every room stood a brazier for charcoal and a divan by it, covered in carpet.

I think Hugh would have made a fuss about it all, and understandably since everything we had brought so painfully from India was left piled in an unused room where it decayed or was stolen, if Charlotte's house had not been so warmly admired. Lady MacNaghten, graciously forgiving Charlotte's lapse, came to call and was evidently much impressed and even Lady Sale, who was very stout and very frightening, stamped about it for a long while and at length pronounced herself charmed. They were followed by all the officer's wives who came crowding and chattering to peer and exclaim, and Hugh suddenly found himself the possessor of the Cantonment's most fashionable house. Of course it led to most awful trouble, because all the merchants in the bazaar immediately put their prices up when the English ladies descended upon them in search of old and wonderful things, but at the beginning it was a triumph and everyone talked of it.

'Everyone' could not of course be said to be very many. There were perhaps some three dozen British officers in the Cantonment of whom twenty or so were married and had brought their families to Kabul. All the wives came to call at once, as punctiliously as if they had been in England, and we sat stiffly on the new divans and drank tea from the new porcelain and were told what a splendid and energetic community we were lucky enough to find ourselves in.

'Not a week goes by,' Mrs Anderson assured us, 'but there is some project to occupy ourselves with. A deal of entertaining you know, and the most amusing theatricals and racing and cricket matches and the embroidery circle—'

I saw Charlotte's eyes glaze for a moment.

'And of course, these poor heathens ever need our help,' Mrs Curtis said solemnly. 'Notably the children, poor little lost souls.'

Lady Sale snorted.

'At least Islam keeps them from drink!'

Charlotte, urged by Hugh, dutifully returned these calls. I would have gone with her except that the fever came back intermittently for a while and I did not seem to be as adaptable as she was to the altitude. So she nobly went alone and came back yawning with reports of conversation on servants and nursery illnesses and the bad behaviour of little Mrs Scarborough who flirted openly with all the bachelor officers and made herself impossible to invite to dinner.

'I feel quite drawn to her,' Charlotte said. 'Much more of this and I shall be imitating her faithfully. The MacNaghtens wish us to dine with them on Friday. Please be better, Emily, for I need you there both to sustain and restrain me.'

'Of course,' I said. 'Of course I'll come.'

It seemed a very incongruous business, putting on our evening dresses and taking trouble with our hair, in order to jolt through the dusty lanes of an Afghan village to dinner in a house made of mud and furnished with European furniture. There was English silver to eat with, and French porcelain, and we drank soup and ate roast fowl and game birds and then a ragôut followed by a salad and syllabubs. If it had not been for the heat and the dark-skinned footmen it would have been easy to think oneself back in Richmond.

I had been kindly placed, by Lady MacNaghten, between two young bachelor officers. They were prepared to be very gallant because there were almost no unmarried ladies in the Cantonment and also, inevitably, because I was Charlotte's sister and she was by far the most beautiful person in the room. There were some good-looking men to be sure, and some pretty women – not many – but Charlotte's looks outshone them all, eclipsed entirely what beauty anyone else had.

'Miss Brent, your arrival here will transform our lives.'

I smiled.

'We are almost entirely cut off here, you know. You must give us news of the world beyond these mountains. Tell us what is doing in India.'

I said, 'You know that as well as I do. Men are always quicker to seize on information of the political kind you seek than we are.'

Captain Carter, who had splendid fair whiskers which he stroked fondly as he talked said, 'Of course the fair sex is hardly interested in political information. Gossip is more your meat.'

I decided to behave as he wished me to. I glanced at him and then at small, dark Welsh Major Roberts on my right and then I cast my eyes down and said, 'Absolutely. Tell me some.'

'How strong a stomach do you have, Miss Brent?'

'A very strong one, Major Roberts.'

He said, across me, 'Shall we shock her with Bewick's latest exploit then?' and Captain Carter guffawed and caressed his whiskers and nodded roguishly.

'You know whom we mean, Miss Brent? Of course you do, he has been lording it there in the Residency ever since the Resident died, a law unto himself and a headache of monumental proportions to everyone else. Including the Afghans. They are wild for him, simply wild. He has parties that would make your hair curl—' he stopped and grinned at me, '– and that sometimes make us all green with envy. The latest one was the night before last when he and his brother and a friend rode out on the Bamian road and captured some women from a village before the men were home at sunset. It's a wonder he wasn't murdered. I expect his poor victims have been. They were returned at dawn I gather, hung with jewellery and very reluctant to go.' He grinned again. 'Have you seen Mr Bewick, Miss Brent?'

'No,' I said, very much interested but conscious it was indelicate to be so.

'It is a chance of a lifetime,' Major Roberts said, applying himself to his plate once more. 'It's so rare to meet a man with absolutely no principles at all.'

'Devil of a good horseman,' Captain Carter remarked.

'Devil,' said Major Roberts, 'is just the word.'

Apart from dining at the MacNaghtens' I hardly stirred those first few weeks. Charlotte made my room comfortable first, and so for a while I simply moved from my pile of pillows out into the courtyard and back again. Richard came almost daily, bringing me seedlings, and we planted a little vine and some huge luxuriant Asian nasturtiums, and tomatoes and aubergines against a wall. It was only when I was truly better and quite strong again, and I was in a chair outside my bedroom door, quite alone for Charlotte had gone out with Sayid for a shooting lesson in Hugh's absence up at the Bala Hissar. Hugh was gone for a part of each day, sometimes only three hours, sometimes six or eight, because of his administrative duties up at the fortress with Shah Suja. Sitting there I suddenly remembered Captain Carter's words and became aware of quite how cut off we were from the rest of the world. There was the courtyard round me, small and white and fringed with young green leaves, and the doorways all round it, leading into rooms whose interiors were now well known to me. Around that was the Cantonment itself, perhaps a square half mile of British and Indian people, and outside that was Afghanistan, mile upon impenetrable mile of peaks and gorges and ravines, inhabited by an unknown and savage race, and quite cut off from everything I knew, even India, by the great prison walls of the mountains.

I couldn't, I realized, even expect a letter from Mamma. No runner would get unmolested through the Khyber, even if he were willing to try, and we were more than a week of rugged marching through most inhospitable country from any place that was even halfway familiar. It chilled me to think that and my wicker chair in the sunshine ceased to be a peaceful haven any more and the courtyard became tiny and vulnerable with me a helpless victim at its heart. I called for Jane and I could hear my voice sound thin and shaking, but she did not hear me, so I got up from my chair and ran about looking for her, suddenly seized with panic and needing a companion desperately.

She was nowhere to be found. I went round and round the courtyard, calling and then I thought she might be hanging out our washing, so I ran up the steps on to the roof. It was empty too, flat and white and hot, and from it I could see other rooftops and other strings of laundry and beyond that the mountains going sheer up to the sky. I could hear a few children in neighbouring houses, and faint shouts and cries came on the still summer air, and then I heard hooves and thought with a clutch of relief that it was Charlotte, hurrying to be back before Hugh.

But it wasn't Charlotte. I strained my eyes to pick out her flying black figure threading its way through the lanes of the Cantonment, and saw only a small group of horsemen, Afghans by their dress, galloping between the houses, it seemed right in my direction. I stayed where I was on the roof, my knees pressed against the low parapet and my hand shading my eyes, and I watched them vanish and reappear among the low houses, all at a breakneck speed.

As they came nearer I could hear that they were shouting to each other and laughing, and more people came out on to the empty white rooftops to see what was going on. A woman, a maid by her dress, two roofs away, waved her arms at me and called something I couldn't hear, and then the horsemen came sweeping round the corner of our lane and thudded to a halt at our gate and one of them called, in faultless English, 'It's this one! I'm sure of it.'

I ran across the roof and looked down into the courtyard. There were four of them and they had swung themselves out of their saddles in seconds and had come bursting through our gate, tossing aside the old bearer who was supposed to be gatekeeper. They had marvellous clothes, tunics and turbans of red and deep blue embroidered with gold, and breeches tucked into glossy boots, and they went striding about our little courtyard as if they owned it.

I called down indignantly, 'What are you doing? This is a private house!'

The tallest of them had his back to me when I spoke, he was bent over my vine. But at the sound of my voice he whipped round and squinting against the sun, made me out on the roof and came over to stand below me.

I had always thought Hugh good-looking. I had also thought Cousin George attractive in his highly coloured energetic way, but this man's face was in a class by itself. I held on to the parapet and looked down at him, at his straight nose and dark brows and small moustache. He had brown skin and brilliant grey eyes and he was smiling at me with all the disconcerting sureness of someone who knows how beautiful they are. I said nothing but just gazed downwards at him, and then he raised his hands and lifted his turban from his head and I saw he had dark curly hair cut short like an Englishman.

He said, 'Mrs Connell?'

'No,' I said carefully, because although his accent was impeccable, he was after all a foreigner. 'I am her sister. Mrs Connell is out riding.'

He laughed up at me, then he bowed and went to the

foot of the outside staircase and held up his hand to indicate that he should hand me down to the courtyard.

'Then until she returns, Mrs Connell's sister, won't you descend and entertain us? Alexander Bewick at your service ma'am.'

I froze on the top step, partly out of embarrassment at mistaking him for an Afghan, and partly because his reputation was so shocking and the tales of his immoral exploits were coming daily to our ears along the Cantonment gossip lines.

I said, 'Alexander Bewick!' and my voice was as horrified as I felt.

He laughed again and came up the steps and took my hand firmly.

'I shall not eat you. In fact you will be astounded at how tame I am. This is my brother Charles, and Edward Tulso and George Rickards who are staying at the Residency. Miss—'

'Brent,' I said and felt quite overawed. 'Emily Brent.'

Alexander Bewick kissed my hand and led me back to my wicker chair and seated me in it. Then he sat on the parapet of the well and the others folded themselves cross-legged on the ground and I saw that though Alexander's brother was brown-skinned, the other two had fair English faces beneath their turbans.

'Miss Emily Brent, how charming you look,' Alexander said. 'I only wish you could be better pleased to see us.'

I was finding it very difficult to take my eyes away from him and when I answered him I stammered a little.

'Wh – why have you c – come?'

'Ah! We have come because of the reputation of this house. I know you are newcomers here, I'm well aware Hugh Connell has only danced attendance on Shah Suja for a month, but your renown has spread far and wide. Sir William MacNaghten even had the temerity to suggest that his wife thought this house superior in taste to the Residency. Now I'm not a vain man, nor a jealous one, but I was curious to see the house that has been made in four short weeks a better treasure trove of Asian splendours than the Residency which I have laboured on three years.'

'It – it has been all my sister's doing.'

'I know,' he said and he smiled again and his voice took on such a disturbing and intimate tone as he said that, that I felt it was perhaps Charlotte herself he wished to see, not the house at all.

I got to my feet.

'I'm afraid you cannot stay,' I said. 'My sister will be gone all morning. I will tell her you called.'

He rose from the well and came over to me and put his hands on my shoulders, gently pressing me down on to my cushion again.

'I *can* stay, Miss Brent. I will behave impeccably, I will do nothing to alarm you, but I have not ridden all the way to the Cantonment for nothing. I know your sister is a great horsewoman. Indeed, there is quite as much gossip about your sister as about her house. It is said she is very beautiful and very talented, that she sits a horse like an Afghan and shoots straight as a die. I did ask Hugh Connell to bring her to dine with me – I should have asked you too, Miss Brent, had I known you were here – but he became immensely pompous and refused. Yet he allows her to roam about with only an Afghan for company.'

I said, quite without meaning to, 'He doesn't know she does,' and clapped my hand to my mouth in horror.

Alexander Bewick laughed.

'I didn't really suppose he would, dear Miss Brent. I am surprised he allows her to keep such a pet in the first place.'

The Sayid question had declined into the unmentionable. Charlotte had refused either to obey or to argue, and Hugh must have resigned himself, because Sayid still padded like an unwashed shadow behind Charlotte, her self-appointed groom, servant and bodyguard. Hugh looked harassed, it was true, but he claimed Shah Suja was proving very difficult and was refusing to ingratiate himself with his people at all, which obviously threatened his security on the throne. On the one occasion I had asked Charlotte about Sayid she had kissed me and told me that I mustn't do Hugh's dirty work for him and gone out of the room, humming.

'That's a bone of contention too, I see,' said Alexander Bewick.

'No-one else in the Cantonment, no *lady*, has a native servant,' I said.

'But it doesn't sound to me as if your sister resembles any other lady in the Cantonment anyway, so why should she in this respect?'

'Sayid is very dirty,' I said firmly.

Alexander Bewick flung back his handsome head and shouted with laughter.

'Is he? Dirty. Dear, dear.'

I said, 'Oh please go away, Mr Bewick. It's wrong for you to be here—' and then Jane materialized in a doorway across the courtyard and came to say that Charlotte was coming.

There was nothing I could do. I thought for a moment of how disapproving Hugh would be, but the situation was not in my hands at all and I was quite helpless. The three companions uncoiled themselves from the floor and went to stand behind Alexander like a bodyguard and when Charlotte came in, he was the first thing she saw, standing there in the bright noonday light in his scarlet tunic and cream-coloured breeches with his followers behind him, like a frieze.

She stopped in the gateway, the long dark figure of Sayid behind her, dressed in her black robes, but with no jewellery because she had been riding, no ornament at all except those long wine-coloured plaits. I stood up to say that this was the infamous Mr Bewick and that I had tried to make him leave, but he wouldn't. But I succeeded in saying nothing. I simply stood as still and silent as all of us there. Then, to my amazement because he had seemed so sure of himself, so arrogant, Alexander Bewick went down on one knee in the dust and Charlotte came over to him, smiling, and held out her hand.

'I don't know you, but I can guess. There's only one European here who dresses like a native, and that's Alexander Bewick.'

He kissed her hand and held on to it, still kneeling there.

I said, 'He's come to compare houses, Charlotte. He's heard how lovely you have made this.'

'I did come for that,' he said slowly, and rose from his knees. 'But I shouldn't have. If I'd known.'

'But I like to have my house admired. I never wanted to make a house pretty before. Did I, Emily? I wasn't interested.'

He held out his arm for her to take.

'Show me,' he said.

So we trailed round behind them like some royal progress, in and out of all our little rooms, and they kept stopping while Alexander said, 'Now that's one of the finest Bokhara I ever saw,' and 'That's a better lamp than mine.' When at last they had finished, he looked at me for the first time since Charlotte had come and said, 'Well, Miss Brent, I have to concede that Lady MacNaghten is right.' Then he turned back to Charlotte and said, 'But if the casket is beautiful, she never told me what jewel it held.'

Charlotte said nothing but her eyes looked as they did when Hugh had reluctantly translated the nautch dancer's song for her.

'When will you dine with me? Today?'

She looked quickly at me.

'Today we go to the Sales, don't we Emily?'

'Yes,' I said. 'And tomorrow the Sheltons.'

'Cut them,' said Alexander Bewick. He bent and whispered something to Charlotte. She laughed and shook her head.

'The day after tomorrow, then,' he said.

She nodded. I thought of Hugh and how much he would disapprove. If he disapproved enough, he would forbid her to go, and then there would be an argument and the household would be set by the ears, as it was over Sayid. I thought too of Charlotte's reputation. Lady MacNaghten could not reasonably be expected to forgive Charlotte everything and I knew she had intimated to Hugh that Charlotte should not ride about with only a Pathan for an attendant. I saw her point of view, just as I used to see Mamma's but I also saw how happy Charlotte was, how fulfilled.

'We would love to come.'

'I shall send you an escort. If Hugh thinks himself above such things, you must come alone.' He bent down to her and said, his face close to hers, 'But *you* must come. You *must*.'

Charlotte said, 'But you would hardly miss me. Gossip says that women are the one thing you have no shortage of.'

'Oh,' he said. 'Women,' and from the way he spoke, he made a clear distinction between women and Charlotte.

'Promise me,' he said to her, 'you will come.'

He turned and said something to Sayid, and Sayid stepped forward and knelt as he sometimes did to Charlotte and replied in his eager hoarse tones. Alexander turned back to Charlotte.

'You see?' he said. 'You'll be made a prisoner.'

'Only if I want to be.'

They remained looking at each other for some moments after this, and then Alexander's companions bestirred themselves from their silence and began to shuffle and clear their throats and I wished to say something to them and did not know what, feeling very Richmondish by comparison with their glamour. I suppose we should have remained like that some while, Alexander and Charlotte gazing and the rest of us looking at our feet and feeling superfluous and awkward, had not Sayid decided that this suspended moment had

85

gone on long enough and shouted for the Residency horses.

Alexander did not say goodbye to Charlotte, he simply kissed her hand. Then he turned to me and said, 'Perhaps now that you have evidence of my docility, Miss Brent, you will put about in the Cantonment that I am not such a bad lot as they say.'

I had never actually met anyone who seemed less docile. He might have behaved with gallantry and charm but he gave the impression of something coiled and dangerous waiting to spring and devour. I managed to look up at him and hold out my hand.

'Goodbye, Mr Bewick.'

He laughed and kissed my hand in a perfunctory way and I felt a little jump of excitement when his moustache brushed my skin which I was most indignant at myself for feeling. We watched them while they swung themselves easily into their saddles and then Alexander paused one moment for a last look at Charlotte, like someone refreshing themselves at a spring before plunging across a desert, then he dug his heels into his horse's sides and there was a clatter of hooves and clouds of white dust and they were gone.

Of course Hugh was adamant. We both knew he would be, though I think Charlotte always had a feeling she would win him round.

'There is no question of it, of course. It is the one house in Kabul I entirely forbid you to enter. I know the young bachelor officers go there but none of the married people would even think of it. The stories—'

'What stories?' Charlotte said.

Hugh looked uncomfortable. For a man who clearly knew what ardour was, he was strangely reticent, even priggish.

'It is not important.'

'It is important. If you will not let us go you must at least be courteous enough to give us good reasons.'

Luckily for Hugh, at this moment Richard came, bringing me a little yellow canary in a wonderful Chinese cage with bells on its upswept roof corners. I was entranced with it and it was not for some time that Charlotte could drive us back to Alexander Bewick's wild parties. Richard coloured a little and looked at me rather apologetically.

'I was there last week,' he said.

'Tell us what happened!'

'There – there was a deal to drink. French wine mostly. Nobody but Bewick has much left, but there was enough champagne to float a ship and claret, superb claret. We were waited on by – by Afghan women and then after dinner – well, after dinner—,' he stopped and looked at me again. 'It wasn't really my sort of evening, Emily. I came away about midnight. I gather there's been an awful fuss about it and the Kabulis have been throwing rocks at our soldiers all week. Bewick doesn't care about anyone's opinion but he did say to me he thought we should keep more of an eye on the Afghans than we do. He thinks an uprising is a matter of months and we should be very watchful of Akbar Khan, son of the deposed ruler. He doesn't think any of us are taking Akbar seriously enough. Akbar bitterly resents his father's deposition and is adamantly opposed to a pro-British puppet on the Afghan throne. He's also a man to be reckoned with in terms of courage and intelligence and the power to draw followers to him. Bewick says Akbar could eat Shah Suja for breakfast if he chose—'

Hugh said, 'Nonsense. Ludicrous theories. Bewick isn't sober enough long enough to know anything.'

'He knows more about Afghan intrigue than any of us, Hugh. He knows what he's talking about.'

'He'll be the first Englishman cut down,' Hugh said and I saw Charlotte's eyes harden for a moment. Then Hugh stood up and adjusted the belt of his uniform tunic.

'You only confirm what I knew, Richard. Bewick may

debauch Afghan women if he's fool enough, but he shan't do the same to mine.'

So we dined with the Sales that day and Charlotte was so good and never said another word about Alexander Bewick. She looked so lovely and asked all the ladies about their children and praised the water ice and flattered Lady Sale, and Hugh was in a high good humour. The next day she did not ride with Sayid at all, but sat in the courtyard with Jane and me and actually held a bit of sewing. She did not stitch once, but it was miracle enough to see her sit so tranquil and quiet while Sayid squatted in a corner and picked his teeth and later sighed. We dined at the Sheltons and Charlotte wore her wedding pearls and was once more the model wife, only forgetting herself once when she picked a piece of chicken out of her pilau with her fingers and gave it to the Sheltons' dog.

Even the following day she did not ride. She persuaded me to come with her to the bazaar it is true, a thing I did not like at all, for I both feared and loathed the stinking labyrinth at the heart of Kabul, but we jolted there in a rough sort of chaise some soldiers had made which Hugh felt was a much more seemly way to travel. We haggled for spices we did not really need, coriander and cumin and cardomom, and I saw Charlotte was desperate for an occupation, desperate enough to invent this hot and trivial errand.

The afternoon came and our cook was told to prepare dinner. Hugh returned from the Bala Hissar in great agitation and said that Shah Suja had ordered a number of prominent Kabulis to be thrown into gaol for failing to show him respect.

'If he is not argued out of it, there will be an uprising. The families of the imprisoned men are restless already. I have to go back tonight and continue the attempt to talk him out of it, or there will be bloodshed before morning.'

'Of course,' Charlotte said in a low quiet voice and I looked at her quickly, expecting to see a gleam in her eye, but she was as submissive as she sounded.

'It may take all night,' Hugh said worriedly. 'Bar the gate when you retire. I'll come back the moment I can, even if it isn't until dawn.'

Then he went round the table and kissed Charlotte and smiled at me and went away to where his horse was stamping in the courtyard.

'What should you like to do, Charlotte?'

She did not answer. She sat in her red bamboo chair and gazed at the lamp on the table, and the flame threw purple shadows on the rugs and hangings and long fingers of yellow light on the rough, white ceiling.

She sighed at last, then she said, 'What should *you* like, Emily?'

What I really wanted was to go to my room and read my tiny luxurious ration of Charles Lamb, and talk to my canary and perhaps think gratefully of its donor. It wasn't that I needed to be alone, not that I didn't want to be with Charlotte, but it was only my room, my small carpeted, cushioned chamber that gave me any feeling at all security in these deep blue Afghan nights.

Charlotte said, 'Dear Emily, you want to go away and read and think about Richard and you feel that you mustn't because of me. Well, I promise you that I shall be quite happy, entirely happy. I shall finish my sketch of Sayid and then I shall go to bed and plan where we shall ride tomorrow. I haven't ridden in two days, Emily. It wouldn't be so very wicked, would it, to ride tomorrow?'

I said I never thought her riding wicked and I meant it. It always seems to me more wicked to waste the talents you have than to exploit them unconventionally, though I suppose it is easy for me since the things I am good at are not the things that are liable to shock society. Charlotte got up and came to me and put her arms round me.

'Would you always love me, Emily? Whatever I did?'

'Of course,' I said.

Then she kissed me and called Sayid and went drifting out into the dusky courtyard. I sat for a long time in the lamplit dining-room and thought about love and Charlotte and Hugh and Richard, and I felt very happy and calm when I had finished, so I got up and went to my room and found it warm and welcoming.

I didn't even read my two pages of Lamb. I climbed on to my bed holding him, and lay watching Jane while she hung up my clothes or folded them into the red boxes, and then felt so full of sleep and contentment that I slipped into slumber with never a word read. Jane must still have been in the room when I fell asleep because when I woke, later, my lamp had been extinguished and there was a bright blade of moonlight slicing between the bed curtains.

I sat up, not sure what had woken me, but feeling that I had heard the dull thud of our gate banging. So Hugh was come home and I waited to hear his boots pass my room on the way to his. There was no sound, only a nightingale somewhere, romantic and lovely in the black and silver night. I got up and opened my door. The moonlight filled the courtyard with pale light and all the leaves of my plants were bleached to grey. I thought I would go and see if Charlotte was still lying wakefully planning routes to ride around, so I put on my Kashmiri shawl and stepped out into the white moonshine.

The black bundle in the corner was Sayid, asleep with his rifle as a pillow. He always slept there a few feet only from Charlotte's door. I tiptoed past him, waiting for him to wake and recognize me, but he lay limp and still, and then I saw it was not Sayid at all but the old gatekeeper, and his head was not on a rifle but on his crutch for he had lost one leg below the knee. This was odd and not at all usual, and I felt a clutch of apprehension and ran to Charlotte's room, wrenching the door open quite without knocking.

It was black inside, quite dark, but the moonlight from the courtyard came in with me and showed me Charlotte's bed, quite empty and unrumpled, the cushions smooth and plump. The light crept on as I pushed the door wider and I saw that on a chest were tossed the clothes Charlotte had worn at dinner, grey-blue silk with the flounces piped in velvet, and that above the chest was an empty brass hook, the hook where her black robes were used to hang. Her pearls lay gleaming in a lacquer tray but her queer barbaric jewellery of silver and turquoises was nowhere to be seen. It was plain where she had gone; robes missing, jewellery missing. Sayid missing, the thud of the gate, the old gatekeeper in a stupefied slumber – Charlotte had gone to Alexander Bewick.

I thought of calling Jane, of sending bearers to the Residency, to the Bala Hissar, to Richard, but I did none of them. I suppose I wanted Charlotte to be happy more than anyone, even if I was fond of Hugh and sorry for him, so I stood in her room for a while and prayed that Shah Suja might take all night to agree to let the prisoners go and then I crept back to my own room and closed the door.

CHAPTER SEVEN

Hugh did not come back until the sun was well and truly risen. I had hardly slept so anxious was I, both for Charlotte's safety and for Hugh's peace of mind, but I had heard her soft return when the first light made a pale line beneath my door and I must have slept then a little, in sheer relief. She did not come to breakfast so I ate my bread and drank my tea in solitude and wondered what I should say to her, for it would be impossible to conceal from her that I knew she had gone.

Hugh came in before she woke. He looked exhausted but relieved and said that Shah Suja had at last agreed and the Afghans were to be released at noon.

'We are all summoned to the Bala Hissar,' he said. 'All the officers and their wives in the Cantonment. It's some sort of reception. Would you be interested to go?'

I knew Charlotte would want to. She was very scornful of the Cantonment's own attempts at amusements and when offered the part of Viola in a forthcoming production of *Twelfth Night* had laughed as if the suggestion could not have been made very seriously. Mrs Anderson, who had clearly wanted the part herself and had been sacrificing her own desires to the cause of Art in asking Charlotte in the first place, became very resentful and angry and told her friend Mrs Shelton that Mrs Connell had had her head quite turned by admiration.

'If that were the case,' I said firmly, 'my sister would have accepted the part in order to be admired further. She refused because she does not particularly enjoy English occupations unless she is in England.'

'Shakespeare,' said Mrs Anderson impressively, 'is beyond such confines. England, Illyria, Afghanistan, his words are as true. I have never before heard Shakespeare defined as a mere occupation.'

I saw that whatever I said would do Charlotte no good in the eyes of these upright matrons, so I contented myself with smiling at Mrs Anderson's little Mary, an enchanting child of three, who, not knowing what an unsuitable person I was on account of my swollen-headed relations, smiled back.

'Well?' Hugh said now. 'Should you like to go to the Bala Hissar?'

'Did you say all the officers?' I asked. 'Wouldn't that be dangerous, not to leave any here?'

'You sound exactly like Richard,' Hugh said impatiently. 'The Afghans are as firmly controlled as if they were British themselves. They know quite well we are a superior strength. They would never dare to attack in our absence.'

I refrained from pointing out that Hugh had spent a whole night in attempting to avert just such an uprising, because he had had no sleep and I was sorry for him on account of Charlotte. She came in just then, fresh and smiling in a blue cotton gown, and kissed Hugh and then me with every appearance of someone with a comfortable conscience.

The servants brought her tea and toast, and eggs for Hugh, and she asked him how he had got on and seemed much pleased at his success. Then he suggested going to Bala Hissar and, as I knew it would, her face lit up.

'Oh yes, Hugh, oh yes! How wonderful!'

He rose and smiled down at her.

'I thought you might like an Afghan treat. I didn't want you to think that I had not noticed you had refrained from riding alone these last few days.'

Out of the corner of my eyes, I caught a glimpse of Sayid squatting in the courtyard outside the open doors of the dining-room.

'It pleases me,' Hugh went on, 'to see that you understand that one must defer to convention sometimes. It gives me hope that you will soon see I also speak sense about that Pathan.'

Charlotte said nothing. She had been looking up at him with a smile, but the smile faded now and her eyes went light and hard.

'You should catch up on your lost sleep, Hugh,' she said.

He bowed slightly and left us. There was some small sudden movement of his right boot as he went out into the sunlight and I wondered if he had had a sudden urge to kick Sayid and restrained it. Charlotte, I think, saw nothing because when I turned back to her, her eyes were fixed upon me and she was smiling. She leaned forward a little and reached out for my hand across the table.

'Oh, Emily!' she said. 'It was wonderful! Emily darling,

don't furrow your brow. Of course I know you know, in fact I almost told you when he came for me, but you were sleeping so beautifully with Charles Lamb tight in your arms that it seemed a pity—'

'*He* came for you?'

'Oh yes. Why else should I have gone?'

'But – but Charlotte, was it *safe*?'

She laughed at me for this and patted my hand with her free one and then laid it on the table again.

'Darling Emily. Never more safe.'

'But didn't you think of being discovered? Of – of something happening to you?'

'No. Why should it? I was doing what it is entirely in my nature to do. I could no more *not* have gone than I could have stopped breathing.'

'But why? Why? Because of the adventure?'

Charlotte got up and went to the doors which had been pushed wide open to let the sun in on the russet and black carpet, the black lacquered table, the brass spoons and forks with their handles of mother of pearl, the blue and white Chinese porcelain on which the crumbs of our breakfast were scattered. She stood there for quite a long time and I had a sudden vision of sitting just like this, pushing a crust around my plate, after breakfast in Richmond, watching Charlotte's back view at the window and feeling just as I did now, that some huge force was boiling within her frame and that I shouldn't know what to do with it when she told me what it was.

She turned round and said, 'No, of course not. I went because of him.'

I knew it before she said it, of course I did, but I felt very shaken all the same to hear her say it.

'Be – because of him.'

'When things are right, Emily, your whole self rushes out to meet them. When they are wrong, it cringes away into itself and is frustrated and unhappy. I knew he was right when I saw him over there in the courtyard, by the well, even though he hadn't said anything and I knew he had come for me. He came that first night and the second night to see if I had really gone out to dine and then he came last night to fetch me as he said he would.'

I kept on thinking of the dull things, the conventional little questions that my mind fed relentlessly into my mouth.

'But did he know Hugh was gone to the Bala Hissar?'

Charlotte came back to the table and took the chair beside me.

'Of course. He had been to see Shah Suja yesterday afternoon and persuaded him to let those men out in no time. Hugh needn't have gone at all. They agreed on noon today because Shah Suja said if they were in for a shorter time his authority would seem to be being mocked at. Alexander can do anything with him.'

I wondered if Alexander had also persuaded him to set up the charade of Hugh's going to the Bala Hissar so that Alexander might abduct Charlotte. Presumably a man with hundreds of concubines has few scruples, if any, on such a question.

'Emily, don't look so horrified, I can't bear you to. I've done nothing shocking. I simply went to the Residency – which is beautiful and full of the most wonderful old Chinese things you ever saw – and we sat on cushions together and were brought wine and delicious strong Turkish coffee and a hookah for Alexander and we talked. I suppose we talked for six or seven hours but it seemed like as many minutes. He knows everything about Afghanistan, everything. He spent weeks in disguise in Bokhara where there is a terrible mad Amir who hates white men and saw prisoners being thrown into the bug-pit, and he dined with Dost Mohammed here in Kabul before he was driven from the throne and he led a band of soldiers who managed to drive the Persians away from Herat, and if it wasn't for MacNaghten and Lord Auckland and their two-faced policies and their everlasting changes of mind—'

'Charlotte!'

'I'm sorry,' she said, but her face was glowing.

I picked up the teapot and poured out a cup and pushed it towards her. Whatever else its failings, Kabul supplied the most delicious tea I ever drank, pale and scented, from the highlands of Western China.

'He's a Scot, Emily. He has a house called Castle Bewick on the West Coast. It's on a loch and there are hills all round and deer and sheep and a river full of salmon and he grows apricots there just like Kabul, because the climate is so mild. The house is quite new, it was built by his father about forty years ago and it has turrets and spiral stone stairs and a great hall in the centre like a medieval hall with galleries at each end and fireplaces big enough to burn whole trees. He hasn't seen it for eight years, nearly nine. He left it just after he was thirty and his mother is there to look after it and she is very beautiful and stern and none of the servants dare take advantage of her,' She paused. 'Emily – are you angry?'

'No,' I said, 'not angry. But I can't help thinking the things Mamma would have called sensible. I don't mean to, I just have that sort of brain. But – but you are married, Charlotte, you can't dine with other men alone, however fascinating and powerful—'

'Oh, but I have to,' she said simply. 'I have to.'

She finished the tea and rose.

'Shall you tell Hugh?' I persisted.

She came towards me and put her arms round me.

'No. We shall not,' she said, and kissed me and with that kiss, sealed my complicity with her deceit.

Richard came later that morning. Hugh was still asleep and Charlotte had gone out saying she had promised to call on Lady Sale, for a great friendship had sprung up between them out of mutual recognition of each other's spirited courage and strength of character. She took only Sayid, as usual, though she wore European dress, and because of our conversation at breakfast I doubted her truthfulness for the first time in my life and wondered if she were really going anywhere near Lady Sale. I was angry with myself because of my suspiciousness, and miserable for fear I might be right, so I snapped at poor Jane for no reason, then apologized, then snapped again and eventually took myself into the courtyard to prod irritably at the earth and hack at the plants until I was prevented by the very welcome sight of Richard.

He knelt beside me and said, 'You shouldn't really touch an oleander now, you know. Out here you really ought to leave it.'

I dropped my scissors and felt absurdly that I might cry. He was so large and gentle and he touched the little shoots I had cut off with such compassion that I had a sudden violent urge to tell him what was happening and ask him what I should do. But chasing on this urgent desire came the thought that Charlotte's situation was very new and raw and might be only temporary, a sort of romantic whim, so I said nothing and concentrated on looking as contrite as indeed I felt, about the poor oleander.

'I shouldn't really have pruned it at all. Can't think what came over me.'

He helped me to my feet.

'Don't worry. It will recover. Emily, you look tired.'

'We didn't seem to have a very peaceful night somehow. Hugh was away with Shah Suja and I suppose that made one restless.'

'Are you afraid here, Emily?'

I looked about me at the courtyard and all that was in it seemed very comfortable and domestic after our three months in Kabul, and then I looked up at the great mountains soaring above it and the little white village of Bemaru poised above us as if it could suddenly plummet down on us like a bird of prey.

'Not really,' I said.

Richard waited until I had settled myself in my wicker

chair, and then he sat on the edge of the well. It was shady in the centre there because of the maple tree with a curious lovely twisted trunk that looked as if it were made of hempen ropes. Richard thought it was probably an Oriental maple. He looked up into its jagged shade now as if he were seeking some sort of inspiration and he stayed like that for so long that at last I said, 'Should I be afraid?'

'Hugh thinks not, MacNaghten thinks not, so does Elphinstone, and clearly so does Lord Auckland, though what he knows about it, tucked up safely in his palaces in Calcutta or Simla, I can't think, but I don't think it's all as calm as they imagine and I know several of the young officers agree with me. Bewick has been saying all year that British complacency is dangerous but although he is probably the best informed of all of us out here, MacNaghten would as soon heed him as the devil.'

I said, deliberately suppressing my urge to catch up his reference to Bewick, 'I suppose the Afghans don't want an Amir selected for them by us, and only kept here by us. Their country is occupied after all—' my voice tailed away as I suddenly began to imagine what Afghan resentment might lead to, a horde of furiously angry Sayids armed with knives and rifles and perfectly careless of life, their own or anyone else's.

Richard reached out and took one of my hands.

'MacNaghten has been made Governor General of Bombay, Emily. He's delighted of course because Bombay is only one step from Lord Auckland and Governor General of India. He wants to leave Kabul in the early autumn and as I am on his staff, I am supposed to go with him.'

'Of course,' I said, 'you must,' and then we sat and looked at each other for a long time and didn't speak.

Then Richard said, 'Do you know if Hugh plans to stay for – for much longer? It's always perfectly possible to find a replacement after a year or so of duty up here if you are only seconded as he is and your own regiment has gone.'

I knew he was actually asking me a far more important question and so I said, 'I don't know about that, Richard. Hugh wouldn't talk to me about his plans. But I must stay with them, with Charlotte. I must stay – at the moment.'

'Yes,' he said, just as I had to him a moment before, 'of course,' and then he kissed my hand and put it back very reverently on my lap.

'Tell me more of what is going on, Richard, apart from MacNaghten leaving.'

'Trying to leave. I doubt he'll be able to. He's just cut in half the subsidy we have been paying to the tribes in the Khyber Pass and that will hardly be a popular move. It's the surest way to turn them from neutral Pathan tribesmen into enemies of Britain and Afghan patriots at one blow. He seems bent on economy because he's also sending back one of our two British brigades and can you imagine the time the poor devils will have in the Pass with the tribesmen on their half subsidy?'

'But what about you, when you go with Sir William?' Richard looked at me very meaningfully.

'It isn't me I'm worried about. If things boil up as Bewick surely says they will, I'll move heaven and earth to stay. Of course Bewick would like MacNaghten to go because that gives him a strong chance of stepping into his shoes. Heavens, Emily, don't you sometimes feel this is a very claustrophobic place? All these mountains hemming us in, all so landlocked. I suppose it's my being a Cornishman. I can't get used to being without the sea.'

'A Cornishman?' I said, my heart immediately full of the violent homesickness the word aroused.

'Yes. A North Cornishman. I have a house at the head of the Camel estuary. My uncle left it to me as he had no sons.'

'And a garden, Richard?'

'Oh yes,' he said and smiled, 'a glorious garden. The lilies are my pride, I have just the place for them, a small sunny walled garden with an old Turkey fig in it and a pink camellia on the north side which is a perfect vision in bloom. Camellias like a northern aspect, which always surprises me. Emily – do gardens mean much to you?'

I held my hand out to him again.

'They are beginning to mean a great deal,' I said, and then there were clattering hooves outside and Charlotte's voice and she came into the courtyard a moment later alone while some of the hooves went stamping off again.

'Lady Sale was in wonderful form!' she said, and tossed her hat to Jane. 'She said MacNaghten has "insufficient moral courage" and called the Afghans "rascals". I don't believe she is afraid of anyone or anything.'

'I rather wish she was in command,' Richard said. He had risen when Charlotte came in and was standing behind my chair so that I could sense his comforting bulk behind me. 'She would be a flogger, it's true, but she has excellent judgement and is entirely intrepid.'

Then he took his leave and held my hand a little longer than usual and I discovered that I was most reluctant to see him go. Charlotte went in to change out of her habit, leaving me dreaming by the well, and when she came back she said, 'Lady Sale isn't the only one who thinks Sir William has rose-coloured spectacles. Alexander has thought so from the beginning.'

'Oh?' I said, hazy still with my own inward pictures.

'He rode home with me. I was just leaving Lady Sale when an Afghan came suddenly upon me out of a side turning wearing Shah Suja's livery and it was Alexander. Wasn't it clever? No-one could have spotted him. It's such a good thing he is as dark as he is.'

I thought of saying something admonishing about such a risky escapade in broad daylight but knew it would be useless. Charlotte began to laugh and I knew she could read my thoughts so I smiled at her and she said, 'There's a cricket match tomorrow Emily, and Richard is expected to get a century. Shouldn't you like to go and watch him?'

'He didn't say anything about it!'

'Of course not. He's much too modest. And in any case, from the look of you both when I came in, he had other, better things to say.'

In the end, much to my relief, it was only a small party that left the Cantonment to go up to the Bala Hissar. Lady Sale thoroughly disapproved of Shah Suja whom she regarded as lacking in gratitude to the British who had after all put him on his precious throne and were now keeping him there.

Charlotte had been brave enough to say that we had put him there for our own ends, but Lady Sale thought our ends were irreproachable anyhow so she could wave Charlotte's objection away. Lady Sale refused to go, forbade her daughter, Mrs Sturt, to go, and was generally very influential in reducing the party, which I for one was most grateful for, as I did not like to think of the Cantonment abandoned without a sizeable complement of reliable British left behind.

All the ladies were put into a series of litters, except of course for Charlotte who rode as usual, and went swaying off through the Cantonment. As we passed out of it I could not help noticing that it had no more fortification than a soft bank of heaped up earth and that the two little forts we went out between had nothing in them but grain sacks. A detachment of sepoys in Shah Suja's own livery were waiting for us there because in the last few weeks British soldiers had been stoned in Kabul and it was thought we needed more protection than usual.

Kabul lay about two miles from the Cantonment. I had ridden there perhaps three times only since the early summer, across the flat stony plain in its ring of astounding mountains. The Bala Hissar was out of the centre of the city, on a little foothill and although it looked like any Afghan fort from the outside, the inside, said the soldiers who had lived there before Shah Suja brought in all his wives, was a royal palace and had a wonderful audience chamber.

It was a truly beautiful day, one of those late summer days when everything is golden and sleepy and the sky was deep, soft harebell blue behind the white peaks of the mountains. I pulled back the curtains as we went so that I could look out past the poor sweat-soaked backs of the litter-bearers and watch Kabul, low and dun, as it came nearer. Two of the sepoys in Shah Suja's livery flanked me on each side, as they did each litter, and after a while one brought his horse up beside me and said my name.

I suppose I might have guessed that Alexander Bewick would hide himself in any gathering that held Charlotte, but I was startled all the same and stunned anew by his face, which I had not seen since that morning in the courtyard.

I said, 'Why are you dressed like that, Mr Bewick?'

He smiled and shrugged.

'I had an invitation, Miss Brent, and I was commanded not to accept it. I am supposed to be unfit company for the ladies.'

I said nothing.

'You won't, of course, ask me why I have disobeyed and come, but I shall tell you all the same. My chief reason is your sister, as well you know, but my other reason is that I wish to keep an eye on things. I don't like to miss anything, Miss Brent, and in such a situation as we are in now, I cannot be too vigilant.'

'I gather you don't think things are as tranquil as they look, Mr Bewick.'

'You gather this, I think, from the excellent Captain Talbot. And you gather quite rightly. Not to put too fine a point on it, I am waiting for the lid to blow off. When it does, Miss Brent, I think you may be quite glad to know me, however obnoxious you find me.'

I wanted to say that I did not find him so much obnoxious as disconcerting but that I did disapprove very much of his pursuit of Charlotte, but somehow each sentence I framed in my mind sounded more priggish than the one before.

'I should like your good opinion, Miss Brent. I don't say that not to have it would alter my course, but it would be a pleasant thing to have. Would your feelings be in any way changed if you knew that in the last three weeks, for the first time in five years – in fact since my arrival in Afghanistan – there is not one single black-eyed damsel at the Residency? I have turned out the very last one, bag and baggage.'

'I hope,' I said in a rush, quite without meaning to, 'that you don't mean to replace them with – with—'

'Only if she wishes it as fervently as I do,' he said. 'I'm no bully, Miss Brent.'

I tried to look as daunting as I could from the undignified position of sitting in a litter.

'Mr Bewick,' I said. 'My sister is married.'

He smiled down at me, his teeth white under his black moustache and his grey eyes brilliant with amusement.

'Why, so she is, Miss Brent,' he said and bowed and spurred his horse to a canter.

The Bala Hissar was huge when we got to it, a massive windowless fortress of stone, the tops of its walls finished in irregular crenellations. We went in through a great gateway between lines of sepoys and into a courtyard paved with stone slabs and surrounded by towering walls. We were put down here, and all set about shaking out our skirts and unfurling our parasols, and then Hugh came and offered an arm to Charlotte and to me. I looked at him to see if he had recognized Alexander Bewick in our armed guard, but then realized that he did not know he should resent him anyway since Charlotte had as yet roused no suspicion. How she did it I couldn't think, for if there was anything the Cantonment loved even better than cricket or amateur theatricals, it was gossip. But she seemed, by the simple

103

expedient of taking very little trouble over concealment, to be successful so far.

We left the great forbidding courtyard and walked into another almost as grim except that the huge archways by which we entered and left it had been draped in gold-fringed crimson cloth. It seemed that these curtains signified the entrance to the palace within the fortress because we then began upon a bewildering series of wide high-ceilinged passages, hung with tapestries and lined with salaaming attendants.

'It's like a city in itself!' Charlotte said.

I remembered Richard saying once that he wished we were all safely inside the Bala Hissar still, and not vulnerable in the undefended Cantonment, and when I looked at the massive thickness of the walls around us, and their height and the huge thick doors bolted and studded with iron, I felt keenly how right he was.

We came at last into the vast audience chamber. It felt as if we had walked almost a mile but the room was so huge and sunlit and wonderful after that maze of passages that I felt I should gladly have walked twice as far. The walls were whitewashed and then painted to represent cypress groves, the tall greenish-blue spires stalking elegantly round the walls and interspersed with garlands of roses and flocks of birds. One whole wall was windows and through them, in that beautiful honeyed light, one could see the immaculate Royal gardens, the flowerbeds laid out between paths of white pebbles, and here and there the gleam of a fish pond. At the end of the room was a fairy-like structure of fluted columns and Moorish arches, painted white, a sort of gazebo, and inside this on a golden throne sat someone apparently wearing an armour of jewels.

I heard Charlotte gasp. It was small wonder. I gazed in awe at this blaze of green and gold and white and then we were summoned forward to curtsey, and when I raised my eyes I saw that Shah Suja was wearing a tunic of emerald silk embroidered with golden flowers and that the flowers were studded with jewels. On top of this he had a kind of breastplate, solid with diamonds, arranged like two giant fleur-de-lys, and his arms were stiff with huge emerald bracelets. His crown must have been almost a foot high, winged and turreted and so brilliant with jewels that it gave off a kind of rainbow aura, like a halo.

I suppose he must have been about fifty. Charlotte had told me with her new knowledge of Afghanistan gleaned from Alexander that he had been King of Kabul years ago, when he was only twenty, and had had to flee almost at once. Then he had lolled about as a guest of British India for almost thirty years and now found himself back where he had begun, but in most peculiar circumstances.

He smiled down at us. He was not a handsome man, but impressive in his heavy, black Afghan way and very dignified. His eyes rested for more than a moment on Charlotte who wore her wedding dress and whose face was illumined at her pleasure in being there. Then he bowed a little and we curtseyed again and went to take up our places against the wall in front of a line of sepoys.

We watched the other British come up and bow and curtsey. The men looked quite fitting in their scarlet and gold, but there was something stiff and unsuitable in the ladies' dresses, all that frilling and layers of flounced collar and great puffed sleeves. They looked for the most part unnatural and artificial and their bonnets were absurd beside Afghan turbans.

I turned my head to watch Mrs Mainwaring who was reputed to be carrying a child but who looked far too graceful and slender to be in such a condition, and out of the corner of my eye, caught a glimpse of the sepoy standing behind Charlotte. It was Alexander, upright and magnificent in his scarlet turban, and only inches from the man he had every intention, it seemed, of injuring. I turned my head a little more, determined to let him know I had seen him, and he met my eye easily and smiled. I could not see Charlotte's face which was quite obscured by Hugh, but I began

105

to feel that she knew who stood behind her as well as I did.

We stood there for a long while and I felt it to be very tense and awkward. I kept wishing to steal glances at Hugh to reassure myself of his ignorance, and thus his tranquillity, but I thought he might feel my behaviour peculiar and suspicious so I looked before me and saw Richard come in with a brother officer and bow, just as all the men before him had done.

Then it was announced that if we would like to see the Shahi Bagh, the Royal Gardens, we might, and Richard came across to us and offered me his arm, and we walked together out into the sunlight. Charlotte and Hugh came behind us, and the sepoys melted away from the walls and began to form a guard of honour into the garden. I deliberately did not look to find Alexander. I saw Charlotte and Hugh together as we moved among the rose beds, but I really wanted to listen to Richard and of course he was very much interested in the roses, so I did not observe them very closely. We wandered happily on in the golden sunlight among beds of crimson and peach and pink and scarlet and the scent that was all about us was quite wonderful and so strong you felt that you could touch it. I looked up once and saw Hugh alone with a group of officers. Alarmed, I looked about for Charlotte. Then Richard began to say something that I very much wished to hear, and when I had listened to it and replied and remembered Charlotte, she was nowhere to be seen.

CHAPTER EIGHT

It was after that day that I began to be frightened. When it came to the time to leave the Bala Hissar after sherbet and cakes had been passed round, Charlotte reappeared again at the very moment that I could feel panic rising in me to the pitch where I should have to tell Richard. She looked radiantly happy and quite composed and Hugh seemed, by some freak of good fortune, to assume she had been with a party of ladies who had gone down to a little ornamental lake at the end of the gardens to exclaim at the size of Afghan goldfish. I looked at her as gravely as I could and she laughed without a trace of self-consciousness, and as she was helped to mount in the courtyard, I could hear that she was humming.

She was very gay during dinner and made Hugh laugh, but I saw she hardly ate at all and covered up her uneaten rice with a chupatti. When Hugh rose to go out into the courtyard and smoke I thought she might follow him so as not to be left alone with me, but she seemed entirely at her ease, and if I had not noticed her lack of appetite, I think I might have accused myself of imagining the whole episode.

'Shall I tell you first, Emily, or shall you scold first?'

'Tell,' I said. 'You know what the scolding will be.'

So she told me how Alexander had materialized beside her in the garden and in the press of people and soldiers and attendants, had guided her away up a series of narrow staircases as small and twisting as corkscrews to a little terrace high in a tower where there was nothing beyond them but the sky and the mountains. They had talked, she said, simply talked, but I knew that there was more than that because her eyes began to blaze with memory and she seemed bursting with a sudden vibrant energy. Perhaps they had been there ten minutes, perhaps more, then he had led her down the staircases once more and between high hedges of oleander and there he had left her and she found Mrs Mainwaring and several others standing picturesquely on a bridge over a little lake and pointing out the fish to one another.

When she finished I rose from my chair and walked about the room for a while. I was torn with feelings both in favour of what she was doing and against it, but above all those feelings I was now feeling fright. She was clearly going to take larger and larger risks to see Alexander, her belief in the 'rightness' of their feelings for each other was growing stronger and stronger, and as both these things happened she was going to slip further and further from me and see my reactions as simply obstructive.

I had as much as told Richard that I couldn't come to Bombay with him because I must stay with Charlotte. That was truer than ever now because she seemed heading for making herself an outcast and would need every friend. I looked out into the darkness, for the nights had begun to fall much more quickly, and saw the glow of Hugh's cigar far across the courtyard and felt my pity for him mingling with my fear for Charlotte.

Behind me, Charlotte said, 'You mustn't worry, Emily. I won't make anyone unhappy.'

I gestured towards the cigar glow.

'But it's inevitable! You have to!'

'You must trust me, Emily.'

'It isn't a question of trust. You can't do the impossible. You are bound to break Hugh's heart.'

We were talking in low whispers now and although Charlotte's voice was not angry, it was very decided.

'Listen to me, Emily. I have found what I was looking for. I thought it was this journey, this place, this adventure, and in a sense it was, it still is. But in him I have found someone with whom I fit like a – a foot in a shoe, a hand in a glove. I am miserable away from him, even for an hour, I feel thirsty. But that pain is mine, Emily, and I wouldn't try to ease it by inflicting another. I won't break Hugh's heart, Emily. You should know me well enough to know I won't.'

Then she rose and went out, calling for Sayid, and she did not kiss me good night.

My fear did not go away. Indeed it grew worse each day as Charlotte vanished more and more often and told me less and less upon her return. She took to riding again in her black robes and would sometimes be gone a whole morning, vanishing in the dawn just after Hugh had left for the Bala Hissar and before the civilians in the Cantonment were awake. Then she would return in the early afternoon when all the ladies were indoors out of the sun, and if there was any racing or cricket or a concert she was always there, smiling and lovely, appearing immaculate in European clothes from heaven knew what escapade.

If I had felt that life would at least go on as normal apart from Charlotte, I should not have felt so alarmed, but I knew from Richard that we were all trembling on the lip of a volcano and that Sir William, who with Lord Auckland took all the decisions, refused to see the need for the smallest anxiety. Outwardly, things were much the same, except that the soldiers now went about in Kabul in groups of three or four; but alarming news had come that the British brigade MacNaghten had sent back to India had been almost blown to pieces by the tribesmen in the Khyber Pass.

Hugh insisted that it was nothing.

'My dear Emily, we are still an immeasurably superior fighting force. We will punish those Pathans as they deserve—' here he shot a most meaningful look at Sayid '– and there will be no more nonsense. You are becoming what Sir William calls a croaker.'

'Then Richard is one too, and Captain Eyre and Captain Sturt and – and so many more.'

'MacNaghten has done a most impressive job, Emily. We have had none but the most minor troubles and he has reduced the administrative costs significantly.'

'If he hadn't stopped paying the tribesmen on the Pass,' I cried, 'Brigadier Sale's brigade would not have been attacked by the tribesmen!'

Hugh came over to me and took me by the hand as if I were very young or very infirm.

'My dear Emily. No harm shall come to you. I promise you that.'

*

Charlotte came to my room late that night. I was on my penultimate and precious page of Lamb, having spun him out frugally all summer, and as she never came to my room now, I thought she must be Jane with some of my clothes, so I did not look up. Then I felt the pressure of her body as she sank on to the edge of my bed.

'Emily,' she said, so faintly I could hardly hear her.

I looked up and I was horrified. I had scarcely seen her all day and had dined alone because she had not returned, and Hugh had gone to the Bala Hissar as usual. I had told him Charlotte was with Lady Sale – indeed she might have been for I no longer knew where she went – and he seemed quite contented. But she was sitting on my bed now as white as milk, her light brilliant eyes as dead and dark as stone, her face drawn and terrible.

I tossed Lamb aside and struggled out of my quilts to put my arms around her. She clung to me the moment I touched her, but she did not cry, she simply hung against me, limp and dead. I rocked her as one would a child but I didn't speak because I knew she would tell me everything now and if I spoke first I might be clumsy and hurt her more.

At last she sighed, shudderingly, and then she drew away from me and tried a faint, unsuccessful smile.

'You can go to Bombay with Richard now, Emily. You must.'

'Why, Charlotte? Why now? What has happened?'

'You told Richard that you wouldn't go with him to Bombay, didn't you, because you thought you should stay with me in case my behaviour ostracized me from everyone, even Hugh—'

'Charlotte, Charlotte, how did you know – it wasn't like that – of course I wanted to go with Richard, but I wanted more to stay with you—'

She put three fingers across my mouth. They were deathly cold.

'It doesn't matter how I know. But I do and I think you

110

and Richard are heroes. But it's all over now, it doesn't matter. You must go to Bombay and – and then you won't be here if any trouble starts and I shall know you are safe and happy.'

'Charlotte, what has happened?'

'Oh,' she said, 'happened,' and then she slid off my bed and crouched on the floor, her arms resting on my quilt and her face buried in them. When she spoke again her voice was so muffled that I had to hang over her to hear what she was saying.

'I told you I wouldn't break Hugh's heart, that I wouldn't relieve my pain by causing another. And I won't. I've given terrible pain to Alexander but he will have to bear that too, I can't see how to relieve him. He asked me to come and live at the Residency with him and then either he would get another posting or, more likely, since the Government wouldn't care for such an irregular arrangement, take me home to Bewick and I should try to obtain a divorce—'

I felt myself utterly bewildered and simply echoed Charlotte's last words.

'A *divorce*!'

She raised her head.

'Yes, Emily. A divorce. He wants me to be his wife, and I want to be his wife more than anything on earth. And at first I said yes – yes, how wonderful. And then I thought of Hugh, and you and Richard – and Mamma and I realized – I realized – oh Emily! I'm not a monster, I know you think I've been behaving like one, but I'm not so cruelly selfish, nor am I giddy and foolish enough to think it's all worth it for the glamour of behaving romantically. I've never tried to make a grand gesture before and I'm sure it will seem better later. In time perhaps it will fall into perspective, it won't hurt so—'

I whispered, 'You – you have broken with him?'

She nodded.

'Oh Charlotte!' I said and I thought I should cry. I got

off my bed and knelt on the floor beside her and put my arms round her.

'Thank God you are here, Emily.'

'And I'm staying.'

'Oh, no. *No.* That's one of the reasons I've done it. I am back to being respectable Mrs Connell now, Hugh is in no danger and the Cantonment won't have any fault to find with me. You can go with Richard now, you *must.*'

Tears were rolling down my face and sliding off my chin on to my lap. Charlotte put up her black sleeve and began to blot them off my cheeks.

'But I don't *want* your sacrifice,' I said. 'I can't *bear* it.'

'Darling Emily, you will have to. For my sake. If I can't think some good has come out of – of tonight, I might as well be dead.'

Then she rose from the floor and pulled off her black robe and stood there, just in her petticoat and bodice.

'Can I sleep with you tonight, Emily? Will you tell Hugh I'm not well, that I might disturb him?'

'Of course,' I said.

I did not have to feign an illness for Charlotte. By the morning, she was so devastated by fatigue that she was quite unable to rise. I couldn't remember her being ill before, except those childhood illnesses which we had always shared and which she had enlivened by drawing little people with a piece of charcoal around our chicken pox spots and by telling hair-raising ghost stories when our room was permanently darkened on account of the measles. I knew she wasn't really ill now, just wounded all through, and that like some injured animal, needed to be left in as much of a haven as I could provide to recover.

Hugh was of course very anxious and sent immediately for the doctor. Doctor Turnbull was luckily a most intuitive and sympathetic man, and whatever he said to Charlotte he said to no-one else. I was in the room when he came, naturally, but he asked me to leave towards the end and so I went to join Hugh who was pacing about the courtyard.

'Emily – Emily I think I must get her to India. I should not like – anything to happen here.'

Then I saw that he thought she might be going to have a child and I felt so sorry for him that I could hardly bear it and wished passionately that *his* wish might be true.

Then Doctor Turnbull came out and said Charlotte was suffering from heat exhaustion and he gave me a sleeping draught for her and said she must stay quietly at home for some weeks.

'There!' Hugh said loudly, as if masking his disappointment, 'It's all this endless riding in the sun. I thought at one time she had given it up. Now she will have to.'

'Yes,' said Doctor Turnbull. 'She will have to give everything up,' and went away.

So Charlotte stayed in bed and slept or came out and sat in my wicker chair in the sun, but mostly she slept, greedy, luxurious sleep induced by the opiate and she craved it pitifully, that oblivion. Then poor Jane fell ill of some fever and began to have severe cramps in her stomach and I had to run between the two of them so that I had scarcely any time for anything else. I found a sergeant's wife from the lines, a Mrs Bates, and she came in every day to do the heavy work and help to wash poor Jane who had gone quite yellow with the sickness which made her black brows stand out alarmingly.

Charlotte was not really well all September. I became so busy that I had hardly time to notice what was going on in the Cantonment or in Kabul and was often too tired to listen to the news that Hugh or Richard brought, even to Lady Sale who was a faithful visitor and came to hearten Charlotte with bracing speeches. All three of them kept talking about Akbar Khan, the son of Dost Mohammed the deposed ruler, but I really only registered him clearly at one unhappy moment when Lady Sale had the misfortune to say to Charlotte that Akbar was almost as handsome as Alexander Bewick and Charlotte went as pale as a lily.

Mrs Bates would come early every morning and she was always full of gossip, but as it came from the lines and was usually extremely indecent, I would try to deflect her with an enormous list of duties needing urgent attention before she began. One morning I failed and she was in full flood on a most unattractive account of the aftermath of Sergeant Bates' discovery of an illegal still somewhere in the Kabul bazaar when she suddenly broke off and clapped one hand to her mouth and another to her pocket.

'Why Miss Brent, I a'most forgot. I've this letter, see, and wot wiv one thing an' another—'

I held my hand out. Mrs Bates fished about in the pocket of her apron and produced a crumpled letter.

'Sorry, Miss, bit the worse for wear 'n' all.'

'Where did you get it, Mrs Bates?'

It was addressed to me in a clear, firm, educated hand.

'It were giv' Bates, Miss. 'E were up at the Palace. It were giv' 'im and 'e was told to giv' it you without fail.'

'Thank you, Mrs Bates,' I said, and I indicated the bucket of soapy water between us. 'I'm much obliged to you.' Then I took the letter and went out to sit on the well wall and read it.

It was from Alexander Bewick. He had heard Charlotte was ill, he wrote, and he was frantic with worry even though rumour reached him that she was on the mend. He would have come to us in the Cantonment except that she had expressly forbidden him to, and although there was no-one else's command on earth he would hesitate to disobey, he held any wish of hers sacred. Would I then for an hour put aside my feelings of repugnance towards him and be merciful enough to meet him at a place appointed on the following day, and reassure him of Charlotte's continued good health? If I could not bring myself to face him would I perhaps write a line or two to be handed to his brother whom he would send to guide me to our meeting place? His peace of mind hung entirely on my compassion.

For about the hundredth time I nearly broke faith and told Richard. Later life has proved to me that if I have a prop to lean upon, I lean upon it shamelessly, so perhaps it was as well that I did not adopt my prop too early. Thoughts of whether this might be a plot, whether I was doing right by Hugh in going or wrong by Charlotte in not going, whether it was dangerous to leave the Cantonment at the moment, whether Alexander Bewick had any right to any solace in any case all chased themselves round my head as I paced about in the sunlight and when Richard came later that morning, I very nearly told him everything. But something held me back. Perhaps it was the sweet submissiveness in Charlotte's face as she thanked Richard for the roses he had brought, a submissiveness so unlike her and so touching, perhaps it was Richard's warm and flattering admiration for the way I was handling my two invalids and which gave me a sense of great independence – whatever it was, I held my tongue. So, late the next day, after our early dinner while Hugh and Charlotte were playing backgammon, I made a pretext of slipping round to Mrs Shelton for something she had promised that might give some relief to Jane, and put on my cloak and went out into the lane beyond our courtyard.

There were two men waiting for me, one holding a lantern in the dusk, and by its glow I could see he was Charles Bewick, Alexander's brother. The other was a servant, an Indian, and both were in uniform.

Charles Bewick bowed and said, 'Miss Brent?' in a low voice.

I nodded.

'We have not far to go. My brother has the use of a room nearby.'

If it had not involved someone as dear to me as Charlotte, I should have found this mission most romantic. As it was, apprehension quelled romance and as we went softly along the lanes between the low houses of the Cantonment, all very similar to our own, I began to wish most urgently that I had told Richard and that his consoling person were there in the thick twilight beside me. It was beginning to be cool at night now, by mid-September, and the air had that sharp clean taste to it as if winter were crouching on those mountain snows already, waiting to spring. Afghan winters were savage, Richard said, and he had made us buy poshteens already, huge, hooded leather coats lined with fur and stinking abominably.

We came at last to a door in a courtyard wall, much like any other, where Charles Bewick stopped and rapped sharply, three times. The door was opened at once, and we went across a small dark silent space and towards a red glow of light on the opposite side. It came from a pair of doors like those on our sitting and dining rooms, left slightly ajar, and Charles Bewick stopped and said softly, 'Miss Brent, Alexander' and then he and his servant vanished into the darkness.

The doors were flung wide in an instant.

Alexander Bewick was there alone, silhouetted against a small bare room with a charcoal brazier glowing in the centre and two divans either side of it spread with carpets.

'Miss Brent,' he said. 'And seldom has anyone been more welcome.'

He took my cloak from my shoulders, then he led me to one of the divans and seated me on it.

'I am quite overwhelmed with gratitude that you came. I did not think you would.'

He was wearing European clothes, breeches and polished boots and a dark riding coat over a white shirt and stock. His face seemed drawn and tired, his eyes darker and ringed with fatigue, but even so, it was still a face that astonished one at every view of it.

He asked, 'How is she, Miss Brent?' and his voice sounded strange and hoarse.

'Much better, Mr Bewick. Quite recovered I think, except for always seeming so tired. But you needn't be anxious now, there is no danger.'

'What was it? A fever?'

'Oh no,' I said and I raised my eyes and looked into his. 'It wasn't an illness of – of, it wasn't a bodily illness.'

He said. 'Oh my *God*,' in a savage tone and then he said, 'Forgive me, Miss Brent' and got up and leaned his arms against the wall and put his head on them. He reminded me poignantly of Charlotte crouching by my bed, her own head sunk on her arms, and I felt a surge of pity for him rise in my throat. He looked so graceful and strong leaning there, his black head and clothes dark against the white wall, and yet so broken and vulnerable too. I rose and went over to him and put my hand on his arm. He took no notice for a while and then he raised his head and looked at me and I had a sudden wild urge to drag him back through the lanes and cast him at Charlotte, Hugh or no Hugh.

'I am not the devil incarnate, really, you see,' he said and his voice was low and gentle. 'I've been wild, I know, very wild, but then I didn't know what was good for me. How could I, when I had not met it? I have never wanted anything as much as I wanted – *want* – your sister and my longing for her has taken away all my longing for anything else. Oh yes, I'm going about my work, of course I am, otherwise we British will be mincemeat to the Afghans shortly, but that is all. *All*, Miss Brent.'

'You don't need to convince me,' I said. 'not any more.'

He smiled sadly.

'Convinced or no, it's too late, isn't it? Charlotte is as good as she is beautiful and she made a decision only the good *could* have made. I thought of capturing her – don't gasp, Miss Brent, I didn't do it – but then I thought that would be against her view of what was right and I suppose it must be proof to you that I love her truly if I respect her wishes more than my own.'

I said suddenly, 'Oh, I wish there was something I could do for you!' and he laughed and took my hand from his arm and kissed it.

'You have, my dear Emily, you have. Charlotte is well now, and it seems she loves me. Those are larger crumbs of comfort than I dared hope for. I won't molest her in any way and even though I long for her to know you have seen me, I forbid you to tell her. I don't want her to have one more second of disquiet than she does already. Perhaps, perhaps if anything were to happen to Hugh Connell, you might—' he stopped and looked at me. 'But I should know. Worlds away, I should know.'

Then he went to the door and shouted for his brother.

'Emily, I do thank you from the bottom of my heart.'

He put my cloak around my shoulders and took my hand again.

'Goodbye,' I said and my voice was not at all steady. 'And – and God bless you.'

He pressed my hand and let it go very gently.

'Captain Talbot is a lucky man,' he said.

CHAPTER NINE

Two days later, Jane became much worse. At first it seemed that her decline was only of moment to Charlotte and me, for all the men were occupied in despairing over the new commanding officer, Major General Elphinstone who, they claimed, was hopelessly undecided and always swayed by other people's opinion. I had heard Lady Sale declaring to Charlotte scornfully, 'General Elphinstone vacillates on every point,' and though I had thought at the time that that was clearly a disadvantage, I was too much occupied with poor suffering Jane to care about the weaknesses in General Elphinstone's character.

Doctor Turnbull had come each week to see Charlotte and as his fourth visit, in early October, coincided with the second day of Jane's redoubled weakness, I asked him for his opinion. He was with her only moments and then came back to me, looking very grave.

'You should have called me sooner. She has cholera and I fear there is little hope. She must be isolated at once and your sister must not, in her weakened state, approach her.'

He gave me an opiate, solemn words about the risk I took myself and left me to shake with remorse and alarm. I tried to persuade Charlotte to go home with Lady Sale who was still impressively ensconced in our sitting-room, but she was adamant.

'I can't do without you, Emily. If you go, I'll go, but as we can neither of us leave Jane, having dragged her all the way to Kabul from Hanover Square, we shall neither of us go.'

Lady Sale seemed to feel that was the right decision but warned us that the other ladies of the Cantonment would feel they must protect themselves and their children and so we should become quite isolated.

'My daughter is nearing her confinement, also Mrs Mainwaring. You will see their position.'

We said of course we should. I think Charlotte was sorry to have to say it because now that she was stronger, she welcomed visitors as a diversion from her thoughts, and her illness had made the ladies of the Cantonment much less harsh towards her and more reconciled to her beauty.

So she had to sit all day and paint or simply think, and I hated to see her do that because of the awful darkness in her eyes. It was growing much colder now and we had to have the braziers lit night and day, and when Hugh wasn't there, Charlotte would let Sayid into the room with her and he would squat in a corner, his jezail balanced across his knees. If Alexander had been frantic while Charlotte was ill, I think Sayid had run him a close second, and was now more of her shadow than ever before. Richard said that as things grew more uncertain, he for one was very glad to know Sayid was with us but he did not say it in Hugh's hearing. Since Charlotte's illness, Hugh had said no more about Sayid but I knew from looks and half-started sentences that his feelings were as strong as ever.

I dosed Jane faithfully and after a few days, began to think she was reviving. Cholera, said Lady Sale, was a quick killer, and Jane had now been ill for almost two weeks. But it was only her determined Cockney constitution that fought so long against the idea of dying in a heathenish place, and the cholera proved itself stronger even than that. Jane died in the second week of October, and was buried in the little civilian graveyard on the edge of the Cantonment. I packed all her clothes away, her neatly mended grey gowns, very long grey gowns for Jane had been a tall woman, almost as tall as Hugh, and her shawls and caps, and then I went to Charlotte in the sitting-room and burst into tears.

She put her hand on my hair.

'Don't be frightened, Emily. It isn't an omen. It's sad, so sad, that she should die far away from London and we shall miss her, but you mustn't feel that the ground is giving under our feet because of it.'

'Oh, but it is, it is,' I said. 'Everyone says so but Hugh. Jane's dying is only the beginning.'

'But it won't be the end,' Charlotte said, and her voice had some of its old life. 'I'll see to that. Don't smile, Emily. I haven't tested my resources for a long time but they are still there. Not dead, Emily, only sleeping.'

Hugh was very gentle with us after that. He had been

much softer since Charlotte had been ill, but I think he saw Jane's dying as the severance of a link with England as indeed I did – and understood how desolating was the effect. There even came a bitterly cold night, the second of November, when Sayid failed to creep into the courtyard upon Hugh's return, and although I saw them notice each other, Hugh said not a word.

Hugh did seem in a high good humour that night. He ate dinner with relish, teased me about Richard, actually asked if he might smoke in our presence, instead of making a pompous performance about withdrawing when he knew we didn't mind, and then cast himself into a chair and drew great sighs of satisfaction.

'You have made this house so charming,' he said to Charlotte.

She smiled. She had picked up her pencil and was sketching his profile and I wondered idly what had happened to the *Hero of the Himalayas*.

'This sort of comfort,' Hugh went on, 'makes one appreciate what that poor devil Bewick must be enduring. I've never seen the dungeons at the Bala Hissar but I imagine—'

'What?' said Charlotte. Her voice snapped out like a pistol shot.

'Bewick's in prison. I suppose we are honour bound to negotiate his release but it's a delicate matter. The Afghans have been wanting him for ages, you know, after his treatment of their women, and he was in some scuffle, the usual thing, late last night and some of the chiefs surrounding Shah Suja took their chance. Understandable really, but difficult for Sir William and Elphinstone.'

Charlotte was chalk white. I was terrified lest she should speak and betray everything so I went quickly over to her and sat beside her, gripping her arm tightly. I looked down at her sketch.

'Hugh has more nose than that,' I said, 'and I'm

afraid rather less hair. Do you really mean, Hugh, that we aren't going to try to get Mr Bewick out of prison?'

Charlotte's arm in mine was shaking violently.

'He's been a thorn in our flesh for so long. I think Sir William's view is that he's best out of the way for the moment. Shah Suja has apparently promised that they won't harm him, they just want to know where he is for a while. I suppose if there was any threat to his life, we would act.'

In a tightly controlled voice, Charlotte said, 'How supremely good of us,' and Hugh laughed and stretched his legs towards the brazier.

Then Charlotte smiled at me and her arm relaxed so I rose and went back to my place.

Later that night when she came to kiss me good night I looked at her most anxiously, fearful that the news might bring on a relapse, but she said, 'Don't speak of it, Emily. Don't worry – but don't speak of it either.'

Of course the incident could not be left isolated and quiet like that. As a result of Alexander's being thrown into prison – and even I could hardly bring myself to think of what he was enduring – we heard that Afghan and British soldiers had begun to fight in the streets of Kabul and then there was a skirmish that resulted in the British Residency being burnt to the ground.

'All his treasures,' Charlotte said softly, but she said no more.

The British Residency seemed to matter more to Mac-Naghten and Elphinstone than Alexander. They made a formal complaint to the insurrectionists who merely laughed and burned down two more British houses and murdered their occupants. At this Kabul was in an uproar. In the biting wind one November night, Charlotte and I donned our poshteens and with Hugh climbed on to the roof of our house and watched the flames of the city two miles away and heard the thud of guns and the steady roar and crackle of the fire.

'It's happening!' I screamed at Hugh, senselessly trying to punish him for my own terror. 'You said there was nothing to worry about, that they were under control and look! Look!'

Hugh, tight-lipped, took us down again and left us huddled round our brazier. I think I was too sick with fright to notice how excited Charlotte was, but I did observe that her eyes were brilliant again as they had not been for weeks. We sat there, Charlotte alert and upright, me dozing and shivering by turns until Hugh came back with Richard and told us that Kabul had quite gone over to the rebels and that the poor defenceless Cantonment was under siege.

At first, all we had to get used to was the noise. It never stopped after that first night, while the Afghans tried to occupy the forts around the Cantonment and the British tried to drive them back. The little village above us, Bemaru, that I had always looked upon as a potential threat, proved a great ally and the commissariat officers obtained all our food from the villagers and wood and charcoal to keep us warm.

It grew colder and colder. Charlotte and Sayid spent large parts of the day on the roof watching the fighting and I had all our beds and braziers moved into the sitting-room for economy and warmth. Hugh, now that he could no longer get to the Bala Hissar in which Shah Suja had virtually been made a prisoner – I wondered if he were allowed to wear his emeralds and diamonds still – had become a real fighting soldier and was off each day organizing his men into reinforcing the weak defences around the Cantonment, a job they had to perform under a hail of jezail bullets.

I said to Charlotte, 'Doesn't Sayid want to go and fight for his countrymen now?'

She translated my question for Sayid, and they both laughed.

'We want to *fight*, both of us,' she said. 'But now that I

123

have taught him to say God Bless Queen Victoria, I think he feels that she and I are one and he will defend us to the death.'

Then in mid-November, Charlotte called down to me urgently from the roof. I had been swathing the plants in the courtyard in old sacks against the frost as Richard had told me to do, and I went stumbling up the steps to join her.

'Look, Emily.'

She pointed to the north-west, and I saw to my horror a huge force streaming out of Kabul and making for the hills behind us.

'The Afghans mean to take Bemaru,' she said.

They not only meant to, they did. It was not until later that I heard Richard had been up there in the thick of it, desperately trying to rally men who were hopelessly confused by Shelton's extraordinary and blundering orders, but also vastly outnumbered by the Afghans who kept pouring endlessly out of Kabul in their thousands. He came the next day and showed me the holes where bullets had gone singing through his coat. I flung myself into his arms and burst into tears.

'Don't cry, my dearest, don't cry. It isn't me you should be crying for. I'm whole, look at me, solid as ever. But it isn't going to be easy from now on because food is going to be very short. And Akbar has finally come.'

Akbar. It was a name we had first heard almost a year ago but it wasn't one I had ever given much heed to. But now it was on everyone's lips a dozen times a day. Akbar had come to Kabul.

He was no longer a violent myth bent upon revenge skirmishing away in Turkestan, but a real presence, a powerful, angry man who had rallied all his ragged forces together and led them against his father's old enemies, the British. He not only led them, he inspired them, and his howling mobs of tribesmen had screamed into Kabul and overthrown it, seizing the throne in the Bala Hissar and hurling Shah Suja into one of his own dungeons. Akbar was, as Alexander Bewick had said fruitlessly for months, a force seriously to be reckoned with. And Akbar was now going to starve the British into submission and out of his country.

'He is a barbarian,' Hugh said, crouched over our braziers.

'No,' said Richard. 'He is a patriot. He is said to be extremely courteous, a skilful negotiator, authoritative and humorous. He does tend to lose his temper violently though. Bewick told me. Bewick knew him well. I would give a good deal to have Bewick out of prison and arguing for us. Very bad luck to be thrown into prison for misdemeanours you have ceased to commit. They say he hadn't given a party in months.'

I looked at Charlotte in anxiety and saw that her eyes were tightly closed as if she were praying.

'Food's running out,' Hugh said. 'There's an order to slaughter all animals that aren't serviceable.'

I suppose I had never been really hungry before. Of course I had known that pleasurable slightly faint anticipation which precedes food when you haven't had any for a long time, but I had never experienced the savage clawing dizzying feeling of real hunger. It made one sick and faint and one's brain became obsessed with food and revolted by the thought of it all at once. Hugh came back one day with the news that camels' hearts were on offer to the officers.

'Ugh,' I said.

Charlotte looked at me.

'Don't worry,' she said.

Soon after that Sayid began to disappear. Not for long, perhaps only a few hours at a time, but a sack of grain arrived in our kitchen, two chickens, a cabbage. They were followed by eggs, a huge jar of goat's milk, joints of tough but so welcome mutton. We kept some for our household because our poor Indians, used to a world of heat, were petrified enough by the cold as it was and hunger rendered them almost insensible, and then we sent out the larger part to the houses where children and babies were.

I once asked Charlotte where it all came from but she merely smiled at me and said, 'I don't know, Emily, I really don't. But Sayid is doing it for Queen Victoria – Charlotte.' Then she paused and her eyes clouded. 'I only wish he could take some to – to Bala Hissar.'

The temperature plunged below zero. Despite Sayid's efforts we were all hungry always, and growing thinner and Hugh ordered all our furniture to be chopped up for firewood. I thought Charlotte would be distressed to see all her lovely red and black lacquerwork reduced to kindling, but she seemed hardly to notice. There was much to-ing and fro-ing in the Cantonment all day despite the ceaseless gunfire, people running in and out of each other's houses with scraps of news, offers of help. We wore our poshteens all day and all night for the winds that came slicing down from the Hindu Kush were like knives.

About a fortnight before Christmas, when all our spirits seemed to flag on account of the cold and our hunger and the noise, Hugh came home to say with as much satisfaction as if he had arranged it himself, that Akbar had met MacNaghten on the banks of the Kabul River and that all would be well.

'Oh?' said Charlotte. We were sewing blankets as lining into old coats for the servants and she stopped, needle poised and looked at Hugh.

'The siege is over, my dearest. Quite over. That will teach people who have had no faith in MacNaghten. He said he would evacuate Kabul in three days time and Akbar has agreed to give us safe passage and provide us with food. All he wanted in return is four officers as hostage which I am pleased to tell you includes neither myself nor Richard. We shall be in Jalalabad for Christmas.'

'Oh,' said Charlotte, again and went back to her sewing.

CHAPTER TEN

Three days came and went and no food came down to the Cantonment.

'It will come,' Hugh said.

'No,' said Richard. 'It will not. He means to starve us into submission.'

Hunger does make one submissive. We still had some food, for Sayid made daily forays out of the Cantonment, but by the time we had given most of it away, the remainder was pitifully small for three people. Charlotte usually manoeuvred things so that she had almost none and Hugh could have a reasonable amount. He never asked where it came from; I suspect he knew and would rather not think of it because of hating to feel indebted to Sayid for anything.

Three days before Christmas a message came from Akbar. I couldn't help thinking about Christmas; last year, somewhere in the Punjab, Christmas had seemed quite irrelevant in that stupefying heat, but here with the snow being whirled about by the icy winds, Christmas seemed more appropriate, more of a reminder of home. A silly convention, I knew, since snow hardly fell in Bethlehem any more than in Delhi, but a strong convention all the same, and I was sitting thinking of Mamma and England, rolled in my poshteen and a cocoon of rugs by our brazier, when Richard came.

'There's a plot,' he said.

I tried to feel interested as well as cold and hungry.

'What sort of plot?'

Richard sat down beside me and held his hands out to the brazier. Even he was thinner, considerably thinner, and the bones of his big frame were beginning to push through his flesh.

'Akbar says he will take Shah Suja out of captivity and restore him to the throne as long as he, Akbar, may be his chief minister, his wazir, and we pay him some astronomical sum: £300,000 I think he wants. He says the British may stay for six months then leave as if it was our commander's own decision, thereby saving face. MacNaghten—' Richard stopped and put his head in his hands for a moment. 'MacNaghten has signed a paper in agreement.'

I said, 'How do you know it is a plot?'

Richard took my hand.

'Dearest Emily. Would Akbar really betray his own people? Would he be content to serve Shah Suja instead of having the throne himself? I and several others spent all this morning begging MacNaghten not to sign, to see that Akbar was laying a trap for him, but what else could we do?'

'Doesn't he suspect *anything*?'

'I think he must, even he. But he's quite worn down with the siege and is afraid for his career. If he bungles Afghanistan, he won't get Bombay. He should have left a month ago – and me with him,' Richard smiled at me. 'At least I have to thank the siege for that.'

There was a blast of petrifyingly cold air as the door was pulled open and Charlotte came in.

'MacNaghten's signed!' she said.

Richard nodded.

'He's to meet Akbar outside the Cantonment tomorrow.'

Charlotte came and sat down on my other side. She was pale, but her eyes were bright with excitement.

'Richard – do you think this will precipitate something? Do you think we shall have to flee?'

'Yes,' he said.

'So do I,' said Charlotte, and looked at him keenly. 'I think we shall find ourselves thrown out. Hugh doesn't. He believes Akbar will keep his word, he thinks MacNaghten will save us. I'm glad you don't, because living in a fool's paradise like that only makes it all the more painful when the axe falls. We should act, not just sit here. We should storm the Bala Hissar and – and let Shah Suja out.'

I put out my free hand and took hers, so that we were all sitting linked together, like the three wise Chinese monkeys.

'I hate just sitting here,' she said. 'I hate to feel so – helpless.'

'You are the least helpless woman I have ever come across,' Richard said to her, smiling.

She nodded. 'In most respects, yes. In – in all respects but – but one—' and then she looked quickly at me and I saw that her eyes were bright with tears now, not excitement, and I squeezed her hand.

She stood up.

'I am going to Lady Sale,' she said. 'She is a positive mine of rumours and I want to know every one. Yesterday's was that Akbar's chiefs are going to round up all the British women and throw them into the Bala Hissar as hostages. At least I'd be inside the Bala Hissar not outside and—' she bit her lip.

'Look after Emily,' she said to Richard and pulled the door open. When she had gone, Richard put his arm around me and I leant against him.

'We are so lucky,' I said, 'to have what we want without much pain.'

He stared into the fire.

'We have to get out of here first,' he said.

The Afghans killed Sir William MacNaghten. I was trying to do some washing with stiff, blue, painful hands and Charlotte came flying home on her pony, her face quite white and her eyes blazing blue and told me what had happened, and I was listening to her so aghast that I quite forgot my hands and they were within an ace of freezing in the tub.

I said 'Richard?' and dreaded her reply.

'He's been taken prisoner. Along with Mackenzie and Lawrence. Trevor is dead. And Captain Carter. The Afghans had laid carpets on the snow and Sir William rode up with his staff and dismounted and gave Akbar an Arab charger as a present and it was all very friendly and then Akbar suddenly screamed "*Bezeer*"!'

'*Bezeer*?' I said choking. I could feel hot tears slipping down my cold face and my heart lay sickeningly heavy in me.

'It means "seize him"! MacNaghten was carried off, so were Mackenzie and Lawrence – and Richard. Sayid saw—' she stopped and put her arms around me, 'Sayid saw MacNaghten's trunk – and – and Trevor's hanging in the bazaar. They've dismembered them. But Richard is still alive. Sayid says so – Emily, they are both in there together now. Richard and Alexander. We have to get them out. We *have* to. We shall leave here soon, we must, we can't stay, not after this. And we can't go without them. I *won't*.'

I don't remember much else of that day. Charlotte gave me some opiate, something Sayid had obtained in Kabul, and I slept heavily, a frightening thick sleep full of red and black images and sounds of gunfire. I woke at moments and once found Hugh there watching me most kindly, and somehow his pity was too terrible to bear, I suppose because he unknowingly needed more pity than anyone, and I let myself slip away from him into my nightmares again.

Next morning, it was snowing again and I woke to the full knowledge of what had happened and knew what it was like to feel fear for a loved one, which is much worse than fear for yourself, and what Charlotte had been bearing for weeks, ever since she had known Alexander had been made a prisoner. I lay under my rugs and stared at the ceiling and thought of him leaning in despair against the wall of the house where I had seen him last and then I thought of Richard, going with Sir

William MacNaghten because it was his duty although he knew it had to be a plot, and I thought of poor Lady MacNaghten waking this morning, and of Charlotte and Hugh and all the things they wished for and couldn't have – and then I wondered why I had woken at all since the world was full of such terrible things.

I struggled out of my rugs and saw that Charlotte's bed was empty and neatly made and then I heard her outside, calling for Sayid, her voice thickened and muffled by the snow. I went to open the door and as I did so, saw my lovely pagoda bird-cage, and my little yellow canary was lying still and stiff at the bottom, killed by the cold, and suddenly it was the end of everything and I couldn't bear it any more and I wanted to be like the canary and not cold and hungry and savaged by wretched anxieties. If Charlotte had not come in then, I don't know what I should have done, but she did come, and as always, when she came, there was a glimmer in the blackness and a purpose in going on.

She found errands for me all that day. What she did herself, I scarcely noticed, but she seemed much occupied and I observed Sayid was not at home and that she seemed very anxious and restless for his return. I made soup on her instructions and carried it through the snow to various houses and took our few spare blankets to Mrs Mainwaring who had had her baby and was being wonderfully courageous in view of the alarming circumstances in which she and her new child found themselves.

I met Lady Sale in one of the lanes well wrapped in a poshteen and all manner of strange shaggy furs.

'You must not worry, my dear Emily,' she said. 'And even if the worst comes to the worst you will have the consolation of knowing that Captain Talbot did his utmost to prevent yesterday's atrocities. Eye witnesses said he almost perished trying to save Sir William when the Afghans fell upon him.'

131

Reflections of this sort seemed to fill me with frenzy rather than console me, but I stammered out some kind of thanks.

'It's a pity Elphinstone isn't a prisoner himself,' Lady Sale continued. 'He refuses to believe Sir William is dead and merely insists he has gone into Kabul for further talks with Akbar. Akbar! Do you know, my dear, what he has suggested? He says he will exchange prisoners for all the women and children in the Cantonment. Is it credible? Captain Anderson said he would prefer to shoot his wife first and my son-in-law said that they should only take my daughter at bayonet point. I rely at least upon your sister not being taken and I could only wish we had all profited by her example and learned to shoot as accurately as she,' and then, with this cheerless news, she nodded to me and swept off through the snow.

When I told Charlotte, she said, 'I believe I should like to be taken prisoner,' and her voice was not altogether steady. 'I've tried to fight it, Emily, I've tried and tried. But it isn't any good. I can't think of anything else. He's probably starving, he's certainly cold and – wretched—'

'Charlotte,' I said and my voice was only a whisper. 'You won't – you won't put yourself in danger. Will you? Oh Charlotte, *please*—'

'I shall do what I have to do,' she said and went up on to the roof to search the Cantonment for a glimpse of Sayid returning.

I don't think there can be a worse condition than to be bored and frightened all at once. The next few days were endless, a ceaseless wearying round of trying to keep warm, and to devise food out of nothing, all the while on edge for some new noise, some unfamiliar happening. Gangs of Afghan bandits prowled round the edge of the Cantonment, sniping away at our poor sepoys who were, for some reason, forbidden by General Elphinstone to fire back. We ceased to be able to sleep properly and Charlotte, thin now as a lath, chafed so much at our imprisonment that she reminded me of some poor lovely wild thing kept in a cage. Between thinking of her and of Richard, I had no energy or time to think of anyone else, not even poor Hugh who was gaunt and sunk in despair.

'I blame myself entirely, Emily,' he said. 'I should never have brought you. Never.'

'Charlotte would never have forgiven you if you hadn't,' I said.

'That was why she—' he began and then he stopped and gave me a sad twisted smile like a clown and went off to hearten the men.

Christmas morning brought grey skies and a wind so sharp that it felt as if the skin was being flayed from one's face – and also the news that Akbar said we must all go, every one of us and we must leave behind all our money and all our field guns but six. If we complied with both these requests, Akbar said he would see us safely out of the country.

'He won't,' said Charlotte, and looked at Hugh as if she expected to be contradicted.

But he said nothing. He simply sat and stared before him. I wondered how much money he would have to leave behind and then thought that money wouldn't matter to him anything like as much as the humiliation of abandoning guns to the enemy, worse even than the disgrace of losing regimental colours.

Akbar hadn't said when he would let us go, he had simply announced he would do so when all arrangements were made, but that we should be ready at twenty-four hours' notice. So we spent the rest of the day packing our possessions and I have not, in all my long life, ever spent such a tense, unhappy and endless day as that Christmas Day of 1841. Almost everything I put into my box made me want to weep at the sheer poignancy of the memories it aroused, yet those memories seemed the only thing seductive enough to lure my mind from the thought of having to leave Richard in a cell in the Bala Hissar or even to a worse – but my mind shied away at that point always, in blind panic.

Dusk fell in mid-afternoon. I sat on my packed box and looked about at my desolated little room and wondered what sort of a Christmas dear little Mary Anderson had spent in such conditions. It was almost dark and I was beginning to feel quite paralyzed with cold yet too apathetic with misery to stir myself when I heard Charlotte's voice outside, warm and excited.

My door opened.

'Emily,' she said, 'I was feeling very bad at having no present to give you, but there seemed no point in giving you something that would be a burden to carry. But, as luck would have it, I've found the very thing,' and then she laughed and stepped aside and a large, beloved, familiar figure filled the dusky doorway.

'They set me free, dearest,' said Richard.

When I look back on that evening, I always marvel at Charlotte's generosity. If she felt any envy at seeing Richard and me together again after only three days apart when she had endured almost two months, she gave no sign of it. She made some amazing dish out of potatoes and a cabbage and a knuckle of salt pork Sayid had returned with and Hugh found two bottles of wine and we had a celebration. It was a real celebration too, despite the cold and the fright and the smallness of the knuckle of pork and this terrible journey that lay ahead of us.

Richard had not been harmed. He had been kept in a cell separate from Lawrence and Mackenzie but apart from the bitter cold and the filth, it had been bearable. He had been fed twice a day on a kind of thin gruel and rice but he had not been chained nor had his possessions taken from him, and his gaolers had left him a small lamp so that he was never in utter blackness.

It was only when he had told us everything and I was leaning against him, full of contentment, that I saw

Charlotte's face, up to then so full of pleasure, fall for just a moment as if her own thoughts had suddenly twisted her with pain. I looked at Hugh beside her, swirling the pale wine in his glass, his poshteen collar turned up around his narrow head – and I decided, abruptly, to chance it.

'Richard – did you hear anything of Alexander Bewick?'

Charlotte never gasped, she simply froze. Richard said, 'Yes, yes, I did. I think the gaolers regard him with some warmth, there were a lot of stories of Sekundar Iskandar as they call him—'

'What stories?' Charlotte said.

'It appears he talked his way out of assassination. I can't think how. But he was sentenced to die and then there was some plea made to Akbar – my command of the language isn't good enough to know the details – and Bewick is still there and there seemed to be some competition to be his gaoler. Of course, if MacNaghten had paid him the slightest heed, none of this—'

'That's enough,' said Hugh. He stood up and belted his coat round him. He was white and strained and there were long lines beside his nose and mouth. 'I'm thankful you are safe, Richard, thankful. But I can't stand all this "if only . . . if only . . ." They're all doing it, Eyre, Sturt, Shelton, everyone. There's no point to it, none at all—'

I saw Charlotte's face turned up to him, streaming with tears. He didn't look at her, or at us. We edged apart, as if by tacit recognition of the unsuitability of parading our happiness and Richard stood up, holding out a hand to Hugh.

'Steady—' he said, but Hugh brushed him aside and flung the door open. He paused on the threshold as if he were going to say something but changed his mind and plunged out in silence, slamming the door violently behind him.

'He feels guilty,' I said to Richard. 'He thinks he should never have brought us. He can't bear our army crawling back to India with its tail between its legs. And he's hungry too, and we aren't sleeping any more, not well—'

'Listen to me,' Charlotte said sharply.

I turned to look at her. When Hugh had gone, I had wanted to go to her but couldn't for Richard knew nothing and it seemed worse to betray her than to neglect to console her. She had stopped crying now and was sitting bolt upright on the divan, her hands clasped tightly in front of her.

'Three days ago, Emily – it seems years – I said to you that if Akbar made us leave I shouldn't go leaving Richard and Alexander in prison. Some miracle has happened and Richard has been freed. Perhaps a second miracle will happen for Alexander but I doubt it.'

Richard was still standing. I looked up at him, fearing to see shock on his face as he took in what Charlotte was saying, but his expression changed only to startled comprehension and from that to sympathy.

He said, 'He's not in a cell like I was. He's in a dungeon. Underground.'

'I know,' Charlotte said. She looked up at Richard and I saw that she meant him to know everything, that she needed him in some way and that he like most men, would not resist her, could not, would even suspend all ordinary reactions and opinions for her if necessary.

'Sayid found out,' Charlotte said. 'He's been around the Bala Hissar most days for weeks. He knew Alexander had escaped death, he can tell me exactly where he is, he even knows most of the gaolers. He told me you were to be freed – Emily darling, I only didn't tell you because I knew the surprise would be so glorious and it was, wasn't it? – and he thinks he knows a way that he and I can free—'

'No!' said Richard. He almost shouted it.

'I must,' Charlotte said.

Richard stopped and took her shoulders.

'You are not in a three-act melodrama, Charlotte. You are in a dangerous, hostile, unreliable country. If you are caught, you will die. Probably horribly. Sayid

136

is a great help to you but he will be shunned if it is known among the Afghans here that he serves a feringhi, shunned and probably murdered. The Bala Hissar is a massive fortification. You cannot do it. You must not.'

'I shall pick my time,' Charlotte said. 'I shall do it. I must. If it doesn't succeed, I'd rather die. Much rather.'

Richard sat beside her.

'Charlotte, please be reasonable. Life isn't a question of high romance and dramatic gestures. The most we can hope from it at the moment is to get out with whole skins—'

'I shall do that,' Charlotte said. 'And Alexander's skin too. I wouldn't have breathed a word to anyone, not even to you, Emily, except that I need your help. I want Jane's clothes adapted so we can disguise Alexander and when you find I have gone I want you both to divert Hugh, calm him, invent some errand I have gone on. You won't stop me, Richard. If you do try, you will find it quite useless. My rescuing Alexander is quite inevitable and if you betray me you will damage three lives, mine, his and Hugh's. You held your tongue once, Emily. You must do so again.'

Richard looked at me and said 'Emily!' His voice was an appeal. Charlotte took no notice.

'I shan't tell you our plans. I have a superstition that if I tell anyone they won't work, and in any case I think, from the best of motives, you might bungle them for me. I haven't told you this much because I want your sanction or even your sympathy, but because I need your help. Hugh mustn't know and – and I'm not much of a needlewoman as you know. It's the only way to get him out safely. Emily, I need your help, I *need* you.'

I said, 'Of course. You shall have it.'

She let out a long breath and then she smiled at me and her eyes were glittering with tears again.

'And mine,' said Richard.

'Then I shall succeed,' Charlotte said.

I wanted to ask her what she meant to do if – and I could not believe her plans would work, even though my faith in her was mountains high – she did extract Alexander from the Bala Hissar. What about life after that – and Hugh? But I didn't because it seemed so typical of me to be prosaic and sensible and I saw from her face that she was on another plane to me, a plane where anything is possible if you have faith, and where faith is the essential ingredient and must not be damaged. So instead of saying what was in my mind, I said, 'What a good thing Jane always wore grey and was so tall. I can run two of her dresses together. Do you suppose he will want her stays?'

Then Richard came over to me and pulled me to my feet and turned to encircle Charlotte with his other arm, and he held us there in an embrace like a bear, laughing all the time.

We waited a week. The snowstorms stopped and a brilliant cold sun came out in the noon and for a few hours our world was so brightly blue and white that it was almost too dazzling to look upon. The mountains were so beautiful it hurt, glittering so pure and clean against the deep midday sky and such a contrast to the Cantonment, trampled into mud with the frozen puddles thawing into evil pools in the brief warmth. When the icy grip of the night relaxed for a few hours awful smells were borne in from the horse lines and the barrack huts where the poor sepoys huddled, as camels and ponies weakened by disease died in the snow and were left there, rotting.

On New Year's Day we ate only a small bowl each of a kind of porridge made from some maize Sayid had brought, and a handful of dried apricots. We looked at our firewood situation and found we had one bedstead and two chairs to go and then we should have to chop up the divans which were now our only furniture. The only thing there was plenty of was rumour. One ran that Shah Suja had appealed to the British not to abandon him to Akbar.

Lady Sale snorted at his cowardice.

'The Afghans do not wish to put him to death, but only to deprive him of his sight.'

Only! I thought, biting off a thread. My adaptation of Jane's clothes was proving a lifeline, a duty which was the most welcome distraction imaginable from my thoughts and from enforced idleness.

'They will murder him,' said Charlotte.

Lady Sale shrugged as if the life of a barbarian such as Shah Suja was neither here nor there. I tried not to think of him as I had seen him last that summer day in his blaze of jewels, his face so dignified, so composed because the contrast to what he was now must be so terrible.

'One should never abandon – people,' Charlotte said. 'We should rescue him.'

'The time for that, my dear,' said Lady Sale, 'is well past.'

Charlotte shook her head slightly, but she did not reply.

For four more days I sewed. I took two grey dresses of stout English wool quite to pieces and then, using Richard as a rough guide, I cut one into long strips and inserted them across the shoulders and down the bodice until I had made the most unbecoming great square garment imaginable. Jane's bonnet fitted Richard perfectly, so I added a heavy grey frill to the brim in order to disguise the wearer's face. There was sufficient material left to add a flounce to the hem which would mask large masculine feet and smaller frills to the cuffs though, as Charlotte pointed out, poor Jane's hands might have been mistaken for a man's at any time.

When it was done, we dressed Richard up entirely.

'I have never felt better clad,' he said and was most good-natured about our laughter.

*

The next afternoon it happened. Hugh came back from the lines, his blue eyes brilliant in this thin tired face.

'We are to march tomorrow,' he said. 'Tomorrow morning. At seven.'

Then he turned to Charlotte and took her hands.

'Take as little as you can, my dearest. Everything warm, nothing luxurious. It will take us all night to rally ourselves together. You can't move 17,000 people in a twinkling. Can I leave your packing to you and to Emily? I'll be back at dawn.'

'I'm coming with you,' Richard said.

'Of course,' said Charlotte. 'Leave everything.' Then she kissed Hugh's cheek and it seemed to me like some kind of farewell and I had to look aside because of the sheer poignancy of it, just as I had at their wedding.

Then the men went away and I crept into my room to repack all the things that had already been packed for weeks so that I should not notice what Charlotte was doing. I did not hear her go, I did not see Sayid, I tried to comfort myself by saying that quite truthfully I *hadn't* seen her, I *didn't* know . . . But I *did* know, and because of that I never slept but sat up all night by the brazier, my eyes and ears straining for a sight and sound of her. Ten, eleven, midnight came and went. The fire died down and I felt the cold creep into my limbs like a deadly poison, so I managed to rouse myself and piled on our last chair legs, the only remaining claw foot of my great black bed. Two, three, four o'clock. The sky outside was still inky black, dawn wouldn't break till after we had gone. Three hours to go, then two. Where was she? And where was Hugh?

I fixed my swimming gaze upon the brazier and forced myself to count the iron rivets that held the bars, then the white circles in the russet stripes of the rug on which I crouched, then the black diamonds between the stripes, then the tassels of the fringes, then the studs on the back of the door, the number of planks of wood it was made of, the bolts in the hinges, the·beams in the ceiling, my own fingers, my finger-nails—

The door opened. I could see nothing in the blackness, only feel the awful air, cold enough to kill you.

'Hugh?' I said, and my voice was a hoarse whisper, 'Richard?'

Charlotte said, 'Where is the dress, Emily?'

CHAPTER ELEVEN

We dressed Alexander in my room, for if Hugh came back and was looking for us, he would knock there. It was also warmer, although the brazier was burning low and Sayid brought a lamp which threw a golden glow around the room, bare now except for rugs.

I could hardly rise from where I had sat all night on the floor and when I did, I couldn't stop trembling, every limb, every nerve seemed to shudder uncontrollably, even my face and lips had a shivering life of their own.

'Emily,' Alexander said and held out his arms to me.

He was pitifully thin and as white as the moon. His eyes seemed almost as dark as his tangled hair and the beard that grew thickly around his mouth and over his chin. The hands he held out to me were as filthy as Sayid's but he was smiling, his teeth brilliant in his dusky face.

'I never seem quite able to please you, do I, Emily. Unprincipled before, black within and white without, now – now—' he glanced at Charlotte and caught his breath, 'now much improved within and as black as coal without. But I've so much to thank you for – so much – your sewing, the support you've been to—' he swung round and caught Charlotte to him then he took one hand away and held it out to me.

141

'Emily,' he said again.

I took his hand then.

'We must shave you,' Charlotte said, her voice muffled against the Afghan tunic he wore. 'Beard, moustache, everything. You're to be a lady's maid.'

He said into her hair, 'I'll be anything you say. Anything.'

I looked round for Sayid. He was squatting by the brazier, no cleaner, no tamer-looking than he had ever been, but his face was illumined with pleasure, his features that always reminded me of a bird of prey, softened somehow and gentle. I released Alexander's hand and went over to Sayid. He looked up at me.

'Is good,' he said.

'Yes,' I said. 'It's very good. I thank you.'

Before six, we were ready. Alexander, washed and shaved, his face vulnerable as a child's without his moustache, and dressed with strange dignity in Jane's ill-assorted garments, had devoured all the food that remained to us, some maize porridge, a cupful of cabbage soup, a stale egg, a few dates and dried apricots. All the while he ate, he held Charlotte with his free hand grasping her wrist, and Sayid crouched beside them like some queer contented parent bird with two chicks.

'Tell me,' I said. 'Tell me everything.'

Charlotte had gone to him, in her black robes, as a whore.

'But your eyes. Your blue eyes!'

Sayid laughed softly on the floor.

'Alexander the Great's Macedonian hoplites came this way,' Alexander said. 'There are a number of blue-eyed Afghans—'

'But a – a *whore*—'

It had seemed the best and most obvious way. Alexander had charmed his gaolers as he had charmed so many before them. They could not do much to relieve his physical misery beyond seeing that he did not actually starve, and he had been ill—

'It was the filth. There never was such a hole. I did get a glimpse five years ago into the bug pit in Bokhara and I don't think there was much to choose between my dungeon and that, except that I didn't have snakes for company, only rats—'

Charlotte shuddered. 'Oh, that was the only moment when my courage failed me when I thought I might—'

'Don't,' he said.

Sayid, slipping in and out of the Bala Hissar, had become a familiar figure. He had begun simply by bringing rumours, the gossip for which they were all greedy, and then he had moved on to presents of liquor which the gaolers, Moslem though they were, were too bored and frustrated by inactivity to refuse. He had also taken Charlotte's jewellery, piece by piece, to the gaolers, professing to have stolen it from the feringhi, the white-skinned unbelievers, and at last as a reward, he had come to see Alexander, chained to a slimy wall, for the gaolers wished to show off their prize exhibit, Sekundar Iskandar.

'There was nothing I could ask for that would not arouse suspicion. We thought about it for weeks, knowing we must have a plan ready to use the night before Akbar ordered you to march because that night all eyes would be on the Cantonment, the Afghans would be assembling for an escort. And we had to use it that night because I think I should have been mincemeat otherwise as poor Shah Suja will surely be—'

'Is no eyes,' Sayid said softly from the floor.

Alexander held out his hand to me once more.

'Don't cry, Emily. Try not to think of it. He was brought up to believe life is a much more nasty, brutish and short affair than we were.'

I took his hand and rubbed a handful of my skirt across my face.

'Tell me more.'

'Because I knew I was condemned, I asked the gaolers for one last favour, a final pleasure for a doomed man—'

'He asked for a woman. It was a good idea, wasn't it? And of course Alexander asked to be unchained for this – this purpose and they saw no harm, deep there in the bowels of the earth.'

So Sayid had brought Charlotte down to the dungeons, but she was not the only thing he brought. Under his tunic bulged a wineskin full of some lethal spirit distilled from rotting peaches and when Charlotte and Alexander had been locked in together, he produced his treasure. There were three gaolers and perhaps a quart of liquor and Sayid was well armed with satisfying stories of how the lily-livered feringhi in the Cantonment quaked now for fear of what the Afghans might do. The gaolers began to boast and shout and crow with triumph and toast each other lavishly for their courage. Sayid talked and laughed and poured spirit into the brass tumblers, bumper after bumper.

'You can imagine!' Charlotte said, smiling down at Sayid. 'Within an hour they were elated, belligerent, confused and finally unconscious. Sayid simply took the keys and came down to us and there we were, me in my black robes, Alexander in those native rags Sayid had found in the bazaar. One of the guards was stirring as we went past, but of course, by then we were all three Afghans and there was nothing strange in our being there. We left the keys on the floor—'

'I wanted to leave a message in English, saying thank you,' Alexander said. 'But I was persuaded to see by your sister who is the wisest as well as the most adorable person upon earth, that that was dangerous bravado. So we sauntered on through the fortress arm in arm with Sayid, talking together in Pushtu and the doors opened for us and we were bidden good night and there we were, outside, Emily, *outside*—'

'But you'll be followed!' I said in panic. 'It will be all over Kabul, they will be looking as we leave, you can't just extract a notorious prisoner and hope that will be an end to it!'

'Oh Emily, Emily, will you never relent? Will you see me as notorious even if from henceforward no maiden aunt behaved as faultlessly as I shall? Of course it isn't safe, my dear. Why else am I clad this way? But it's safe enough—'

Boots thumped in the snow outside. Alexander and Sayid tensed immediately, their eyes wary and hard. Charlotte never took her hand away from Alexander, she simply turned towards the door and called, 'Hugh?'

'No,' Richard's voice said, thick with relief, 'I've come back to fetch you.'

Sayid leaped up to open the door. Richard was livid with cold despite his poshteen and an army greatcoat he wore tied around his shoulders by the sleeves.

'My God,' he said looking down at us, then his face contracted for a moment and I wondered if he were going to laugh or weep, but he did neither, simply knelt and kissed Charlotte's hand. Then he rose and said, 'We are off, my dears. We are to be gone, all of us, by noon. Charlotte and Emily, you have ponies, I'm delighted to tell you, and you're to ride behind the cavalrymen for protection. Bewick—' he paused and then a great smile lit up his face and he held out his hands – 'Bewick, my dear fellow, what are you doing in *my* gown?'

CHAPTER TWELVE

It was terrible confusion, our leaving. I never saw so many people in one body in my life before and realized how vast an existence had been played out in the Cantonment all around me for nearly eight months while I was too absorbed in our own dramas to notice. I don't suppose more than a quarter of that great unwieldy caravan were soldiers, and almost all of them were the wretched shivering Indian sepoys, but the rest was a horde of followers such as I had never dreamed existed, and their families and their endless bundles.

We were to leave the Cantonment by the gate nearest to the Kabul River. It was savagely, viciously cold even though a faint bloom in the sky to the east showed that somewhere the sun was struggling. I was so swathed in clothes against the wind that I could scarcely mount my pony.

'Not much like leaving Bombay, eh?' said Hugh. He was greenish-white with fatigue but he had greeted us smilingly, a smile I could hardly return, I felt so false. I did not look at Charlotte when they met. I could not. If she had greeted him with unconcern, gaiety even, I should have come close to hating her and that I could not do.

As if he read my thoughts, Richard said, 'We can't run with the hare and hunt with the hounds, Emily. We have cast our lot—'

'I can't bear to think of what will happen when she – she—'

He looked at me sternly.

'You must not think of that. You don't even know what she means to do. You must save every ounce of energy, mental and physical, for what lies ahead. You must not relax your determination until we reach Jalalabad.'

Outside our house, Alexander and Sayid had vanished utterly. I knew they were going to mingle with the great ragged mob of followers, twelve thousand of them who intended, for they had no option, to plod alongside the main body of the army. There were enough turbans and outlandish bonnets in that scarecrow caravan for both Sayid and Alexander to disappear comfortably, but all the same I could not help feeling that Alexander must be very careful, must not forget for a moment that he was a marked man, not for miles and miles, even to Jalalabad.

146

I sat on my pony and watched the red coats in front of us and the camels and gun carriages, and in spite of Richard's warning, I found that I wanted all of them to be happy, Charlotte and Hugh and Alexander; that I didn't want any of them to fail in their heart's desire and that I could see everyone's point of view, quite clearly. Then somebody shouted above the clattering and jingling and there were blasts on a bugle and the whole unwieldy procession began to lumber forward into the raw dawn – and those were the last proper thoughts I had.

'India, here we come,' said Hugh and his voice was exultant.

I suppose there were about thirty of us, wives and children of officers – a tiny group of English people in a jostling horde of Asians, a horde so vast that it spread over the plain outside the Cantonment like a human blanket – and we were the lucky ones. The rearguard of the army was swooped upon by Afghan troops as it formed up to leave the Cantonment and we heard furious gunfire behind us as we plodded on through the deep snow in the teeth of the screaming winds. My clothes felt like paper, even my poshteen seemed a frail barrier against the blast.

Charlotte had taken little Mary Anderson to ride in front of her saddle, partly to comfort her and partly to warm her, and the child was clinging to Charlotte, her face buried against her out of the gale. Above the wind I could hear Charlotte singing. What it was I couldn't hear, but she was smiling as she sang, one arm tight about Mary, the other hand on her reins.

It took two hours to cross the Kabul River because a muddle had happened, the first of endless muddles, and the icy water was jammed with men and guns and camels, and when we had struggled across, dazed with cold and effort, bullets began to sing and whine about us from the banks of snow either side of the track.

'Some protection!' Charlotte said. 'I suppose this is Akbar's idea of safe conduct. Emily, will you take Mary for a while – she's wonderfully warm and I would like to have both hands free.'

I was so stiff and sore from hours in the saddle, I hardly knew if I could lift the child, but Mary came scrambling across from pony to pony like a little monkey and pressed herself to me as she had to Charlotte. I looked across at Charlotte and she was still holding her reins with one hand but the other now loosely clasped a pistol lying across the pommel of her saddle.

'Alexander's,' she said, following my gaze and then she twisted in her saddle and looked at the huge struggling mass of humanity behind us. 'I wish at this moment Jane's clothes had been bright yellow. Something really visible—'

'Charlotte,' I said firmly – and then I lost courage. 'Are you – are you very tired?'

She looked at me in amazement and her face, though thin now, was so full of vitality that the energy seemed to burst through her skin.

'Oh Emily, Emily, you should know me better than that!'

If it was a terrible day, the night was worse. The sun sank about four and the whining wind rose to a howl, slicing and carving its way round us until we were quite tortured with cold. Lady Sale had brought a small tent which Hugh and Richard made valiant attempts to put up, but there were not enough pegs and the ground was as hard as iron. We huddled together as best we could, Mrs Mainwaring valiantly pressing her baby to her in an attempt to stop the poor little thing freezing to death, and I don't remember much of it, except the grinding wretchedness. I dozed and woke, woke and dozed in the inky, icy, blackness. Richard was right. We had been away from Kabul for hardly twenty-four hours and already all my energies were needed simply to keep going. Often when my mind surfaced for a moment, I could hear Charlotte's voice, warm and encouraging, the only note of comfort in the bleakness.

*

We tried to make a fire in the morning but the few sticks the men found us were sodden with snow.

'The sepoys have terrible frostbite,' Hugh said. 'They've no notion how to keep warm. Mackenzie said some of them were actually burning their clothes last night for a few moment's warmth.'

'Look,' Richard said. He was standing beside us as we crouched over our tiny fire, the dry bread that was his breakfast portion in his hand.

Charlotte stood too and shaded her eyes against the morning sun.

'Akbar's escort,' she said softly.

The snowy heights around us were black with them, some on foot, some on horses, their jezails making little diamond points of light where they caught the sun.

'Perhaps he will keep his word,' Hugh said uncertainly.

We watched as the turbaned columns came down the steep slopes towards us, the whole army seemed to be watching, holding its breath, cold and hunger forgotten for that moment. Then there was a wild scream that rang echoing around the peaks and the cavalry columns of Afghans broke into a trot, then a gallop and thundered, howling and firing their weapons into the rearguard of the army.

That was only the beginning. The day broke into a mad scramble as we all stumbled in panic to our ponies, leaving precious bread to be trampled in the snow. Our neat close band behind the cavalrymen became invaded with followers, plunging forward in terror. A woman was dragging at my stirrup, screaming, a mad, pathetic hideous woman in a tawdry bonnet and a plaid shawl and I saw her poor clawing fingers slipping inexorably away and her waving limbs crumple among the horses as the whole body pressed forward. The air was full of the sound of firing, the mountains on either side still thick with whooping, galloping figures. I felt a thud on my arm and looked down to see, with quite impersonal surprise in the din and confusion, two neat holes in my poshteen where a jezail bullet had gone into my sleeve – and out.

There was no hope of stopping. Our ponies were screaming too, their eyes rolling white, there was nowhere they could bolt in their frenzy as the mountains were beginning to hem us in, closer and closer, pushing us into the deadly funnel of the Khurd Kabul Pass. I looked round to see if there were any familiar faces around me but I could see none, only a press of faces as blind with panic as I felt my own must look. I began to pray, stupid, desperate, frantic prayers and then someone put a hand on my bridle and a voice said, 'I'm pulling you into the edge, Emily. Right up to the cliff. They can't pick you off so easily there—'

It was Alexander.

'Charlotte—' I said, gasping.

He pointed ahead.

She was perhaps twenty yards in front, riding beside Mrs Mainwaring and her baby, pressing them into the cliff wall as close under the overhang as she could get them, and every so often she would raise her pistol and take aim and fire.

'She's hardly missed one,' Alexander said, and then he smiled at me and said something else, but I never heard it for a shattering volley of rifle fire exploded into the gorge and before my eyes, only feet away from me on the path I had just left soldiers began falling, red coat after red coat buckling into the snow, jerking and twisting, while the whiteness became dabbled with blood and the awful deafening noise went on and on. I could not bear to look. I put my hands into my sleeves and concentrated on Alexander's fist that held my pony's rein. Every so often he would glance up at me and his eyes were brilliant with the same excitement Charlotte's held. I suppose we struggled on like this for an hour or more, between the soaring, awful walls of blue-grey rock while the Kabul

River boiled yellow below us and the road swooped and plunged underneath the terrible crags that loomed above us and hid Akbar's marksmen.

Then Alexander shouted something and abruptly flung away my reins and stumbled out into the deadly hail of bullets in the middle of the path. I looked up in alarm and saw him bent over someone, something, there, a something in folds of dark cloth, a broken limp something. He picked it up and came back to me where I stayed, pressed against the splintering rock wall, and his face was full of fury.

'Look!' he shouted angrily. 'The bastards! It's Mrs Curtis, I never saw her in the mêlée. I'd have put her on the pony with you—'

I slid off the pony and together we laid Mrs Curtis on the stones of the roadway. She was a pale, prim woman in her forties who had disapproved very much of Charlotte and whose every waking moment in Kabul had been devoted to showing the Afghans the error of their heathenish ways. Now she lay on cold, wet inhospitable Moslem earth, still and dead, shot through the body.

I crouched over her, holding her still faintly warm hand, sickened and horrified, and I thought of Major Curtis, grave and courteous and humourless, somewhere among the cavalrymen ahead, ignorant of his loss. From heaven knows where, Alexander found a mule, its panniers crammed with bundles, and across these he laid Mrs Curtis; and we covered her poor dead face with the shawl she had knotted round her shoulders and then Alexander motioned me to mount again, and we moved onward, myself in front and him coming behind leading the mule.

Without Alexander at its head, my pony jibbed so that I had to dig my heels into him and as I did so I felt him shudder all through his frame and he seemed to go slack underneath me, heavy and limp, and to sink. There wasn't even time to realize fully what had happened before I felt an arm about my waist and myself being heaved out of my saddle and set on my feet and then we lurched forward and I almost fell but for that iron arm.

'Hell!' He shouted. 'The army's broken!' And I saw that all the path before us was littered with bundles and weapons and ammunition and crumpled, flung-about bodies, red and white and pitiful in the snow.

I couldn't see Charlotte now, I couldn't see the mule, I couldn't see anything. There were people and animals all around us jostling and pushing, and then there was an icy stream to cross and I felt the water biting at my legs and knees, and I wanted to stop and just sink down, but Alexander had me up and propelled me on while the roar of rifle fire crashed on. People seemed to be running in all directions, madly, pointlessly, anywhere rather than plod on under that deadly fire. We seemed to go stumbling on for ages, my head bent, my eyes almost closed, but he held my waist firmly all the time and I began to feel through all my terror, a calm beginning, a strange powerful, confident calm, the kind of calm Charlotte gave me.

The wives and children that had survived the gorge were packed together that night in a mass so solid no-one could even turn. Charlotte and I put Mrs Mainwaring between us, and the baby, and there we lay in our shredded tent, dumb with fatigue. In the darkness there was some scuffling and tugging at our tent and then nightmare moans and howls and we realized that some of the followers and the sepoys, maddened with cold, were trying to force their way in. When morning came, and we struggled, half dazed with fitful sleep, into the bitter air, the ground about the tent was littered with the poor men, quite literally frozen to death.

I said, 'Oh Charlotte—' but she wasn't listening. She was looking away from me at an officer whom I had last seen as Orsino in *Twelfth Night* listening to a lute on a pile of cushions and who now stood haggard and bloodied, his eyes fixed on Charlotte and full of weary sympathy.

'I'm so sorry, Mrs Connell. So sorry.'

She shook her head wordlessly.

I said, 'What is it, what's happened—' and she turned her head slowly towards me and her blue eyes were as dark as thunderclouds.

'He's dead,' she said. 'He died yesterday. In that gorge. And I was too stupid with tiredness – and remorse – to – to tell you yesterday—'

A figure pushed through the people around us, an incongruous striding figure in a grey habit. Charlotte gave a little cry and put her hands out as if she wanted to be guided, to be led.

She said, her voice catching, 'He's dead. He was killed in – in the gorge. And – and I saw him and I did nothing, I couldn't.'

'It was just before the army broke, where the river crossed the road and he had come back from the vanguard to see if I was safe, to help me, and I saw him—' she stopped and choked. I waited for Alexander to move towards her but he did nothing, simply waited, expressionless and still. 'He came towards me, I could see him, battling between all the men struggling the other way and he caught sight of me and waved and then I saw him fall, I saw the blood on his head and then my pony bolted and I got carried quite past the place and I couldn't stop the pony and I couldn't see Hugh and I could hear myself screaming. I can't think about anything else, I'd give my life to go back there, to have been by him, to have tried to save him, I can't bear to think of him all broken there in the mud, poor Hugh, poor Hugh—'

I looked up at Alexander's face thinking to see triumph, but there was nothing there but pity.

'Ah, my dear,' he said. 'My very dear,' and in front of all the watchers, he took her in his arms.

Lady Sale said later that morning that she had known the tall woman in grey had been a man all along and by early afternoon she confided to me that she had known he was Alexander Bewick too.

'What is more, I believe your sister is the only woman alive who could tame him.'

It was the only light-hearted moment of the day. We had struggled on from our camp, leaving those poor stiff corpses in the snow and three thousand dead in the gorge, and had stumbled wearily on, too worn down by cold and hunger and misery to feel the terror of yesterday, while the Afghans rode up and down beside us sniping away at our flanks. Just as I had persuaded myself that Richard too lay in that bloodstained death-trap, he found us. He was severely wounded in the shoulder and grey from loss of blood, but as he said gallantly, with a head and a heart still and a pair of legs.

Alexander had no reason to leave us now and I spent the greater part of the day dragging myself in his wake, for he and Charlotte had become a sort of talisman to me, a lucky charm that it would be perilous indeed to lose. And then, as the sun began to slide down behind the crests of the mountains, we were commanded to halt. At first it seemed Elphinstone had decided to pitch camp for the night and then we saw, on a rising patch of ground, a group of Afghans and General Elphinstone was among them.

'Akbar!' Alexander said.

I tried to stand on tiptoe and crane to see but I was too tired, too weak from lack of food. Behind me Lady Sale was reciting a poem she said she couldn't get out of her head, a poem by Campbell—

> 'Few, few shall part where many meet,
> The snow shall be their winding sheet,
> And every turf beneath their feet
> Shall be a soldier's sepulchre.'

154

Charlotte looked round, smiling, though her face was as weary as I ever saw it and still streaked with tears.

'Oh no,' she said. 'No sepulchre. Not when we've come this far. Not now—'

And then the news broke. Akbar was to take us, all the women and children that remained and a few severely wounded officers with us, and we were to go with him to the enemy lines, among the Afghans.

'It is the only way,' Elphinstone said, his voice cracking with strain. 'It is the only way you will not die of starvation or frostbite. We must pray, pray most fervently, that Akbar will protect you, will keep his word.'

I looked about me with a sudden ridiculous rush of pleasure, realizing that Richard would come, that Alexander in his absurd clothes might come and then, as I was about to speak, about to point it out, I saw Charlotte wheel round, her eyes wide and frantic.

'Sayid!' she cried. 'Where is Sayid?'

CHAPTER THIRTEEN

'With sleeping nightmares,' Charlotte said carefully, her face averted from me, 'at least they are only momentary, quickly over and done with. But waking ones – waking ones go on and on, don't they – Emily, on and on—'

She kept her voice very low. I think she would have hated the other hostages to see how afflicted she was deep down, for we had all, all sixty of us, come to rely upon her for cheerfulness and resourcefulness and a powerful conviction that things could not go on as they were.

I, for one, desperately wanted to believe her. Once we had been given over to Akbar, all the women and children and a few wounded officers, we had been herded about aimlessly for days through such a nightmare landscape that even now I can hardly bring myself to dwell on it.

Akbar made us ride through the ruins of the army, over all those corpses and parts of corpses, all naked, all mangled, and among them still some poor wounded, starving camp followers quite out of their senses with cold and gibbering idiotically at us. Charlotte tried to stop several times but our guards screamed at her and raised their jezails.

And then Akbar brought us at last to a village called Budeabad, to a small and ancient fort, and we were crammed into five, icy, cell-like rooms pell-mell, men and women and children all jumbled up like cattle. Lady Sale was magnificent.

'Your promise was to take us to Jalalabad,' she said firmly to Akbar. 'We are to be taken to my husband's brigade.'

Akbar had simply smiled and shrugged.

'We are bargaining counters,' Charlotte said. 'He won't kill us because he will have the wrath of British India to contend with if he does. But he'll keep us until every last red coat is out of Afghanistan.'

Mrs Sturt had whispered to me then, 'How brave your sister is! I do not believe she minds all this at all!'

How really brave she was, no-one knew except myself because one cannot share a straw mattress with someone every night – and not know. She never wept, or if she did, she did it only when I slept, but she clung to me in the darkness in a most uncharacteristic way, as if I were somehow the last thing left to her. In a way I suppose I was. Hugh was dead, Mamma was thousands of miles away and, thank God, ignorant of our plight, Sayid had vanished – and so had Alexander.

Our last sight of him had been when he was standing by Charlotte as General Elphinstone told us that we should be Akbar's hostages. Charlotte had turned to smile at him, sure as I had been, that Jane's clothes would enable him to accompany us.

'And he looked back at me so – so deeply, Emily, not smiling but really looking, and then I turned to say something to someone else, I can't remember who, Mrs Mainwaring perhaps, and when I turned back he—'

No-one seemed to have seen him go. He had vanished as utterly into that desolation of wind and snow and suffering as if he had never been there.

'Of course he always loved to be free,' Charlotte said. 'He couldn't bear to be confined, he so loved what was unfettered and — and forbidden. I suppose he couldn't bear to be a prisoner again, not after the Bala Hissar, not so soon.'

But I knew she didn't mean that. I knew she wondered if, now Hugh was dead and she might be his in a perfectly orthodox way, he didn't want her. He mightn't care for a widow that society would sanction his having perhaps, only the wild, romantic, unlawful pursuit of someone else's wife. That was, in her blackest moments, Charlotte's nightmare. Beside it the daily struggle in our bitter little cells with no privies, no hot water, terrible meals of boiled rice and shreds of mutton like old shoe leather — all those difficulties were as nothing to her and she faced them with an ease that made us all look instinctively to her.

There were ten of us in our room, Charlotte and myself, three other ladies, two children and three wounded officers who had hung strips of cloth from the ceiling between themselves and us and had gallantly crammed themselves into a corner hardly big enough for three dogs. Next door Lady Sale commanded an equal number of souls, including — and this I must honestly confess was the only reason I could be any kind of comfort to Charlotte — Richard, whom I had wanted to nurse myself. But Lady Sale had been adamant.

'It would not be in the least proper, Emily. I have dressed several of Brigadier Sale's shoulder wounds and thus am a deal more experienced than you would be. It is imperative that we observe such proprieties as are left to us.'

157

They were indeed, precious few. Our room contained ten straw palliases flung down on mats on the stone floor, a low rough table on which our disgusting meals were banged, a window set in the thickness of the great fort walls which we were obliged to block up on account of the cold, and a crude brazier out of which sparking logs were always falling to the panic of the two mothers. The walls had been roughly whitewashed, the ceiling was made of planks of unplaned wood and the door would not shut properly so that an icy draught from the corridor made a certain corner of the room intolerable to sleep in. The officers had nobly claimed it as their own.

'No,' Charlotte said. 'We shall share it. Turn and turn about. Except of course for the children.'

We obeyed her. As the days went by, we did more and more, and gradually our Afghan warders, who had begun by howling and screaming at us and threatening us with knives and rifle butts, began to succumb as well. The stinking wooden buckets that were dumped in every room became rapidly intolerable. On the sixth day Charlotte had a brisk exchange in Pushtu with the warder on our door, and the bucket went out into the corridor.

Charlotte shook her head. It was not enough. The guard shouted and Charlotte smiled and persisted. Within an hour all five buckets from all five rooms had been taken down the corridor and left discreetly between the buttresses of a small courtyard in the open air.

The buckets were only a beginning. Brass cans appeared in which we could boil water on our braziers, bundles of newspapers from the garrison at Jalalabad, so old as to be almost history but wonderfully welcome all the same were thrown into our rooms, and Charlotte went on a visit to Akbar himself. Even I was not apprehensive when she went, but helped to dress her and to adorn her with a few pieces of jewellery we ladies had left. Captain Eyre and several others had escorted her and when they returned and we clustered round them full of questions, his face was illumined with admiration.

'I never saw anything like it, Miss Brent. We should have sent her to Akbar in Kabul. He's a handsome dog, you know, and must have his pick of pretty women, but his jaw fairly fell when Mrs Connell came in and I think he would have granted her anything within reason. She was so clever too, spoke to him in Pushtu, all smiles and reasonableness, and there he was smiling back for all the world as if they had known each other for years and the upshot is, Miss Brent, that we are allowed to have our Hindu servants back with us, and what is more, they are to be permitted to cook for us.'

To crown this triumph – and in a way this was the bravest deed of all – she persuaded Lady Sale that I should be with Richard during daylight hours at least and be allowed to nurse him.

'I'm – I'm very much afraid I don't dress this half as well as Lady Sale.'

We had an audience every morning of nine pale little children who had adopted Richard as a kind of honorary uncle.

'I'd a thousand times rather have you do it, Emily. You know that. In any case, I think you manage wonderfully. I don't suppose you ever bandaged a wound before.'

Of course I hadn't. I couldn't even remember seeing blood before except for pricked fingers and Charlotte's knee when she had climbed the plum tree in Richmond and fallen, and an awful burn once when Annie had scalded herself with boiling jam. But blood was now a commonplace, an awful one it's true, but frightening and sickening no longer.

'I suppose in the end one gets used to anything,' I said to Charlotte and then I could have bitten out my tongue.

'Almost anything,' she said and then she went away very quickly as if she could not trust herself to stay.

The days dragged into weeks. We became numb to almost everything, the cold, the confinement, each other, even the vermin. There had been appalling screams from Mrs Sturt early on in our captivity and we had all rushed to her aid, sure we should find her pinned to the wall by an Afghan madman, and discovered her pointing tremblingly at a small flea which had emerged from her bodice on to her sleeve.

'Light cavalry only, dear lady,' Richard had said to her. 'Wait until the infantry arrive.'

'Infantry?' Mrs Sturt said quaveringly.

'Lice, ma'am.'

There was little we could do about them and gradually we all stopped screaming.

'I admire your resolution,' Captain Eyre said to us and we felt complimented indeed.

It needed even greater resolution when the earthquakes began. Charlotte and Lady Sale were hanging out some washing together on the roof when a violent tremor rippled the earth under the fort as if it had been no more substantial than cloth, and the roof on which they were standing caved in beneath them.

'It just collapsed, fell away as if someone had opened a hatch,' Charlotte said. 'Thank goodness the room below was where they stored the rice, all those great sacks—'

After that we felt the earth heave like some malevolent subterranean dragon every day. Charlotte drew the dragon for the children on the walls with a piece of charcoal and then she took down one of the strips of cloth that made a screen in our room and draped it over a line of children so that they could caper about, playing at being an earthquake.

When anyone felt sick, as they were bound to do in such conditions, she proved a tireless nurse and even assisted at two confinements, returning elated at having shared in a birth.

'Think what heroes they will be, Emily! What a way to start a life!'

People were always talking about her, always asking for her, even people who in ordinary circumstances would have resented her capability as they resented Lady Sale's, just as they would have found her beauty and her courage an obstacle to feeling comfortable with her.

'She is magnificent,' one of the officers said to me. 'I don't know where our morale would be without her.'

He, of course, had no idea of the state of her own morale. As the days lengthened into weeks and then drearily into months, I began to have less idea myself. She seemed to be busier and busier, refusing ever even to touch upon anything personal in our whispered conversations late at night and I began to wonder if she was healing, if she was finding real solace in what she did to lighten our captivity.

And then, one day in April, I needed her for something, some trivial little thing, a scrap of cotton to patch a gown, and I could not find her. I roamed up and down our corridor, looked into all those dismal little rooms, as familiar now as if I had known no others, climbed on to the roof, explored the parapet. I was just about to summon Richard, whom I had left in the delighted discovery that a warder would obtain aubergine and melon seeds for him, when I saw her. She was at the far end of the parapet where the fort wall turned south towards Jalalabad, her grey dress almost invisible against the mud of the building. She had knelt down by the parapet and put her arms upon it, but instead of gazing southwards as I should have expected, her head was buried in her arms and her shoulders, thin and sharp as wings now through her clothes, were shaking convulsively.

I said, 'Oh *Charlotte*,' to no-one in particular and ran along the wall to comfort her.

Three days later a parcel came. It was a huge unwieldy parcel done up in a strip of red cloth, and it turned out to contain bundles of clothes for us all.

'From Jalalabad!' Lady Sale announced. 'From the garrison there!' From my husband's brigade!'

161

We plunged in among the cloaks and shawls with as much excitement as if we had been wafted to Paris.

'Look!' I said and held out to Charlotte a magnificent huge deep blue shawl, the colour of summer night sky. 'This would suit you wonderfully, and your grey dress is in rags. Let me put it round you – like this – over your head—'

Uncharacteristically, she pushed me away.

'No, don't Emily. I don't want it. Give it to Mrs Mainwaring, it would become her just as well.'

'Then this cream one, look, you always look lovely in cream. It isn't so big but it's very fine and soft—'

'No,' she said and her voice was harsh. 'I don't want it. I don't want anything. I – I don't *care* for anything.'

I dropped the shawls and came towards her. A little awkward pool of silence had fallen round us, created by the unfamiliar sound of Charlotte's irritability, so I said in a low voice that only she could hear, 'What is it, Charlotte, what is the matter? Dearest Charlotte, tell me, do.'

She stared at me for a moment and I saw how thin her face was now, making her eyes as huge as lamps, blazing lamps against her white skin between her braids of dark red hair. She stared without speaking, her eyes as hostile as if I were some stranger, and then she turned and fled away, out of the room, along the passage, her footsteps ringing on the stones.

'Let her go, Emily.'

'No!' I said and tried to wrench my arm free. 'Something is the matter! I *must*—'

'You must consider her dignity,' Lady Sale said firmly.

She would not let me go. She turned and commanded the other ladies to return to the bundle of clothes, then she led me out of the room and along the corridor to the staircase which led tortuously down to the courtyard where we were allowed to exercise and where I had left Richard contemplating his prospective melon bed. He was still there, pacing thoughtfully up and down the south facing wall while an Afghan warder watched him benignly. Lady Sale marched me over to him almost as if I were a child being brought for punishment.

'There is no time to be lost, Captain Talbot!' she announced. 'Something must be done for Mrs Connell.'

Richard looked at me inquiringly. I explained as well as I could, daunted by Lady Sale's presence, that I thought Charlotte had now been too unhappy for too long, that she might break under the strain of it—

'We must obtain news, Captain Talbot,' Lady Sale said. 'We all need news, heaven knows, of what is going on, what will become of us all, but I do believe Charlotte needs news of a most particular kind.'

'We are not permitted letters,' Richard said. 'And this morning's bundle is our first real communication from the outside world—'

'But not the last.'

'No, ma'am,' said Richard and kicked at a clod of earth with his boot. 'The first of many I trust. What do you think, Emily?'

I couldn't think anything. I stood stupidly between them, looking from one to the other and despairing of myself for being so useless, so helpless, so idiotically female, and then I heard my voice say quite calmly, as if my brain had instructed it, 'It's perfectly simple, Lady Sale. The newspapers. We must use the newspapers.'

The strip of red cloth went back to Jalalabad neatly folded and tied with a length of cord to make it a manageable parcel. With it, visibly, went a written request for some smaller clothes and with it, invisibly, folded into the fabric, went several sheets of newspaper with letters of the alphabet carefully marked to form a message. Richard and Lady Sale had devised the message and Captain Eyre had been used as a guinea pig in deciphering it. It had taken him five minutes.

'Not a method likely to be detected by an Asiatic,' he had said and I had felt absurdly pleased.

If it was a system that might be too much for an Afghan, it certainly wasn't for an Englishman. The next bundle of newspapers were rich with information, transmitted in the same manner. The outrage of Akbar's behaviour and the news of the massacre of our army had at least reached India, and when spring melted the snows in the Khyber Pass, Major General George Pollock was going to lead an Army of Retribution to Kabul.

We were wild with excitement. Not only were we all to be avenged but we were also to be rescued it seemed. Further down the page we carefully spelt out the news, in an article on the replacement of Lord Auckland as Governor General of India by Lord Ellenborough, that Brigadier Sale intended to march upon Akbar the moment General Pollock marched upon Kabul.

'Oh, Charlotte, Charlotte, isn't it wonderful? We are going to be freed!'

'Of course,' she said and her voice was dull and mechanical.

'The next messages,' Lady Sale said later, her eyes upon Charlotte, 'will have to be a good deal more specific.'

They were. We asked for detailed news, spelling Alexander's name out twice to be certain. Had anyone heard of him since January, or of Sayid? The smallest detail was significant. We said the matter was urgent, as indeed it was, for Charlotte, though she involved herself as much as ever with all the hostages, did so now without life, without the warmth that had saved us all from despairing in the first few weeks. I suppose hope had kept her going then, an unreasonable but powerful hope that in the confusion of our retreat from Kabul, Alexander had gone astray deliberately, to hide, to defend himself against possible re-capture and that he would surely appear again, drawn to her by the same irresistible force that had drawn her out of marriage and accepted behaviour to him. And then the weeks had passed, and then the months, and he hadn't come and hope had burned down like a candle until the light had gone out altogether, drowned and dead.

The newspapers came back. There was no news of Alexander, except the crumb of information that he had been seen in an Afridi village in the Khyber Pass in the first week of February. Since then it seemed he had vanished utterly – and nearly two months had passed.

'You will say nothing to your sister, Emily,' Lady Sale said firmly.

I was about to cry indignantly that I of all people should not dream of inflicting any further hurt upon her, but I saw that Lady Sale's own eyes were misted and that we, in this respect at least, were one in our feelings. So I simply said, 'Of course not,' and went down to the courtyard to help Richard find stones to edge his melon bed.

Thanks to the newspapers we knew when our rescue was likely to be. Brigadier Sale sent word that he was barely thirty miles off, perhaps two marches, and that his brigade, which had been decimated by wounds and disease, was now up to strength and straining to retaliate against the Afghans after a winter of disaster and humiliation. We were all elated, we could not hide it.

'I only hope our guards put it down to spring fever,' Richard said.

His shoulder was quite healed now, though he would always have a jagged scar as we had not been able to stitch the wound. As for Charlotte's wounds, it was impossible to know how to heal them.

'It will be better out of here,' I said. 'Much better. Everything is out of proportion here, it must be, we are so isolated. You will be comforted by things being normal again, being ordinary—'

'You forget,' said Charlotte, smiling faintly at me, 'that that is precisely what I am unfit for. Normal things—'

We could pack up nothing, prepare ourselves in no way for fear of arousing suspicion among our warders. We had to eat and sleep and do the laundry and play cards and loll around just as we had done since the middle of January. Richard even continued to dig his garden and the other officers to tease him about it, and all the time our ears and eyes were straining to catch some sound, some sight that would tell us that Brigadier Sale had come.

It happened in the dawn. We knew, from our information in the newspapers, that it would be in early April, but the days had ticked on, days filled now with thin spring sunlight, and we had woken morning after morning to find ourselves just as before. And then one night I dreamed that I was standing on the roof of our house in Kabul and I had heard a most extraordinary noise above me, and I had looked up and seen hordes of people streaming out of the village in the mountain, among them the Rector's lady from Richmond and the Misses Adams all wearing purple stoles around their necks, and Mamma and Cousin George and Hugh in his uniform, and I began waving at them madly, and then Jane came up and took my arm and said, 'Come on, come *on*', and I thought she meant me to come and greet them so I turned saying. 'Oh, I'm coming! I'm coming!' and found myself being shaken awake by Charlotte and all our room in uproar.

'Emily, it's happening! Brigadier Sale has come! Oh you must wake at once, you must!'

The air was full of explosions and shouts. People were running everywhere, I could hear the clump of boots on stones, and some of the babies and children were crying.

'Quick Emily, just put your clothes on anyhow, it doesn't matter. We must be ready to go at once. Put your gown over your night things, *hurry*!'

I was dazed with sleep still. I could feel my slumbering fingers limp and hopeless on my buttons, my arms crumpling feebly as they sought my sleeves. Charlotte began to dress me swiftly and competently as if I had been a doll.

'Emily, we must help the others. We must help the children first.'

Outside our one small window the sky was silvery, shot across with flashes of rose and apricot from sunrise and gunfire. I crawled from our mattress and set about the first child I came to, a little thing of two or three still bundled in its night clothes and composedly sucking its thumb. Beside me Charlotte was bundling up baby clothes and when I raised my head to look at her, I saw that her eyes were alive for the first time in weeks. Nothing normal, she had said, that's what she couldn't manage. She could deal, without thinking, with Pathans and prisons and gunfire and dawn raids, but she couldn't manage domesticity, monotony, predictability. I sat back on my heels, one little boot dangling by its laces from my hand, and gazed at her in awe.

At that moment, the uproar outside became quite drowned by the confusion within. There had been no sign of our gaolers during those minutes while I had fought my way to consciousness but now they materialized in our corridor, screaming at us as they had done when we were first in their charge. Ours, whom we had become quite used to, if not exactly fond of, came into the room and began to herd us out into the corridor using his rifle butt as a kind of flail and howling at us as he did so. The children burst out crying and two of the mothers, so stoical and brave for so long, broke down entirely and clung weeping to the young men who had slept inches from them all these weeks.

Charlotte swung round to me.

'He says Akbar is taking us away!' she said. 'He

wants to get us out of here before the British storm the fort.'

The weeping round us broke into hysterical screams. There was a scuffle in the doorway and Richard broke through the Afghans gathered there.

'At all events, Lady Sale and Akbar notwithstanding, I shall stick close to you this time.'

Charlotte smiled at him and said something in the din. We leaned closer to hear her.

'I'm not going! I'm staying here—'

Someone shouted something imperious out in the corridor, a clearly heard voice above the clamour. The rifle butt that had been jabbing my shoulder blades fell away and in seconds the room had cleared and we could hear the sobbing protests being driven on down the corridor.

We looked around us in amazement. There were just the three of us, standing in a litter of mattresses and abandoned clothing, quite untouched and quite alone. I looked questioningly at Richard. He jerked his head towards the doorway. Two Afghans stood across it, their backs to us, their shoulders almost touching so that I could not see beyond them into the corridor.

'We are not going free, I fear. Perhaps they are taking the mothers and children first, the swine – forgive me, Emily—'

Charlotte called out something sharply to the two guards. The shoulders of the taller one moved slightly but neither of them replied.

'What did you say, Charlotte? What did you ask?'

'It's perhaps unwise to anger them at this moment', Richard said, 'although I entirely sympathize with your feelings—'

'*Oh!*' Charlotte said impatiently and then she called again, louder this time. Still they took no notice and then a faint scream came down the passage and I heard my own gasp after it.

Charlotte left and went firmly across the room.

'Charlotte—' Richard said in warning, but it was too

168

late. She was speaking again, imperiously this time, inches from those implacable backs, and then she put her hand out and took hold of the sleeve of the taller guard and pulled it, hard.

We waited in horror. The Afghan swung round slowly, very slowly and as he turned he said. 'Why am I keeping you? So that no-one else shall have you, my darling, that is why.' And then Richard's voice beside me, stunned and far away, said 'Bewick—' and the tall Afghan took Charlotte in his arms.

I burst into tears of joy. Nothing seemed to matter for that brief and marvellous moment, not our predicament, not Charlotte's past grief, nothing, because they were together again, she was in his arms, he was holding her. When I could speak I said, 'But where have you *been*? Where did you go? You nearly broke her heart—'

He looked at me across the room and if I had not known that men like Alexander Bewick don't know how to weep, I should have said that his eyes were full of tears.

'I was here, hard by, all the time,' he said, and then his eyes dropped to Charlotte and he gathered her so closely to him that she seemed almost swallowed up. 'But even I couldn't storm a fort single-handed. I had to wait for Bob Sale and his merry men. I was with Sayid's people in the Pass above Landi Kotal at first and then we went down to Jalalabad to push Bob Sale into coming to rescue you. I've been urging him for months—'

'You haven't!' I shouted, beside myself. 'You weren't in Jalalabad! We know you weren't. No-one had heard of you! We asked them there, in the newspapers—!'

Alexander released Charlotte and swung round on me. His eyes were cold and furious.

'What newspapers? What do you mean? Of course I was in Jalalabad, I've been there since February. If it wasn't for me, Bob Sale wouldn't be here today!'

I began to scream at him. Richard put an arm around me from behind and closed his large firm hand across my mouth.

'We have been in communication with Jalalabad for some time, Bewick, a sort of code devised out of old newspapers. Emily invented it. We asked them for news of you, specifically, and they said there was none, you had vanished—'

Alexander swore. Behind him, Charlotte said, 'I thought you had gone.'

He seemed to make a visible effort to control himself then he turned and drew Charlotte to him and said in a voice rigid with effort, 'I know nothing about the newspapers. I did not know the garrison had any communication with you. All I knew was that you were still here and that I should rescue you if it were the last thing I did, and that getting Bob Sale to move was like shifting a mountain. Damn his eyes!' he shouted. 'Damn him to eternity! He kept it all from me with his priggish views on marriage, his infernal sanctimoniousness! He *knew* you were safe and he—'

Smiling, Charlotte put up a hand and silenced him.

'It's over, Alexander. Over. There's no use in wasting anger on what is past.'

'But that you should think me indifferent for one moment, one second. That you should imagine I thought of anything but you—'

'I didn't,' Charlotte said. 'I never doubted you,' and then she quelled at a glance my rising objection to her lie.

'To have and to hold,' Alexander said passionately to her. 'To hold, to hold and hold—'

Richard put his arm around my shoulders and I heard his voice, comforting and full of laughter, and then something tugged at my skirts and it was Sayid. He was kneeling on the floor, grinning up at me, filthy and familiar.

'Is good?' he said.

I looked across the room at Charlotte and Alexander and then at my left hand, firmly clasped in Richard's, and then I held out my free one to Sayid.

'Oh yes,' I said. 'Oh yes, it's very good.'

Alexandra

CHAPTER ONE

'Alexandra! Alexandra!'

At the sound of her mother's voice, faint but even at this distance still accusing, away down there on the snow-covered lawn, Alexandra drew away from the window into the shadows of the room behind.

'Alexandra!'

She knew why her mother sought her outside. She had been down to the lochside in the early morning with a basket of crusts and potato peelings for the water birds and had left a row of neat black boot prints in the snow. She had then come back past the stables to pay a visit to her father's huge slobbering wolf hounds so the tidy boot prints didn't have a returning track beside them.

'Alexandra!'

The voice was fainter now. She stepped forward to the window again and looked down from her turret, whence she had the view of a seagull, on to the sweep of snow, blanketing terrace and steps and lawn, rolling on white and smooth to the ruff of black shrubs on the lochside, and then beyond that the grey water, still as glass, gleaming like steel. On the far side, the hills rose again, white fortress walls of snow, broken here and there by smudges of low trees, and at their foot the jolting road to Inverary, empty now in the grip of January.

Everything was empty, the lawn, the loch, the heavy dove-coloured sky, everything except for the break in the shrubs where the garden gave on to the water and where her mother now stood, leaning on her stick, screaming for her. Alexandra could imagine her face, white and drawn, her eyes shut against the effort of calling, the effort of standing there with almost all her weight on the one leg that was any use to her.

'No,' said Alexandra out loud.

The mice in their home-made cage on the table by the window sprang to life at the sound of her voice and began to scutter desperately around their dwelling.

'Don't worry,' Alexandra said, 'I wasn't talking to you.'

She looked down at the table. On it lay her attempt at drawing the mice. It wasn't very good, she knew that, she didn't seem able to capture the vulnerable, and at the same time intensely alert, look of their eyes and ears. It was about her twentieth attempt too. It hardly seemed fair to keep them in the cage she had made out of an old claret case she had dragged up from the cellar. She really was more than half-minded to take them downstairs again and post them through the hole in the mahogany skirting board of the dining-room where they could lie in wait for crumbs of bread and cheese and apple peels that she would be careful to drop . . .

But then, she might somehow get the drawing right, just as she had dreamed of playing the clarinet exquisitely enough for an important conductor, conveniently marooned in a snow drift, brought half-dead to Castle Bewick and hearing those magical notes drifting from her tower, to stagger from his couch and say, 'Ah what notes of fairyland do I hear?' What if, say for local example, the Principal of the Glasgow School of Art, his leg broken while foolishly roaming the hills in the amateurish manner of town dwellers, and also brought half-dead to Castle Bewick should spy, carelessly hidden beneath a sofa-cushion, a drawing of such rare and touching brilliance that he too, broken leg notwithstanding, should limp forward, eyes blazing, the paper shaking in his hand . . .

'You'd be much better off in the dining-room,' Alexandra said to the mice.

The clarinet lay dusty on a shelf beside a *Lamb's Tales from Shakespeare*, a sheep's jaw from which she had meant to begin a study of anatomy, and a rough tangle of embroidery wools with which she had resolved to emulate Penelope, stitching and stitching as if her life and virtue depended upon it. Below it stood the childhood doll's house she had intended to renovate for posterity and the guitar whose broken strings had halted her on the path to world fame as a singer of gypsy ballads, in a costume of scarlet and yellow sewn with little mirrors.

'Alexandra!'

Her mother sounded nearer now. Alexandra shut her eyes. She would be down there on the terrace, in her black flannel coat and skirt, clutching her plaid shawl round her shoulders, her skirt hem clogged with snow . . .

'Alexandra!'

She had won, as usual. She was right below her window now, gazing up those steep granite walls.

'I wish I were you,' Alexandra said, 'I wish I were a mouse,' and then, drawn inexorably, she leaned forward across the table and looked down through the closed window at her mother's upturned face below.

It was ten minutes before they met. Alexandra's reluctance to descend from her tower, Iskandara's lameness as she negotiated the stone stairs to her sitting-room, fiercely beating off all help with her stick; both these things delayed them. Alexandra, dawdling along the gallery that led to the sitting-room, could hear the drag and gasp of her mother's ascent and put her fingers in her ears.

'Why did you not answer me?'

Iskandara always chose the wing chair that had been her mother's, covered in wine-red leather and studded with brass nails as big as gull's eggs. She sat in it as if it were a throne, her back bolt upright inches away from its back, her black flannel skirts smoothed to disguise the fact that only one foot could be conventionally booted.

'I was drawing.'

'Drawing!'

Alexandra always felt that the room itself conspired against her. It wasn't simply her mother, ramrod straight in the red chair, but her grandparents too, those glorious, improbable beings whose beauty and courage and glamour were so legendary. They seemed to range themselves behind her mother somehow, their portraits, hung either side of the huge stone fireplace, seemed to glow with energy and disapproval.

'Drawing!' Iskandara said again with contempt.

Alexandra stole a look at her grandmother, beautiful celebrated Charlotte Bewick with her wine-red hair full of the diamonds her husband had given her, dressed in a flowing thing of cream silk and wrapped in furs.

'Even – even the man who – who painted Grandmamma must have had to practise, you don't simply become a genius overnight—'

'A genius!'

Alexandra could have sworn her grandfather snorted. She did not look up at him, she didn't dare. He had been painted in wonderful Afghan clothes, a tunic and turban of deep blue and red embroidered with gold, clothes he had brought back from the exploits during which he had found Charlotte, the fabulous exploits that had been Alexandra's bedtime stories every night, every single night in childhood, haunting her sleep with nightmares of cruelty and savagery in wild, barbaric places.

The Afghans had called him Iskandar. That was why her mother had this outlandish name of which she was so proud and which Alexandra had tried to keep from her few childhood friends. Indeed he accounted for Alexandra's own name but not, unfortunately, for her looks. She knew without looking at him, every line of his looks, his blazing handsomeness, his grey eyes, dark moustache. But of course, her father had confused those looks for her, given her hazel eyes and hair whose redness owed more to carrots than claret . . .

'Listen to me,' Iskandara said.

'Oh please—'

'Listen.'

Alexandra sank on to a stool and bowed her head. I know what's coming, it's always the same, please God make her stop, help me bear it, let me think of a poem to say as a distraction, make this all go away, Charlotte, Alexander, Mother, everything, only not father, not the farm—

'Listen!'

'I am, Mother.'

'You go up to that room, deliberately, because you know I cannot follow. Why your father ever sanctioned making it comfortable for you, I cannot imagine, because all you ever do in it is idle. Idle and dream. Do you realize that by your age your grandmother was a national heroine? Can you imagine yourself in her place, reckless of her own safety, involved in escapades that left the public gasping, braving death to rescue your grandfather yet always solicitous of the meanest person's welfare? And you . . . *you*. Marooned in that room or dawdling on the shore. Achieving nothing. *Nothing*. Dreaming, dreaming always, endlessly supposing some Act of God will lift you out, make you remarkable through no effort of your own. Alexandra, if I had two legs as you have, if I were whole and young and healthy, do you suppose I should be content to moon through the days, dabbling at this and that, as you do? Do you imagine I could bear to live with these glorious examples before me and not strive to emulate them, not strain every sinew to make Bewick still a name—'

'My name is Abbott,' Alexandra said.

Iskandara flung her hands across her face and began to weep. Alexandra sat and watched her. The dark hair inherited from her father was streaked with grey now, and when she wept, it would loosen itself from the neat coils in which she pinned it over pads called 'rats' every morning, as if in sympathy, and strands would creep down over her hands and cheeks.

She was much older than most mothers. Even in

Alexandra's sheltered life she knew that. In three years she would be sixty — and Alexandra would be twenty-four. The servants believed there was some blight on Iskandara and her mother — they had gossiped across Alexandra in her nursery when she was supposedly too small to understand — some blight so that only daughters were born to these remarkable women who craved sons, and lone daughters at that, born late, at a time when most women were coming to an end of their childbearing.

'Please don't cry,' Alexandra said.

Iskandara took her hands away from her face and glared at her daughter with the same light, bright aquamarine eyes that looked out from her mother's portrait.

'You make me cry!'

'No. No. I — I don't mean to. I can't be what you want, you know I can't. I haven't it in me, I'm not a Bewick by nature, I'm an Abbott. We've been through all this before, so often. You can't behave in 1905 as you could in the 1840s, I couldn't rush about India doing good and performing wondrous deeds, it's absurd—'

'Absurd!'

'Yes, absurd.'

Slowly and stiffly, Iskandara rose from her chair, found her stick and limped to stand beneath her mother's portrait.

Alexandra stayed on her stool and watched her. She had never seen her mother's withered leg; indeed, imagining it had fuelled some of the worst nightmares of her childhood, worse even than Afghanistan which was at least safely half a world anyway, not just down a corridor, released from its sheath of leather and metal, grotesque and awful.

'Look at her,' Iskandara said.

Alexandra rose obediently but she did not cross the room.

'What must she feel about you? How can you stand before her and offer her the nothing, the *nothing*, that you are? How do you suppose I feel, crippled, helpless—'

Alexandra took a step back, towards the door.

'Mother, please. Please don't—'

Iskandara raised a hand and touched the pale painted hand above her. It was so like an act of worship, so supplicating, that Alexandra could not bear it. She spun round, almost falling over the voluminous folds of her skirts, and made for the door. As she pulled it behind her, reckless of whether she slammed it or not, she could hear her mother's voice again.

'Alexandra! Alexandra!'

Her father was where he always was in the afternoons of mid-winter. The home meadows were not so much white with snow as grey with sheep, a bleating, heaving block of woolly bodies, gathered in from the hills in the autumn and brought down to the Castle for feeding and safekeeping in the snows. There were several shepherds out there carrying loads of hay on pitchforks, but her father was working with them, his wrappings of leather and tweed and sacking indistinguishable from theirs, his voice as thick and soft, his movements every bit as practised.

He paused when he saw her by the iron railings that separated mown lawn from pasture. She waved and then crossed her arms to lean on the fence and thus indicated to him that there was no hurry, there was nothing urgent. Her heart was hammering hard but she knew that if she breathed slowly and deeply and looked long and intently at the comforting ritual of man and beast before her, the thudding would subside.

Beyond the few meadows on this apron of land that girdled the house on the lochside, the hills rose again, hills as individual and familiar to her as people, whose slopes and habits she knew intimately, walking them year in, year out with her father, the gun he had taught her to use broken carefully in the crook of her arm. The snow made her a prisoner, diminished her world, took away the pleasure and the freedom—

'Well, my lass?'

James Abbott held the crook he carried every working day, the crook that had been his father's when he was shepherd here, head shepherd to Alexander Bewick.

'A bad day, father.'

James looked towards the house briefly.

'You'll get a fork, then.'

'Yes, father.'

'You'll see to the small ones at the back here. They're lucky to get so much as a mouthful. You'll have to push in, they'll not be looking your way for food.' He looked at the sky. 'More snow on the way. It's a bad winter this one and I've known them all here, man and lad.'

The hay had been brought up on a wain in front of which two of the farm horses stood, blowing plumes of steamy breath. As a precaution, Alexandra took her fork round to the far side of the wain, in case her mother should be looking from a window, and plunged and twisted it in most expertly in order to bring out a huge wedge of tawny grasses, cut last summer in these very meadows. Then she followed her father back towards the flock, where the sheep at the rear, desperate at the sight of hay ahead and too stupid to look for it from any source except the one they all sought, were scrambling on to each other's backs in panic.

When Alexandra was nine she had had her only birthday party. She knew her father had pleaded for her, had said she was too solitary and that her mother had refused to allow the shepherds' children to come, the children she liked to play with. The children who did come were not familiar. They came from the big houses down the loch or over the pass towards Loch Lomond, or the castle at Inverary, from miles and miles, little girls in furred and caped coats and dresses gathered into heavy bows behind the cascades of ringlets. Alexandra had been very shy, had wanted to run out to the stables and hide, but she had had to stay, unhappy at the head of the table while all the little girls who knew each other from Christmas parties and dancing classes, from the complicated social traffic among their parents, chattered and giggled among themselves, as if she wasn't there. Then at last, desperate, Alexandra had leaned towards her nearest neighbour, a pale aristocratic child with thin mouse-coloured hair tied up in blue ribbons and said, meaning only to establish identity, 'Who is your father?'

The child, staring, had replied coldly, 'At least he isn't a shepherd.'

There had been no birthday parties after that. The servants had taken pity on Alexandra, old Elsie especially who had nursed her as a baby and who now kept the linen cupboard, and helped in the kitchen; and she had learned that her mother had married beneath her, far beneath, but that being over thirty and a cripple, she was, in a sense, lucky even to get James Abbott, if a man was what she wanted besides all she had already, castle and land and sheep. James had been head shepherd and farm manager since her parents' death, he had guided the young Iskandara through the pitfalls of estate management, helping her to hire and fire, to plant with trees the slopes that would not take sheep, to deal with poachers on the river, maintain the roads and fences. And then, after twelve years she married him.

Once over the first fright of finding out that this was an unconventional arrangement, Alexandra found it less surprising that her mother should have married her father, than vice versa. He was indifferent to the house, indeed almost disliked the grander parts of it, preferring the fire in the hall where he could drink his dram in company with his dogs as if he were by the croft hearth of his childhood. He seemed to take no interest in his wife's wealth as such; in fact Alexandra could never remember him buying anything unless it was for the farm or some little thing for her.

It was the farm that was the key. Alexandra had come to see that, perhaps two years after the disastrous birthday party, finding her father in the midst of the

flock at lambing time, naked to the waist like the other
shepherds, his right arm streaked with the birth slime
of the lambs whose arrival had been difficult. He had
looked so utterly contented then, surveying his growing
flock, his flock, not just the flock he had care of, but his
own, Abbott's sheep driven down to market on the Isle
of Bute by his men, shepherds in his employ.

If he had married Iskandara for her sheep, he had given
good measure in return. Alexandra sometimes found his
patience with her mother hard to bear, but he would
brook no criticism even from his beloved daughter.

'We've no way of knowing what she must bear, we've
no burdens like hers.'

He had, of course, known those grandparents whose
glamour made Alexandra's existence so difficult, but he
saw them in a light so different from his wife's that they
seemed hardly the same people.

'He was no farmer,' he would say of Alexander. 'Knew
not one end of a sheep from the other. She could shoot
straight, mind, straighter than most men but she could
no more keep house than fly to the moon . . .'

He did not believe in dwelling on things. When she
asked him if they had really been as beautiful as angels,
he had told her abruptly to look at the portraits, just as
now, sensing that she had been hounded out of the house,
he had given her something to do, a task to occupy her
hands and head.

A few thin snow flakes began to fall, drifting silently
down out the leaden sky. She put her fork down and
looked up, letting the quiet wet snow alight on her face.

'You'll go in!' her father shouted.

She hesitated. She was only wearing a threadbare old
cloak she had seized from the hallway as she came out,
but she was quite warm after the exercise and she didn't
want to go in, alone, back to the remnants of her mother's
angry despair.

'I'm telling you!' he shouted again, 'I'll want to find
my tea ready!'

He had given her the excuse as usual. Pulling her cloak around her and laying her fork carefully along the wooden pegs on the side of the wain, Alexandra climbed the iron railings, already cold and slippery with new snow, and went off in the direction of the kitchen.

CHAPTER TWO

Tea was laid twice, as was customary. Her mother's was on a tray with fine china, nothing to eat, slices of lemon for the pale, scented tea she liked laid out on a glass dish like a shell. It was often her task to carry it up to the little sitting-room, followed by Mary from the village, who came in as a daily maid, bearing a silver jug of hot water and matches to light all the lamps.

Her father's tea was set at a corner of the kitchen table, a pile of oatcakes, cheese, a cold wing of game. He never ate between breakfast and sunset, but could not last without tea until the meal he clearly still found extraordinary, eaten by wax candlelight in the dining-room at an hour when all his shepherds were asleep.

'Will you be taking up your mother's?'

'Not today,' Alexandra said.

Elsie, spooning black tea into the fat pot her father preferred, said, 'She could do with company. You were up there alone in your tower all morning and you've been away out an hour or more—'

'The post's come,' Mary said.

Alexandra looked at it indifferently. It was always farming circulars for her father, copies of the newspaper to which he occasionally contributed articles on sheep, seldom anything for her mother beyond invitations the senders knew they were safe from her accepting, or appeals for money from charities, the Scottish Women's

Institute, funds to save a painting for the Glasgow Art Gallery.

'I'm having tea down here today,' she said. 'I'm cold. It's snowing again.'

A bell on the wall, one of a row on curved metal springs above black glass plates announcing, in gold letters, the rooms they belonged to, sprang jangling to life. Silently Mary put some of the letters on to the edge of the tray, wedged against the silver teapot, and carried it from the room. As the door swung back behind her, an icy draught whistled into the room from the black corridor beyond.

'It's not kind-hearted,' Elsie said reprovingly.

'I know.'

'You're a bairn no more. You must put yourself out. She's a sick woman.'

'I – I think I make her worse.'

'By hiding yourself away you do. You could be a companion to her. A young lass like you, full of life, you could amuse her.'

Alexandra sat down at the huge scrubbed table at which she had watched twenty years of bread and pastry being made.

'Could I have some tea?'

Elsie put a mug before her, not a cup and saucer. It was a rebuke in itself.

'It's time you were married, lassie.'

'Married!'

'At your age, I'd been married five years. If you'd a husband and bairns to occupy yourself with, there'd be none of this drawing and tootling on flutes. You've done nothing in five years, nothing since that Miss Gracie left.'

Miss Gracie had been the last governess, a pale sad woman who had lived for the brief holidays she could get away to spend with a beloved brother and his family in Stirling. She had taught Alexandra all the history she knew from an intensely Scottish point of view, and French with a cramped and ladylike accent. She had been no worse and no better than the three women who had preceded her in Alexandra's life, all driven away in the end by the isolation and the powerful ghosts.

Elsie dumped a pile of peeled carrots on the table and began to chop.

'Cook's sister's not well, not at all and she's gone into Inverary to look to her family, so I said I'd get dinner. No word to your mother mind, she's not to be upset by thinking things aren't as they should be.'

Alexandra picked up a disc of carrot and bit into it.

'Whom do you suggest I marry?'

'You'll not find him sitting here.'

'Where then? Glasgow?'

Elsie stopped chopping.

'You'll not use that tone with me. You're to me as my own and I'll not stand cheekiness from either. It's a pity you've money, you'd be a deal better off if you'd a living to earn, teaching or nursing.'

Alexandra put her carrot down.

'I know.'

'Well, then.'

'Elsie, I don't know how to start. I don't know how to do anything, not properly. I can't cook or clean because you all do that, I don't even sew very well because you do it better, I can't play or draw, not really—'

'You could learn.'

'Where?'

'Not here, lassie. If you'd a mind to be a true child to your mother, you could, but if you haven't, you're best out of it. And quickly.'

The outside door beyond the kitchen scraped open and was banged shut.

'Your father,' Elsie said. She jerked her head towards the range whose temperaments ruled all their lives. 'You'll fetch him his tea.'

As she set the pot on the table, her father came into the kitchen, his beard dark with melting snow.

'You down here, my lass?'

'I was talking to Elsie.'

Her father and Elsie exchanged smiles. They had been children together at the village school in the 'fifties, staying at home whenever their parents needed them, finishing with the whole business of education at twelve when a wage might be earned.

Above their heads, the same bell jangled abruptly again.

'That'll be your mother,' James Abbott said. He took off his jacket and tossed it across a wooden bench by the fire.

'Tell her I'll be up when I've eaten,' he said. 'Tell her Jamie found four more sheep in the drifts up above the pass and they're alive. That'll please her.'

'Of course,' Alexandra said in a low voice.

Her father reached for the tea pot.

'That's my lass,' he said.

In Iskandara's sitting-room, a lamp had been lit beneath the two portraits, as if they were altars, and the lamplight gave the two faces an eerie look of real life. Alexandra felt the six accusing, disappointed eyes turned upon her as she came in, three Bewicks who despised her for her inability to be one of them.

'Mary says you have been helping to feed the sheep.'

'Yes, Mother.'

'That is better. Better than mooning in your room. But not really suitable, not for you, not for my daughter.'

Iskandara had changed into an afternoon dress of soft black wool with huge puffed upper sleeves and rows of little jet buttons down the bodice.

'You are still in your coat and skirt, Alexandra.'

'I'm sorry. But – but you can't feed sheep in a gown.'

'I had rather you did not feed sheep.'

'Father says four more have been dug out of a drift and they are still alive.'

Iskandara smiled faintly. 'That will please him.'

'Did you want anything in particular, Mother?'

188

'I had hoped you would bring up my tray.'

'I – I saw the post had come,' Alexandra said desperately, 'I wondered if there was anything – interesting, anything at all—'

Iskandara picked up the few envelopes and looked at them disinterestedly.

'A request to subscribe to a building to re-house some people in the Gorbals, an invitation – which of course I shall refuse – to lunch with Lady Laughlan. And a letter from your Great Aunt Emily to say she is not well again. It is extraordinary to imagine that she and my mother could ever have been sisters, they were like beings from different species. My mother loved her dearly of course, she was so infinitely tender-hearted, but she was a frail-spirited thing by comparison, totally dependent on my mother—'

'Is she very ill?' Alexandra said. Great Aunt Emily was the only person who had remembered her childhood birthdays, sending parcels from Cornwall full of exquisite doll's clothes made with her own hands of which Iskandara had been suitably scornful.

'She always imagines herself so. She had to be carried into Afghanistan that fateful summer because she could not face the rigours of the journey and took refuge in illness. I expect she is simply disliking the winter.'

'She is quite old,' Alexandra said, 'And she lives alone—'

'Alone? My dear child, Richard Talbot would never have left his widow alone. She has more servants than she knows what to do with. My mother spoiled her, Richard spoiled her, her servants spoil her. She lives in Cornwall like a queen and complains if she has the smallest twinge. It is so like her to ask if you may go and nurse her until the spring, like her self-indulgence—'

Alexandra said, 'She asked if I might go to Cornwall? She asked for me?'

Iskandara sighed.

'She did. She used to ask my mother too, endlessly attempting to work upon her soft-heartedness, whenever

189

she so much as had a headache. She never asked me, she knew better. I have never been to Cornwall. I would not go.'

Alexandra was holding her hands so tightly, the one gripping the other, that she could feel bone grind on bone.

'Oh may I go? Just once, just to see her, just to meet her? She may not live long and I won't ever have known her. And she may be really ill and need me—'

'Need you? I need you here. There is no question of your going.'

Before dinner, Alexandra brought the claret box down into the dining-room and released the occupants. There was no-one in the room at the time for Murray had only newly lit the fire and the table was still unlaid apart from the great branching candelabra like silver trees. When the mice had scattered across the carpet and melted into the shadows by the wainscoting, Alexandra picked up their home of five days and carried it back to her tower room.

She put it down on the floor beside her guitar. It was very cold in the room, for Iskandara had given orders that a fire was not to be lit there as a matter of course and Alexandra was shy of asking Mary or little Annie to bring up a bucket of coals for her. Often she carried one up herself and sometimes her father, without comment, brought one, but tonight there was nothing, not even the glow left from the morning's fire.

She looked round the room, at the haphazard stacks of books, the half-finished drawings, the partly-made toy theatre, boxes of paints, pieces of unfinished embroidery, the dust-covered instruments. Pictures were pinned on the walls, copies of pictures she admired, notably Millais and Holman Hunt. She wondered if she really liked them any more, if they still struck her as both noble and imaginative in the highest degree.

She put her hand under John Ruskin standing by a waterfall and tore him off the wall.

'And you,' she said to the next one. 'And you, and you. All of you. I'm going to start again, everything, everything new, all different—'

She crammed the stiff, shiny paper into the fireplace.

'Now,' she said and stood looking resolutely at the rest of the room, 'I will finish the theatre. I will get my guitar mended. I will do half an hour clarinet practice each day. I will learn another language, perhaps German. I will not put up any drawing that is not my own. I will finish that chair seat. No – not German, Spanish so that I can learn flamenco songs in Spanish. I will begin tomorrow—' and then she crumpled up softly on to the cold floor and began to weep.

She did not weep silently like her mother in a web of hands and hair, but noisily, like a child, with great sobs and huge tears that splashed down on to the brown wool of her skirt to which little bits of hay still clung from the afternoon. She sat there for a long time rocking backwards and forwards and giving herself up to howling, letting her gasps for breath shake her to pieces and leave her shuddering.

Far away a clock struck seven. She wondered whether to stay where she was, cold and tear-stained, and let her father find her and pick her up to comfort her as he did when she was small. But he wouldn't do that now, he hadn't picked her up for twelve years. She would only bewilder him quite as much as she would distress him. It was sheer self-indulgence to stay.

So she got up slowly from the floor, the last few sobs still springing unbidden up her throat, and without looking round at the disordered room once more, she picked up her lamp and went down to her bedroom to change.

There was game soup for dinner, and haddock cooked in milk with a bay leaf, and blackcock with carrots and potatoes and a pudding Alexandra detested flavoured with marmalade. Iskandara had changed into black taffeta and her mother's diamonds and James wore plaid trousers and a velvet jacket and a collar he loathed almost as much as Alexandra loathed the pudding, a high stiffened wing collar around which Murray had tied a bow tie of black grosgrain. Alexandra wore green velvet and hoped her eyes were not pink.

'No, thank you,' she said to the pudding.

Murray waited beside her, his pale eyes fixed enquiringly on his mistress.

'A little,' Iskandara said.

Alexandra made no move to help herself. Murray cut a small neat slice and put it deftly on her plate. Alexandra bent her head.

'You eat that,' her father said, 'and you shall have a wee dram with me.'

'James!'

He smiled at his wife.

'Malt whisky never did anyone anything but good.'

'It isn't suitable. There's no question of it.'

'I imagine,' Alexandra said with difficulty, her swimming eyes still fixed on her plate, 'that in most households, people of twenty-one are not required to eat food they detest as if they were children.'

Her father said softly, 'That will do, my lass.'

'James, I am glad about the sheep.'

He smiled at his wife again.

'I knew it would please you. When the snow clears a little, I'll drive you up there to see for yourself. Drifts as high as a house Jamie said.'

'Eat, Alexandra,' Iskandara said.

'If she mayn't have a dram,' James said, 'What might I tempt her with? What would you fancy, my lass?'

Alexandra ate her pudding in two savage mouthfuls and gulped as if she was swallowing medicine.

'Father, I'd like to go to Cornwall. Aunt Emily has asked for me. She's over eighty and ill and she asked Mother for me. I want to go.'

'Well?' James said down the length of the table.

'Of course she can't go. Emily is practised at exploitation. She began with my mother, attempted unsuccessfully to go on to me and now feels Alexandra is old enough to be the next victim. She likes to have people at her beck and call—'

'But she's ill?' James said. He ran a finger around his neck and shook himself like a dog settling itself inside its collar.

'She's always fancying herself ill.'

Alexandra tried not to look imploringly at her father. She took a mouthful of water to drown the lingering memory of marmalade.

'Alexandra should go, Iska.'

'No!' She almost shouted in her surprise at his opposition.

'Yes, she should. It's no life for her here. It may be no better there, but it'll be different.'

'No! No! I can't spare her, I can't—'

'You've me.'

She put her hand out to him down the table, imploring him.

'Please James, don't make me, don't—'

He got up and grasped her hand.

'I don't make you do much, Iska. I've no mind to. But in this I have. You think I don't notice much out there with the sheep, you think I don't concern myself with what goes on between you and the lass, but I've noticed, I've thought about it. She's twenty-one now, she's no bairn. I could wish the first chance that came her way wasn't nursing some poor old woman with a weak chest. But it's a start. Your Aunt Emily lives more in society than we do. Cornwall's another way of life. She can come home if she wants to, as soon as she wants to, but go she will.'

'Father—!' Alexandra said.

'There'll be no gloating from you, my lass. I'll drive you to Glasgow the minute the snow lets up but I'll not hear a word about it.'

Iskandara had put her hands to her face again.

'Come now, Iska. Here's your stick. I'm coming to sit

193

with you tonight, I'll take my dram with you and those parents of yours.'

He helped her to feet, and drew her free arm through his. Since her last cry of 'Don't!' she had not uttered a word, and now she went out of the dining room on Jame's arm without once looking back at Alexandra.

CHAPTER THREE

'You look young for your age,' Aunt Emily said.

She was sitting up in bed in a profusion of little pillows. The room had a pinkish pearly glow like the inside of a shell, its pale draperies lit by the steady warmth of a coal fire.

Alexandra smiled.

'So do you,' she said.

'I'm eighty-four,' Aunt Emily said. 'I was over sixty when you were born. That's the only time I saw you, at your christening. I stood godmother to you though I don't think your mother wanted me too much. It was Charlotte's wish really and when she wished something we all fought to fulfil it for her. You hated your christening. You wept and wailed all the way through. I can see your poor little furious red face now, glaring at me and the tears kept running down your cheeks into your ears and I remember wondering if one's brain could become waterlogged. Alexandra, we must do something about your hair. And your corset.'

Alexandra's hands fluttered immediately between her head and her waist.

'I don't go in enough, I know, and my hair – well, it's not a pretty colour—'

'Oh, it's pretty enough. But you pull it back so tightly. It should be much softer. You don't really look like a Bewick at all you know. They are extremely beautiful,

Bewicks, but fierce-looking too. I'll never forget seeing your Grandfather for the first time, I couldn't believe any human being could have a face like that.'

'And Grandmamma too.'

There was a small charcoal drawing by Aunt Emily's bed, buried in a forest of medicine bottles and flasks of eau de cologne. Aunt Emily picked it up.

'And Charlotte too.'

Alexandra leaned back in her chair and looked about her. She was warm, deliciously warm, all over, for the first time since leaving Scotland, and when she had arrived, but an hour before, she had come straight up to Aunt Emily's room with no injunctions to change her boots or smooth her hair, and been given a tray of tea and toast cut into little fingers and tiny biscuits flavoured with almond. There had seemed, in the carriage ride from Bodmin, to be no snow in Cornwall, and the air when she stepped out in front of Aunt Emily's door had a faint, sharp tang of salt, a whiff of the sea.

'Did you think you should find me very ill?'

'Mother—' Alexandra began, and stopped.

'Said I should only be pretending. I do pretend a little, especially since Richard died. I suppose it amuses me and I never needed to be amused before, not when he was here to do it. Now you will amuse me and I shall be well at once. Staying in bed seems a very sensible occupation for January and February, like a tortoise. We have such an amiable tortoise here, he spends the summer under the fig tree and the winter in a box in the stable. I always look forward to his waking up, he looks so antediluvian he makes me feel only a girl again. My dear, it is a great treat for me to have a girl in the house. Did the journey alarm you?'

'Only – only before I did it. Driving to Glasgow I wondered how easy it was to get lost and end up in Wales or Norfolk or somewhere, but once it began, it was so exciting and I saw one couldn't get lost, not even if one tried. And – and I liked being alone.'

Aunt Emily eyed her.

'Some Bewick in you after all, then.'

'Oh Aunt Emily! Travelling in a first-class carriage, waited on hand and foot and endlessly interrupted by kind ticket inspectors who wanted to see if one was quite happy! It's hardly being alone in the Bewick sense!'

'It's a beginning.'

'Yes,' said Alexandra, 'It's a beginning.'

The door opened.

'Janet,' Aunt Emily said without looking round, 'I suppose you have come to take Miss Alexandra away.'

'That's right ma'am.'

Alexandra prised herself reluctantly out of the chair and stood looking down at her Great Aunt. That round, soft face with its clear blue eyes and straight nose, those small, pretty hands, the plump frame swathed in shawls, all that had actually gone to Afghanistan 60 years ago, had taken part in the adventure that had provided the myth and the burden of Alexandra's childhood.

'I can't quite believe I'm here.'

Her bedroom was as unlike her bedroom at Bewick as it could be. She was used to draughty spaces, soaring walls, a nightly ritual of wraps and hot bricks in winter. To open a white painted door, its handle and finger plate of white porcelain rimmed in gold and painted with fat roses, and find herself in a low warm room where every surface was cushioned and padded, designed for comfort, was a revelation indeed.

Her trunk had been placed at the foot of her bed, whose curtains, in harmony with those at the window, were of heavy glazed chintz patterned with flowers. There was a chaise longue upholstered in velvet, a plump dressing-table stool to match it, a bureau with a padded chair. Rows of silver and china objects filled the mantlepiece and the top of the dressing-table; there were looking-glasses there and two, framed in mahogany, fixed to the wall, either side of a great gleaming wardrobe so that everything was magnified by reflection, the cushions, the lamps, the fire, the flowered fabrics, the rugs laid on the carpet. It was wonderfully luxurious – and slightly stifling.

She had only been there a few minutes, revelling in the multiplicity of objects and fabrics, when a little maid crept in and indicated shyly that she would unpack. Alexandra had packed her own trunk – Iskandara had required it – and she wondered now if her methods were fit for public scrutiny.

'I'm to wait on you, Miss. If that's all right, Miss. Seeing as you've no maid of your own, Miss.'

She was perhaps fifteen, small and sturdy with a bright complexion and crooked teeth.

'What is your name?'

'Lyddy, Miss.'

'Lyddy.'

'Yes, Miss. D'you have your keys, Miss?'

Father had said Cornwall might be different and in little more than an hour, how different it was. At Bewick she would not have dreamed of sitting by a fire in idleness while her clothes were sorted and shaken and put away in drawers and cupboards, which, when opened, gave out breaths of lavender. She closed her eyes and tried to picture herself, but three days ago, in her mother's sitting-room, making up the fire, carrying trays, standing apprehensive in the doorway dreading a fresh outburst against her selfishness in going away. But the image wouldn't come, it was softly blotted out in this warm, rosy room with drawers and cupboards being gently closed upon the last of her possessions and Lyddy asking her which dress she wanted laid out for dinner.

She ate dinner alone before a fire made of driftwood that sent salty blue flames leaping up the chimney. The windows were barred with white painted shutters covered with curtains of crimson velvet, her feet rested on a Turkey carpet and the walls were as thickly covered with pictures as if they had been pages in a stamp collection. Two dogs came in to share her solitude, absurd, dignified little Pekinese who regarded her gravely with their blue-brown eyes like marbles and then lay before the fire and ignored her.

She was waited on by Penman. Aunt Emily had said he was Janet's husband. He did not speak much but smiled broadly when she thanked him. He brought her soup in a paper-thin china cup, a morsel of fish in a flotilla of pink shrimps, chicken creamed in a silver dish, peaches and grapes on a glass plate.

'I do hope you weren't lonely,' Aunt Emily said later, 'I do hope you had enough to eat.'

'It was wonderful,' Alexandra said solemnly. 'Wonderful, and so pretty. Everything is so pretty.'

She stooped to kiss the soft crumpled cheek.

'Alexandra, I have something for you.'

Aunt Emily fumbled beneath her pillows and pulled out a small fat volume bound in red morocco.

'I'm sure you know that all good little girls should keep a diary. I used to keep one. Charlotte never bothered. She would always rather live life than write about it. But I kept one when we went to India, I kept one about Charlotte. You should read it. Not tonight, because travelling always distorts one's feelings for a time, but at your leisure, when you feel settled. You should know about her, the real her. Because you are her granddaughter, there is something of her in you.'

'I don't think so,' Alexandra said. 'That is what makes mother so miserable, that I don't resemble her in any way.'

'You wait,' Aunt Emily said. 'You wait and see.'

When Lyddy folded back the shutters in the morning, bright cold winter sunlight bounced into the room like an explosion.

'There's a few snowdrops out, Miss,' Lyddy said. 'To welcome you, Miss, to Bishopstow.'

'Snowdrops? In January?'

'Oh yes, Miss. Always in Cornwall.'

She sat up in bed. On the chaise longue lay her brown wool skirt, neatly brushed, and beside it her pink striped blouse with a white collar that needed to be fastened on with studs. Next, in the order in which she would need them, were her flannel petticoats, her cotton bodice and frilled drawers, her black woollen stockings, her long boned stays and the combinations that had so irritated her skin when she was small. They had been covered with a square of spotted muslin, for decency she supposed. The muslin square was not her own.

'I've polished your boots, Miss,' Lyddy said.

'I – I usually dress myself.'

'No, Miss,' Lyddy said firmly.

It was strange and awkward, being dressed by someone else, seeing Lyddy kneel to put on her stockings, lace up her boots, feeling the steady foreign strokes on her head of a hairbrush wielded by another hand.

'You've lovely hair, Miss.'

'No,' Alexandra said. 'It's red.'

They surveyed it together in the dressing-table glass, heavy, thick stuff falling to her elbows, the colour of barley sugar.

'Not my notion of red, Miss,' Lyddy said.

She buckled a stiff hard belt around Alexandra's waist and stood back to admire the effect. Alexandra felt smooth and neat and tight and regretful that, with Lyddy to keep a stern eye on standards, she could not secretly leave off her stays when the weather got warmer as she did occasionally at Bewick.

Breakfast and the Pekinese awaited her in the dining-room. It too was full of sharp yellow sunlight, and the sideboard was laden with food, a ham on a china column, fish and eggs under silver domes, muffins, coffee, sweet pale butter, a honeycomb running syrup on a green plate like a leaf.

Beyond the window the garden sloped in terraces,

intricately cultivated, and beyond that green fields rose to a gentle hill, each one outlined with a grey stone wall.

'The sea?' Alexandra said to Penman. 'Is the sea over there?'

'A mile or so, Miss Alexandra. You can see it from the fields up there. It's the mouth of the estuary.'

'The estuary?'

'The river Camel, Miss Alexandra. Down that way. Running to the sea.'

It suddenly seemed a waste to be sitting over muffins and honey.

'Can I get to the river?' Do I go down through the garden? Is it far?'

Penman refilled her coffee cup.

'Mrs Talbot asked for you, Miss Alexandra. You're to go up when you've done breakfast.'

'Of course,' Alexander said and cast a regretful glance out of the window. 'Of course I will. I intended to anyway.'

Aunt Emily said, 'And did you sleep well?'

She was wearing a different lace cap, another fine soft shawl.

'Oh yes,' Alexandra said, 'So well. But I dreamed a good deal.'

'That's travelling, my dear. It shakes up one so.'

'Penman said just now that there was a river down there, beyond the garden, and that if one climbed the hill one could see the sea. Our loch is a sea loch, but that isn't the same as the sea, it's much tamer—'

'The sea is why you slept so well.'

Alexandra said, 'I'd love to see it.'

Aunt Emily patted her head.

'All in good time. We have so much to do. You must have a good corset first, it's of the greatest importance. I shall ask my dressmaker from Bodmin to come out and we will see about some new clothes for you. Lyddy has done splendidly with your hair. And then of course there are all the people round who will want to meet you. I'm a very poor caller in winter, but you shall do it for me, everyone will be so pleased to see you.' She paused and then said, 'Don't pull a face, my dear.'

'Aunt Emily, it isn't any good. It would be a waste of time. I don't know any people, we don't at Bewick, we don't see anyone except the shepherds and Mother's lawyer every so often. I shouldn't know what to say.'

'And that is how you will remain, is it? Unable to speak to people, awkward in company—'

'Am I awkward?'

'Yes,' said Aunt Emily, 'very.'

Alexandra went over to the long glass on a mahogany frame that stood in the bow window and looked at herself.

'In what way am I awkward?'

'You look as if you weren't in proper charge of your arms and legs, as if your clothes were uncomfortable.'

'They are,' Alexandra said. She caught Aunt Emily's reflected eye and laughed.

Aunt Emily said, 'You are a dear child. I don't want to make you different, merely easier.'

'You mustn't feed me so well, then. It will only make my clothes much worse.'

'Where do they come from, Alexandra?'

'My clothes?' Well, Mother's from Glasgow and then mine are copied from those. By Mrs McPhee in the village. Her husband is the carpenter at Berwick.'

Aunt Emily looked intently at Alexandra's skirt.

'I can understand the connection,' she said. 'You shouldn't wear brown, it makes your eyes like boot buttons. I think you should wear peach and cream and pale green, sage green, and grey perhaps. Should you like a new dress?'

'Not particularly,' Alexandra said with truth.

'If I have to look at you,' Aunt Emily said without rancour, 'I should like to see you in a new dress. I am used to looking at pretty things, they give me pleasure.'

'I – I didn't mean to be ungrateful. Or – or rude. I just

201

find it difficult to be interested in clothes or how I look. I don't like how I look very much.'

'I do', Aunt Emily said, 'What do you like instead?'

'I should like to go and look at the sea.'

'Then I will give you two things,' Aunt Emily said. 'I will give you new frocks and some company manners, whether you like them or not. And I will also give you a good deal of freedom to look at the sea.'

CHAPTER FOUR

Imperceptibly almost, Aunt Emily began to get up. Alexandra would find her by the fire in the drawing-room in the afternoons, the Pekinese guarding her against invisible dangers, then she came down in the mornings and needed letters written, wools held. The dressmaker called, and the merciless corsetière, and two obsequious men from Bodmin with bolts of wools and flannels and silks which they laid out across the drawing-room sofa for Aunt Emily to see. She did not consult Alexandra when choosing.

'This won't give you any pleasure, Alexandra, so I shall give some to myself.'

A grey coat and skirt were made trimmed with darker grey silk braid, and a pearl grey silk blouse with a tall frilled collar. It was followed by two afternoon dresses with tiny waists and lace inserts and huge pleated upper sleeves like bellows.

'For calling in the afternoons,' Aunt Emily said. 'You will need them.'

Then came a box of hats, huge, wide, heavy affairs swathed in pleated velvet and accompanied by an army of pins to secure them. And two little silk handbags on gilt chains, and gloves and a box of spare collars with bows and rosettes to fasten them with.

'Please stop,' Alexandra said. 'It's so kind of you. But it's not what I came for.'

'It's part of the process,' Aunt Emily said.

Lyddy insisted on doing her hair over at least twice a day. She would have liked to do it a further time, after luncheon, but Alexandra was adamant.

'No, really, no. It's as smooth as anything. My head won't bear more brushing.'

Aunt Emily made her practise walking in a hat, sitting down gracefully in her sweeping skirts.

'You must glide, Alexandra, not march. Think of moving from the hips. Imagine yourself infinitely tall.'

And then there was the piano. Alexandra had confessed about the clarinet and the guitar, at her inability to persevere with either.

'I will persevere for you,' Aunt Emily said. 'We will play what is delightful, Mozart and Chopin. A little time every day.'

'Did – did Charlotte, I mean Grandmamma, play?'

'No,' Aunt Emily said. 'She drew a little, but apart from that she didn't like sedentary occupations. Have you read my journal?'

Alexandra took her hands off the keyboard.

'No,' she said. 'not yet. I'm waiting for the right moment.'

'What sort of moment?'

'When – when I feel – I feel even the smallest bit like her, when I feel in sympathy.'

'Have you felt any yet? Any at all? Does she seem any more real to you here, more real than at Berwick?'

'I don't know about real,' Alexandra said, 'but less frightening certainly. Less remote.' She paused and looked down at her lap. 'I don't think I like sedentary occupations very much either. Perhaps that is why my perseverance is so poor.'

There was a brief silence, broken only by the tumble of a coal in the fireplace.

'You may go out,' Aunt Emily said, 'When you have earned it.'

203

After three weeks, the first callers came. Alexandra, in her new afternoon dress, her hair parted in the middle and drawn up by Lyddy into a series of padded puffs and curves behind, waited in the drawing-room on the edge of the sofa. A huge fire was burning, and beside it sat Aunt Emily, dressed in heliotrope and a number of shawls. A bowl of daffodils stood at her elbow, the first bright heralds of spring, and the room smelt of their freshness, along with the beeswax of the furniture polish and the comforting smell of the coals.

Aunt Emily said, 'There is no need to be so stiff, my dear.'

'I feel stiff.'

'Is the dress too tight?'

'No. I am. Inside.'

'That will pass,' Aunt Emily said. 'All the people round here are so charming. You will forget to be shy.'

When Penman opened the door to the first knock, Aunt Emily said, 'You will see how easy it is.'

'Yes,' Alexandra said, 'yes, I expect so,' and then the door opened and Aunt Emily looked up and said, 'Mrs Burrows! How good you are to come! My first visitor of the year!'

Alexandra stood up, found she was standing on her own hem, bobbed a little to release herself and confronted a large, commanding woman pulling off brown suede gloves.

'My niece, my *great* niece, Alexandra Abbott.'

Alexandra held out her hand. Mrs Burrows took no notice.

'Daffodils already my dear! Of course, I should expect them in this house. I shouldn't be in the least surprised to see daffodils in September here. Are you a gardener Miss Abbott? Your aunt and your late uncle were famous gardeners, the best west of the Tamar. Do you garden?'

'No,' Alexandra said and blushed. 'I'm afraid not,' she corrected herself.

To Mrs Burrows, she then became perfectly invisible. Talk of the Rector and his unruly family, of her wild Harry's doings at Oxford, of the poor hunting season it had been, all flowed between her and Aunt Emily and when she rose to go, and Alexandra held out her hand in farewell, Mrs Burrows stalked past her to the door as if she had no more real existence than an armchair.

'Very modest,' Aunt Emily said when she had gone. 'Very proper. Not at all a bad beginning.'

The next visitor was made more alarming by bringing with her two daughters, perhaps a little younger than Alexandra, who both seemed to have no trouble at all in managing their skirts and hats and gloves.

'My daughters, Miss Abbott,' Mrs Langley said, 'Rose and Grace.'

Rose said, 'We go to Scotland every autumn, don't we Grace? You know, to fish and Papa to shoot. Don't we Grace? But what do you do all year, if you live there? What is there to amuse yourself with?'

'I shoot too,' Alexandra said.

Rose and Grace Langley exchanged glances.

'I mean, I shoot in season. Of course. Father taught me.'

'We like archery,' Grace said, 'Rose is rather good. But guns—'

'I've never used a bow and arrow—' Alexandra said.

Rose interrupted, 'That's what I mean. Even if you knew how, I don't suppose there is anyone up there most of the year to shoot against. We saw not a single sign of any fun last year. Did we, Grace? No archery, no parties, no hunting, no nothing, just mountains and rivers and rain and those awful midges. Do you remember the midges, Grace? When we were on Skye I thought I should have died of the irritation of them.'

'What do you do in Scotland all year?'

Alexandra spread her hands.

'I – I don't know really. The time passes—'

'Did your gown come from Scotland?'

'No. It's a present from Aunt Emily.'

'We have to wear such awful clothes in Scotland. Don't we, Grace? We hate them, all tweeds and so heavy. We usually go to London in the winter but the house is having alterations done to it so we can't. Do you hunt?'

'I – I ride,' Alexandra said.

'Don't you hunt?'

'I haven't ever—'

'Have you met Harry Burrows?'

'No, no I haven't met anyone. I've only been here a little while, looking after Aunt—'

'Oh, he's the best fun in the world. We had the most wonderful Christmas party, didn't we Grace? Harry and our Langley cousins and both the Trethowans and all the houseparties they had staying. It was glorious. We even sent an invitation to Michael Swinton as a joke just to see what he'd do, but it was hopelessly disappointing, he simply pretended he hadn't had it—'

'Have you seen him?' Grace demanded.

'Who?' Alexandra asked, bewildered.

'Michael Swinton.'

'No, no I haven't—'

'Well, of course, you wouldn't have, he's a recluse, a hermit practically, on account of being so peculiar and gloomy. The villagers won't go near him, except for mad old Meg, but then she's almost a witch herself. Harry Burrows rode round his house on Midsummer Eve in a white sheet pretending to be a ghost, we nearly died laughing when he told us—'

'So we won't see you at the meet on Tuesday?' Rose said.

Alexandra shook her head.

'Our cousins are coming. Our Langley cousins. At least some of them, George I think and perhaps Piers. Why don't you come?'

206

Alexandra said almost in a whisper, 'I haven't ever hunted. I haven't a horse—'

'I can't understand it. That huge estate in Scotland – I've been listening to Mamma and Mrs Talbot with half an ear, you never know what you might miss – and you don't hunt.'

'No, I don't.'

'Who do you live near in Scotland? The Campbells? The MacPhersons? Do you know Reggie MacPherson? He proposed to Grace last season in London. We nearly died laughing, didn't we Grace?'

'No,' said Alexandra, 'I don't know him.'

'Oh,' said Rose, 'Don't you?' and then she looked at her sister and they both looked at their laps and a heavy silence fell.

'Who – who is the man you tease?' Alexandra said with some desperation. She felt she was honour bound, as hostess, to keep the conversation going, and the mention of the poor man who had had to endure Harry Burrows moaning in a sheet beneath his windows had been the only topic to cling to her memory.

Grace said, 'Michael Swinton? Oh, don't worry about him. He doesn't count.'

'Nobody ever asks him to anything, that's why we did, for a joke. Papa says he's a gentleman but we know he paints, pictures you know, so Mamma says he can't be.'

'What sort of pictures?' Alexandra said.

Rose stared at her.

'Heavens, I don't know. Does it matter? He's extremely odd. I've never seen him but Grace has, haven't you Grace—'

'About a year ago. We trespassed on his land. Piers said it was by mistake but I know it wasn't and he came wandering out of the wood, all black and shaggy like the Beast in the fairy tale in the most peculiar clothes, very ancient, and dreadful wild hair like pictures of the Prophets.'

'Was he angry?' Alexandra asked. 'Did he shout at you because you were on his land?'

'Shout?' Grace said and looked in amazement at her sister. 'At us? Of course not. He simply said something about it's being his land and Piers told him we had made a mistake and we all rode off as hard as we could because we were bursting with laughter—'

Alexandra said quietly, 'Poor man.'

'Poor?' They chorused.

'To be teased.'

Rose giggled.

'Don't you like fun?'

'I don't know,' Alexandra said, 'I didn't know that's what fun was.'

Mrs Langley called across the room to her daughters. They rose at once, extremely eagerly, shaking out their skirts and smoothing their waists with graceful gestures.

'We shall look forward to seeing you soon, Miss Abbott,' Mrs Langley said.

Alexandra blushed. 'Thank you,' she whispered.

'So fortunate that you are so close in age to Rose and Grace. The young people in these parts have the best times in the world. Shall you be hunting on Tuesday?'

'She doesn't hunt, Mamma,' Rose said clearly.

'No,' Grace added, 'She hasn't a horse.'

'May we not lend you a mount, Miss Abbott?'

'Thank you,' Alexandra said, crimson with mortification, 'I do ride, I mean, I can ride, but I haven't ever hunted. I – I shouldn't know what to do—'

Mrs Langley eyed her in silence for a while.

'I see,' she said and then she bowed, very slightly, and Rose and Grace did the same and then all three moved out of the drawing-room, upright and daunting.

Aunt Emily had her eyes shut.

'I'm tired now, child. Tell Penman will you, that you will see any further callers. I'm going to my room.'

'Not on my own,' Alexandra said. 'Not without you!'

Janet had come in and was assisting Aunt Emily to her feet.

'You can manage quite well, quite well. Come and see me after tea, when I have rested.'

Alexandra did not move from the sofa but sat on it quite rigid, her ears straining for the dreaded sound of wheels on the gravel of the drive. Her new corset dug savagely into the soft parts at the sides of her waist and seemed to crush her ribcage in an inexorable grip. She seemed pulled out, elongated by it, so that her shoes, her new bronze slippers with rosettes on the toes that Aunt Emily had said she must keep hidden at all times if possible since legs and feet were highly indecent, seemed far further away than the five and a half feet she knew separated them from the crown of her head.

The door knocker sounded like a knell. Alexandra heard herself gasp. Her eyes fixed themselves in terror on the door. It opened, and Penman said.

'Mrs Chamberlin, Miss Abbott.'

'My dear, don't get up. Please don't. I'm the Rector's wife, I should have come weeks ago, I knew perfectly well you were here, I know everything in this village. All the children have had measles, all five, you cannot imagine what hard work it is, day and night and their poor eyes so sore as well as the rash and the fever. I do hope your aunt isn't ill again, I quite expected to find her up, her card, you know, her card indicated she was ready for callers again.'

Mrs Chamberlin was most consoling in appearance. She wore an oatmeal flannel coat and skirt which even Alexandra could see was badly cut, and a heavily pleated cream blouse, the collar fastened with a huge hideous brooch made out of a green polished pebble set in silver. Her hair escaped in wayward fronds from beneath her brown velvet hat, and her eyes, of the same brown, were full of friendliness.

'She is better, thank you,' Alexandra said, 'but tired. We have had two — no four, callers already—'

'Who, my dear? Do tell me who came. I'm going to sit right on this glorious fire and get warm all through to my bones. I suppose it would bore you to come and see my poor children, but they do need amusing, they are at that stage of convalescing when nothing is entertaining for very long and Mamma is certainly not entertaining at all, so a pretty thing like you would be a breath of fresh air. Now, tell me who came. I've no business to ask, but I do like to know everything that's going on here, and what with the measles, I've been so dreadfully out of touch.'

Alexandra told her and then added with enthusiasm, 'I should *love* to come and see your children. I really should.'

'The Misses Langley, eh? And how did you find them, I wonder. In my view they need good steady husbands as soon as they can be found, and Harry Burrows needs a commission in the army and to be sent somewhere really uncomfortable. Should you really, my dear? It would be kinder than you know. There are so many sick in the village, February is a wicked month, and it seems to take me all my time to get round the cottages and then when I am back, I am extremely tired and I fear I'm not as patient as I should be, poor little creatures and the baby still in his petticoats. Tomorrow? Would you come tomorrow?'

Alexandra thought of tomorrow afternoon, presumably in her other new dress, waiting in the drawing-room for the thud of the knocker.

'Yes,' she said firmly, 'I should be happy to.'

'Shall you mind a walk? It's not far, under a mile, the grey house beside the churchyard, the one with those disagreeable laurels I long to have cut down but the Rector says no, they give us some privacy and I suppose, as usual, he is right. I imagine you are used to walking, coming from Scotland. We went to Edinburgh on our wedding tour and I thought it beautiful but I think that my state of mind at the time was such that I should have thought anywhere beautiful. Shall I expect you at three?

Don't wear that pretty dress because the children do romp so, it's only affection but it's detrimental to one's clothes all the same. No don't get up, my dear, I'm thoroughly toasted now, warm as a new loaf—'

'Thank you for calling,' Alexandra said, and smiled.

'I shall look forward to tomorrow,' Mrs Chamberlin said, 'I shan't tell the children until luncheon otherwise they will plague the life out of me. Did I leave my umbrella in the hall? I expect I did, but I never know, I'm so afraid of losing things that sometimes I take them into the most unsuitable places. I took a basket of eggs into church last Sunday because I was so afraid I should forget to give them to old Mrs Baldwin on my way home. You must see my hens, I'm most proud of them, your aunt doesn't keep hens, I can't think why. It would be so easy to have hens here, and a cow and a goat and even a pig or two. Give your aunt my love and tell her I shall see her soon, very soon.'

When Mrs Chamberlin had gone, hurrying into the gloomy February afternoon, her oatmeal figure bent resolutely against the wind, Alexandra looked round the drawing-room and saw it had an animated, unsettled look, as if the last caller had stirred everything to action, all the silver photograph frames, the vases and pin-cushions, the rugs and cushions and shaded lamps. Smiling to herself at the thought, and confident that it was now too late to be interrupted further, Alexandra went upstairs.

'I don't think you will care for it at the Rectory,' Aunt Emily said. 'There are five children and all woefully undisciplined. They will tear you to pieces. I wish you wouldn't go, it will quite ruin your new clothes—'

'I shan't wear them,' Alexandra said. 'I shall wear my Mrs McPhee coat and skirt. That was built to last if anything ever was. And I shall like the walk—' she stopped abruptly. After all Aunt Emily's generosity, it seemed churlish to point out how stifled she was, cooped up in the warm, soft, comfortable house, fed like a lapdog and learning to be a lady. To cover up her ingratitude, she held out her gros point.

'Aunt Emily, do you think that is better? Is it more even?'

Aunt Emily leaned sideways from her pillows. 'Better, but not perfect. And it has to be perfect before I shall allow you to go on to petit point.'

Alexandra's heart sank. Petit point was clearly seen as a reward, not a threat.

'I wish you would not walk, my dear. Murphy will take you. The horses have done nothing all winter and it would do them so much good. I do rather crave a motor car. Mrs Burrows has one and Mrs Langley says she will give Mr Langley one as a birthday present. I always did like anything new, as long as it was comfortable.'

'But I should like to walk. I should like the exercise.'

'Exercise!' Aunt Emily said in horror, and fell back among her pillows.

As she stepped out of the front door, Alexandra felt like a bird finding its cage door opportunely left open. For almost a month she had remained in the house, eating and sleeping and sitting, submitting to Lyddy's hairbrush, practising her daily ration at the piano, performing her daily ration upon tapestry canvas, running endless little errands for Aunt Emily, trying to make her handwriting more ladylike, her movements more graceful.

The sky above her was weak pale blue, misted with clouds through which a dim sun struggled to shine, but the air was soft and fresh and the damp black earth along the edges of the drive was pierced with the sharp green points of spring bulbs. The lane from Bishopstow village came right up to the drive gates and ended there between stone gateposts crowned with lichened pineapples. Alexandra stood between them and looked down the lane, sunk between high fields, and saw the church tower rising among leafless trees and the blue slate roofs that clustered round it. It was a pity her way lay away from the sea, not towards it. She imagined she could hear it at her back, behind the house and the soft green swell of land that shielded it, could hear the breaking thud of the winter waves on the shore she had not yet seen.

By the time she reached the village her face was pink with air and exercise and she felt that her nose was too. She had walked fast, comfortable in the old corset she had firmly told Lyddy was quite sufficient for visiting the Rectory children, and as she passed the church, the clock struck three sonorously into the still afternoon air. The village street was empty, the pump deserted, for all the domestic chores were done by midday and the women were indoors now, assembling greens and bacon for tea or hooking rugs out of old rags.

The Rectory drive was dank and dripping between its lugubrious laurels. The gravel was carpeted in bright green moss and leaves lay sodden and dark under the shrubs. Alexandra saw a wooden hobby horse abandoned in the gloom, one wheel missing. She went boldly up to the door and let the huge brass knocker fall with a thud. There was an immediate squealing from inside, like a horde of piglets seeing a trough of scraps, and the door was pulled open, revealing a little red-nosed maid and a tumble of children.

She was towed in like a liner by tugs, her hands and skirts clutched and pulled. Mrs Chamberlin fussed round them.

'Oh, Miss Abbott, how good you are, don't pull so, Robert, how can poor Miss Abbott possibly come as fast as you? Helen, you mustn't tug her skirt so, you will quite part it from the waistband. Do mind the baby, children, oh dear, he always wants to join in and he invariably gets trodden underfoot—'

The children pulled her irresistibly into a large square room at the back of the house whose floor was covered

213

with a threadbare brown carpet. There was a huge brass fireguard before the fire, hung with innumerable little garments, and a table in the centre draped in a green chenille cloth down to the floor. The floor itself was littered with wooden bricks and fragments of doll and lead soldiers.

'Can we play mothers and fathers?'

'Can we play camping in the Canadian backwoods?'

'Will you read to us? Will you, will you, will you—'

'I want to play lions and tigers, can we play lions and tigers, I want to be a lion, I want to be a lion—'

The baby stumbled on a brick and fell heavily into the folds of the table cloth.

'Ah, poor Jack! Poor little Jack! Did it tumble then, did it hurt its little self?'

The baby struggled purposefully out of its mother's arms and made for Alexandra.

'You go,' she said to Mrs Chamberlin, 'You go and do all the things you have to do. I'll amuse the children, I shall be perfectly happy.'

'Shall you, my dear, I'm sure I don't like to leave you all on your own, not at first—'

'Lions and tigers! Lions and tigers! Lions and tigers!'

'Please go,' Alexandra said, fielding the lion as he plunged at her, 'I'll call for help if I need it. Really I will.'

The door closed behind Mrs Chamberlin and silence fell at once.

'Now,' said Alexandra.

They gazed up at her, all five of them, pale with illness still, their confidence vanished with their mother's going.

'Listen,' said Alexandra.

They were listening already. Helen, never taking her eyes off Alexandra, craned sideways so that she could wind a finger round and round in a hole in her black stocking.

'This table,' said Alexandra, 'Is a log cabin. Those

214

chairs are a forest nearby where a lion lives. A *terrible* lion. The fireplace is a volcano. Robert is a trapper and Helen is his wife and they live in the log cabin. They have a child – yes, Jack, you will be the child, a very brave remarkable child who gets ravished away by the lion. Richard you are the lion and you, Arthur, you are a Canadian Mounted Policeman and when the lion threatens to throw the baby into the volcano, you will come galloping up on that hobby horse – that one there, the one with bells – and rescue him.'

Arthur took his thumb out of his mouth.

'What will you be?'

'Who will be the winner?' Robert demanded. 'I want to be the winner?'

'It is not a winning game,' Alexandra said. 'It is an acting game and I shall invent the story. Now I want you to find something that will do for guns and fur caps and a saucepan for Emily to cook wolf stew in—'

'Tiger stew! Tiger stew!'

'Very well. Tiger stew. Go on. And then we will draw the curtains and pretend it is arctic night and we will all be the wind and howl and moan.'

Arthur plugged his thumb in again. He now removed it briefly to say, 'You are a nice lady,' and then went off in search of a gun.

More than an hour later, Mrs Chamberlin opened the door to find all her children under the table eating tiger stew out of an old bowler hat doing duty as a cooking pot, save one, who was crouched on top of the table growling ferociously. Alexandra was standing on a chair and most of her hair had come down on to her shoulders.

'He's a lion,' she explained, 'Richard is a lion. They don't know he's there because the wind is howling so loudly. At least it was, but I'm rather out of breath.'

'You are a miracle, my dear,' Mrs Chamberlin said.

At the sound of her voice, all the children surged

out from beneath the table and began to jump up and down and scream. The baby staggered to Alexandra's chair and hung on to her ankle with grim determination.

'How do I reward you? Dear Miss Abbott, how do I possibly reward you?'

Alexandra said shyly, 'I should like to see your hens.'

'My dear, the very thing! And just before it's too dark and they have to be shut up. Don't, Robert, you will quite pull poor mamma over. Yes, you shall take some eggs back to your aunt, my Rhode Islands lay such beautiful brown speckled ones with yolks like marigolds. Helen, don't cry my pet, Miss Abbott will come again, I am sure, and Richard, that is enough roaring now, quite enough, you will make your throat quite raw. Mind the baby, Arthur, how can Miss Abbott get down if you are to stand just there?'

The hens lived in the orchard. The light was thickening but the twisted silvery grey trunks with their crusted bark showed up clearly against the long grass where some of last autumn's apples still lay, puckered and brown. The hens moved carefully about, picking their way on their spindly yellow legs, muttering comfortably to each other and darting their heads to the ground every so often in pursuit of something delicious. They were a beautiful colour, rich, glowing, russety brown and their combs and wattles were pure clear scarlet.

'Oh!' Alexandra said in delight.

'Aren't they splendid! I'm so glad you appreciate them, so few people do, they leave them to gardeners and such like, it's such a pity, they're so characterful—'

'How many would one need,' Alexandra asked, her eyes on the hens, 'for just a small household, say eight people? How many hens?'

'Roughly two hens a person, my dear. These Rhodes lay like clockwork, though of course they all have a poor period, a sort of resting period. I give them a hot mash too, as well as letting them scratch about here, we cook up all the scraps in the kitchen. Did you not have hens in Scotland?'

'Yes, we did, but they were part of the farm, the shepherds' wives looked after them. I didn't.'

'They don't need much looking after, that's the joy of them. I do shut them up at night because of the stoats and the foxes, but they put themselves to bed, I only have to shut the door. Come out of that tree, Arthur, you make Jack want to follow you. My dear, I don't in the least want to hurry you but I think you should go. The days are lengthening a little, but with this gloomy weather you hardly seem to notice it. I can't thank you enough, really I can't, and I hope you will come whenever you feel like it.'

Alexandra stooped and kissed the children in turn.

'Yes,' she said, 'I should like to. I should like to very much.'

That night, sitting by Aunt Emily's bed before going to her room, she said.

'Would – would you let me keep hens, Aunt Emily? Just a few, six or so. They needn't be any bother or trouble and of course I should buy them myself—'

'*Hens*, my dear?'

'Yes. Yes, I should so much like to. Mrs Chamberlin has more than a dozen and she gave me such beautiful eggs to bring home. It would be such a pleasure and I would promise you that they would be no inconvenience to you. I should keep them out in the orchard. Oh, please may I? Please!'

Aunt Emily smiled at her in a puzzled manner and picked up a letter which lay on the quilt.

'I suppose you may if you want to so much. We never had hens, the local farm has always been so obliging. But certainly you may if it means so much. Now look at this, Alexandra! Now we are really making progress! Guess what this is? It's a letter from Mrs Burrows asking you to dine next week! Isn't that a stroke of luck? Murphy shall take you and you may borrow my pearls. Dear Alexandra, I think things are just beginning!'

CHAPTER FIVE

Alexandra sat in front of her mirror in her new cream silk gown while Lyddy folded her hair carefully over the pads. None of her was comfortable. There was no denying that the new corset had an impressive effect on her waist, but the dress disconcerted her – the first true evening dress she had ever had – because it left her shoulders quite bare as well as a considerable amount of – of, well, upper bosom, and all her arms. The skirt was lovely, there was no doubt of that, swishing down rustling folds to the deep ruffle at the hem, but she was doubtful about managing the small train, even after an hour of practice in front of Aunt Emily. She had cream silk stockings and cream satin slippers with waisted heels and bows of stiff cream ribbon on the toes.

Lyddy put the final touches to her hair and slipped two ropes of pearls carefully over the finished edifice.

'There, Miss,' she said, her voice rich with satisfaction.

'My dear child!' Aunt Emily said from the doorway in much the same tone, 'My dear Alexandra! What an utter transformation! What a triumph.'

'You have been so kind,' Alexandra said unsteadily. 'All these clothes, and shoes and – and lending me your pearls—'

Aunt Emily waved a shawled arm.

'It is my pleasure, dear child. Tonight it is absolutely my pleasure.'

Once in the carriage, Alexandra stopped feeling merely

apprehensive and became sick with fright. She sat with the blood thudding in her ears, just as it used to do when her mother began a tirade, and prayed for the impossible, for the carriage to be overturned, for it to be the wrong night, for her to develop a sudden and dangerous illness. It seemed only minutes, desperately short minutes at that, before she was riding smoothly up a huge curved drive towards a house whose long windows were ablaze with light. In front of the shallow steps that led to the door were parked two – no three, motor cars.

Murphy climbed down to open the door for her.

'You – you will be back at eleven?'

'Prompt, Miss,' he said and seemed gone at once, leaving her only halfway up the steps, with the great door still to negotiate, not to mention a butler and a huge hall beyond and all the alarming noise made by people who know each other very well.

'Ah, Miss Abbott!'

'Why, it's Miss Abbott. She doesn't garden you know. So unlike her aunt.'

Her new velvet cloak was whisked away, and she found herself in a large red room full of lights and people.

'I say, that's a very jolly dress, you know—'

'My son, Miss Abbott. Harry, this is Miss Abbott, Mrs Talbot's great-niece. She comes from – from Scotland,' Mrs Burrows said with emphasis.

'Do you,' Harry Burrows said, grinning. He was square and solid with curly brown hair and a neat, thick moustache. 'What a jolly life you must have. In Scotland.'

'No, I don't,' Alexandra said truthfully. 'That is why I came here.'

'Did you, by jove! I say, do you smoke?'

'No!' Alexandra said, shocked.

'I say, have I shocked you? Plenty of girls do, you know. And you look so topping in that dress that I thought you might be a sport. Mind if I do?'

'Not at all.'

'Have you met the Langleys? Awfully jolly people. Rose

219

and Grace ride to hounds like nobody's business and their cousins are simply topping. Cambridge isn't big enough to hold them. I'm an Oxford man, myself. Best fun in the world. Trinity, of course.'

'Of course,' Alexandra said faintly.

'By jove,' he said, 'haven't you met an Oxford man before?'

He took her in to dinner. Mrs Burrows was careful to indicate what a privilege this was, her only son and she, Alexandra, a nobody and a temporary resident at that. Behind her in the procession to the dining-room was Grace Langley on the arm of a languid young man with a monocle, several couples of strangers, and then Rose Langley in pink, giggling, and a young man like a ferret.

The table was enormous and gleamed redly in the candlelight. There were baskets of flowers with long green trails of smilax all down the length of it, and by every place, above the glittering phalanxes of silver and the shining forests of glass, were engraved menu cards, each held in a little silver fist.

Alexandra counted desperately. Nine courses. *Nine*. Already she felt she couldn't breathe, laced into this frock like a second skin. After nine courses would she simply explode, like a too-fat sausage—?

'Piers Langley,' said the young man with the monocle. 'And you're Alexandra Abbott and you don't hunt. I've asked.'

He sighed.

Alexandra said tartly, 'Then there's nothing more to say, is there?'

He said, 'I say, I didn't mean to upset you. I didn't hunt until I was ten. I was supposed to be delicate.'

'I'm twice that and still I haven't hunted. I don't know what you do.'

A plate of greenish soup descended over her left shoulder.

'Turtle,' Piers Langley said gloomily.

Alexandra picked up her spoon.

'I say!' Piers said in alarm.

She looked at him questioningly. He cleared his throat.

'Lady Pemberton hasn't started yet.'

Alexandra looked uncomprehending and moved to put her spoon in her soup.

'I say, you shouldn't,' Piers said, 'not until she does. She's on Mr Burrows' right, after all.'

Blushing and slowly understanding, Alexandra laid down her spoon.

'Now you can,' Piers said a moment later.

Head bent, Alexandra concentrated miserably on her soup. When she had finished she said to Piers, to hide her confusion, 'I – I always think how odd it is that turtle soup doesn't taste of turtle.'

He gazed at her.

'It isn't turtle. It's mock turtle.'

Alexandra looked quickly away. All down the table, white-gloved footmen were removing the soup plates, the men's all empty, the ladies' all – all but her own – three quarters full still. She was hot with shame.

Fish came, and game, and beef in pastry and a cheese soufflé. She dared not eat any of them. When ice cream was offered her, a marvellous thing like a fairy castle, she was afraid to touch it and shook her head.

'You should, you know,' Harry Burrows said. 'It's pretty good. Mater's very hot in the fodder department. Here, I'll give you some.'

He put a huge wedge of gleaming white pudding on her plate.

'You could come hunting with me,' he said. 'I'd look after you, only the easy fences and all that.'

Alexandra picked up a spoon, remembered, shot a mortified glance at Lady Pemberton and blushing, laid it down again.

'It – it isn't the fences, it's the manners.'

Harry let out a breath.

'You don't want to give a fig for those.'

'I don't,' she said, 'but other people do.'

'Then we're two of a kind,' he said encouragingly. 'How awfully jolly!'

'Yes,' she said, 'how – how jolly,' and then she put her spoon suddenly into her ice cream and the whole glistening thing slid smoothly off her plate on to the shining red table.

'I say!' Harry said, 'what fun!' But there were tears in Alexandra's eyes and a lot of the older people had stopped talking to watch. A footman came and did something deft with a spoon and a plate and a linen napkin. Conversation began again.

'It helps, you know,' Piers Langley said slowly, 'to use a fork. Spoons are for soup. Pudding is eaten with a fork.'

'Yes,' Alexandra whispered. A hot tear made a dark spot on the cream silk of her bodice.

'I say,' Harry Burrows said, 'I say, I really will take you hunting you know. When I say a thing, by jove I go through with it. And that really is a topping dress—'

Alexandra cried all the way home, quite unrestrainedly. Her smooth cream front became quite blotched with dampness because she made no effort to check her tears, just let them run down her face and drop wetly on to her bodice. Her hair came loose at the back where she rolled her head against the cushions and the locks slipped down against her neck and got cried on to as well.

To her relief, Aunt Emily had not waited up. But Lyddy had. She was there in Alexandra's room with hot milk flavoured with nutmeg and the fire lit and Alexandra's nightgown spread on a chair before it to warm.

'Why, Miss, whatever—'

'No, Lyddy,' Alexandra said with difficulty, 'not a word, not a single word. And especially not to my aunt.'

'You all right, Miss?'

'Physically, perfectly. I just want to go to sleep and forget – forget it.'

Lyddy picked up an envelope on the dressing-table.

'This came for you, Miss. Mrs Talbot forgot to give it you.'

She held it out. It was postmarked Inverary and bore her father's handwriting. She tore it open in a frenzy; she would go home, at once, tomorrow, at least she was appreciated there, well anyway by her father, at least she didn't make a fool of herself—

'Your mother and I are so pleased you are so happy. A letter from your Aunt Emily told us how much she likes having you and how accomplished you are becoming. Don't get too fine for us, my lass. I've not mentioned it to your mother yet, but since the thing is such a success, I think you should stay, through the summer at least. Your aunt says there is a chance of you hunting, which is grand, and you'll catch the tail of the season. So don't fret about us here. We're all well and your mother has been out a good deal. You stay where you are and enjoy yourself and maybe we'll see you after the summer—'

Lyddy said, 'No bad news, Miss?'

'Not very,' Alexandra said and threw the letter, so cursorily read, on to the fire.

Lyddy gasped.

'Oh Miss—!'

'It's all right, Lyddy, I didn't want it, I just want to sleep and sleep.'

'Yes, Miss.'

'Lyddy.'

'Yes, Miss.'

'No word to my aunt, please, nothing at all.'

'Yes, Miss.'

CHAPTER SIX

Aunt Emily sent for her after breakfast. She hadn't eaten anything, just pushed a piece of ham around her plate to placate Penman and crumbled up a muffin. Looking at herself in the looking-glass on the stairs she saw how small and pink her eyes looked, their lids still puffy and her skin was tired and lifeless.

'Well?' Aunt Emily said. She looked to Alexandra disgustingly spry and healthy, rosy and refreshed after an excellent night and full of happy anticipation at hearing of the dinner party.

She patted the bed.

'Come and tell me all about it. My dear, you look tired. Of course it is always difficult to sleep after great excitement. Now, who did you sit next to? What did you eat? Were there ices? Mrs Burrows is famous for her ices, she uses cream from her own cows—'

There was nothing for it but to pretend it had all been as Aunt Emily would have wished it to be. Once embarked upon the fabrication of an imaginary dinner party, Alexandra found it quite easy.

'– and I was placed between Harry Burrows and Piers Langley and they told me all about hunting round here and really it was so interesting that I hardly noticed what we ate, some sort of fish and pheasant I think and, oh yes, there was an ice but by that stage, you know, I didn't have the smallest corner to put in so much as a mouthful—'

Aunt Emily said with real warmth, 'I am so glad, my dear. I know your mother scoffs at social life but I don't think she realizes what pleasure she is missing, how delightful it can be to be among amusing people.'

Alexandra smiled bravely. A small sharp throbbing was beginning in her temples and her eyes felt sore and gritty.

'I – I know it's silly Aunt Emily, but I'm – I'm so little used to late nights that I do feel absurdly tired. I – think if I had some fresh air today I should feel much better, if I went down to the sea, perhaps.'

'Of course,' Aunt Emily said comfortably. 'After luncheon. When my letters are done and you have told me how your parents are and whether your gown was admired. After luncheon. When I am resting, then you shall go.'

After luncheon she said to Penman, 'Can I walk anywhere? Does it matter?' And Penman, removing her untouched pudding with a troubled air said, 'If you go straight through the garden and over that rise, Miss Alexandra, the shore all before you belongs to Bishopstow House. But up to your right, where the estuary flows into the sea, that's Mr Swinton's land and although I know no harm in him myself, they say – they say he doesn't like trespassers, Miss Alexandra. He's a very solitary gentleman.'

'Yes,' she said, 'I'll be careful.'

The air outside was marvellous after the close warmth within, sharp and sweet, and the sky a pale, soft grey like plucked feathers. She went down the garden with a buoyant step between the neatly trimmed shrubs her uncle had so lovingly planted, past the magnolia, black and wet and knobbly, and through the rose garden the Talbots had laid out together in the manner of an Elizabethan one, formally-shaped beds edged with fat hedges of box. A solitary yellow leaf hung here and there, still in the windless air.

At the end of the rose garden an iron gate between grey stone pillars gave on to the fields beyond. Drops of water hung on it and the latch was stiff with lack of use. There were no cows in the fields that sloped up gently before her, no sheep, nothing except empty tidy green grass and neat grey walls.

'What a waste,' Alexandra said aloud. 'All these home fields and nothing in them. What a waste.'

She set off across the rough turf towards the low hill brow ahead. The first wall had a stile in it of stone slabs set like a crude staircase at intervals into the sides, rough with golden lichen. Alexandra climbed carefully up the first side and then leaped from the top on to the grass below. She looked back briefly at the house behind her, low and grey with its long eighteenth-century windows and its sheltering clumps of trees, then she picked up her skirts and began to run up the slope towards the sea.

She heard it before she saw it, murmuring louder and louder with the squeals of gulls cutting shrilly across the regular soft booming of the waves. Alexandra came stumbling, panting, over the crest of the hill and then the ground ran sheer downhill before her, covered in tawny winter grasses, down to the bleached pale strip of sand and the heaving, shifting steely mass of the sea. Ahead of her, straight ahead, she could make out the grey hills on the far side of the estuary and to her right where the land first widened out and then melted away altogether, the sea flowed to the ocean, limitless, miles of moving, salty water.

A little round hill, a sort of headland, thrust itself out into the estuary slightly to her right, and beyond it, she thought she saw a great bay, a giant bite out of the smooth slope of grassy shore. She began to run again, down towards it, jumping from tussock to tussock, and then her hat came loose and she snatched it off, scattering pins as she did so, and ran on, holding it in her hand and every so often bowling it ahead of her like a hoop.

It was indeed a bay, a vast expanse of ribbed brown sand over which the water was just beginning to creep, a gleaming line on the outer edge. She set out across it, wishing she had a dog with her and admiring, over her shoulder, the neat prints of boot sole and heel that she left behind her as she walked. Every so often there was a little crab corpse or a twist of sand thrown up by a sandworm or a streak of brilliant green weed like the hair of a water nymph and sometimes a smooth small rock and beside it a still, clear, tiny pool with mussels, blue black and pearly. Alexandra began to sing.

At the far side of the beach the rocks began, some humped with brown weed, some slatey and treacherous, breaking away in thick flakes. She looked hastily up at the rising land behind her, saw nobody, and hitched her skirts up to tuck them into her waistband. It was absorbing work, scrambling over the rocks, especially hampered by a hat in one hand, so after a while she left the hat on a dry plateau beside a pool and pursued her way unencumbered. She went steadily on, from foothold to foothold, only stopping to peel off her glove now and then and push a finger into the wet fringed mouth of a sea-anenome, but mostly she concentrated on the next step, the next handhold, with the sea on one side of her, the swell of grassy land the other.

She was so absorbed that it was not for some time that she realized that the sea on her left was no longer the water of the estuary but had become the ocean. She stopped for a moment, and gazed at it with pleasure, and saw how huge it was, surging against the rocks with far more power and energy than it had in the shelter of the estuary, flinging plumes of spray about in a reckless manner and dragging back to gather itself for the next rush forward.

She came to a little patch of sand, the bottom of a miniature canyon, and on the far side of it there was a smooth grey rock, sliced neatly off at the top to make a platform. Alexandra dug her toes into fissures in the canyon wall and pulled herself on to the platform which was dry and flat and sloped slightly towards the sea. It was the perfect look-out. Glowing now after her exercise, she sat down on the rock and pulled her skirts over her knees, hugging them to her so that her chin could rest there while she gazed.

It was perhaps the most luxurious moment she had ever known. Vibrant with exercise, alone, firmly pushing aside all thought that oppressed her, she sat and watched the sea, while the salty air buffeted softly against her cheeks and the gulls wheeled overhead, slightly paler than the pale sky. She could hardly see where sea and sky met far away in the soft grey mistiness, but she let her mind wander out there and find ships and whales and foreign shores.

'On a monument, I see,' a voice said below her, 'but not, I hope, smiling at grief.'

She felt as if she had been woken from a deep sleep and was conscious of pulling her mind back, painfully, as if it had been a kite out there, held to her by only a string. There was a man on the sand below her platform, a black-haired stocky man with a beard, dressed in an old cloak and hatless, who was gazing up at her with powerfully blue eyes, astonishing in his dark face.

'I'm sorry,' he said. He had a deep resonant voice and she caught a glimpse of white teeth in the dark forest of his beard. 'I see you weren't grieving, only musing. I shouldn't have disturbed you.'

'I wasn't – thinking at all—'

'No,' he said, 'I see that. I regret interrupting you. It was just such a surprise to see you here. There is never anyone here, the shore is always quite empty. I'm afraid curiosity got the better of me and now I have broken your mood. Please forgive me.'

Guilt and apprehension rushed over Alexandra's face. She attempted to get up, was foiled by her skirts and clumsiness, and ended up on her hands and knees looking down from her platform directly into his face.

'I – I didn't mean to trespass, I didn't think, I'm so sorry, I just went scrambling on, not thinking, I do apologize Mr – Mr—'

'Swinton,' he said, 'Michael Swinton.'

'Yes.'

'You know?'

'I – I've heard—'

He grunted. Then he moved a little up the canyon to where the jutting rocks made a rough natural staircase and held out his hand.

'May I help you down, Miss—?'

Alexandra got to her feet with difficulty.

'Alexandra Abbott. I'm so very sorry—'

'There is nothing to be sorry for. Not on your part.

It is I who am so sorry for disturbing you. Come, take my hand.'

She hesitated, putting her hands to her bare head, murmuring 'My hat—'

'I'm thankful you have lost it. Come now, whatever you may have heard of me, this is a perfectly ordinary hand, not a centaur's hoof or a goblin's claw.'

She blushed. She stepped carefully from her platform to the first foothold and put her hand in his. Even through her glove, she could feel his warmth and he guided her down a step or two and then, at the last moment, let her go in order to put both hands at her waist and swing her down.

'There,' he said, 'most elegantly done. And you are smaller than you looked up there.'

She nearly said, 'And you are larger,' but didn't, only looked up into his face and saw that he was not a young man, perhaps even as much as forty. He had thick brows and a nose which was so curved it was almost hooked, and she felt apprehension rise in her like sickness.

She said, 'I must – I must go back. Thank you for your kindness. I won't – I won't disturb you again—'

'I should like you to disturb me a little longer.'

'Oh no!' she said in fright, 'no – I mean, I mustn't think of it, I should go back, I was very wrong to walk on your land—'

'I am asking you to walk on it further. Come,' he said and held out that strong, flexible hand again, 'come and see my house. Come and see the sorcerer's kitchen where I brew up the grotesque potions that make me a legend here.'

Instinctively she looked up at the sky.

He said, 'I'll see you safely home before dark. Don't worry. Where is home?'

She said almost in a whisper, 'Bishopstow House.'

'Ah, the charming Mrs Talbot. I hardly ever see her now because she doesn't go out and neither do I. But I used to see her when her husband was alive, indeed they

229

were almost the only people I ever saw. For choice, that is. She is your—?'

'Aunt,' Alexandra said faintly.

His blue eyes were full of mockery.

'Come and see the wizard's lair, Miss Alexandra Abbott. I have a man, quite as terrifying as myself, and I will send him to tell your aunt that you are quite safe and that I will restore you to her by nightfall.' He held his hand out and this time he did not wait for her to respond, but grasped her hand firmly and began to lead her, with great skill and speed, over the rocks towards the cliff.

At the top of the cliff, Alexandra said breathlessly, 'I didn't mean to be impolite. I didn't mean that I don't want to see your house. Of course I don't believe the silly stories—'

'You don't?' he said sceptically. He was not in the least short of breath. 'You don't? What stories?'

'Oh!' she said, 'you aren't fair! You know what I mean, you have made fun of them yourself already—'

He was laughing. He said, 'There are some stories which say that I am not quite right in the head and some that I am full of evil powers. Those stories circulate in the village. And there are other stories, and these of course are *much* worse, and they have currency in the houses of the local gentry, and *they* say,' – he lowered his voice and spoke in a shocked whisper – 'that I cannot be a gentleman because I am – a *painter.*'

Alexandra coloured.

'I know,' she said, 'I have heard them.'

'And you will chance your luck?'

She smiled for the first time at him.

'Yes,' she said.

His house was a grim, grey dwelling, appropriately masked in creeper. A broad terrace ran round it with tufts of herbs growing on it and broken steps leading down on to the ruins of a lawn. From one of the chimneys only rose a thin, faint streak of smoke, but although it was a sunless day and darkening already, the black windows sent out no gleam of lamp or fire.

'Do you think it suitable for me?' he asked. 'Properly abandoned and forbidding?'

She hesitated.

'I see you do. I am just as neglected as my house. I have my man and a bent old crone from the village who drinks my whisky which she thinks I don't notice. We live in the kitchen together and I live in my studio alone. There, there are my studio windows.'

Facing out towards the sea and the cold north light were the largest windows Alexandra had ever seen, huge soaring panes of glass reaching from the terrace to the guttering below the slates.

'The view and the north light, that's why I bought the house. Come in. Come in and see.'

The kitchen reminded her strongly of Bewick, lofty and castle-like, except that the order which prevailed at Bewick had no chance here. The table was strewn with books and papers and candle-ends jammed into empty bottles, and the floor was similarly littered, but with boots and boxes. The dresser was crammed with a thousand things beside plates, old envelopes and letters, mousetraps, rags, pipes and screws of black tobacco in papers, and every chair was heaped with clothing, shirts and coats and cloaks. There was a huge range on which a vast kettle simmered like a cauldron and beside it a gun rack where four guns rested, gleaming with care and beautiful.

He shouted, 'Punch!'

A man came out of the pantry beyond, a small man with a sharp clever face, in an apron and gaiters.

'Miss Abbott, this is Punch. I picked him off Newbury racecourse after he had broken most of his ribs under the flying hooves of his competitors. Punch, I want a chair cleared for Miss Abbott, and tea. While you do it, I shall show her the studio.'

If Punch was astonished, he gave no sign. He made a sort of ducking movement to acknowledge his orders and tipped up the nearest chair so that its burden of garments slithered to the flagstones.

'Ten minutes, Punch,' Michael Swinton said.

He guided Alexandra out of the kitchen and along a passage so dark that if it had not been for his hand on her elbow, she would not have known where she was going.

'Now,' he said, 'the heart of the matter.'

He flung open a pair of doors she had not even noticed in the gloom and revealed the largest room she had ever seen, endlessly high, and filled with the grey light of the sea. It was curiously ordered after the kitchen, with canvasses in neat stacks along the walls, and in the centre a table, clearly from its size once a billiard table, covered in piles of drawings, pots of brushes, bottles and jars and a huge battered shallow leather case, full of tubes of paint like silver fish. Everything had been arranged with strict symmetry except for the giant easel standing on a square of Turkey carpet by the window, and everything, canvasses, table, marble busts, was covered with dust.

He didn't say anything. He simply stood aside and let her enter. She walked all down the room on the bare boards, looking at the paintings on the walls, breathing the smell of paint and turpentine laced with the richness of linseed oil. She walked up and down for some time, looking and sniffing, but not touching, and he waited by the door in the shadows and watched her. And then she said, in a simple, firm tone, with no gush to it, 'It's wonderful.'

He let out a long breath.

'How very satisfactory you are, Miss Abbott.'

She said, 'May – may I see what is on the easel?'

'No,' he said.

She recoiled a little at the sharpness of his tone.

'You wouldn't understand it. It's one of the things I

232

try to do for selfish pleasure, glorious, indulgent, selfish pleasure, rather than for money.'

'Money!' she said and her tone was shocked.

He laughed again and she could see his teeth gleam whitely across the room.

'Ah, Miss Abbott. Money. That stops me being a real artist in your eyes, doesn't it. Money. Dear, dear. Miss Abbott, I must peel the scales from your eyes entirely. I must tell you that once, fifteen years ago or so, I made a lot of money. A lot. I painted the young Lloyd George, I painted most of the Cabinet, I even painted two of the royal grandchildren. Now I don't paint so fashionably, but I still sell. I have an exhibition in London each spring and Punch makes wooden crates to pack my canvasses in and we put them tenderly on to the train in Bodmin. I don't go with them.'

'Never?'

'Never.'

'Wouldn't you like to hear the praise? Wouldn't you like to see the admiration on people's faces?'

'I have seen and heard it. I don't want it any more.'

She said in a rush, 'I – I used to dream about being famous, I used to imagine how wonderful it would be, to feel that you mattered, that people knew who you were, that you were *somebody*.' She remembered the sketches of mice and the dusty clarinet and blushed at the recollection.

He came forward into the room to stand close to her and bent to look into her face.

'Ah, my dear,' he said with great gentleness.

Alexandra took a step back, a lurch of fear jumping up her throat again. Michael Swinton straightened up and ran a hand over his rough black head.

'I'm afraid fame is not like that,' he said. 'At least, it was not like that for me. The more celebrated I became the worse I painted and the more false I felt. It was a very simple process and very powerful.'

'So – so you came here?'

'Yes. Just like that. I came here.' He smiled again. 'I can't appal you with gothic stories of ill-treated wives and neglected children. Never had either. At least — at least — I don't know what it is about you, Miss Abbott, but you make me want to bare my soul to you — I did have a wife once, years ago, when I was very young, but she left me, not I her, to live with someone else. She died soon after, coughing her lungs out.'

'How dreadful!'

'Yes. Yes, I suppose it was. It's twenty years ago, long before I came here. And the mention of twenty years reminds me that that must be the number of summers you own to, Miss Abbott and that being young and having spent the afternoon in the sea air, you must be hungry.'

The litter on the kitchen table had been pushed back to leave a clear corner on which a cloth, clean but creased, had been laid, and on it were two unmatching plates and two cups which bore no relation in design or size, to their saucers. There was a white milk jug, a rough block of butter, a loaf on a wooden board and a fat teapot, just like the one her father used every day—

'Miss Abbott, what is it? Your eyes are full of tears. Is it the crudeness of everything here? Does it distress you?'

She said hurriedly, 'Oh no, not at all, it's just that the teapot — the teapot gave me a pang of homesickness, just a pang. My father uses one just like it. That's all.'

He took her hand in his warm clasp for a moment and then he said, 'You must pour from it at once and lay the ghost. Pour for both of us. Punch, will you ride to Bishopstow House forthwith and leave a message to the effect that Miss Abbott is here with me and that I will return her within the hour.'

Punch said nothing but slid at once from the room. Michael Swinton cut bread, thick satisfying slices and speared one of them on to Alexandra's plate.

'He will be there in minutes. He always rides as if he were winning the St Leger. I suppose it is a habit.'

Remembering the turtle soup, Alexandra said in confusion, 'I'm – so sorry but – but I really am dreadfully hungry.'

He looked at her in surprise.

'Of course you are. I knew you were. I expect you to be.'

She ate gratefully and ravenously.

'When did you last eat, Miss Abbott?'

'L – last night.'

'And why no breakfast and no luncheon? Food at Bishopstow House was always excellent. I remember it with great nostalgia.'

Looking at her plate she said, 'It was at a dinner party. At – at the Burrows' house.' She paused and then because he said nothing, but only kept a silence full of sympathy and put more bread on her plate, she burst out, 'I did everything wrong that I could. I drank all my soup, I didn't hunt, I don't know about fashionable Scotland, I dropped ice cream on the table, I didn't know when to begin to eat. But you see at home, it's so isolated we never see anyone, I never learned how to behave properly. I mean, I'm sure my mother does but I never believed her, I was always afraid of being like her and I'm such a disappointment to her, so hopeless and not beautiful, not like my grandmother. And my father was her shepherd so nobody asks us to their houses, so I never met people like this before and Aunt Emily is trying to bring me out and she's so sweet, so generous. She keeps giving me clothes – not this dear old awful thing, Mrs McPhee at home made this – and making me practise manners and the piano and I couldn't tell her about last night, I couldn't, I can't disappoint another person, not after my mother—' and Alexandra put her head down on to the slice of bread on her plate and burst into tears.

He didn't speak or try to touch her. He sat quite silently until she had cried enough, and then he waited until she had pulled herself upright again when he handed her his handkerchief, cleanish but crumpled like the tablecloth.

'I shall give you more bread,' he said. 'You can't eat damp bread. It is probably indigestible.'

He cut another slice and then he leaned across and buttered it for her, as if she had been a child.

'Eat that, my dear.'

She did as she was told, sobbing every now and then, rubbing the handkerchief across her eyes. When she had finished the entire slice, and he had refilled her cup, he said, 'There is a way out of this, you know. It doesn't have to be fame. That is probably the worst solution.'

'I couldn't think of any other.'

'I know. It is most understandable. But I think a more modest aim would make you just as happy, just as satisfied. What is it that you really like to do?'

She thought for a long time, not looking at him, but at the glowing red centre of the range. She thought of all the things she didn't like to do, the sewing and painting and practising, and then she tried to think of the days at home she had enjoyed most and unbidden, pictures came to her mind of the farm and the sheep and the days on the hill with her father. She said slowly, 'I like *doing* things. I liked helping my father with the sheep. I liked shooting with him. I like his wolfhounds but my mother wouldn't let me feed them.' She took her reddened eyes from the fire and looked at her host. 'A week ago I played with the Rectory children. I liked that. And I saw Mrs Chamberlin's hens and they were splendid and Aunt Emily says we may keep some and I shall make sure it is me who looks after them, not Murphy.'

He smiled at her.

'You see, my dear, you don't really need advice at all. You are beginning to work out your own salvation. For yourself.'

'Am I?' she said. She sounded genuinely surprised.

'Follow the hens with a goat, or perhaps a cow and a pig or two—'

'All those lovely empty fields!'

236

'Precisely,' he said. He stood up. 'I must take you home, Miss Abbott.'

She said, 'I – I am sorry about the handkerchief. I will get it washed and return it to you.'

He looked at her very intently for a moment.

He said, 'Perhaps I have a salvation too,' and his voice was so low and his look so piercing that she felt a sudden clutch of fear, just as she had in the studio.

Perhaps he saw it, for his face relaxed at once and he held out an arm to her.

'Pray take my arm m'lady and I shall convey thee hence in the twinkling of an eye.'

She smiled and put her hand in his arm.

'Thank you,' she said. 'And thank you for tea.'

'Do not thank me,' he said. 'Do not ever thank me. It is I who thank you.'

CHAPTER SEVEN

'You must have been a success,' Aunt Emily said. 'I knew you would be. Mrs Burrows called this afternoon while you were on the shore and said that Harry was most anxious you should take part in some theatricals the young people want to perform at Easter. She said he would have come himself but he had to go Oxford of course. He was only home for the weekend. He won't be down again until next month.'

Alexandra wondered if Mrs Burrows had said anything else, but she gazed at the tapestry on her lap and said only, 'She – she is most kind. But I don't think I will. I've never acted and I'm sure I should be extremely awkward. Worse than usual.'

Aunt Emily said firmly, 'You have plenty of time to change your mind.' Then she added, 'You must call on the Langley girls tomorrow. It's only proper.'

'Oh, please!'

'There is no question. And you are immeasurably more poised than you were. You won't find it in the least difficult.'

Alexandra stitched in silence. After a while, Aunt Emily said,

'And what did you make of Mr Swinton?'

Alexandra said, 'He was very kind to me. I trespassed quite by mistake and he was most generous about it.'

'He is generous,' Aunt Emily said. 'Your uncle admired him very much. We used to see something of him, but of course, he never mixed, he is too odd, too difficult. He used to come and dine here sometimes, just on his own, and he and your uncle would talk and talk. He came here as quite a young man, perhaps twelve, fourteen years ago, but we never knew anything about him, where he came from, who is parents were. Of course we knew he was a celebrated painter, everyone did, and I think the neighbourhood felt quite disappointed when by moving down here he became less celebrated. He almost refuses to work which seems so oddly deliberate in view of his talent.'

'There was a painting on his easel, but he wouldn't let me see it. He said I shouldn't understand.'

Aunt Emily looked away from her into the fire.

'He was undoubtedly right. Your uncle maintained that he was a man of immense depth, a very philosophical creature in the classic sense. He once did something quite extraordinary for me. I told him about Charlotte and he said would I describe her, in the smallest detail that I could. I was of course, delighted, and as I could recall her face more clearly than anyone else's, except perhaps Richard's, I was able to comply. Two days later, he brought me a charcoal drawing of her, very lightly done, a sort of dream-like impression and it was so like her, it captured the essence of her so minutely, that I could not believe he had never seen her, only listened to me.'

'The drawing by your bed,' Alexandra said suddenly.

238

'The very one. She is more vivid in that, more vital, than in any of the countless, expensive portraits Alexander had done of her. That is why I keep it by me. Which reminds me, have you read my journal yet—'

'No', Alexandra said hurriedly. 'I nearly could today, very nearly. But there will be a better moment. You mustn't feel that I don't want to read it, but I am a little frightened of reading it after, well, after mother and her feelings for – for her mother and for me.'

Aunt Emily said, 'If you read it, dear child, it will take away your fear,' and Alexandra, stubbornly remembering Michael Swinton's saying that she seemed to be working out her own salvation and feeling that the decision to read the journal must be part of that working out, shook her head and sent her needle stabbing in and out of the canvas.

After a while, after a silence broken only by the whispering of the fire, she raised her head and said, 'May I really have some hens soon? If I were to get half a dozen hens and half a dozen pullets, because I think you would like their little tiny eggs, would that suit you?'

Aunt Emily shook her head in puzzlement, but she smiled.

'Yes, yes. Of course. Such an extraordinary desire, but of course you may. What harm could there be?'

At two thirty precisely the following afternoon, Murphy and the carriage and the stout, gleaming pair of bays were ready before the front door. At two thirty-five, the front door was opened by Penman, and Alexandra, in a green wool crêpe dress with a lace jabot and a good deal of complicated silk braid around the hem, under a coat of similar fabric, slit to the waist at the back and sides to allow for the movement of her skirts, and a hat swathed in green gauze and decorated on the left hand side with brown velvet pansies, came down the steps and climbed in.

239

Penman said, 'Langley Dene', to Murphy who indicated with a faint grimace that he knew his destination perfectly well already, and closed the door of the carriage firmly upon Alexandra.

She sat very upright and looked down at her green lap and the bronze toes of her boots, and the brown silk handbag on a gilt chain which contained a handkerchief, a phial of sal volatile and some of Aunt Emily's calling cards in a mother of pearl case, since she had none of her own. She thought, 'I shall count, very steadily, all the way there and then I shan't have a chance to be afraid,' and then the carriage turned right out of the driveway and went past the orchard wall and with a leap of pleasure, she thought, 'In two days the hens will be there! My hens! My own hens! Under the apple trees!' and when she thought again about her fright, it had quite vanished.

They were going inland, behind the little fishing village of Rock, towards Wadebridge, past little green cushions of fields and hedges of tamarisk and white cottages with blue slate roofs and windows made tiny against the weather. She sat and watched it all slip past, and thought how she must persuade Murphy to let her cook up the hens' mash on the saddle-room boiler, for Dora would hate her to do it in the kitchen, and how she would need a galvanized bucket and an old ladle and a door on the old donkey shed in the orchard to keep out the foxes.

In the fields to her left, a man was riding, or perhaps it was a boy, for the figure was very small. She craned forward to look more clearly and saw it was Michael Swinton's man, Punch, and that he was putting his horse, a great mangy thing, at the walls of the fields and leaping them and going on to the next as if he were steeplechasing. It was lovely to watch, the effortless, rhythmic flowing of the horse's limbs and then Punch turned his mount and came thudding towards the road. Alexandra thought they couldn't stop, not possibly, but they did and she saw

Punch's face, two yards away, look towards her, blank with unrecognition until she smiled and waved her hand and then he too grinned, and ducked his head at her and swung his horse away from the wall again.

'Of course he wouldn't know me,' she thought. 'How could he? I must look a different being to yesterday. I wish it *was* yesterday, I wish I was just climbing over the rocks in dear comfortable Mrs McPhee who doesn't mind getting wet and lets me breathe—'

Murphy had swung in between two newish and very neat grey gateposts. The gravel under their wheels was new too and very yellow and smoothly raked. Little young shrubs lined the drive growing in finely sifted black earth behind a neat strip of cropped grass. And then the drive curved and the house came into view, a huge solid new house, built of the same neat grey blocks as the gatepost, with enormous sash windows staring blankly out and a shallow slate roof with heavily moulded eaves.

Murphy climbed down and opened the door for her. Mindful of the stable-room boiler and the bucket, she gave him a brilliant smile as she stepped down and then she said, 'Twenty minutes, Murphy,' and he grimaced faintly again, as if to say he knew perfectly well she would be twenty minutes, ladies calling always were.

A stout butler led Alexandra across a hall floored in gleaming yellow wood and lined with large dark paintings, and announced her at the drawing-room door. Mrs Langley rose from a chair by the fire and Alexandra was aware of her daughters and someone else on a sofa in the great square bay window; and even as Mrs Langley was greeting her she could hear Rose say clearly, 'Well, whatever else she hasn't got, she certainly has elegant clothes,' and Alexandra, stung out of all terror quite suddenly, said crisply, 'I will tell my aunt how much you admire her taste. She has chosen all of them for me.'

Rose gave a tiny stifled scream and the third person

in the bay window proved itself to be a young man by throwing back his head and shouting with laughter.

Even Mrs Langley looked a little confused. She said hastily, 'Miss Abbott, may I present my nephew George Langley. You will forgive him rising but he had a bad fall yesterday and has damaged his ankle. The doctor has forbidden him to put any weight on it.'

Alexandra said, emboldened by her success, 'Then perhaps it is as well that I don't hunt.'

George Langley held out his hand.

'I'm awfully sorry not to get up. I failed to get myself introduced the other night. It was the jolliest dress you had, in that I will agree with my cousin, though I don't in much. Do I, Rose?'

Rose said, almost accusingly, 'You missed a really splendid day. We found in the first covert and then twice more, I can't remember so many good runs in a day before, not all at once.'

Alexandra was not sure if she should sit down before she was invited to, but by now she hardly cared. She seated herself in the bay window and said to George, 'Are you not supposed to be at Cambridge? I thought it was still the term time.'

He pulled a face of mock terror at his aunt.

'It is. I should be. But Aunt May won't let me go because of this confounded ankle. I daren't disobey her, Miss Abbott – dare I, Aunt? – because you see, my brother and I have been in her care since we were boys and stand in the greatest awe of her imaginable.'

Mrs Langley said fondly, 'George. What nonsense.'

Grace spoke for the first time. She said almost tentatively, 'You sat next to George's brother, to Piers, at – at the Burrows.'

'Yes,' Alexandra said, 'I remember. He too, plagued me about hunting.' This spirited behaviour seemed to be quite easy, now she had embarked upon it. She said, 'I like to ride for my own pleasure, but I'm not at all sure I want to hunt. I'm going to keep hens.'

For the second time George Langley burst out laughing.

'Oh, but I can imagine you, Miss Abbott! In a charming little bonnet and a print pinafore standing in your model farmyard and calling your devoted flock by name—'

'I am perfectly serious,' Alexandra said.

'So am I,' George Langley declared. 'I think it is a delightful amusement. I shall borrow the carriage – may I, Aunt May? – and come and witness this pastoral idyll before you get tired of it.'

Alexandra said calmly, 'I shan't get tired of it. It isn't a game, I am going to learn about hens and I shall look after them entirely myself.'

Mrs Langley said faintly, 'Hens—' and Rose, startled out of the remnants of her confusion said, 'Why can't – can't the gardener do that?'

Alexandra looked at her. 'I should like to do it myself. And then I should like to buy a cow perhaps and maybe a pig.'

'Oh, my hat!' said George Langley in delight.

Alexandra turned to Grace.

'I saw Mr Swinton yesterday. I met him quite by chance when I was rambling on the shore. And I didn't think him in the least like the Beast in the fairy tale although his hair and beard need a little trimming perhaps. He was very courteous and very kind. I went to his house and saw his studio and we had tea in his kitchen. He is a very famous painter, you know.' She looked at Mrs Langley. 'He painted two of Queen Victoria's grandchildren when he was younger.'

Mrs Langley seemed to grope for words.

'Yes—' she said at last, scarcely audible.

Grace and Rose said in chorus, 'You saw Mr Swinton?' and their voices were shrill with incredulity.

'Yes,' Alexandra said, 'I told you. We talked together for about two hours. And I can assure you,' she said with emphasis, 'that he is a gentleman.'

George Langley said in a fervent tone, 'You were

wasted on my brother the other night, Miss Abbott. Quite wasted.'

She turned to look at him. He was of the same cut as Piers, tall and dark, but his face was more animated, his eyes not so heavy-lidded and languorous.

She said, 'I think you would probably have scolded me just as hard, Mr Langley,' and then she gathered up her handbag and rose to her feet.

'Don't go!' George Langley begged. 'Please don't go! Aunt May, be as firm with Miss Abbott as you are with me. Make her stay!'

Mrs Langley seemed flustered. She said, 'Why George, my dear, I think – I am sure Miss Abbott – but of course only too delighted—'

'I must go,' Alexandra said, 'I have a very busy afternoon ahead.'

'But you will come again? Soon? I don't know how long I shall be laid up with this wretched ankle. Please say you will come!'

'Yes,' Alexandra said, and smiled at him. 'Of course I will,' and she smiled at Mrs Langley and held out her hand and smiled at Rose and Grace, and then she went swiftly from the room and across the hall and down the steps to collapse shaking into the carriage.

'The Manor House, Miss Alexandra?' Murphy inquired through the open door, 'Mrs Burrows? Or Pemberton Park?'

'Neither, Murphy', she said, 'The Rectory. Take me to the Rectory.'

Murphy said doubtfully, 'Very good, Miss Alexandra,' and closed the door upon her.

The carriage had hardly halted in the Rectory drive before the door was torn open and the children came tumbling out with Mrs Chamberlin behind them vainly trying to exert some sort of control. Murphy forgot to be stately and was off the box as nimbly as a boy in order to prevent his precious carriage being invaded by this horde in battered boots and smudged pinafores. They danced up and down on the gravel and shouted and sang out Alexandra's name.

'My dear!' Mrs Chamberlin said as Alexandra stepped down, 'You look quite ravishing! A living fashion plate! Children, children! You are entirely forbidden to touch Miss Abbott when she is dressed like this, entirely forbidden. Robert! Did you hear me? Arthur! Arthur! There will be no jam on your bread today if you so much as lay a finger—'

'I don't mind,' Alexandra said, 'really I don't. They are only clothes, after all.'

She was towed into the house as before and taken straight to the nursery despite Mrs Chamberlin's protests that dressed like this they should take Miss Abbott to the drawing-room, the parlour at least, she insisted—

'I am quite comfortable here,' Alexandra said. 'Please don't trouble yourself. I came to recover from calling at Langley Dene. I think I behaved extremely badly. I seemed possessed of some extraordinary mad courage. I think – I think I said some shocking things.'

The children began to clamber on to her, calling for games, demanding she be a lion too this time, begging that they could all be mounted police, even the baby.

'No,' Alexandra said firmly, 'not now. I shall talk to your mother first. Then I will play. If you interrupt, I shan't play at all.'

They subsided at her feet. Their mother said, 'I don't know how you do it. I can't, to be sure. They have talked of nothing but Miss Abbott since you came last, nothing at all. Now, my dear, I don't know about *saying* shocking things – and I must confess, although the Rector would be horrified to hear me say it, that I should be very tempted to say shocking things at Langley Dene, such very new money my dear, everything so dreadfully bright and shiny – as I was saying, I don't know about saying shocking things, but you are certainly doing them. The village is buzzing – Arthur you must never, *never* put objects up your nose, it is quite dreadfully dangerous – as I was saying, that gossip is loud today about you. In fact, I can't remember when it was last so vociferous. Rumour *says*, my dear, that you actually took tea with Mr Swinton!'

'Yes,' Alexandra said, 'I did.'

Mrs Chamberlin spread her hands.

'There now! And I have spent all morning saying it cannot possibly be true, that you devote all your time to your aunt, that you have scarcely left the house in over a month and all the time you were doing just what you were rumoured to be doing! Of course, old Meg is not to be relied upon at all, owing to her unfortunate fondness for the bottle, and when I heard that she was the source of the story I said that it couldn't possibly be the case, that she didn't know what she had seen, as usual—'

'Old Meg?' Alexandra said, puzzled. The baby had been endeavouring with grim determination to haul himself from the floor on to Alexandra's knee, gripping handfuls of her skirts to assist himself and heaving with astonishing strength. Alexandra now lifted him on to her lap, where he immediately settled, plugged his thumb into his mouth and gazed pityingly down at his brothers and sister.

'My dear, do put him down. You mustn't let yourself be exploited though he is a dear, aren't you, Jack? Mother's own one. My dear, Meg works as a cleaning woman for Mr Swinton. I think he allows her considerable freedom over her – her weakness, you know, and so she is quite content to work for him whatever the village may say of him, and they do, to be sure, say some very foolish things. At least, I am sure they *are* foolish. It seems that Meg was washing up in the pantry yesterday when Mr Swinton came in from the shore as is his custom in the afternoons, and you were with him! And then he gave orders to Punch for tea to be prepared and they had a terrible time finding any china that wasn't cracked or broken and then she went on working in the pantry as quiet as a mouse and she could hear you both talking as clear as clear. And then of course, when she came into the village to buy the few things they need – it is astonishing how modest Mr Swinton's needs seem to be, she hardly buys any comforts at all but I gather his man is an excellent gardener and they keep a pig for bacon—'

Alexandra said a little sharply, 'And I suppose she also told you everything we talked about?'

Mrs Chamberlin coloured. 'My dear, I never meant to offend you. It's simply my tongue. Of course, she didn't. She said – she said she did not understand a word you said, either of you.'

Alexandra said, 'He is the most interesting person I ever met in my life.'

A voice from the doorway, a tired, kind voice, said, 'I am so glad to hear it. It is what I have always felt.'

'My dear!' Mrs Chamberlin said. She sprang up and all the children rushed towards their father save the baby, who was not, even for that prize, going to chance losing his throne.

'Miss Abbott,' the Rector said, advancing into the room, his legs severely hampered by the clinging children, 'you will think me abominably lax not to have called upon you since your arrival. I feel most conscious of the lack myself. But the truth is, we have all been unwell, I'm sure my wife will have told you, and there is so much sickness in the village—'

He looked so tired, his thin face drawn below tufts of reddish hair, that Alexandra smiled at him warmly.

'Please don't think of it, Mr Chamberlin. I feel just as guilty because I have been here five Sundays and not come to church on any of them. Aunt Emily likes me to read morning prayers to her, but I should have come all the same.'

He seated himself beside her, seemingly unaware that a rag doll and two lead soldiers had occupied the chair before he reached it. Helen let out a wail and plunged for her doll. Apart from a look of mild surprise, the Rector seemed unaware of the toy being pulled roughly from under him.

'I am so glad, so very glad, that you have spoken to Mr Swinton. I feel him to be a lost soul, a good one, an excellent one, but a lost and unhappy one. Of course, so few are aware of his background and he being, shall we say, a little unorthodox in his dealings with people, never seems to think of it or to realize that in some circles it might be of – of help to him. His father, Miss Abbott, was a Sir Thomas Swinton, of an exceedingly ancient family who have lived at Swinton – the Somerset Swinton, you know, spelled as Swynetoun in the Domesday Book where the manor is described in detail – since before the Conquest. Mr Swinton is Sir Thomas' third son and he was unable to persuade his father that art in any way constituted a life's work. Sir Thomas, you see, was so very much a local philanthropist, a local administrator, indeed he was Lord Lieutenant I believe, some time in the 'seventies. I understand there was some kind of rift and Mr Swinton is not recognized by his brothers, the eldest of whom has now assumed the baronetcy. So you see, Miss Abbott, though he might never, on account of his birth, want for money, he lacks sadly the human love that lucre can in no way replace. It is really wonderful to think that someone, a young person like yourself—'

'Forgive me,' Alexandra said, feeling a recurring surge of the courage that had invaded her at Langley Dene, 'but I think – with respect, I think that everyone is making too much of my meeting Mr Swinton. I trespassed on his land and he was most kind about it and, as I said to Mrs Chamberlin, he is extremely interesting to talk to. That is all.'

The Rector blinked at her. She wondered if she had gone too far, so she turned to Mrs Chamberlin and said with real enthusiasm, 'Imagine! Aunt Emily has no objection at all to a few hens! Isn't she good? They are to come from Grove Farm, just as you recommended, 12 Rhode Islands and 6 pullets. They are to be delivered on Friday.'

Mrs Chamberlin smiled with real warmth. 'My dear! I am delighted. They will give you such pleasure and satisfaction. I cannot think why Mrs Talbot never chose to have any herself, there is really something special about a poultry yard.'

Alexandra disengaged Jack with difficulty and rose to her feet.

'Play! Play!' the children clamoured.

She looked down at them.

'I did say I'd play. I know I did, but I think not today, not dressed like this. I'll come tomorrow and we will play at Indian princes and elephants—'

'And lions and tigers! And mounted police!'

'All of them,' she promised, 'Every one.'

Outside on the drive Murphy was waiting, the carriage door open.

'Pemberton Park, Miss Alexandra?' he said doggedly. 'The Manor House?'

'No, thank you,' she said. 'Neither of them. Just home.'

Once the carriage was in motion, she closed her eyes, tired now and a little dispirited. How odd people were, how unpredictable and curious, how difficult it was to know how to behave so that one pleased oneself and society as well. It had been a confusing afternoon as well as a satisfying one, but one thing was clear, quite clear. She could not, evidently, repeat her chance and happy encounter with Michael Swinton.

CHAPTER EIGHT

The day the hens came, squawking faintly in a crate from Grove Farm, Aunt Emily received a note from Mrs Langley.

'Listen, my dear,' she said to Alexandra, summoned

flushed and impatient from the orchard where she had been settling her new charges in and attempting, as tactfully as possible, to exclude Murphy from the process, 'Mrs Langley says George is heartened beyond anything by your visit. He was so depressed, poor boy, at falling in the first place – all Langleys ride as if they were born to it – and then at not being able to return to Cambridge for the last few weeks of term, and his aunt was quite at her wit's end to know what to do with him. And then you called and he enjoyed your visit vastly and Mrs Langley says that while he is laid up, with the girls hunting two days a week, would you be sure to go and see him—'

'Please, aunt—' Alexandra said desperately, twisting her hands together. If she stayed indoors much longer, Murphy would have taken over her tasks and have filled the old beer crates they were to use as laying boxes with straw, and be collecting the scraps from the kitchen, that Dora had reluctantly promised to keep for her. She knew he would. He was stiff with disapproval at the notion of her carrying buckets of steaming hen mash about the place like any farmer's daughter in the first place and any chance to cram her back into what he considered her proper place as a lady, he would take.

'Dear Aunt Emily, please may I go? Of course I'll call to see George Langley, anything, only please—'

'I am delighted for you, Alexandra. It is all turning out just as it should. The Langley girls hunt on Tuesdays and Thursdays and Mrs Langley will expect you then, and to stay a little longer than usual. Perhaps George will teach you chess. You ought to play chess—'

The faint but unmistakable sound of an outraged hen came through the closed drawing-room windows.

'Anything, aunt!' Alexandra gasped. 'Of course, Tuesdays, Thursdays, anything, I promise, of course—' and fled.

In the orchard, Murphy was standing beside the trough Alexandra had appropriated for the hens' use. In his hand was a bucket, the very bucket she had chosen in which to cook up the scraps. Around his feet the red-brown hens surged in anticipatory ecstasy while the smaller, paler pullets scrambled frantically round the edges of the group, certain they would be the losers.

'Murphy!' Alexandra said sternly from the gate.

He started guiltily.

'I told you, Murphy, that although I am immensely grateful to you for helping me to repair the shed to make a hen house and for finding me the things I need, these are my hens and I shall look after them. You are not to concern yourself with them at all.' She marched forward and took the bucket from him.

'Tisn't proper, Miss Alexandra. Hens is dirty things, that bucket's 'eavy. Tisn't right you should touch them things.'

Alexandra put her free hand under the end of the bucket and tipped the contents into the trough. The hens clambered in, cackling with delight and greed. She looked at them for a moment with pleasure and then set the bucket down and turned to Murphy.

'Listen to me, Murphy. I know what's bothering you. You don't want me in the harness room, do you. You don't want anyone prying into your private domain and observing quite why there were so many conveniently empty beer crates for us to use. Well, I will tell you now, Murphy, that as long as you continue to do properly the job for which you are paid I don't care how much you drink nor shall I tell anyone about it, not anyone. I shan't inspect the harness, I shan't poke around the stables. All I will do is to come in after breakfast every day and put my bucket on the harness room boiler to cook up, and an hour later I will take it away. I will do it even when it snows and when it rains. I won't interfere with you and you, Murphy, won't interfere with me. Is that clear?'

Murphy, whose face had gone through a perfect pantomime of reactions during her speech, now nodded silently, his complexion purple.

'Then you may go.'

He made a move to pick up the bucket but saw Alexandra's glance in time and withdrew his hand unhappily. He went out of the orchard most uneasily, turning every so often to look at her as she contemplated her hens. Then he shut the gate and ambled off to the house, shaking his head in perplexity, to complain to a sympathetic Dora in the kitchen.

'Now,' Alexandra said to the hens when he had gone, 'come with me and I will show you where you will sleep.'

The following Tuesday, Murphy brought the carriage to the door with his usual punctuality. Alexandra came down the steps in her new green clothes, under which she had managed to put her old comfortable corset when Lyddy had left the room to polish her boots, wearing a smile that was partly triumph at her illicit comfort and partly the satisfaction of having taken five hens' and four pullets' eggs to Dora in a little rush basket that very morning. Dora, kind-hearted even if disapproving, had promised to make a soufflé for dinner, which Alexandra had assured Aunt Emily would be superior to any she had ever tasted before.

When the carriage stopped at Langley Dene, the butler seemed more deferential as he opened the door and Mrs Langley, instead of merely rising from her chair, came halfway across the drawing-room to welcome Alexandra. George was on his sofa in the window as before, and beside him was a table littered with books and cards and fruit and bottles.

He said, 'It's seemed like a year, waiting for you to come again. I made Aunt May write the moment you had gone. I was wondering how on earth I should endure these hunting days, especially when they all came back and crowed over me about the jolly time they'd had, and then I thought, by jove, there's Alexandra Abbott and she doesn't hunt and she made me laugh more than anyone has for years. So I exercised an invalid's moral pressure, you see, and here you are!'

252

Mrs Langley, who had stood over them while he spoke, forbidding in burgundy taffeta and garnets, said she was sure they could amuse each other very well without her.

'I shall be at my desk, George,' she said levelly to her nephew, 'so I shall not be far away.'

When she had rustled off, Alexandra said with genuine simplicity, 'Why does it matter where she is? What might you do?'

George's colour rose hotly.

'I say, Miss Abbott, you certainly go to the heart of things—'

'Won't you call me Alexandra?'

'I should like to above anything. What a sport you are. It's an awfully jolly name, you know. I suppose you were named for the Queen.'

'No,' she said flatly, 'after my grandfather. He was wonderfully handsome, incredibly dashing, astoundingly brave and entirely fascinating.'

George Langley said, 'Why do you say it like that? In that – that dead sort of voice? My grandfather—' he glanced at the impressive dark red back at the far end of the drawing-room and lowered his voice, 'My grandfather was a fat, red manufacturer of mill machinery with a strong Lancashire accent. It must be splendid to have a grandfather like yours.'

'It isn't,' Alexandra said.

He leaned forward.

'Why?'

She shrugged.

'It doesn't matter. Aunt Emily said you should teach me to play chess.'

'I say, I'd love to. Then I might have a chance of winning, at least for a week or two. Don't frown, Alexandra, it makes me think you didn't want to come.'

She smiled at once.

'Oh, I did! I wasn't – I wasn't at all sure your aunt would want me here again, but of course I wanted to come. It must be so frustrating to be laid up like that.'

George leaned forward again so that his bright, good-looking face was only inches from hers.

'Between you and me, Alexandra, Aunt was much impressed by your performance last time. She made a lot of conventional noises, of course; she had to because you can't have Rose and Grace getting any sillier than they are already and they might have taken it into their heads to copy you, but I could see she thought you had real spirit. You do, too. How are the hens?'

'Nine eggs today,' Alexandra said proudly. 'Farmer Dawes said it might take them a few days to settle down but they were laying on the second day.'

He laughed.

'Splendid! And who won, the servants or yourself?'

'I did.'

'I thought you would. You are just about a match for anyone, aren't you?'

'I shan't be at chess.'

'I'm relying on that. You have to let invalids win, you know, otherwise they have relapses.'

She found the chess-board under a pile of books and manoeuvred it out.

'You aren't a real invalid.'

'I'm going to be from now on,' he said, 'now that I've made you come. If you keep coming, I shall be an invalid for weeks and weeks. We can have an infinite chess game which will go on for months. Chess is like that.'

She looked about her.

'Where are the men?'

'Under there.'

There was a wooden box under his table. She picked it up and set it on her knee, then began taking out the yellow and black wooden pieces and setting them on the board. George watched her in silence for a while and then he said in a low voice, 'I say did I offend you just now? I'd do anything rather than offend you, you know. It was when — when we were talking of grandfathers. Did I put my foot in it? I'd hate to do that, so tell me where I blundered and I'll know not to do it again.'

Alexandra put down a black and a yellow bishop side by side on matching squares.

'It wasn't anything you said, I promise you. I can't tell you why I spoke like that, I – I don't find it easy to talk about I'm afraid. But it was nothing to do with you and you mustn't reproach yourself. Now then, how do I set up the board? The pawns all go in front of the others, don't they, in a line?'

'Yes,' he said. He looked at her keenly. 'You will come on Thursday, won't you?'

'Yes,' she said, 'of course I will,' and smiled at him.

She went straight home from Langley Dene although her aunt had instructed her to call on Mrs Burrows. She said, 'Home directly please,' to Murphy and this time he did not sigh or look pained at all, but simply said, 'Very good, Miss Alexandra,' and obeyed.

The house was very quiet when she reached it. Janet, tiptoeing out into the hall when Penman had opened the door, said that Aunt Emily was resting and would come down at tea-time. Alexandra nodded and went quietly up the stairs and down the landing, past the bowls of pot-pourri and prints of wild flowers framed in black and gold, to her own room.

Lyddy was there at once. Alexandra took the long pins out of her hat and laid them in the red glass tray on her dressing-table.

'I shall get into something comfortable,' she said, 'and then I shan't want anything for the whole afternoon.'

'I'll make up the fire, Miss, and bring up some more coals—'

'No thank you, Lyddy. The room is like an oven already. I don't want a single thing but solitude.'

When Lyddy had gone, Alexandra went to one of her huge wardrobes and from beneath a pile of linen drew out the little morocco volume Aunt Emily had given her the evening of her arrival. The covers were very worn, as if it had been travelled about a good deal, and on the fly leaf was written 'Journal 1841' and then, in a different coloured ink, 'And 1842' and then, below that, carefully, 'Emily Brent'. Charlotte had been Charlotte Brent, Alexandra's mother had Brent somewhere in her name, even she, Alexandra was a little bit Brent, somewhere, some part of her.

Taking the book to the chair by the fire, Alexandra sat down with it in her hand. Then she eased off her shoes, put her stockinged feet on the fender and began to read.

She supposed she must have risen at some point to light a candle on the mantlepiece. She couldn't recall stirring but when she came to the end of the journal and looked up, bemused and far away, not recognizing her surroundings for a while, the room was faintly glowing with fire and candlelight and the sky beyond the windows was inky blue. She sat quite still, the little book in her lap and gazed up at the pale candle flame, hardly seeing it, so busy was her inward eye upon the scenes that had held her in thrall for two hours or more.

As if sensing she had finished, Lyddy came softly in and began to light lamps and draw the curtains, gently pulling Alexandra back to reality.

'Mrs Talbot wants you downstairs, Miss. She's ordered tea late for you. There's a gentleman come. You're to go down as soon as you can, Miss.'

Alexandra nodded, still silent. Lyddy knelt and put on the shoes she had kicked aside and then brought a hairbrush. Alexandra moved her head away.

'No – no, don't Lyddy. I am perfectly tidy—'

'There's a gentleman come, Miss.'

'I am tidy enough for him, too.' Alexandra said, and drifted from the room, the journal still in her hand. She went along the landing and down the staircase, still in a waking dream, crossing the hall and seeing Penman there, waiting to open the drawing-room door for her, as if it was someone she was watching perform, not herself but another being altogether.

The drawing-room seemed very hot and bright. She dimly saw Aunt Emily by the fire and the silver tea service winked on a table beside her, and there, in front of the fire, standing there as comfortably as if it were his own fire, she saw with no surprise at all, that it was Michael Swinton.

Aunt Emily and Michael Swinton spoke to her together and then laughed and she saw that he looked quite different, much younger, that his hair and beard had been trimmed, that his expression was full of vitality. He said, 'What have you been doing all this time?'

Silently she held out the journal.

'I thought as much,' Aunt Emily said. 'I knew you would read it sooner or later. Show Mr Swinton.'

Obediently she put it into his outstretched hand. He was smiling and his eyes were very blue.

'Well, my dear?' Aunt Emily said, 'What did you think?'

Alexandra sat down.

'Just as you thought I should. That she was really fascinating, really, truly fascinating – and lovable as well. I couldn't see how she *could* be lovable. But now I do.'

Michael Swinton said, the book open in his hands, 'And did the journal end there? Christmas in Bombay in 1842?'

'Yes. I never wrote another word. There was Richard, you see.'

He put the journal on Alexandra's lap and went to sit down in the chair beside hers.

'Well, Miss Abbott, is it all a great relief to you?'

'Yes,' she said.

Aunt Emily said, 'She is quite like my sister, you know, Mr Swinton. She wouldn't hear of it to begin with, but I see more evidence of it every day. Come and pour out for us, my dear. Is it not rather a triumph actually to

257

have Mr Swinton here? I thought you had given up drawing-rooms entirely.'

'I have,' he said. He took up his cup from Alexandra and smiled at her again. 'Miss Abbott will tell you that I don't even possess one of my own to entertain her in.'

'I don't mind,' Alexandra said, 'I like kitchens. I would spend more time in Aunt Emily's except that Dora doesn't like it. But I have made her promise to teach me to cook a little even though at first she said she wouldn't think of it.'

Aunt Emily said, looking into the fire, 'You see, Mr Swinton? My sister never gave twopence for convention either.'

'Why have you come?' Alexandra said suddenly, standing before him with a plate of wafer thin bread and butter that he had already refused.

'How sensible you are, Miss Abbott. When you want to know the answer to something, you ask outright. I have come to thank you. Nothing more, nor less.'

She sat down, balancing the plate of bread and butter on her knee.

'Why?'

'Alexandra, really,' Aunt Emily remonstrated. 'My dear, please—'

'I enjoy it, Mrs Talbot. She is the least self-conscious creature I have ever met. Miss Abbott, when you came to my house the other day and wandered round my studio and let me see something of your thoughts, it was as if a gale had blown through all the dust and cobwebs, all the mouldering old habits that were growing up round me like ivy, and when you had gone, I tore that canvas off the easel and smashed it—'

'Oh!' Alexandra exclaimed, shocked.

'Wickedly wasteful, I know, but I smashed it, and set up a new one and I have painted upon that new one the first thing that has given me real pleasure for years, oh, years and years. It is magnificent for me to feel that way again. So I have come to thank you.'

'You certainly look quite different,' Alexandra said, catching his mood and smiling.

'I've had a haircut,' he said, teasing her. 'At least, Punch did to me what he does to the horses in the spring. I'm no judge of whether it suits either of us.'

Alexandra looked at him.

'It does,' she said decidedly.

He returned her look with a glance so suddenly intent that she felt a flash of absurd panic, and rose hurriedly to busy herself with the teapot. Behind her back he said, 'Punch saw you the other day, going out in a carriage. He was exercising a horse. I let him keep young ones for sentimental reasons since I don't need them for practical purposes. He said you looked like royalty.'

Alexandra's face was fiery. Aunt Emily said, 'She is making a very satisfactory silk purse, Mr Swinton,' and they both laughed.

'And the farming plans?' Michael Swinton asked, forcing Alexandra to turn back to him.

'A dozen hens,' she said and her voice was full of pleasure, 'and six pullets.'

'Excellent!' he said. 'Mrs Talbot, when will you allow her to keep a cow?'

'A cow!'

'Yes!' Alexandra said. 'Oh yes! A cow—'

Aunt Emily closed her eyes.

'It is hardly fair to me to encourage her, Mr Swinton. She insists on looking after the hens herself. Imagine, with a cow—'

'A rustic bonnet, perhaps,' he suggested, 'and a yoke with two pails. And a little three-legged milking stool.'

Alexandra ignored the teasing.

'I should like that.'

'So should I. I will come and paint you while you do it. It will be a rural idyll. The Academy will love it.'

He put his cup down and rose to his feet.

'Mrs Talbot, that was the most delightful hour.'

'You will come again, Mr Swinton?'

259

He hesitated for only a moment, then glanced briefly at Alexandra and said, 'I should be happy to.'

'My husband would have been so pleased. He would have liked to know that you still came to see me. Wednesdays, you know, Wednesdays are my afternoons.'

He bent and kissed Aunt Emily's hand. Then he turned and said simply to Alexandra, 'My dear, thank you,' and was gone.

CHAPTER NINE

Until mid-March Alexandra faithfully visited George Langley on Tuesdays and Thursdays. Even when his ankle was much improved, the fracture knitting itself together most satisfactorily, she still went and would find him hobbling around the conservatory which was raw and bright, being still too new for the vines and jasmines to have masked its bare white ribs. They played chess and bezique and silly paper games, Alexandra attempted sketches of him which convulsed him with laughter and read comic poems to him. She tried reading him Wordsworth and Tennyson and Browning but he would sigh and interrupt her when she did, so she went back to the lighter Kipling poems and he would lie and grin happily to himself and make her read his favourite passages over and over again.

Twice a week, with equal fidelity, she went to the Rectory, partly for poultry conversations with Mrs Chamberlin, and partly to play Mowgli with the children whom she had introduced to the *Jungle Books* with wild success. When she arrived they would clamber in a body on top of the nursery table and standing there, hands on hearts, would chant to her—

'For the strength of the Pack is the Wolf, and the strength of the Wolf is the Pack.

The Jackal may follow the Tiger, but Cub,
    When thy whiskers are grown,
Remember the Wolf is a hunter – go forth,
    And get food of thy own!'

And then they would spring down with a howl and rush to embrace her.

On Wednesdays, to please Aunt Emily, she stayed at home to receive callers. It was tedious, but no longer alarming, and as she contrived most mornings to slip down to the shore for gulps of sea air, though she was careful now never to go beyond the rocks around the headland, she did not chafe at the confinement as once she had. Mornings had indeed developed into quite a happy routine of little errands and duties for Aunt Emily, the hens and the sea; and if she felt now, as quite often she did, an incomprehensible longing for something wilder and freer and more satisfying than this domestic round, she put it down to needing to be in the open air more and gave herself, next morning, a longer spell on the smooth buff sands of the bay. When she wrote home, as she now did regularly, she wrote believing herself to be very contented.

The week before Easter, a week in which the air suddenly lost its sharpness and became soft and spring-like, Harry Burrows and Piers Langley arrived home from university. Langley Dene erupted into chatter and activity and the Manor House, around which Mr and Mrs Burrows had moved in stately solitude all term, echoed with shouts and thundering feet. Harry brought friends with him, the family carriage was despatched to Truro to meet a London train bringing Mrs Burrows' oldest friend, a widow with a daughter who was reputed to be an awfully jolly girl, and a motor car rolled up to Langley Dene with more cousins, swathed in veils and goggles and long motoring coats, come to celebrate Easter.

Alexandra stopped visiting George.

'But why, my dear? Mrs Langley says she wishes you would go. You have been so good to George and you deserve a little reward now that all the young people have come. She came yesterday afternoon, even though she knew it wasn't my afternoon, hoping to find you, but of course you had gone to the Rectory, and begged me to persuade you to go to Langley Dene on Saturday. They have immense plans for you all, and then you shall dine there. You may have the carriage all day and take Lyddy with you so that there will be no difficulty about dressing—'

Alexandra, sorting tapestry wools, looked up from the muddled skein in her hand.

'Dear Aunt Emily. I really don't want to go. *Really*. I have nothing in common with those people, I should be bored and cross.'

'But it would be so much better for you. I don't like to think of you spending so many afternoons playing panthers and bears with those Chamberlin children. It's very kind of you but – but so *odd*. I had so hoped, when you started to visit George Langley—'

'I know exactly what you hoped,' Alexandra said, 'and I like him on his own. I expect I should like all of them on their own. But not together.'

Aunt Emily sighed but said no more.

The following day, two unexpected allies of Aunt Emily came in the shape of Harry Burrows and George Langley. Harry had driven his friend over and was in boisterous good spirits at having been the first person to be allowed to take George away from the house.

'By jove, Miss Abbott, it's simply topping to see you! You look awfully – awfully – doesn't she, George? I say, George, you're a lucky dog to have – to have——. D'you know what we've come for, Miss Abbott? Sh, George, don't spill the beans. Quite the wounded hero, isn't he, Miss Abbott? I say, what a jolly house this is. Do you know, I've never been inside before, simply splendid to be near the sea—'

'Why don't you come near me now?' George demanded, lowering himself carefully into a chair by Alexandra.

She said frankly, 'I don't care for crowds.'

'Pooh, nonsense, Miss Abbott,' Harry Burrows exclaimed, striding about the drawing-room and picking up Aunt Emily's treasured objects. 'Crowds are the jolliest thing, you know. You'll find that out, won't she, George? Come on, George, you tell her why we have come.'

George said, 'We are going to put on a play, Alexandra. There's the perfect place at the Manor House where the front and back drawing-rooms meet with curtains. We're going to do *Maria and Murder in the Red Barn*. It's the funniest thing you ever heard of. I've put in to be a corpse already and then I can laugh my head off on the floor all the way through—'

'We want you to take part, Miss Abbott. I say, may I call you Alexandra too? How jolly sporting of you. We're all agreed, Rose and Grace say they think you'll be simply topping and I've some awfully jolly people staying who are just waiting for me to bring you back with us so that we can decide on the cast and get started. By Jove, it's going to be the best fun in the world! Get your hat, Miss – Alexandra, and let's be going!'

Alexandra said, 'You will both think me the poorest – sport, but I'm going to refuse.'

'No!' they shouted.

'You can't,' George said earnestly. 'You *must* come. We need you. I – it won't be half the fun without you.'

Harry Burrows looked thoroughly bewildered. He made an effort to understand her, wrinkling his honest brow.

'Is – is it because you think you should stay with your aunt? Mother says you are simply splendid—'

'No,' Alexandra said. 'It isn't that. Aunt Emily would love me to go. I just can't—'

The door opened and Penman said in a voice that was not entirely neutral, 'Mr Swinton, Miss Alexandra.'

Both young men froze. In the moment before she rose to greet Michael Swinton Alexandra noticed their fascinated

263

and apprehensive expressions with amusement, and saw Harry dart one swift glance at his friend.

Michael Swinton looked easily at both of them and said to Alexandra, 'My dear, you really are holding court.'

She introduced them all. Harry and George bowed silently, their gazes fixed at some point rigidly below Michael Swinton's chin.

'You have come in the nick of time,' Alexandra told him. 'I was being persuaded to act in some amateur theatricals.'

'Against your will?'

'Was she?' he said to Harry Burrows.

Harry licked his lips.

'Sir. We – we asked her, sir, because we thought it would be – be awfully jolly, sir, to have her with us.'

'Just a bit of fun, you see,' George said, his drawl emphasized by unease. 'Perhaps you would help to persuade her for us.'

Michael Swinton looked at Alexandra, then chose a chair and settled himself comfortably in it. He was wearing top boots and had evidently ridden over, because they were splashed with mud.

'I can't do that, I'm afraid.'

'Why not?'

Michael avoided the questioning look in Alexandra's eyes and turned to answer Harry.

'Because, Mr Burrows, she is promised to me. Miss Abbott is sitting for me, for a portrait. It has to be finished this month in order to be considered for the Academy's Summer Exhibition. As it is, it is late and the Hanging Committee have very kindly allowed me a few weeks' grace. So you see, Miss Abbott has no time. I have commandeered it all.'

George Langley said in a low voice to Alexandra, 'You said nothing of this.'

She said to her lap, 'I – I had not quite got round to it—'

George struggled to his feet.

'But you'll come and see us every so often, all the same, won't you. You can't stop, just because I'm up and about now. I'm not allowed to ride yet, you know, I'm still pretty tied to the house.'

'Of course I will come,' she said warmly.

He smiled at her in undisguised relief.

'Aunt says she hopes you will dine with us soon.'

Harry Burrows shot an aggressive look at Michael Swinton.

'So does Mother. She sent an especial message to you.'

When they had gone, Michael Swinton let a small silence fall and then he said, 'We had better make the lie a truth, I think.'

'Why – why did you do it?'

'You needed to be rescued, didn't you? And I want to paint you. It seemed obvious.'

She smiled at him. The strange, wild feeling that usually drove her down to the sea was beginning to thump in her bosom.

'I certainly didn't want to take part in the play and I am not at all at ease with those – those people. But – to be painted! Oh!' she said in despair, 'I'm blushing, I can feel it. I suppose it's the thought of being painted, of you wanting to, of you looking at me—'

'I shall,' he said. 'Very intently. Beginning tomorrow.'

'Tomorrow!'

'In the morning. The light is best then. Don't look so horrified. Bring a maid if you want a chaperone.'

'Yes – no – I – the village, you see, the village—'

'Will talk. Of course it will. Do you really mind?'

She thought a moment.

'No,' she admitted and then added shyly, 'I – I should like to be painted.'

He looked at her keenly and then stood up.

'Good. I must go now. Aren't you going to ask me what you should wear?'

'Should I?'

He smiled. 'Most women do. In fact, I think all the women I ever painted did. It was the first question usually.'

She stood up too.

'Well, then?'

'Wear Mrs McPhee,' he said, 'and something cream under it, nothing formal. Don't do your hair too elaborately. If you do, I shall simply stand you out in the wind for a while.'

He moved towards the door and put his hand on the handle.

'Give my regards to your aunt. Tell her I was sorry not to see her. And I will see you tomorrow.'

When he had gone, she stood for a long time in front of the looking-glass that hung over the fire, her hands pressed to her cheeks, her face quite alive with excitement. The excitement seemed to spread all down her, in fiery threads, right down to her fingers and toes. Only later, much later, when Penman knocked and asked if she would like tea, did it strike her that she had no idea why Michael Swinton had really called.

It did not occur to her, going upstairs in happy anticipation, that Aunt Emily would do anything other than smile upon the plan. It seemed, after all, a perfectly proper arrangement and one that was, in a way, almost professional.

But Aunt Emily was shocked.

'My dear child, there is no question of it. You cannot possibly go. He may be – indeed is, as I am sure you have gathered – a gentleman, but his being a painter makes him a little – unconventional, shall we say, and it would be entirely improper for you to go to Trelorne alone—'

'But I shan't! I shall have Lyddy! And I have had tea there and no harm came to me!'

'That was an accident,' Aunt Emily said firmly, 'after you had put yourself considerably in the wrong by trespassing.'

Alexandra fell on her knees by the bed.

'Aunt Emily, please, oh please! I am simply going to sit in his studio for perhaps three hours for the mornings of the next few weeks and Murphy shall take me and bring me back and Lyddy shall sit close by me and I will take Janet too if you would allow me—'

Aunt Emily said suddenly, 'How – how did he say he wished to paint you?'

'Oh, so comfortably Aunt Emily! You can have no objection to that. He wants me to look very ordinary, very much as I did the day I trespassed. I am to go in that old brown coat and skirt I brought from Bewick—'

If Aunt Emily had looked shocked before her eyes now dilated in horror.

'You cannot be serious! That dreadful, badly cut shabby old coat and skirt! I am dumbfounded you should even think of such a thing with that lovely new cream gown hanging in your wardrobe and I should have been so happy to lend you my pearls. Have you listened to nothing I have said all these weeks? Have you profited by no example?'

Alexandra cried, 'Oh Aunt Emily—' but her great-aunt lay back on her pillows with finality, holding up a hand and closing her eyes.

'Go away, Alexandra. At once. The whole affair is out of the question. You have exhausted me. Go away and send Janet to me at once.'

Alone in her room, banging the knob of the blind cord against the glass in the window in frustration, Alexandra glared out into the darkening world and raged. She did not rage so much against Aunt Emily but more at herself for being so naive as to agree to and promote a plan that any less raw and unworldly creature than herself would have seen was hardly possible. She had a violent impulse to summon Murphy and go at once to Trelorne and find Michael Swinton, and so strong was this inclination and the need to explain to him that she was personally so very

267

disappointed that she had rung the bell and summoned Lyddy before she realized that such an action was only a perfect sequel in childish impetuosity to her former one of agreeing to be painted in the first place.

'I – I want – paper and a pen, Lyddy.'

'But they'm here, Miss Alexandra. Right in your bureau, where they always are.'

There seemed no point in justifying her mistake still further, so she merely sat down in silence and allowed Lyddy to place paper and ink and a pen before her, just as if she had summoned her all the way upstairs for that very purpose.

She meant, after ten minutes' solemn consideration, to write that she was extremely sorry, and entirely responsible for the change of plan, but she could not now sit for him. She intended to plead her own nervousness and her desire not to be destined for public exhibition and planned to finish by thanking him for the compliment of his request and wishing him well in finding a more practised model.

'Dear Mr Swinton,' she wrote,

'I am bitterly disappointed, for Aunt Emily says that it would not be at all proper for me to come to Trelorne and that I was very wrong to let you think that I might. She also feels it would be highly unsuitable not to be painted in full evening dress. I can think of no way round this dilemma except that you come in person and explain to her that it is an entirely business-like arrangement.

Yours Sincerely,
Alexandra Abbott'

When she had finished, she did not even read it through, but thrust it into an envelope, rang furiously for Lyddy and demanded that the letter be taken at once to Trelorne. Then she sat at her bureau and put her hands to her flaming cheeks and tried to think about the hens, the sea, the possibility of buying a pig, something, anything, rather than the likelihood of not being painted by Michael Swinton.

In the morning, Punch brought a letter from Trelorne, whose contents Aunt Emily did not reveal, but Alexandra found her in the drawing-room after luncheon.

'But Aunt Emily! it is Thursday, not Wednesday! There is no need to leave your room—'

'I am expecting a visitor, Alexandra. I think I should like you to call on Mrs Chamberlin for me. This is usually the time of year she asks for my subscription to the Church of England Orphans and I wonder if she has forgotten me. She must be at least a week late.'

Dawdling down to the village on this spurious errand, Alexandra was consumed with impatient curiosity. When she arrived at the Rectory she found that Mrs Chamberlin was out, the Rectory children had been taken for a walk by the nursemaid, the Rector had asked not to be disturbed for he had both a parish letter and acute indigestion to tackle that afternoon. Alexandra wrote her message on one of her aunt's cards and retreated to the lane. She walked slowly back to Bishopstow House, her eyes on the verge, her thoughts entirely preoccupied, so that when she found Michael Swinton on horseback in the gateway, motionless and watching her, she gave a genuine start of surprise.

'Oh Mr Swinton! I am so glad to see you! I thought – I mean, I supposed it was you Aunt Emily was waiting for, but she sent me out, she thinks I have been very silly over the whole affair—'

'You have,' he said smiling, 'but impulsiveness has great charm and often great effect.'

She put her hand on his horse's neck.

'Oh, did she, I mean, now you have spoken to her, will she let me come?'

He leaned down so that she saw his whole face was alight with a slightly satirical amusement.

'Of course you will come. I explained to her all about the Academy and my standing as a painter and the patience of the Hanging Committee and the uniqueness of you as a model. She agreed at once.' He straightened up. 'I shall expect you in the morning.'

'Mr Swinton, oh, I am so pleased, I mean to say, I—'

He touched his whip to his hat brim.

'I expect you at ten. Don't be late, Miss Abbott.'

The following morning, accompanied at Aunt Emily's command by a trembling Lyddy who was sure she was going to the very mouth of Hades, Alexandra was driven out to Trelorne, dressed very much as she had been when she trespassed along the shore. The house looked grim and dreary in the faint damp rain and Lyddy shivered beside her.

Punch was waiting, small and silent, in his leather apron.

He took them through the cavernous littered kitchen, where an old woman in a grey shawl was mixing something in a basin on the table, and down the dark passage to the studio. He paused there, waited a moment, his ear pressed to the panels, and then knocked.

'Come!'

Punch opened the door and stood aside to let them pass, Lyddy pressing as close to Alexandra as she dared.

At the far end of the studio, near the easel, on a sort of crude platform, an arrangement had been made of what appeared to be boxes under grey blankets. Michael Swinton jerked his head towards them.

'Rocks,' he said briefly.

He was wearing riding boots again and breeches, and over whatever jacket he had he wore a full calico garment like a surplice, liberally smeared with paint.

'Right,' he said. 'Jacket off, hat off, boots and stockings off—'

270

Alexandra and Lyddy gasped in unison.

'Oh – but Mr Swinton, I can't – I – really I cannot—'

He did not look at her but said calmly, 'Why not? It seems to me a perfectly simple procedure. And I see you even have a minion who will help you with the difficult task of unlacing your boots.'

Alexandra's cheeks were scarlet.

'But – but I cannot have – have – bare feet in front of – of you. I can't do it. I mustn't.'

He looked up briefly from his palette, but he did not smile.

'Don't be miss-ish, Miss Abbott. If you were a professional model I should probably require you to take every stitch of clothing off, let alone your shoes and stockings, and, if you will remember, it is on the grounds of the business-like aspect of this arrangement that I have your aunt's sanction to paint you. If you wish to be regarded as a proper model, you must behave like one. Take off your boots this moment, before I lose my temper, and sit down over there. Those are rocks and you are sitting on them gazing out to sea. You are very fortunate that I don't make you actually sit in the real sea. Come on, hurry up.'

In silence, Alexandra and Lyddy turned away and fumbled together in a dark corner. After a while Alexandra turned round and walked with bare feet, her chin high, across the studio and mounted the dais.

'How shall I sit?'

He smiled at last.

'That's more like it. What pretty feet you have. I should expect you to, of course. Now sit, quite naturally, just as you would, alone on a beach in order to dream and gaze at the sea.' He paused and then said quietly, 'Just as you were when I first saw you.'

She chose a rock facing the window, a low rock, and sat down on it, circling her bent knees with her arms and resting her chin on her knees. She heard his step on the

271

floor, and then his hands warm on her own, moving them just a little, and then on her feet, pulling them further from under the brown wool folds of her skirt.

Then he stepped back and said, 'Perfect.' After a long while in which she heard nothing but the rasp of charcoal on canvas and the faint distant booming of the sea, he said, 'Talk if you want to. I may not answer and if I am doing your mouth I shall tell you so.'

'I don't want to talk,' she replied.

'Oh Alexandra!' he said, and his voice was full of laughter.

A little later, he said, 'You really have lovely hands and feet. The same fine boniness that your cheeks have.'

She wanted him to go on, but he didn't, so she simply sat and dreamed and let her mind go floating out into the grey April morning towards the gulls and the sky and the sea. When he said, 'Get up and stretch,' she was quite startled, and when she struggled to her feet, surprised to find herself so stiff.

'One more hour,' he said. 'That's enough for you. And for me. Are you cold?'

'No,' she said. 'May I look?'

'No.'

'Not ever?'

'When it's finished. Even if it's a betrayal.'

'A betrayal?'

'Yes,' he said, 'a betrayal. Now sit down again.'

She sat, simply and naturally as she had done before.

'Good,' he said. 'Excellent. I'm doing your clothes now, your sleeves and skirts. Tell me about the hens.'

'No,' she said, 'I don't want to talk. I'm thinking. At least,' she added truthfully, 'I almost am.'

He muttered something under his breath and she wanted to ask him to repeat it, but couldn't somehow, so silence fell again and lapped peacefully round them so that time seemed quite to vanish. When at last he laid down his brush and palette and came across to help her up, she found that she resented his breaking the mood.

'Tomorrow?' she asked.

'Tomorrow and tomorrow and tomorrow. It's the way I work best, never stopping. It's the way I get the best results.'

She looked at the back of the easel.

'Will – will it be good?'

'Yes,' he said. 'It will.'

CHAPTER TEN

In the first week of May, a golden week full of sunshine and birdsong and bright new leaves, the painting was finished. A fortnight later, when it was dry and varnished, Alexandra was allowed to see it. She was so overcome by what she saw that she burst into tears. Michael Swinton watched her in silence as he had watched her before, only proffering as he had done once before a handkerchief which he had plainly also used as a paint rag.

She saw it was herself, there on the canvas; in fact it was so much herself that she could not believe that she could be both people, one here on the studio floor and one sitting there clasping her knees, her eyes lost in faraway visions, her white feet on wet black rocks against which little waves were breaking in plumes of spray. Her skin looked luminous, her hair was the colour of the pale amber beads Aunt Emily always wore because she said they helped her rheumatism.

'I said it once before,' Michael Swinton said, watching her, 'and I will continue to say it. Miss Abbott, how very satisfactory you are.'

She said sniffing, inhaling the oily smell of the paint from his handkerchief, 'Do I look like that? I mean, I know I do but really – really like that?'

'I only painted what I saw,' he answered and she had again that sudden, stupid stab of fear and pushed

273

his handkerchief at him saying that she must go, she was late.

He said only, 'Punch and I will take it to Bodmin on Friday. I don't have much doubt that they will hang it. Do you like the notion of being in the Royal Academy?'

'Is – is that where I will be?'

'Yes. Will you come up to London with me and see yourself?'

'No – no,' she replied hurriedly. 'That is – I should love to, but Aunt Emily, I can't leave her. And she has agreed to a cow at last, next week, I must—'

He cut in. 'Of course,' he said, 'but I shall go all the same. I shall escort the painting. I've not been to London in twelve years.'

On the way home, she found that she wanted to cry again and could not think of a possible reason why she should. There was a letter from George Langley, from Cambridge, waiting for her at Bishopstow but somehow it did not interest her, she could hardly be bothered to open it.

The next few months saw subtle but definite changes at Bishopstow. Aunt Emily was not exactly ill, at least she had no definable complaint, but she rested a good deal, more and more, and every day seemed happier to let Alexandra take over the household decisions. At first, it was simply the menus, then her sphere of influence extended to household ordering, the overseeing of repairs, the servants, the account books.

The cow came, a soft-eyed Jersey cow the colour of her own rich cream, and a pig, and outhouses were scrubbed out and whitewashed ready for use as a dairy and cheese-room. The old cheese presses which had lain dusty in the stable loft were brought down with difficulty on account of their immense weight and set up on the flagged floor. Alexandra bought a book on cheese-making and ignored Dora's protests that she had helped make cheese at her mother's knee and knew all there was to know about the matter already.

She took a great interest in the kitchen garden too, and calculated with pleasure how many greengages and damsons they would have, how many cherries and pears and strawberries. She spent a good deal of time in the kitchen and bullied Dora into showing her how to make bread and pastry; she would take cookery books up to her room and study the methods of jam making and preserving fruit and vegetables. The little laundry maid who came in daily from the village was dismayed to find Miss Alexandra in the laundry room asking what clear starch was and demanding to be shown how to use a goffering iron.

The days were full now, very full. She rose early and spent the morning with Aunt Emily or visiting the kitchen and garden and orchard and doing the household accounts and the correspondence she had taken over from her aunt. In the afternoons she paid the calls she could not escape from, visited the Rectory regularly, or sat at home on Wednesdays devising domestic plans for the future in between visitors. She sat with Aunt Emily again in the early evenings and read to her, staying with her most nights until she had slipped into sleep when she would tiptoe back to her own room and write home to Bewick or to George Langley in Cambridge.

It was only sometimes, in the warm dusks, that she felt this life was not perfect, not as full to her as it seemed. She would stand at her window in the summer twilights and feel the tug inside her as if something were straining to get out, urging her on with the kind of excitement she longed for and shrank from all at once. But that only happened sometimes and when it did she would take out her account book and force herself to concentrate on its columns till the dangerous exhilaration had gone.

Aunt Emily said, 'Look, my dear.'

She was reading *The Times* with the aid of a magnifying

glass. She hardly ever read it herself now, preferring Alexandra to read it to her, but some mornings, when she felt stronger, she would be propped up on extra pillows and given the paper and her glass.

Alexandra, sorting through the enormous bundle of charitable appeals that Aunt Emily kept bound up with blue tape, asked absently, 'What is it? Something interesting?'

'Yes, my dear. Very interesting. Read it to me, do.'

Alexandra put the bundle of papers on the floor.

'Where, Aunt Emily? Which bit?'

There was no need to ask. The centre headline said 'The Royal Academy's Summer Exhibition,' and below that, the smaller title, 'A Triumphant Re-entry into the World of Art.'

Alexandra sat down abruptly in her chair.

'There was a time,' she read, 'when the acclaim of both the public and his fellow artists was a common thing for Mr Michael Swinton. For the last decade, such accolades have been heard more rarely since Mr Swinton chose a hermit's life in the West Country and no paintings of his have come before the Selection Committee at the Royal Academy since he left London. This year, the phoenix has risen from its ashes, a phoenix in brighter plumage than he has ever worn before. However much we may lament Mr Swinton's recent seclusion, we are forced to conclude that it has done him nothing but good.

'*A. in Reverie* is by far the best painting to come from Mr Swinton's brush. Who "A" is, remains a mystery, but she is a creature of clearly inspirational beauty who has been captured with a fluidity of drawing and subtlety of palette that would be envied by the greatest masters of the French Impressionist School.

'Mr Swinton is reticent about everything to do with the painting except to express his relief and delight at the perfect union of conception and execution. He will find it difficult to escape once more to the fastnesses of Cornwall without a horde of people eager to commission him clinging to his coat tails. Were he to refuse them, as he has done for so long, he would do himself, as well as the public, a grave disservice.'

'There, my dear,' Aunt Emily said and glanced at the little drawing by her bed. 'I knew it.'

Alexandra sat and stared at the paper in silence.

'Are you not delighted, my dear? Is that not immensely exciting? What a triumph!'

Alexandra replied slowly, 'I – I should like Mr Swinton to be admired once more, admired as he deserves. That is, if he would like it too.'

'Perhaps he won't come back to Trelorne,' Aunt Emily said, 'if he gets back his taste for painting duchesses and celebrated actresses. They will be clamouring for him now, my dear, simply clamouring.'

Alexandra felt a sharp cold stone at the pit of her stomach. She said in a small voice, 'Perhaps they will.'

The next day brought her two letters, one from Cambridge, one from London. George had seen the notice in *The Times*, and he was telling everyone he knew who 'A' was, he wrote, because he didn't see why she shouldn't have some of the credit and also because he was awfully proud to know her. He would be back in the first week of July and at home all month until they went to Scotland for the opening of the grouse shooting season on the twelfth. He hoped she would spare some time for him and he promised he would not ask her to act in anything. Piers sent his love and was all for going up to London that minute to see the painting. They would go in a day or two, he thought, and then he could collect his new guns from Holland and Holland on the same trip.

The second letter was from Michael Swinton. It bore no address at the top and simply said.

'My dear Alexandra,

You see, I told you it was good, but you knew it too, I think. You look very lost, hung up there among Royalty and aldermen, and it makes me homesick to look at you, so I don't, too often. I am besieged with commissions, literally besieged. I might even accept some of them.

My regards to your aunt. Punch tells me Bishopstow House is become quite a smallholding.

Yours ever,
M.S.'

For some reason, this letter so unnerved her that she thought she must rush down to the sea at once, and run the thudding in her head quite out of it. But no, she told herself, there is no reason for that, and you have not seen Aunt Emily yet this morning. Her room is where you should be, not rampaging on the sands like a hoyden. So she put the letters in her desk with resolution and went up the stairs to see her aunt.

Towards the end of June, when sitting by Aunt Emily's bed and explaining to her that they grew far too many potatoes for their needs and it would be sensible to grow turnips and swedes instead which would serve as winter food for the animals, Aunt Emily suddenly put out a hand and said.

'Don't my dear. Don't bother. I don't mind what you do. You have taken so many burdens from me, you are so level-headed and sensible. Don't feel you have to tell me.'

Alexandra took the small soft hand in hers and thought that it seemed smaller than ever, frailer, more insubstantial.

'I didn't mean to trouble you, dear Aunt Emily. Truly I didn't. I thought you liked to know.'

'I did, my dear, I did. But I don't seem to now. I seem very tired, all the time. Peacefully tired, you know, as if I were floating. So don't trouble to tell me. Just do as you wish, do everything just as you wish—'

The house grew very quiet after that. Anxious that nothing should disturb her aunt, Alexandra had the hens moved to a small paddock the far side of the stables so that their greedy shouting for breakfast could not be heard in the house. On a visit to Mrs Chamberlin she explained that she did not like to leave her aunt and would from then on come only once a week, and she put it about that for the moment, neither she nor her aunt would be at home on Wednesday afternoons. Eventually, to the amazement of Murphy and the stable lad, she informed them that the livestock were all in their care until further notice and that the carriage horses could be put out to grass. If she needed to go anywhere she would walk.

The days revolved around Aunt Emily, days of gentle routine in her room where the white blinds were lowered most of the day against the late June sunlight. Such meals as she ate were brought to her on trays by Janet, meals that Alexandra and Dora would plan with minutest care in the kitchen. Alexandra talked to her when she wanted it, read to her when she wished, and while she slept in the daytime, sat and did the household correspondence, knowing Aunt Emily liked her to be there when she woke.

'I am just a little ship,' Aunt Emily said, 'drifting farther and farther out to sea.' She turned her head to smile at Alexandra. 'Richard is there, you know, just beyond the horizon. And Charlotte, of course, and Alexander. They are all waiting for me. Charlotte and Alexander have been waiting for years. So has Mamma—'

Alexandra, Lyddy and Janet took it in turns to sit up at night with her. She grew a little confused as to which was day and which was night, and increasingly wanted Alexandra there, calling for her in her faint cracked voice, if she woke and found her customary chair empty. She never noticed if Alexandra was fully dressed or had stumbled straight from sleep in her night clothes but would welcome her always with the sweetest of smiles and a gentle reproof for leaving her alone.

The rhythm of her life grew slower and slower, fewer

meals, longer sleeps, the periods of wakefulness hazy and dream-like. She called Alexandra 'Charlotte' and spoke of far off things, but of Richard even more often, usually as if he were in the room with her. The doctor, on his now daily visit, said simply to Alexandra, 'A matter of time, my dear, a matter of time.'

On the first day of July, just before dawn, Alexandra was woken by a weeping Janet, a Janet whose normal self-control and impassiveness had broken down utterly. Alexandra was out of bed and along the landing, hair flying, in seconds. Even those seconds took too long. As she sank by the bed, pressing her ear to Aunt Emily's heart beneath its layers of lace, Aunt Emily's little boat had already slipped quietly over the horizon.

CHAPTER ELEVEN

'And so Miss Abbott,' Mr Renfrew said, taking off his spectacles and folding them neatly, 'that is the sum of things.'

Alexandra sat and gazed at him. She had never met him before although, as he was her aunt's lawyer, she had written several letters to him in his offices in Bodmin. After Aunt Emily's death, he had informed her that he wished to speak to her and had proposed that he journey to Bishopstow for the purpose. He had come before luncheon, eaten everything put before him with great dedication, looked about him hopefully for the cigar the household did not possess, and then explained abruptly without any preliminaries to Alexandra that she was her aunt's sole heir.

'House, outbuildings, 50 acres and £30,000.'

He had quite stunned Alexandra. She could say nothing.

'It was always left to you, you know. Colonel and

Mrs Talbot drew up their wills after you were born. I remember them going to your christening, up in the north somewhere—'

'Scotland,' Alexandra said faintly.

'Ah. That's it. Scotland. They went up to Scotland for your christening, 'eighty-three, it must have been no 'eighty-four, and when they came down south again, they came to my office and the wills were drawn up.'

He looked round the drawing-room, at the pictures and looking-glasses and ornaments shrouded in black, at Alexandra herself in the first mourning dress she had ever had.

'Stay here, will you, Miss Abbott? Comfortable house.'

'I – I hardly know—'

'£30,000 will bring in a very tidy income, you know. Your aunt never wanted for anything.'

'I wish I'd come years ago!' Alexandra said passionately. 'Why didn't she send for me years ago? I could have looked after her and been with her so much longer then, not just a few months, not just at the end!'

'I imagine,' Mr Renfrew said unexpectedly, 'that it was only at the end she felt the need.' He got up from his chair and put his spectacles into a red leather case which he then returned to his pocket. 'Well, Miss Abbott, you know where I am if you need me. If you decide to sell up, you know, or want to know where the money's been put. Don't hesitate. That's what I'm there for. I'll wish you good day now.'

When she heard the front door shut behind him and Penman's footsteps retreating, she rose from her chair and began to walk slowly about the room, touching the sofas and lamps and tables. Mine, she thought in wonder, all mine. And there, out of the window, all the way to the sea, all mine, the garden, the fields, the trees. And the dining-room and the bedrooms and the kitchens and all the pantries and the pictures and silver and glass and carpets. All mine. And the drive and the carriage and all the animals and the fruit and the gardens and every brick in every wall and every slate on every roof, all mine, every single tiny plant in my land, mine, mine. She sat down in a chair by a table and as she had done once in Michael Swinton's kitchen, put her head down on her folded arms and burst into tears of passionate gratitude.

Callers, suitably and sombrely attired, came thick and fast. The Rector and Mrs Chamberlin, Lady Pemberley, Mrs Burrows and Harry, a tribe of Langleys, George Langley on his own several times, and a host of others Alexandra had never seen, but to whom Aunt Emily had been a fixture for more than 50 years. They stayed only minutes, most of them, pressing her hand and uttering the easy ritual phrases of sympathy and then departing, leaving their cards in the hall until the salver seemed endlessly overflowing. 'I must have my own,' Alexandra said to Penman, gazing absently at the silver tray he brought her, 'mustn't I? I must have my own cards.'

She sat in the drawing-room and received all the callers, genuinely grateful for any tribute to Aunt Emily although there seemed to be, among all the people who came so punctiliously, hardly anyone who had known her really well. Mrs Langley came twice, George more often than that. Even if he had not known Aunt Emily himself at all well, he seemed to have an inkling of Alexandra's feelings and he was, among all those condoling faces, the only one she felt comfortable with.

'This is only the beginning, you know,' he said one day as she walked with him round the garden. 'They'll beat a path to your door now. Aunt May is only the front runner. But then, she usually is.'

'What do you mean?'

'Alexandra, you are a woman of property now. You have become someone of consequence. They'll court you now.'

'They didn't before.'

'No,' he said.

She snorted. 'Then they won't make much headway now.'

He grinned at her, then swished at a shrub with his cane and asked, with studied casualness, 'And will you stay here at Bishopstow? Or will you sell up?'

She said decidedly, 'I shall stay. My parents are coming to visit me—'

'Your parents! I – I somehow thought you hadn't any, like me, you know.'

Alexandra smiled.

'Oh yes,' she said, 'I have parents.'

She had intended, and was obviously successful, that George Langley should think she had asked her parents to come. She had not. They had insisted. She had written to them at once after Mr Renfrew's visit, encompassing them in the great outpouring of gratitude that had flooded her, and received from her father in reply a letter that had shocked her and alarmed her.

'Of course we rejoice with you, we rejoice with you to the full. But I am sure your own good sense will tell you that it is hardly practical nor proper for a girl as young as you still are to run a house alone without a companion of any sort. We shall come south as soon as possible and review the situation and you must prepare your mind for returning with us until some suitable person can be found to share Bishopstow with you.'

Alexandra had gone for a long walk before replying to this letter. Indeed, she walked so far and so long that she was too tired to write anything at all upon her return and did not in fact send a reply until the following day. She wrote to her father alone. Nothing, she said, would induce her to leave Bishopstow, she loved it with her whole heart, it had become her home. She was sure the neighbourhood would initially be outraged at her living alone, despite the presence of more servants than she knew what to do with, but she was proof against their opinion and she would only be a nine days' wonder in any case. He and her mother were more than welcome, she would delight in the chance to show them the treasure that was hers, but leave it she would not. Not even for a few weeks. They might come and see how competent she was to run it if they chose, but short of abducting her, they could do no more than advise.

Silence had fallen for almost three weeks and then her father had written again, with the utmost brevity, to say he would review the situation when he saw it and that they could get away after the harvest.

'They will come in September,' Alexandra said now to George. 'My first September at Bishopstow.'

'It's a long time away,' he said doubtfully. 'Won't you be bored, all that time? Just here, I mean. I would put off going to Scotland—'

She said, 'I wouldn't hear of it. Bored? I couldn't be bored here if I tried.' She paused and looked up at the small gentle fields for the placid yellow outline of the Jersey cow. 'I shall get more cows, I think. And when my father is here, he can advise me about sheep. Look at all that wasted space.'

'What about a horse?' George said. 'A nice little mare for your own use. I could help you there.'

'I want to learn to drive, really,' Alexandra said. 'I don't much care for Aunt Emily's stately old carriage. I'd like a trap or a gig, something light I could drive myself. I don't know why I never drove at home. My father taught me to shoot, I can't imagine why he didn't teach me to drive.' She clutched George's arm in sudden excitement. 'Do you realize, I can buy myself a gun now, and keep rabbits out of my own lettuces?'

George said eagerly, 'I'll find you a nice little gig. I know just the fellow. And something brisk to take you bowling about the place. Sure you don't want a motor car?'

She stopped and looked at him delightedly. It was like a lovely game.

'Perhaps I do!' she said.

Indoors, the afternoon post was waiting for her. So far,

she had answered everything scrupulously as it came, but the volume threatened to defeat her. She riffled quickly through the pile and saw nothing of interest but an envelope addressed to her in a bold black hand that looked dimly familiar. She tore open the envelope, ignoring the paper knife Penman laid ready for her each day.

Inside was a single sheet of paper, thick white drawing-paper with roughly-cut edges. It was undated and had no address.

'My dear Alexandra—
  I meant to write at once. You have been much in my thoughts. And still are. She was a true friend to lose.

                                        Ever,
                                        M.S.'

Alexandra plunged into the wastepaper basket to retrieve the torn envelope. It was postmarked Nottingham. What was he doing in Nottingham? Why didn't he write more, why didn't he say where he was? Didn't he realize how much she wanted to tell him about Aunt Emily's magical generosity and her own longing to have done more for her while she lived—? She stopped herself resolutely. He was a famous painter once more now, not simply a local eccentric to encounter on the beach. She held the letter over the basket, ready to consign it to being thrown away, and then at the last minute snatched it back and put in in her desk.

As if in answer to her thoughts, *The Times* helped her next morning. Mr Michael Swinton, it said, had accepted a commission in Nottinghamshire and would be at B—— Castle some weeks. *A. in Reverie* was undoubtedly the painting of the season, and the portrait he had recently finished of Mrs C——, the celebrated actress, was acclaimed – and not only by the sitter – as the best likeness of her striking looks ever achieved. Needless to say, Mr Swinton was much in demand. It was thought he would take a studio for the London season. It was rumoured that he had even been asked to Sandringham with his sketchbook, some time this coming autumn.

Alexandra read the paragraphs through carefully several times, then cut them out and laid them in her desk with his two letters. Then she went out into the garden to walk around for a while and before she was aware of her own movements, found herself moving briskly, almost running, up the green slope to the sea.

She insisted on driving with Murphy to Bodmin to meet her parents. Murphy wanted her to stay by the first fire of the autumn and be waiting there with the tea table, as Aunt Emily had always done; but he knew, after just over two months of Alexandra's rule, that it was pointless even to look his disapproval. She would not mind it, nor would she take any heed of it. Dora had told him that Miss Alexandra was but a month short of her twenty-second birthday and he had gone out of the kitchen, scratching his head in disbelief. She seemed so authoritative already, so decided, a world away from the desperately anxious girl he had taken to pay her first calls that chill afternoon of February.

Alexandra was extremely excited, over-excited in Janet's opinion. She had spent the previous day helping Janet to prepare Aunt Emily's room for her mother. Janet had at first demurred at the room ever being used again, let alone so soon after Aunt Emily's death.

'Do you really think,' Alexandra had said earnestly, a pile of linen sheets in her arms, 'do you truthfully think for one moment that Aunt Emily would wish this room to be kept like – like a museum? I wouldn't put just anybody in it, but my mother, Aunt Emily's niece, her only surviving direct relation except for me—'

Janet had given way. The medicine bottles were cleared away, the windows flung open, the multitude of little cushions and shawls packed carefully into an old ball dress trunk with a high-domed lid and E. B. painted on it, in white. And now, aired and emptied of its clutter, with fresh sheets on the bed and a bowl of roses on the table by the window, the room awaited Iskandara. Beyond it, the small, bare, white-washed room that Emily's Richard, whom Alexandra had never known but whose benevolence still lay about Bishopstow like an embrace, had used as a dressing-room, had been made ready for her father. James would like it there, he would feel comfortable in its masculine simplicity. Alexandra had gone from one room to the other that morning smoothing pillows and straightening covers and, as a last gesture, putting Aunt Emily's little morocco bound journal beside her mother's bed.

As the train drew into Bodmin, Alexandra found herself clasping her own hands so tightly she could feel the seams of her gloves grinding into her flesh and wished, passionately for the visit to be a success, for them to like her house, approve of what she had done – and above all, to leave her alone to do it. The train slid by, crammed with strange faces. 'They have missed it, they aren't on it, they decided not to come—' At the far end of the train a door swung open and a man climbed down and shouted for a porter.

'Father!' Alexandra screamed, one hand on her hat and one at her skirts as she began to run along the platform. 'Father! Father!'

He had turned back to help someone else out of the train, but at the sound of her calling, he swung round and stood waiting, his arms outstretched and his face, above that dear and familiar gingery beard, creased with the broadest smile.

'Father!' she said, and fell into his arms.

'It's grand to see you, my lass, grand. And looking quite the—'

'Alexandra!'

Alexandra lifted her face from her father's shoulder. Iskandara was in the doorway of the train, her stick

287

in her hand and her plaid shawl over a dark, braided travelling dress.

'Come here,' she said. Her voice was queer and hoarse.

Alexandra went obediently to stand and look up at her.

'Child, you are so utterly, completely changed. I can hardly believe you—' she broke off and looked at James. 'Do we not have a lovely daughter?'

They stayed a fortnight. The house and garden bloomed in early autumn sunshine, soft golden days full of butterflies on the michaelmas daisy clumps, days with misty mornings and deep blue dusks. Alexandra took her father over every inch of her domain and he nodded at her enthusiasm, but if he was at all impressed by what she did, what she planned, he gave no sign.

She told him she wanted to buy more cows. He leant on the wall and surveyed the little Jersey chewing thoughtfully in her field.

'You get her to calf,' he said. 'If you want to learn all about it, you must breed your own. There's no other way.'

'I had rather do that,' she said. 'I simply did not think of it.'

'You'll be needing another hand,' he said, 'if you're to have more stock.'

'Yes,' she said, listening hard.

'Don't overgraze these acres. You've not the space we have at Bewick. Don't walk before you can run.'

'No,' she said, 'I won't.'

He took his pipe out and lit it slowly, squinting at her through the puffs of blue smoke.

'Abbotts make good farmers,' he said. 'We're not afraid of work. And some Abbotts, my lass, get strokes of good fortune. I'm one. You're another. We'll not forget to be thankful.'

She said, 'Oh Father, if only you knew how thankful I am. And most of all, that you'll let me stay. I know you

288

will, because you never would talk about the future like this otherwise, you wouldn't tell me what I need. And you have never mentioned going back to Bewick—'

'I'm still of the opinion you should have a companion. It's not right for you to be here alone.'

'I'll find someone,' she promised, 'really I will. Give me a little time. I'll ask people round here, someone will have an idea, Mrs Chamberlin perhaps. I will find someone, truly I—' She stopped and then said diffidently, 'And – and mother?'

'I'll speak to her. We have talked it over, you know. I think she'll abide by what I tell her.'

He put out a hand with uncharacteristic demonstrativeness and touched her cheek.

'You just had to find the right path, didn't you, my lass. And once that was done, you've stepped out bravely. Never be afraid to step out, if it harms no other and gets you your heart's desire. Now then,' he swung round and contemplated the pig styes behind them. 'You'll be needing more space in there when she has her litter, or she'll lie on them and crush the lot.'

Between Iskandara and Alexandra that fortnight, there reigned an uneasy truce. It could not be said that a peace had been finally made because old habits in Alexandra would not die a final death and made her still reserved, a little wary. But on the first morning of the second week Iskandara came into the drawing-room, where Alexandra chose to write her letters instead of using the boudoir upstairs as Janet wished her to do, and silently put Aunt Emily's journal down in front of her daughter.

Alexandra, her eyes on the stock prices of the farming page in the local paper said, 'I suppose you have read it?'

'Of course.'

She could feel her mother's presence behind her but she refused to turn round or even to raise her head.

'So you see,' she said, 'that you misled me. All the time

289

I was a child. She wasn't so remote, so awe-inspiring. In a way, she was greater than you let me know because she was approachable too.'

A small silence fell.

'No,' Iskandara said after it, and her voice had all the suppressed emotion in it that Alexandra had dreaded all her life. 'No. You are no nearer her. That – that trivial account, those little domestic doings, they simply demean her, belittle her. Your aunt had not the soul to discern the matchless spirit that was my mother's.'

Alexandra sprang up.

'Keep her to yourself, then! Or rather, keep the image you have! Aunt Emily may have been spoiled but she was irresistibly spoilable because she was so generous, so imaginative, she did not try to destroy people's pictures of themselves as you do, but helped them to build them up! I thought when I first came here that I hated what she was trying to do to me and then I came to see that the clothes, the manners, the society, all those things were part of a process, a process to give me enough confidence to do what I liked, not to live in eternal dread of insignificance and error. I am quite sure she was as sensitively generous to her sister as she was to me. I expect Charlotte owed her quite as much as I do and loved her for her undemanding support and affection as I did. You won't, in my house, say one word against Aunt Emily, nor will we ever mention your mother again since she and my grandmother are now, I see, quite different people, torn apart by your distorted view.' She stopped for a breath and took a step nearer her mother. 'You don't see what *is*, you only see what you want to see. I now begin to see what I am, not clearly yet, but more clearly each day. If I were still at Bewick, I should still have my vision of myself quite obliterated by your violent view of how I should be, but I am free now and you cannot put the chains back on, it is too late, I am *growing up*.'

Iskandara had felt behind her for a chair back and now stood gripping it, her free hand clenched about the head of her stick. She was chalk white, as she always was at emotional moments, but her eyes were blazing. Alexandra wondered dispassionately if she would weep, and decided that if she did, she, Alexandra, would leave her to do it. But she did not weep, only said in a low, harsh voice, 'Then you won't come back? You won't come back to Bewick?'

'No,' Alexandra said. 'I won't.'

Iskandara's head went up.

'Then you too are becoming spoiled, I see. This house, your money, the glamour of being the subject of the Academy's most popular portrait—'

Alexandra said fiercely, 'How do you know that?'

'Of course I know. I imagine everyone who reads a newspaper knows. Michael Swinton is not, of course, one of our most distinguished painters, his style is too obvious, too photographic but I imagine that to you it seemed a wonderful distinction.'

Alexandra took a long, slow breath.

'It *was* a wonderful distinction. You have, of course, not seen the actual painting—'

'We saw it in London,' Iskandara said. 'I thought it artificial and mannered.'

With an enormous effort Alexandra said, with a small smile, 'It was better to be artificial than actually to sit in the sea in March. It has done great good to his career. So many people admire his work that he can be quite careless of the few who don't. Mother, I do have work to do. There are several decisions about livestock I want to take while Father is here to advise me, and I must persuade him to come with me to Bodmin market on Thursday. Will you be comfortable here until luncheon if I go in search of him? I will send Janet to you in case there is anything you want.'

Iskandara said nothing, nor did she move from where she stood. Alexandra walked over to the door and when her hand was upon the handle, turned and said, 'I am going to obliterate this conversation in my memory of your visit. I shall only think of my pleasure in having Father and – and you here, and showing you my house. Of course, *you* must do as you please.'

Then she opened the door and passed out into the hall, closing it behind her with a quiet but determined movement, leaving Iskandara staring after her in silence.

If Iskandara said anything of the matter to James, he let it go no further. He accompanied Alexandra into Bodmin Market on the following Thursday and all the way spoke only of practical matters.

'Of course I'd like to see you with a few sheep, my lass, sheep being so close to my heart. But it's cattle you should think of in this country, perfect dairy pasture, rich it is. You could stand a spoon in the cream here, it's so thick. You must concentrate on a dairy and maybe a few tender crops we could never grow up north. Under glass maybe. Give it a thought.'

When they reached Bodmin, he was silent. He followed her swift figure among the pens and observed the number of farmers who nodded to her.

'I haven't bought here yet,' she said. 'No more than the cow and the pig. But I come whenever I can, just to watch and listen. That is why they know me.'

Only when they were returning home in the dusk did James say, 'You'll be right not to come back to Bewick. It's right you should stay here. You'll be making your way, on your own and it's better like that.'

Alexandra said hesitantly, 'You – and Mother—?'

'You know us,' he said comfortably, 'we have worked out our ways too. Your mother takes more interest in the farm now you've gone, she's out and about a good deal more. Come and see us now and then, but don't have us on your mind. Abbotts are best kings of their own castles.'

In the dim light, Alexandra stretched out her hand and felt for her father's.

She said fervently, 'Thank you.'

He said nothing, only grunted, and when he spoke again, it was on the subject of pigs.

CHAPTER TWELVE

The winter began closing in on Bishopstow almost before Alexandra realized it, so swiftly and busily did her days pass. Her parents travelled home in the first week of October leaving her with fields enriched by the presence of a few dozen sheep and enough advice to see her through the cow's first calving and the sow's first litter.

Mrs Chamberlin had sent up Jem Watkins from the village, the younger brother of two hands at Grove Farm, and Alexandra resolved that he and she should learn together. He was given a room in Murphy's lodge at the gates and was the only member of Alexandra's household who did not find her independence disconcerting. This was because, Murphy told him, he had never known a proper lady in the first place.

There had been a little unrest among the servants, particularly in the kitchen and pantries where Dora was resentful of finding Alexandra counting bottles of damsons and crocks of lard, and thrown totally into disarray by Alexandra's demanding to be allowed to stir the jam or weigh out ingredients for chutney made from the vast harvest of plums. There had been a tense week, in which Alexandra came to hear that Dora had wanted the position of head cook at Langley Dene, but she said nothing to Dora, and continued to interest herself in the kitchen just as before, and the matter went away quietly of its own accord.

October and November passed in wild untidy days and wet nights which left the windows plastered with yellow leaves. Alexandra bought herself stout countrywomen's boots in Bodmin and found a dressmaker who would copy Mrs McPhee in thick, practical tweed for her forays around her yard and fields. The cheese presses went into use for the first time in twenty years, Jem attended Bodmin market with butter and lard and eggs to sell once a fortnight, and, with George Langley's help, a little light trap came, of varnished wood, which Murphy, now beaten out of surprise and disapproval, taught Alexandra to drive with a helpful bay mare between the shafts.

On Wednesdays, as a tribute to Aunt Emily, she was at home to callers, and faithfully, once a week, she went to the Rectory and was a tiger for an hour in the jungle under the nursery table. As the nights grew darker and colder, dinner parties grew scarcer and most nights Alexandra spent by her own fire, doing her meticulous accounts, writing faithfully to her father or answering George Langley's breezy and frequent letters from Cambridge, Rose and Grace Langley were in London until Christmas, their hunters idle in the stable and Alexandra's life was both peaceful and satisfying in their absence.

Crossing the kitchen two days before Christmas on her way out to the dairy, Dora said, 'He's back at Trelorne, Miss Alexandra.'

Alexandra stopped, a copper cream pan in either hand.

'Who, Dora?'

'Mr Swinton, Miss Alexandra. I sent Peggy down to the village for yeast and old Meg was at the baker's, first time in months, and she says her master's back.'

Alexandra grasped her cream pans more firmly.

'Indeed,' she said, and went on out to the dairy.

The Christmas preparations seemed endless and unnecessary to her. She had offered Dora and Lyddy a holiday, a chance to go back to their families on their inland farms, but they had refused with dignity. *She* might not know what was proper for a lady at Christmas time, but at least they did. There was nothing that they were going to forget. The kitchen was scented with the rich enticing smell of spices and dried fruits, and Alexandra met Lyddy on the stairs carrying down the cream silk evening gown to be pressed.

'I shan't wear that dining at the Rectory!' Alexandra said.

Lyddy regarded her levelly.

'It's Christmas, Miss Alexandra,' she said firmly and went on her way.

Alexandra thought of calling her back, explaining that Mrs Chamberlin might regret her kind invitation to dine with them on Christmas Day if Alexandra were to upstage the Rectory family in such a way, but then she reflected on the goodness of Mrs Chamberlin's heart and the necessity of living up to at least some of Lyddy's expectations of her.

On Christmas morning, Murphy brought the carriage round to the front door long before Alexandra could send him a message to say she would drive herself to church. Lyddy had laid out the pearl grey coat and skirt that had been a present from Aunt Emily and a fur coat Alexandra had never seen before, heavy and glossy.

'She would wish you to wear it,' Lyddy said, with determination. 'How else are you to appear in church?'

So, befurred and kid-gloved, her hair put up elaborately around her pale grey hat, she went into the Talbot pew in Bishopstow church, her own pew now, and put Aunt Emily's prayer book on the ledge before her, and knelt to say a prayer of profound thankfulness. Behind her was the bulk of Mrs Burrows, also thickly padded with fur, flanked by the stalwart figure of Harry and the morose and drooping one of his father. Across the aisle Lady Pemberley sat alone and behind her two grandchildren wriggled in charge of a governess whose long bony face and ill-fitting clothes reminded Alexandra powerfully of Miss Gracie.

The Rectory children were being confined with difficulty in the pew beneath a brass plate Alexandra could not read without a pang, commemorating a young man who had died in the Charge of the Light Brigade, nearly sixty years ago, when he was only 22, her own age. At a respectful distance behind the Chamberlins on the one side and the Burrows on the other, the village people packed the pews, shiny with scrubbing and breathless with the tightness of best clothes.

The pulpit had been wreathed in holly, ivy had been twined up the lectern, garlands of leaves and berries hung from the gallery where 18th-century fiddlers had played before the organ came. There were candles on the altar, on the pulpit, on the deep stone ledges of the windows, and the glossy leaves gave back the candle flames' reflections. Alexandra gazed about her with delight, folding the Burrows, the Pemberleys, the Chamberlins, the village, everyone, into the warm embrace of her grateful glance, and sang and sang.

The luncheon table was laid as it had been for 50 Christmasses, with a pyramid of polished John Standish apples from Somerset in the middle, flanked by Christmas roses and trails of ivy. Dishes like silver fig leaves held nuts and dates and raisins. Penman had even filled a port decanter, Alexandra noticed, deducing quite rightly, that as she would hardly drink any, Christmas munificence would prompt her to tell him to help himself. She ate quickly, partly because she was so used to eating alone now that it seemed more a practicality than a pleasure, and partly so that the servants might have their own dinner at leisure in the kitchen. She went upstairs to change after luncheon and then took herself to the chair by her bedroom hearth, and said she should want nothing further, all afternoon.

Lyddy seemed anxious.

'Nothing at all, Miss Alexandra?'

'Nothing. Nothing whatever. Except to know by your absence that you are enjoying yourself as you should be.'

She must have slept, almost instantly, lulled by her own

contentment and comfort. She woke to find the room dim with approaching dusk, and without lights except for the glow of the fire. She rose and went to the window, still in the half-real state induced by daytime sleeping, and looked out at the darkening world where the yellow glow of a lamp in the yard showed Jem was milking. A week only, and there would be a calf—

Lyddy interrupted her reverie with the cream silk dress laid across her arms like an offering. Having accepted that she must wear it, Alexandra then set herself to dress for the pleasure of the Rectory children, throwing good taste to the winds and insisting upon hanging herself with all that glittered from the jewel box Aunt Emily had left her, its rose suede depths heaped with treasures from Richard Talbot.

Alexandra's efforts were not in vain. When her cloak was removed in the Rectory hall and she went into the drawing-room which had been lavishly and clumsily decorated by the children on precisely the principle Alexandra had used in dressing, they crowded round her with gasps of delight and wonder.

'Are you a princess?' Helen whispered, running her fingers reverently over the brilliants in Alexandra's bracelet.

'You are a beautiful lady,' Arthur announced, removing his thumb for the purpose, and added as an afterthought, 'not today a lion lady.'

The baby clawed to be free of his mother and pressed to the brooches that studded Alexandra's bosom and Robert, commonly bright-eyed with aggression, stood scarlet and speechless in a stupor of admiration and wonder.

Mrs Chamberlin was entranced.

'My dear, you have the best heart! What a pleasure for them! There, my darlings, is not Miss Abbott a finer sight by far than that tawdry tinsel fairy you wanted for our tree? You see, my dear, we had a little difficulty over which should adorn the top of the tree, the star of

Bethlehem which is of course the only proper thing as well as being the only thing countenanced by the Rector, or an immensely glittering and unsuitable fairy doll someone was so ill-judged as to give to Helen. So you see, my dear, you are a pleasure in more ways than you know!'

When the Rector gravely offered Alexandra his arm to take her in to dinner, Robert's face fell so utterly that she took his arm as well, and moved lopsidedly from the room between her ill-assorted escorts to the unspeakable anguish of the baby. Her place had been set with a wreath of holly, adorned with a place card on which Richard had laboriously written 'Miss Abbitt' in scarlet ink with a liberal spattering of blots. The table was covered in red ribbon streamers and chains of coloured paper and each candlestick bore a large bow of ribbon and a rosette of gold and silver paper. The whole room, scented with the Christmas goose, seemed to glimmer with warmth and merriment and if it had not been for fear of distressing the children, Alexandra would have been happy to burst into tears.

After dinner in the drawing-room the children, fierce now with the determination to stay awake on such an evening – for even though dinner had been very early to accommodate them, they had all been awake since dawn – clamoured for games.

'Miss Abbott's dress!' their mother cried. 'My dears, we cannot ask her, we simply cannot, such finery—'

'Bother the finery,' Alexandra said.

The children cheered and the Rector even forgot the after effects of goose and pudding on his digestion to smile gravely and agreed to join in. They played turn the trencher and Blind Man's Buff and forfeits, during the course of which Robert was required to kiss Alexandra and became entirely incoherent with rapture.

She was reluctant to go. The happy muddle of the Rectory drawing-room, the flushed children, the feeling of belonging, of being part of a group of humans who all wanted her, among whom she could be entirely herself, all seduced her to stay. But the nodding baby, the beginnings of whimpers from Helen who had decided that she minded bitterly that her fairy doll had spent Christmas in a cardboard box, Mrs Chamberlin's gallant attempts to fight her own fatigue, told her she must go home. Murphy was summoned, the Rector put her cloak over the cream dress and the avalanche of jewels and she was driven home alone in the quiet dark night.

In her bedroom she was assailed by restlessness. It was not late, nothing like time for bed, she felt so full of energy, of goodwill, of the need to take some action. She flung aside her heavy bedroom curtains and pressed her face to the cold glass but there was nothing there, just the quiet, empty blackness which enveloped the families all over Cornwall who were turning the trencher in a thousand drawing-rooms.

Alexandra pushed up the window and the cold rushed in and the sharp salt smell of the sea. She had meant to walk down to the sea today to greet it on her first Christmas here, her own sea, her own stretch of wild grey winter water. She thought of the beach and how lovely it was in winter, so clean and cold, and then she thought of the rocks and their pools, icy now in December and how, if the snow fell here, the flakes would melt into the water, the sea would always win.

She shut the window and stood for a moment, her hands still on the bottom bar of the sash, arrested by a sudden thought. Here she was, possessed of more than she had ever dreamed of, this house, its comforts and warmth, those servants whose lives were spent in caring for hers, friends such as the Chamberlins who had taken her to their hearts, this first, unforgettable Christmas with all its bounty and then – Michael Swinton, in that bleak and dreary place, with only drunken old Meg and silent Punch, his loneliness accentuated by the life he had known these last few months in London and in the great houses he had stayed in. No traditions and Christmas games for him, no decorated tables, no candles and dishes of fruits and nuts, only that vast gloomy kitchen and the clutter of bachelor living. Alexandra looked at her clock. It was barely ten. Alexandra rang the bell vigorously.

Lyddy exclaimed in horror, 'But Miss Alexandra, you can't go like that!'

Alexandra surveyed herself in the long glass on the wall.

'Why not?' she said. 'Of course I can. You insisted I must wear this to dine, and I am certainly not going to change again now. I shall go to Trelorne like this, Lyddy. My fur coat — Aunt Emily's fur coat — is wonderfully warm.'

Lyddy said in despair, 'Mrs Talbot'd never have liked it. Poor lady, she'll be turning in her grave to think of you going out on your own like this—'

'I am not going on my own. Murphy will take me. I should like to go on my own but I do see that the gig would be a little draughty at night in evening dress. Now, has Dora everything ready?'

Lyddy thought of the basket that had been ordered, filled with mince pies and a cold chicken, and chestnuts and oranges and the decanter of port, to Penman's misery, carefully wrapped in napkins.

'I'm sure he'll have been provided for,' Dora had said in disapproval. 'I'm sure Mr Swinton won't be starving.'

'It's no use,' Lyddy said. 'She's bent on going. Nothing'll stop her.'

Now she said to Alexandra, 'Yes, Miss Alexandra, it's all ready. The carriage is ordered.'

'Then I shall go,' she said.

She was filled with happiness, driving to Trelorne. She held the basket on her knee and revelled in its contents, the treats she had ordered and checked meticulously, even down to a handful of sugar plums in their nests of perforated gold paper. She wanted to laugh aloud at the prospect of the delight she would give. She could visualize them, all three of them, silent around that vast table in the kitchen, as if they were engaged upon the business of any day, any ordinary day, not Christmas. She pictured them all staring up as she came in and Michael Swinton giving rapid orders to Punch as he had done before, and saw herself putting her basket on the table and showing him what she had brought, the taste and spirit of Christmas from Bishopstow, from her house, her own establishment. And best of all the pictures that flew through her mind so happily as she jolted onwards was Michael Swinton's gratitude and delight, how touched he would be that she had thought of him, how she would seem to him like some sort of Christmas spirit, glittering in a thousand jewels, her arms laden with bounty . . .

Trelorne was quite dark as they approached. It was only the light from their own carriage lamps falling on the neglected driveway that told her they were approaching the house, and the salt smell that got stronger and stronger and seeped through the closed windows of the carriage. When they stopped, in blackness and silence, before the steps that led up to the kitchen door, the only door anyone ever used at Trelorne, Murphy wanted to accompany her inside.

'No, thank you,' Alexandra said. 'Give me a lamp in this hand and the basket in the other and I shall manage perfectly well.'

At the top of the steps, she stopped, and put down the basket so that she could knock. There was no answer. Murphy, at the foot of the steps, waited for her to return to the carriage. Instead, she turned the handle of the door, picked up her basket, stepped inside and closed the door firmly behind her. Through the panes of dirty glass at its top, Murphy could see the wavering light from her lantern as she vanished into the interior of the dark house.

She went steadily through the scullery where only a tap dripped in the quiet, and then stood outside the closed kitchen door, and called. A thin line of light around the edge indicated that at least the range was alight, even if nobody was sitting by it.

'Mr Swinton! Mr Swinton!'

There was no reply. For the second time, Alexandra set down her basket and put her hand on the door handle. It turned easily and she pushed the door open, stepping at the same moment into the kitchen and the rosy glow of firelight and the small flame of a single candle.

The room was empty. She stood there for a moment in confusion, the lantern in her hand shedding a golden light on the creamy folds of her dress where the dark fur had fallen open over it, her hand to her eyes, shading them against the lantern light, her brow creased with puzzlement.

She said uncertainly, 'Mr Swinton?'

From the shadows he said, 'Ah, you *are* a vision, but a flesh and blood one. I could not be sure.'

He came forward into the firelight then and she saw he had been sitting beside the range, in an old rocking chair which he had left tilting back and forth, to take the lantern from her, grasping her free hand in his.

'I can hardly believe it. I thought you were a hallucination you know, a fantasy, standing there all cream and amber in your fur wrappings. Miss Abbott, in the name of all that is improbable and wonderful, what are you doing here?'

She broke from him and picked up her basket.

'I kept thinking today how lucky I was, you see, how blessedly fortunate, with all I have, all that is so comfortable, all that makes me so – so much happier than I was, and then this evening I went to the Rectory and when I returned I was in my room and I looked out at the darkness and I thought of you and how lonely you must be after all the company and society you have known just recently and I thought – I thought—'

His blue gaze went from her face to the basket with its bundles and the white swaddled decanter, and back to her face again. She waited confidently for his smile, his look of wondering gratitude, his stumbling words of thanks, her eyes fixed upon him in happy expectation.

He said furiously, 'How dare you!'

She did not understand him. She said, 'I brought you some port, Mr Swinton, and – and some mince pies, Dora's mince pies are so very excellent—'

His fist crashed on to the table.

'God, how can you? Breaking in here covered with jewels like a Jezebel, babbling about pies and port, coming alone to see me – have you no delicacy? Have you no discretion at all? No tact? How dare you patronize me, how dare you flaunt yourself at me when you know—' he stopped for a moment and shook his head. 'It is horrible,' he said vehemently, 'Horrible. Horrible that you should tempt me so heartlessly and – and *pity* me,' he spat at her. 'Giving me the crumbs from your great table, taunting me with your presence. You should not be here, Miss Abbott!' he shouted. 'In every way it is wrong for you to be here!'

Dismay poured through her like a flood. He was terrifying, towering over her seeming twice the size in his fury, but she would not run. She swallowed several times and tried to speak, but bitter shame held her tongue.

'Get out,' he said.

Her eyes strayed involuntarily to the claret bottle on the table.

He said angrily, 'I am not drunk, Miss Abbott. I have never been clearer in my wits. Nor have I ever been more sorely tried. Get out before – I—'

'I made a mistake,' she said.

He let out a long, gasping sigh.

'I – I am so sorry. I am sorrier than you will ever understand, Mr Swinton, much, much sorrier. I never thought I should be – be improper to come, that you should think me patronizing.' Her voice was shaking badly so she stopped and swallowed once more and bravely went on, 'I have behaved like a child, a stupid, ignorant child, but I never intended it. I just wanted you to have some of what I had had today, some of the joy and warmth, I wanted to give you something—'

'Stop it,' he said. He had turned away from her a little and she could not see his face. She waited, forcing back tears she thought might irritate him further, watching his implacable shoulders.

At last he said, 'We have got ourselves thoroughly at cross purposes have we not?'

'I hope not – any more,' she said in a low voice. 'But – but I should go now. I have behaved so badly, I can't bear to think I have angered you—'

He swung round.

'You haven't. Or rather you did violently, but I judged you too hastily and I am not angry now. I am extremely – oh, a host of things, but not angry any more. Will you not stay a little while, Miss Abbott? Since your reputation is now ruined by your own hand?'

She smiled wanly at him. 'Only in Murphy's eyes.'

He laughed then, his easy familiar laugh and gestured to the fire.

'Come and sit down. Perhaps you wonder why I am all alone. Christmas is Punch's one luxury, Miss Abbott. He will be insensible with drink until the New Year. He began last night and he knows I do not want to see him again until he is sober. And I packed that old witch off to the village. She reminds me more of All Souls' Eve than Christmas. I dined off bread and cheese and this excellent claret. I don't suppose you know much about claret but this Chateau Margaux 1875 is nectar. I am even going to give you some, which I should not do for someone who knows nothing about wine.'

When he had seated her in his rocking chair and put a glass of dark liquid in her hand, he moved her lamp and his single candle so that her face was illumined.

'Don't,' she said. 'I – I feel like an altar.'

'Very appropriate,' he said. 'Don't touch them.'

He pulled a wooden chair away from the table and brought it so that he could sit opposite to her. He was dressed with his usual carelessness, in boots and dark breeches and jacket and a shirt whose collar he had pulled open for comfort. His hair was still quite closely cropped, and his beard now followed the lines of his jaw and allowed her to see the hard fierce lines of his face.

'Beauty and the Beast, are you thinking, Miss Abbott?'

She blushed hotly.

'I shouldn't blame you. You have had enough praise heaped on you this year to last most women a lifetime.'

She said shyly, 'Did the painting really help you?'

He took a swallow from his glass.

'In one way, which is obvious, immeasurably. In another way, which I might tell you of shortly, it has made me damnably unhappy. What is in the glass will not bite you. Put your nose in and take a deep, magnificent breath of it. Then take a mouthful, and hold it there in your mouth for a moment, then swallow it, very slowly, noticing the taste of it all the way.' He watched her. 'Very neatly done. What did you think?'

'I – never drank anything like it before.'

'Of course you haven't. It would be a criminal waste to give it to most women.'

'It was – was a very *big* taste, somehow, a great deal of it—'

'Ah!' he said with satisfaction. 'I may even give you some more.'

She asked without looking at him, 'Were you unhappy to be back with fashionable people? Was it like before, when you were famous and – and couldn't paint?'

'No,' he replied, 'it wasn't like that at all. I can paint anything I want to at the moment, anything, everything. I have never had mastery like this before.' He stood up and picked up the candle and went wandering off into the shadows with it. From across the kitchen he said, 'I don't think anything I have painted this autumn is quite as good as this, but then, I would not expect it to be. Not all my sitters are Miss Abbott.'

Alexandra swung upright in the rocking chair. Across

the room, the single candle flickered in his hand and illuminated her own bare feet on a black rock, her own hands clasped round her bent knees and the brown familiar folds of Mrs McPhee. She stood up.

'But – but that is my portrait!'

'Of course,' he said calmly and came back across the room. 'What did you think would happen to it? Did you suppose I should sell it?'

'I – I didn't think what would happen to it. I didn't think much about it.'

He put the candle down on the table and came to stand close to her.

'Of course you didn't. You never do think much about yourself. Or of yourself. That is one of your most powerful attractions, your unselfconsciousness. The others of course, are legion, your loveliness, your adorable practicality, your kindness, your loving-heartedness, your naturalness. You are why I came back, Miss Abbott. I could have stayed in London of course, eating my heart out for you as I have done ever since you put your head down on to your bread and butter here in this room and burst into tears; but the combination of Christmas, and not having seen you in months drove me to a railway station and this morgue of a house. I packed you up in your painted form as I have done for every move I have made since the Summer Exhibition, and we travelled down to Bodmin together, you and I—'

He stopped. She said nothing, but gazed at him with wide, terrified eyes, then almost involuntarily she made a small gesture with her hands to ward him off and he, taking it as a token of reciprocal feeling, stepped forward and took her in his arms. She felt them go round her, strong and decided against her dress, beneath her coat, and then he put his mouth on hers and began to kiss her, and for a moment she felt that she was flying, and the next minute she was clawing herself free with the superhuman strength of panic and stumbling for the door.

He was there before her. Even as her hand fumbled

to open it, he thrust himself between her and the door, barring her way.

She screamed, 'No! No! Let me go!' and flung her hands out and he caught them and held them firmly. She twisted herself sideways in frenzy, screaming still and trying to wrench her wrists free and then he moved both her hands to one of his and gave her a light stinging slap across her cheek.

She gasped. He said, 'Calm down. I did not mean to frighten you, either by kissing you or hitting you. Come and sit down.'

'No!' she said. 'No! No—'

'Do as you are told. Don't be melodramatic. If we part like this, we shall create the most monumental awkwardness for each other and ourselves. Sit down.'

She obeyed him, sinking on to the wooden chair he had pulled up for himself. He handed her her glass of claret.

'Drink this.'

She gulped and almost choked.

'If you drink my Margaux like that, I shall give you another slap. Alexandra, listen to me. Look up. I wish to speak to your face.'

She raised her head slowly and looked apprehensively at him. He was sitting on the edge of the table and was regarding her with his steady blue gaze.

'Cross purposes, my dear! How right I was. And more crossed even than I knew. You cannot conceive of the feelings that consumed me when I understood – or rather when I thought I understood why you had come tonight, when you said you wanted to share your happiness with me, wanted to give me something. I misinterpreted you, my dear. I forgot how young you are, how inexperienced, in what a simple spirit you saw your generosity. I supposed, during those brief, heady moments after your heartbreaking apology that you had wanted to come to me tonight as much as I wanted you to come. That is why I kissed you. I imagined – wrongly

– that you wanted me too. Now you have shown me that I was wrong, that I was mistaken. That is so, is it not? I was mistaken to think you loved me?'

Slowly, hardly knowing what she did, Alexandra nodded.

His mouth twitched a little. He said, 'I never meant to frighten you and I am sorry that I did, truly sorry. Here,' he held out his hand to her with a little smile, 'take my hand to show you forgive me for alarming you.'

Her own was shaking, she could not seem to stop it. His clasp was as warm and steady as ever.

'If I had been sensible, Alexandra, I should have known I had no chance. How old are you?'

'Twenty-two,' she whispered. 'Just.'

'Then very recently I was twice your age. Now I am rather less. Small consolation, that is.' He stood up. 'Miss Abbott, you must go home. We shall meet in the course of things, I think, and we will do so on just the footing we have always known. Before tonight, that is.'

She rose and stood before him.

'Yes,' she said.

He picked up her basket.

'I shall carry this out for you. I am sure you will understand that the contents would choke me. Take my arm. The house is as dark as Hades.'

At the foot of the steps, Murphy waited, bundled up in an old sheepskin. He looked at the basket in surprise.

'Mr Swinton has so much already,' Alexandra said, her voice almost steady, 'that he asked if you might have the basket for bringing me out here on Christmas night.'

She felt her arm squeezed slightly.

He said, 'My sentiments exactly, Miss Abbott. Now in you get. This is no night for hanging about in the air.'

The door was closed firmly upon her. She let the window down.

'Shall – shall you be going back to London?'

'Yes,' he replied. 'That is exactly what I shall do.'

She said in a small voice, 'Of – of course.'

'Perhaps I may come down again in the spring. Then you can show me your lambs, your first lambs.'

He pulled the window up quickly and it was too dark for her to see him step back towards the house. Murphy swung the horses round and headed them towards Bishopstow, and in the carriage, in her crumpled finery, Alexandra sat and pushed her fists against her mouth to stop herself from crying.

CHAPTER THIRTEEN

On New Year's Eve, it snowed. Alexandra woke on the first day of the new year to a soft white stillness and a grey sky heavy with more snow to come. Her first thought was for her sheep, but Jem was before her, and the barn which in Aunt Emily's day had stood empty, now had a pen in the corner in which Alexandra's little flock was safely confined.

After breakfast, she wandered restlessly about the house, frowning at the snow. She had, for some reason, been restless for the past week, and kept finding herself straying aimlessly about the house and garden without any conscious sense of purpose. The Langleys had asked her to dine with them on New Year's Eve since all the young people were at home, but she had refused and after her note had gone, had wondered why she had refused, why she was being so contrary and felt so unsettled.

With the snow, there was little for her to do. The dairyman from Grove Farm, Jem's elder brother, had said the cow would not calve for some days yet. The hens stayed in the hen house, the sheep in the barn, there was nothing amusing going on in the kitchen, she could not seem to concentrate long enough to read or write. She thought of turning out Aunt Emily's drawers, or rearranging her own bedroom and ridding herself of its rather overcrowded feeling, but disinclination struck her almost before the ideas were formed. Scraps of news filtered to her from Lyddy; they had danced until two in the morning on New Year's Eve at Langley Dene; the Rectory children had been given a toboggan and Mrs Chamberlin said it was almost a better present to her than to them for it kept them so happy and exhausted them so satisfactorily; Mr Swinton had gone back to London.

When the snow had lain for four days, increasing every night by an inch or so, George Langley and Harry Burrows appeared on Alexandra's lawn in snowshoes.

'Where have you been?' George shouted to her through the glass. 'Why didn't you come on New Year's Eve? It was the best fun imaginable!'

Laughing, Alexandra indicated that they should slide round to the front door and come in in a conventional manner. Once in the drawing-room, glowing with exercise, George repeated himself.

'I looked out for you all evening! I was sure you would come. It hardly snowed at all, nothing like enough to stop you. How's the gig? And the mare? Does she suit you?'

'It would have been awfully jolly if you had come,' Harry Burrows said. 'We must have been twenty or so, eh George? Why didn't you come?'

'I really don't know——' Alexandra replied.

'I nagged and nagged at Aunt to ask you. I wanted her to ask you for Christmas, I was sure you would be on your own. You were, weren't you? She said oh, you were so much your own mistress now you wouldn't want to leave Bishopstow, but that's bosh, isn't it, utter bosh.'

'Not quite,' Alexandra said. 'I do love it here, I do like doing things myself.'

'You looked topping on Christmas Day. In church,' Harry Burrows said fervently. 'Simply topping.'

'Aunt says you have sheep now and a pig and you are selling stuff at Bodmin Market.'

'Oh yes,' Alexandra said. 'They must all pay for

themselves. In the end. I'm making cheese, and the cow will calve any day.'

'I say!' Harry Burrows said.

'We have come to kidnap you,' George said. 'No protests this time. You can't possibly play at farming in this weather. We have brought the sledge and we will tow you back to Langley Dene. Aunt almost insists – I think in truth she is a little in awe of you now – and I certainly do—'

Harry Burrows exclaimed, 'So do I!'

'– so you see you have to come. Get your maid to put up a few things, Alexandra. Don't be stand-offish.'

'I'm not,' she said. 'I should love it. I should love to come. I only fidget about here somehow.'

'Of course you do. It's positively freakish the way you live. I don't know how you stand it.'

She said seriously, 'Most of the time, I am absolutely contented, but it has just been this last week or so somehow, the weather, you know, it's probably the snow—'

'Of course it is! Now hurry up, there's a good girl.'

She went to the door and turned to say gratefully to George, her hand on the knob, 'I really am so thankful to you.'

He coloured slightly, glanced at Harry and said with some awkwardness, 'Oh – oh, that's nothing, I mean, it's awfully good fun, that is – that is – well, wild horses wouldn't have kept me away, actually, if you want to know—'

Langley Dene hummed with people. Harry Burrows was staying rather than be snowbound with his oppressive parents; a young husband and wife – she was a great friend of the Langley girls – had been prevented from returning to Bristol, where they lived, by the snow; and a jovial pair from Plymouth, the husband being a business associate of Mr Langley's and equally prosperous, had decided to stay on partly for the sake of their daughter,

311

an uncomfortably vivacious girl who viewed Alexandra's arrival with considerable displeasure.

Alexandra was shown to a massively furnished bedroom with the luxury of its own bathroom adjoining where a huge hooded bath was enthroned in the centre, complete with the astonishing and novel device of a shower. Rose, with vociferous insistence, lent Alexandra her maid and both she and Grace hovered about the room, asking Alexandra if everything were quite comfortable, quite to her liking, and pouncing with squeals of admiration on every one of Alexandra's possessions as they were taken out of her box.

Alexandra, exhilarated by three miles of speeding over the snow and the icy air and now by the festive air that permeated Langley Dene, and the Langley girls' obsequiousness, watched them with sceptical amusement.

She was dressed reverently for dinner by Rose's maid while other maids, in fluttering cap and apron streamers, came silently in and out to light and trim lamps, stoke the fire, carry more hot water, empty the waste-paper basket into which she dropped no more than a screw of newspaper she had found in her coat pocket, a cutting torn from the farming page on the advantages of White Wyandottes over Rhode Island Reds. Rose's maid said reverently,

'Mr Langley says we shall have electricity in the spring. He is going to install a complete electrical system, all over the house. Of course, the London house has been electrified since Miss Grace and Miss Rose were children but there is hardly any electricity down here. Langley Dene will be the first house in Cornwall, I shouldn't wonder. What wonderfully thick hair you have, Miss Abbott.'

At dinner, Alexandra was placed on Mr Langley's right. At his other side was jolly Mrs Durrant from Plymouth; at hers, Piers Langley who claimed he had begged for the privilege.

'Remember the last time we met?'

She regarded him coolly.

'Perfectly, Mr Langley.'

He grinned.

'Good sport, eh? And now, you are a woman of property and in a fair way to becoming a farmer and I'm told, on the coachman's grapevine, that you drive very nicely, very nicely indeed. Why won't you hunt?'

'Because I don't want to.'

He shook his head at her.

'Don't understand it.'

'I don't see why I am the one who is peculiar,' Alexandra argued, 'just because I like my own company and prefer to occupy myself than amuse myself. Why shouldn't you be the odd one instead?'

An arm descended and removed her soup plate in which at least half her lobster bisque remained.

'You've spirit, Miss Abbott, I'll say that for you. Why did you let George help you choose a mare? I'd have been glad to. What George knows about horses, you could write on a sixpence. Why didn't you ask me?'

'Because,' Alexandra explained, 'the last time we met you were so perfectly disagreeable,' and then she turned to her right and smiled at Mr Langley.

He said heartily, 'Mrs Langley and I are very pleased to have you here.'

'You are most kind.'

'In fact,' he added, leaning towards her confidentially, 'I'm glad to have the chance of a word with you. I hope you won't mind my asking a bit of a favour, Miss Abbott, but the truth is, if you could put in a word for me in high places, I shouldn't forget it. I'm not one to overlook favours done me. Here, Miss Abbott, your glass is almost empty. Like champagne, do you? If my father could see me and this house and champagne on my table, he'd think he was seeing things.'

Alexandra's glass was refilled at once.

She said, 'How can I help you, Mr Langley?'

He leaned towards her again.

'It's like this, Miss Abbott. You wouldn't expect me not to know about your portrait, now would you? You can't be the talk of the town and word not get about, now can you? Mrs Langley and I took the girls up to the Royal Academy as we do every summer and there you were, and upon my soul, Miss Abbott, you made a lovely picture, you did indeed, and I speak no more than the truth as is my way. Well, when we had seen the picture, I tried to contact Mr Swinton. I sent a note round to his studio, and pointed out we were neighbours down here and, would you believe it, Miss Abbott, he took not the slightest notice, never even replied. So I called. I got myself a cab and called on him. Now I know you have a way with him and we all admire him, but the fact is, Miss Abbott, that Mr Swinton was, not to put too fine a point on it, downright rude. It's not a smiling matter, Miss Abbott. I was quite put out, I can assure you.'

'I – I am sorry,' Alexandra said, struggling with her smile.

'Well, since then I hear he's been up at Sandringham and he's painted two dukes and many prominent members of society and the fact is, Miss Abbott, I want him to paint my girls. I'll pay him whatever he wants. When I want a thing, Miss Abbott, money's no object. But the difficulty is to get the man to agree to do the painting in the first place. And this is where you could help me, Miss Abbott, having such influence with him after the success of your portrait.'

Alexandra answered in some confusion, 'Oh, I don't think – I mean now – I hardly think I do have any influence. I should like to help you, Mr Langley, of course I should, but I don't think I should fare any better than you did. Mr – Mr Swinton is a very – independent man.'

Mr Langley's large, red face puckered with disappointment.

'I'm sorry to hear that, Miss Abbott. I'd been counting

on you, you know. I said to Mrs Langley that if any-one could persuade Mr Swinton, you could. Won't you even try?'

'He – he is not coming back to Trelorne until the spring, Mr Langley. Perhaps – perhaps not even then. I could ask him, I suppose if – if I do see him—'

'Of course you could. Now, if you could see your way to writing to him before the spring it would mean a good deal to Mrs Langley and to me. There'll be half London hammering on his door by now and I don't want to be the last in the line. Thank you, Miss Abbott, I shan't forget this, I can assure you. Wait till my girls are hanging where you were and see what I shan't do for you. Now, you must have some of this ice. I know the people round here say there are no ices like Mrs Burrows', but just you taste Mrs Langley's and see if you don't find it superior. Much superior.'

Alexandra slept badly. The room seemed very hot, very airless, and the great bed suffocatingly soft after her own at Bishopstow. She got up several times and lit her candle and took sips of water from the cut glass carafe by her bed and paced around the room. Once or twice she went to the window and looked out longingly at the darkness and the blue-white snow and strained to hear the sea. But she was too far inland, too cushioned in the fat comforts of Langley Dene. There was nothing even to read in her room, nothing to occupy herself with except her restless thoughts or the weary counting of fat roses that papered the walls like plump pink cabbages. At last, towards dawn, she fell into a deep, troubled sleep and was woken by Rose's maid at nine, thoroughly unrefreshed and with a blinding headache.

At breakfast, she announced that she must go home. There was a chorus of protest.

'Forgive me,' she said to Mrs Langley. 'You have been so very hospitable, but there are things at Bishopstow I must see to.'

'Of course,' Mrs Langley murmured, 'I – I quite understand you. George and Harry shall take you. It was so good of you to come.'

'Why must you go?' George demanded fiercely a moment later when he could speak to her alone. 'What possible reason is there to go home for? You enjoyed yourself enough last night, didn't you? And we've a thousand things planned for today.'

'The cow might calve—'

'Oh *bosh*,' he said furiously. 'What about all of us? What about *me*?'

She suddenly felt close to tears.

'George I – I am so sorry. But I think I am better alone. You were so kind to come and fetch me and I'm so sorry to be a nuisance—'

He took her hand.

'I say, I didn't mean to upset you. Of course you aren't a nuisance. I'm just so frightfully disappointed, that's all. I have to go back to Cambridge in three days. It's my final year, you know, and Uncle won't like it if I plough everything. I just thought you – you would like it here for those few days. I – I just hoped you would.'

'Oh, don't be kind to me!' she cried despairingly. 'I don't deserve it, I don't deserve anything. Take me back to Bishopstow and just leave me there. Forget me.'

'I can't do that,' he said simply.

They towed her home, almost in silence. When they reached Bishopstow, Alexandra was greeted with the news that the cow had dropped a fine little heifer at two that morning, and that Jem and Murphy had been in attendance but she had hardly needed them. It had been a model birth, Alexandra's first from one of her own animals – and she had missed it.

She went up to her bedroom and sat in dreary contemplation of her own tired face before the mirror. She had sat there ten minutes or more, sighing occasionally and weighed down with disappointment and the feeling she should go and see the calf but could hardly rouse herself to, when Lyddy came and announced that luncheon was ready.

'I don't want any, Lyddy.'

'Miss Alexandra! Of course you do, all morning, out in the air, you must have an appetite—'

'I haven't. I haven't an appetite for anything. Eat it in the kitchen. I am going down to see the calf and then I am going to walk down to the Rectory. A game of lions and tigers will shake me up and be good for me.'

'Oh, Miss Alexandra, you shouldn't walk in this snow, indeed you shouldn't. Even if you keep to the wheel tracks in the lane, you'll get wet and it gets dark so early—'

'Lyddy,' Alexandra said in exasperation, 'stop it. I shall go where I like and do what I like. If I don't we shall all have to put up with my awful temper and none of us will like that. Now, go and find my boots and stop fussing.'

Mrs Chamberlin said, 'Oh, my dear, you are an angel of mercy in truth you are! They all have colds, every one, even poor baby, and I have absolutely forbidden them to go tobogganning and they are as cross as cross and the poor Rector has a headache and it's his day for writing his sermon, he always does it on Thursdays. I suppose it's so he has enough time to think it over by Sunday. Come in, my dear, do. Did you walk all this way in the snow? I blessed the snow when it first came, but now I should curse it if I dared. We don't often get snow here so it's rather a novelty for the children, but oh, my dear, when they can't go out in it—'

In the nursery, the children lay in sniffing lumps in chairs or on the floor and Helen was crying softly into her doll. Mrs Chamberlin said brightly, 'Look who I've brought you!'

'You poor little things,' Alexandra said. 'How miserable you look.'

They struggled up to greet her, the baby launching himself at her ankles with his now familiar manacle hold. She surveyed their white faces and pink noses and eyes.

'I think I should read to you today. I don't think we can play if you can't breathe. I'll read to you about jungles instead of playing at them.' She sat down and lifted the baby on to her knee. 'I feel just as cross as you today, so we can all be cross together.'

Mrs Chamberlin collected her mending basket while Alexandra read. It was difficult to read since tiredness and the dry heat of the room made her eyes swim, but she persevered with *Rikki Tikki Tavi* as much for her own good as for theirs.

'Look,' she said at the end and held out the book. 'Look. There's a picture of him.'

'Speaking of which,' Mrs Chamberlin said, biting off a thread, 'I was wondering where you will hang your own picture. I never saw a more romantic painting, my dear. It will be a wonderful thing to have when you are stout like me and can scarcely recall what a waist was, let alone where it was supposed to be. I suppose one should hang a painting like that in one's boudoir, but it seems such a waste that so few people will see it. I suppose you might make room in the drawing-room, on that wall by the window, where that really rather nasty still-life is that your uncle was so fond of. You could banish it to the dining-room, far more suitable really, all those pheasants and berries, you know.'

Alexandra looked down at Jack.

'I shan't hang it anywhere. It isn't mine to hang.'

'Oh yes, it is, my dear! He has left it for you!'

Alexandra's head came up with a jerk.

'Left it for me?'

'Oh, what a man he is! Imagine not telling you himself. Some people are casual to the point of rudeness. He said to old Meg – I know you think I shouldn't listen to servants' gossip but, my dear, how else am I to know what is going on and tell people things they should know, just as I am telling you – he said to old Meg, "Well, Miss Abbott may as well have herself now", and then he went off to London without another word and left your portrait in the kitchen at Trelorne, and of course poor old Meg didn't know what to do about it and didn't dare come to Bishopstow House and at last asked Cook, here, what she thought she should do and of course Cook came straight to me. So there you are, my dear. I must say I think it very generous of him even if he was hardly gracious in how he gave it to you. It must be worth a fortune. You can send Murphy for it any day because old Meg is up at Trelorne most of the time, poking around you know, and I'm sure she feels the picture is a heavy responsibility. There, my dear. Is not that a lovely surprise?'

'Yes,' Alexandra said dully. 'Lovely.'

'I knew you would be pleased. I am so glad I could tell you. I suppose he has so much work now that he doesn't need you as an advertisement any longer. What a deal of good you have done him! He must be thankful to you.'

'He – he did say something like it. He was very kind.'

She trailed home dispiritedly through the snow, leaving a promise to come the next day to the clamouring children and a further promise that when the snow melted they should all come and see her new calf. When she reached Bishopstow, Lyddy was waiting for her anxiously.

'Why, Miss Alexandra, you look just as tired as when you went out. I thought it'ud do you good, the walk and the children and all—'

'Well, it didn't,' Alexandra said crossly. 'You were quite right. I should not have gone. And now I am going to bed. I know it is early, I know I should eat dinner, but I don't want to. I don't want to do anything but sleep. And be left alone.'

'Yes, Miss,' Lyddy said faintly and watched as Alexandra turned away and wearily began to climb the stairs.

CHAPTER FOURTEEN

The little calf thrived and in early February the sow had a litter of fourteen. Alexandra bought a dozen White Wyandottes and made a successful barter arrangement with the fishermen at Rock for the exchange of dairy produce for fish. She drew up plans for a glasshouse to be erected on the southern wall of the stable yard so that she might grow tomatoes in commercial quantities and had the little downstairs room her uncle had used as a study made into an office for herself with filing cabinets set against the walls between his cases of horticultural books.

The outside world left her very much alone beyond the customary Wednesday afternoons. The mornings she spent with Jem and Murphy, who had to his own amazement found himself with every day less of a coachman and more of a farmhand. His amazement was doubled by discovering he hardly minded; if Alexandra was perfectly willing to carry buskets and fill troughs, he could scarcely refuse to do it himself.

She wrote weekly to her father and received from him equally regular letters full of information and advice which she noted down in a daily journal she was keeping for practical purposes. He would write, 'Your mother sends her love,' but Iskandara never wrote herself. Besides letters from Bewick, she began to look forward to letters from Cambridge, letters from George which were nothing like as breezy as they had been before, and whose unmistakably affectionate tone was a balm to Alexandra. She replied carefully and punctually. Of Michael Swinton she heard nothing, beyond seeing two Punch cartoons of him during March in which he was drawn wearing a flowing cloak and beard and brandishing his palette and described as 'Our Famous Society Artist'. Murphy had collected *A. in Reverie* from Trelorne and had left it, on Alexandra's instructions, shrouded in sacking in one of the back kitchens. Lyddy said it was like Miss Alexandra's modesty to leave it out of sight and Janet had snorted and said it was something else as well.

Most afternoons during the first three months of the year, Alexandra went down to the shore. She went whatever the weather unless a thick sea mist made it utterly foolhardy, and wandered along the huge, empty beach and climbed the rocks right round the headland, knowing that it was perfectly safe to do so now since there was no-one to observe her. On dry days she sat for as long as she could without getting chilled to the marrow on the flat-topped rock, and gazed out to sea, and one day she even climbed the cliff behind it and went up to Trelorne and pressed her face to the great blank studio windows and looked at the dais where she had sat on rocks Punch had made out of boxes and blankets. She collected shells and pebbles on these scrambles and when she got home would put any little pink cowrie shells she had found on the beach below Trelorne into a glass jar on her office windowsill. She found herself regarding them as a kind of talisman.

Shortly before Easter, Alexandra became aware that the neighbourhood was waking up once more. The Langleys came back from London and Alexandra received a slightly aggrieved note from Mr Langley to the effect that he had once more attempted to see Mr Swinton but could only suppose from his manner that Miss Abbott had not found time to write to him and plead the Langleys' case. All the young men came back from University full of plans that now the hunting season was over, they might ride in point to point races. Alexandra received invitations to all the local houses and even one from the Durrants in Plymouth, inviting her to sample the delights of the south coast with them and their daughter for a week.

After the long winter of seclusion, constructive though it had been, Alexandra was pleased at the thought of company. She even went so far as to summon Aunt Emily's dressmaker from Bodmin and spent at least half an hour with the newest fashion magazines, gazing earnestly at the designs. There seemed to be a strong influence of what the magazines called *Art Nouveau* which involved a lot of enamel jewellery and flower embroideries and a good deal of classical draperies and flowing lines. Alexandra ordered a new evening gown and two new day dresses with narrow tulip-shaped overskirts and felt extremely doubtful about the whole thing when the dressmaker had gone.

She confided her doubts to Mrs Chamberlin.

'My dear, I am quite sure you will look perfectly charming and in any case, at your age, one can get away with anything. I don't change because I really can't think how to and I do so like to be comfortable. I never saw you look better, I must confess, than you did in your portrait. Some people pay to dress up, others don't, and if you will not be offended, my dear, you really do look your best at your most natural. I was quite overcome by what pretty feet you had. One never thinks of people's feet you know, one isn't permitted to. Isn't it odd the things that are considered indecent? I should think shoulders were far more indecent than feet, but then I am no arbiter of propriety. Which reminds me, my dear, I mean, speaking of bare feet and your picture, Mr Swinton is back. Cook saw old Meg again and I thought, now, I must tell Alexandra because you have never had a chance to thank him for the picture have you, though I am sure you have written to him, and I am sure he would be pleased because old Meg says he is hardly in the best of tempers and you have been so good at cheering him up in the past. And you must hang it up, my dear, think how offended he will be to think of it stuck in a pantry. Why is it stuck in a pantry?'

'Because I don't like myself much,' Alexandra said, her heart thudding.

Mrs Chamberlin regarded her.

'What a strange child you are,' she said.

The day the dresses came and Alexandra was despairing at herself for having attempted to be any way ahead of fashion, George Langley, extremely spruce in grey flannel and yellow kid gloves, came to call.

'Oh, George, look!' Alexandra said unhappily, waving her arm at the dresses spread over the drawing-room sofas, 'aren't they hideous? I shall never wear them. I can't imagine what I was thinking of.'

'You will look splendid,' George said loyally. 'You always do. I say, I have worked like a beaver this term. I can't tell you what a help your letters have been, really splendid of you to write so often. And guess what? Uncle says if I manage a second – which really will be punishing the old brain cells – he will give me a motor car. Piers is green, quite sick with envy. He's got a year to go and hasn't done a stroke of work so far, but I'm sure he'll buck up if Uncle makes him the same offer. It's pretty handsome of Uncle, isn't it?'

'Very,' Alexandra agreed.

'I – I suppose you could get yourself a motor car any day you wanted, couldn't you?' George asked a little awkwardly. 'Uncle says you are an example to us all, not splashing your money around. He's a bit sore about this painting thing, though. He really wants Swinton to do it.'

Alexandra sat down.

'I know he does, but I can't ask, I simply can't. I dare not.'

'I suppose he has a wicked temper, hasn't he. We always thought he did. In fact, until you came and seemed to charm him, we thought he was a bit, well — you know, not quite like other people. But you seemed to make him quite human. Aunt said she actually saw him riding once or twice. But you could charm the birds off the trees if you wanted to—'

'One thing is certain,' Alexandra said. 'I can't charm him. Not any more.'

'Bother him. Who cares about him? I certainly don't. He's only a painter after all. I say, Uncle's changed his mind about having me in the business, you know, his shipbuilding business. He always said he wouldn't because I wouldn't work, but my tutor's report this term was so good that Uncle has softened up like anything.'

Alexandra said, 'Should you like that? Shipbuilding?'

George came to sit by her on the sofa.

'I don't suppose I care much about ships but I might get to, I should think. It isn't the actual business, you know, it's the prospect of making some money. Piers and I haven't much, you know, our father didn't have Uncle's golden touch. I think enough was left for our education, that's all. We always knew we should have to work for our livings.'

Alexandra said tartly, 'Poor you.'

'I say, don't tease. It's all very well for you—'

'Do you think I don't work?'

He coloured.

'I know you do. That isn't what I meant at all. Farmers round here are beginning to notice you — you know they are. It must be jolly comfortable, though, to work for pleasure rather than because you have to.'

'It is,' Alexandra said frankly. 'I know just how lucky I am.'

He hesitated and then said in a low voice, 'I wonder if I shall ever be so lucky.'

'In the same way?'

'No,' he said, looking at her intently. 'In another way.'

She smiled at him.

'What other way?'

His hands were clenched together. He said hurriedly, 'I say, Alexandra, I didn't mean to come for this, though heaven knows it's been on my mind for months. I just came to see how you were, you know, and thank you for those marvellous letters. You don't know what it meant to me to get them, it made all those hours of swotting worthwhile. And I was a bit worried that you were angry about something at Christmas. I wanted us to have such fun, as we always do—'

'Yes,' she said, 'we do, don't we.'

He rushed on, hardly looking at her, 'I'm sure you will think this is awfully impertinent of me, but you must know what I feel about you. I mean, I thought you were so awfully kind when I was laid up and you have written me these really sporting letters and, well, Alexandra, I keep thinking about you, that's the fact of it and I seem to do it more not less. I never meant to say all this today, truly I didn't, but you are being so awfully sweet to me and it's so wonderful to see you and I should hate you to think it's your money that makes the slightest difference to me, though obviously it would help with me not having a penny. The thing is, Alexandra, the – the thing is – oh hang it, Alexandra, I really do love you awfully and it would mean everything in the world to me if you would marry me.'

For a moment, she went on smiling at him, smiling and being on the point of putting her hand out to him, of touching his hands, of saying, 'Oh George, of course—' and then, just as she was about to lean towards him and do these things, an abrupt cold horror fell upon her like a cloak, a horror of how close she was to a really catastrophic mistake and she heard herself say, in a voice she despised, a cool, remote voice,

'Oh, no, George, I am afraid I can't do that.'

The colour fled from his face. He stared at her.

'You – you can't? But I thought – I mean, you've been so sweet to me, we have had such fun – I mean, I know

325

I'm a worthless oaf, but I'd work myself to a standstill for you, honestly I would—'

She did touch him then, leaning forward and putting her hands round his clenched fists.

'I know you would, George. And I know I – I have led you on. The mistake is quite mine, not yours, and I am terribly sorry, painfully sorry. Of course we have had fun, wonderful fun, like a brother and sister—'

He said bitterly, '*I* never felt like a brother.'

'I expect that was my fault, too,' she said soberly. 'I just had no experience. I don't want to hurt you, George, I am far too fond of you, but I should hurt you far more by marrying you and not loving you as a wife should.'

'I shouldn't care!' he cried. 'I'll make up for both of us. Alexandra, I've never felt like this before—'

'But you will again,' Alexandra said, hating herself. 'You are awfully young. As young as me. We are both young and silly. We are a recipe for disaster. I – I don't blame you at all for what you say you want. And I see entirely that the money would be a help. Of course it would, it's only natural.'

He muttered, 'It isn't the money.'

'It must be a little. It would be to me if I were a man in your position.'

He looked at her.

'You are the most honest creature I have ever met.'

She said, 'I think I run you a close second,' and smiled.

He stood up.

'I suppose I had better go. You are a brick, Alexandra. Even after – all this, we can still be friends, can't we? I mean, I do understand your point of view even if I think I could make it all right for us.'

'Of course we are still friends,' she said and then added, with a touch of bitterness, 'that is one thing I have learned anyway, how not to make too much of things.'

'I suppose,' he said, looking down at her, 'I suppose

there is always a chance, isn't there, that you might change your mind?'

She stood up so that she could look directly into his eyes.

'No, George, there isn't,' she said. 'I won't change my mind.'

He shrugged. 'Then I shall have to bear it, shan't I? I say, Piers and I are riding in the races next Saturday. At Wadebridge. Will you come and cheer us on?'

She smiled broadly at him.

'Of course I will,' she said.

She lay awake that night, flooded with a curious calm. She had told Lyddy to pull the curtains back so that she could look at the pale April night sky, and she lay tranquilly against her pillows with her hands folded across her breast and knew that she had done perfectly right in refusing George Langley. She was remorseful, deeply remorseful about having led him on, however unconscious she had been of what she did, but she had made no mistake in saying she could never marry him. It was better to marry nobody than to marry the wrong person. She knew, from her childhood, what it was like to live with the wrong person, and George would have been the wrong person, and George would have been wrong although they might have been comfortable enough together in an unremarkable way.

She realized, lying there and looking out at the stars, that she had turned to George for comfort, that she had used his affection to bind her own wounds, wounds she had inflicted on herself out of her own inexperience, her fright at the unknown. Her father had said to her in the autumn, before, 'Never be afraid to step out if it hurts no other and gets you your heart's desire.' Well, she had hurt George, there was no denying that, but until she hurt him she had not seen clearly what her heart's desire was.

Now she saw it. The next move was the stepping out, and she was the only one who could do it. If she did step out and ask for her heart's desire there was always the terrifying chance of rejection, but it was worth the risk, it was worth any risk. Alexandra turned her head on the pillows and looked at the pale oblong of Charlotte's portrait, the little charcoal sketch Michael Swinton had done for Aunt Emily and which she now kept by her bed. Charlotte would not have held back. Charlotte had said to her sister that when you knew a thing was right, your whole soul went out to meet it, you could not stop yourself, any more than you could stop yourself from breathing.

She was quite correct, Alexandra thought staring at her, it's just that I didn't know she was, because I had not recognized what was right for me before, not till this afternoon, not till George proposed to me. Now I have. Now I know what it is I want. And tomorrow I shall go and ask for it.

CHAPTER FIFTEEN

''E's out,' Punch said laconically. He was leaning against the door he held half open and made no move to invite Alexandra inside.

'Has he gone? Where? Has he gone back to London?'

Punch regarded her. She felt her face betrayed everything and also that it didn't matter in the least if it did.

'No,' he said, ''e ain't.'

'Then where is he?' Alexandra demanded. 'Where can I find him?'

Punch shrugged.

'On the shore mos' likely.'

'Where on the shore? On the beach here, below the house?'

Punch took a deep breath and said in a burst of

communicativeness, ''E's got 'imself a dinghy. Bought it in Rock. 'E's scraping 'er ready for revarnishin'. Like I said, 'e's on the shore.'

'Thank you,' Alexandra said.

She went round the broken terrace, picking her way over piles of rubble and avoiding the gaping holes where slabs of stone had been ripped up for use somewhere else. It was a soft blue, twittering day with a cleanwashed spring sky, but the neglected lawn below the terrace was still rough with pale winter grass and the stunted shrubs at its edge were leafless still.

Alexandra picked up her skirts and made her way towards the cliff edge. She had dressed with enormous care that morning, amazing Lyddy who felt quite done out of the half-hour of bullying and cajolery that went into making Alexandra look as she felt she should – and then, the moment she was dressed, she had torn all her clothes off again and insisted that Lyddy get out that dreadful old brown coat and skirt she had brought from Scotland. Lyddy and Janet had agreed what a pity it was Miss Alexandra should have been painted in that shapeless skirt and the cream blouse whose collar was a disgrace and whose sleeves were too old-fashioned to bear thinking about – why not in evening dress and those lovely pearls? And now, Miss Alexandra was casting aside the pretty new pink-striped blouse and the nicely cut skirt her aunt had ordered for her and climbing resolutely into those terrible old garments that were hardly fit for a lady to wear at any time, even to feed the hens in . . .

Penman had reported that she had not touched her breakfast and Jem was astounded to hear that he must perform his morning duties alone. For one fleeting moment of bliss, Murphy had thought she might want the carriage, but no, only moments later he was asked to have the gig ready at once – Miss Alexandra would drive herself.

Now standing at the top of the cliff below Trelorne,

clutching handfuls of Mrs McPhee in clenched fists, Alexandra strove to be calm. Down below her on the beach was an upturned dinghy, resting on trestles above the high-water line, an old wide-bellied dinghy, its flaking varnish the colour of butterscotch. Michael Swinton was bent over it, a foreshortened figure from where she stood, jacketless in a shirt and waistcoat, and from above she could hear the faint rasp of scraping.

Slowly and carefully, she began to pick her way down the cliff. The path was narrow and shaly, the smooth places slippery in the damp spring air, and halfway down she nearly slipped and sent a handful of pebbles bouncing noisily down the beach. He stopped working then and looked up and saw her and waved in a friendly, abstracted way and then bent over the dinghy again. Alexandra put her hands up to her head, pulled out the long pins and removed her hat. She set it down beside the path, straightened her jacket, took a deep and steadying breath and went carefully on down to the beach.

She crunched her way over the small pebbles towards him and it wasn't until she was but a yard away from the boat that he stopped what he was doing and looked up. He held a piece of broken glass in his hand with which he had been meticulously scraping the old varnish from the hull. Alexandra went round to the opposite side of the dinghy and surveyed him across it. He smiled at her.

'Miss Abbott, good morning. And what a very good morning it is too. This is the time of year when Cornwall comes into its own.'

'Yes,' she said, 'I suppose it is.'

He began to scrape again, using light careful strokes, and Alexandra watched the little curls of old varnish drift down on to the pebbles like feathers. The sea was playing gently among the rock pools ten yards away and the few gulls, wheeling effortlessly overhead, made the only other sound to be heard on the beach.

'Mrs Chamberlin told me you were back,' Alexandra said.

'I have been back a week. And to a right royal welcome at that. Beyond that old witch in my kitchen, I haven't seen a soul.'

'You never do,' Alexandra retorted. 'You can't expect people to line the streets and cheer. You make no effort for them.'

He grinned at her.

'Nor I do, Miss Abbott. But one hopes, you know. I see you have lost none of your edge. How is the farming going?'

She leant her hands on the warm wood of the boat.

'Very well, thank you. I now have a dozen sheep and seven lambs, a cow and a calf, a sow and fourteen piglets, more than two dozen poultry and a tomato house. I sell butter and cheese and eggs in Bodmin Market and that is only a beginning.'

He said quietly, 'You have come a long way in a year, my dear.'

'Yes, I have. And I have you to thank for it really. You pointed out the way I should go.'

He stopped scraping and straightened up, leaning his arms on the boat so that they faced each other across it.

'Did I now? How nice you are to acknowledge it, Miss Abbott. The least I can do is to reciprocate and say that thanks to the success of my painting you, I now have enough commissions to keep me working from dawn until dewy eve, every day until about 1910.'

'Mr Langley—' Alexandra began.

Michael Swinton gestured and put his jagged morsel of glass on a nearby rock.

'Dreadful man. Claimed he knew you. In fact, Miss Abbott, he even had the gall to say that you especially requested me to paint his daughters.'

'He asked me to.'

'Ah. Well, I shan't. I shan't pick up a brush for a month.

331

I used to be rather competent with boats and I am going to see if the skill lingers.'

Alexandra leaned forward across the dinghy.

'I know the Langleys quite well.'

'Do you now,' Michael Swinton said without interest.

'Yes, I do. They live in a very – handsome new house on the road to Wadebridge. I expect you have noticed it, very square and grey. They have two daughters, the ones Mr Langley wants you to paint, and two nephews who are their wards and who have lived with them since they were small. They are called – George and Piers.'

He shook his head at her.

'I am sure they are, Miss Abbott. I am very pleased to think you have friends. Youthful romps and so on. But I am still not going to paint that man's daughters.'

Alexandra said patiently, 'I'm not talking about painting. That isn't what I am trying to tell you.'

He leaned forward too now, so that their faces were only a foot apart.

'Forgive me for being obtuse, Miss Abbott. What are you trying to tell me?'

'It's about George. George Langley. I met him over a year ago when he had had a fall hunting and we became friends and he taught me to play chess and really, he has been very kind to me and I do believe him when he says it isn't entirely my money he wants, but all the same, when—'

Michael Swinton cut in abruptly, 'What in heavens name is all this about?'

'Yesterday George Langley proposed to me.'

He pushed himself off the boat and swung round so that he was standing with his back to her. She watched him in trepidation, but after a moment he turned back and said easily, smiling as he spoke, 'Well, Miss Abbott, I do most sincerely hope that you will be very happy—'

'No!' she shouted. 'No! That's not it at all! I refused him. I refused him because I – I – Oh, Mr Swinton, I was so stupid at Christmas, so hysterical, and I've been so miserable since and I didn't dare to write to you and anyway you are so busy and famous now—' She stopped, for tears were beginning to blur her vision, she could hardly see him. Brushing them away with one hand and using the other to clutch the boat as she stumbled round the bows towards him she said, choking, 'I – I expect you despise me now, I deserve it, I mean you didn't take my picture with you so I thought you – you probably no longer – but I had to ask you, I have to, I mean, and it wasn't till George asked me to marry him that I – that I – Oh, *Michael*—'

He said something indistinct she could not hear and then, not caring for anything at all, not even caring if he pushed her away, she flung herself at him, and felt with a leap of utter thankfulness, his arms go round her, wrapping her against him as closely as if she had been a part of his own body.

Some time later he lifted his head and looked down at her in silence.

Returning his gaze, she said, 'I don't think I want to live up here, though. Not at Trelorne.'

He released her so that he could put his hands either side of her face. With his own face only inches away he said in wonder, 'Miss Abbott, Alexandra – are you making me a proposal of marriage?'

She tried to nod, but his hands restrained her.

'Yes, I am. Is that very improper?'

He said unsteadily, 'It's the properest thing I ever heard in my life. And I accept with my whole heart.'

She pulled his hands away from her face so that she could reach up to kiss him.

'Miss Abbott,' he said sternly. 'How have you become so practised? Whom have you been kissing?'

She coloured a little.

'Nobody,' she said. 'Only – only you.'

He gathered her into his arms again.

'Alexandra, we have a great future.'

She blushed more deeply.

'Painting and farming, a matchless combination. You will have to build me a studio if I am to live at Bishopstow, and you will have to come to London with me. I shan't leave you alone for a moment you know. I warn you that I am exhausting to live with.'

'Yes,' she said, happily.

He went on, his cheek against hers, 'Thank God you came, thank God. I could have throttled you just now, coming coolly over the beach dressed as you always are in my imaginings and your lovely hair, just as it is in the portrait—' He stopped and took his face from hers. 'Ha! That reminds me! What in the name of the devil is the best painting I have ever done doing in your scullery? It's mine, damn you, mine. You have no business to have it. It has nearly killed me to be without it all these months though I hoped it might cure me. How dare you take it and how dare you leave it neglected among the potato peelings?'

'How do you know where it is?' she asked in amazement.

'Punch worked it out of old Meg. I ordered him to. I am absolutely furious, Alexandra, now I come to think of it, furious.'

She released herself from his arms and stepped back, holding out her hand.

'Come with me, then. Come back to Bishopstow and hang it where you will. I only kept it out of my sight because I could not bear to think you did not want it with you any longer. And I thought from something I was told, that you didn't want the picture any more at all, that I could have it, so I imagined you didn't want either of us. But now you – you do – now you have both of us you can hang it exactly where you like.'

He smiled at her then and caught her hand and kissed

it, and together as they had done before they began to climb the cliff path up towards Trelorne, while the gulls cried overhead and the sea, not caring for anything, went on with its gentle splashing game among the rocks on the shore.

Cara

CHAPTER ONE

July 1939

'Where's Cara?' someone said.

They all stopped lolling across their desks and sat up.

'I don't know. Who saw her last?'

'She was with Matron an hour ago. Saying goodbye. Matron was crying like anything.'

'She can't *still* be there—'

'It's leaving prayers in ten minutes. She absolutely mustn't be late for that.'

'Perhaps if you've been late for every single thing at school since you were eleven, seventeen – nearly eighteen – is a bit late to reform—'

'I'll find her,' Alison Burrows said.

They all exchanged glances.

'Oh, Alison—'

Alison blushed.

'I know you think I'm silly, always running after her, but someone has to—'

'Your tunic's rucked up.'

Alison yanked crossly at her tunic, whose flat pleats, falling from a shallow yoke, made no allowances at all for a budding bosom.

'I *hate* this uniform!'

'Last day, my child!'

'I shall burn it. And that awful panama hat. I shall dance on the flames.'

'You wouldn't dare. You'll have to get Cara to do it for you.'

Alison stuck out her tongue.

'Actually, I shouldn't think Cara would flinch from

burning down the whole of St Faith's as a farewell gesture—'

From the doorway a voice said, 'It would never catch fire. I never saw anywhere so waterlogged. Everyone I speak to bursts into tears.'

'Cara, you're nearly late, it's leaving prayers at three—'

'I know,' she said.

She shut the door carefully behind her and leaned against it.

'I've been into Hall of course. To have a look. Got shoo-ed out at once but not before I'd seen who was there.'

'And? And?'

'My parents, naturally. And both my brothers—'

'Even the one who's at Cranwell?'

'Even Alex. In uniform, of course.'

There was a brief and disapproving silence. Cara was the only one of the Upper Sixth at St Faith's who had not joined the Senior School Peace Movement. It had been founded 15 months before, after Hitler had marched into Austria in March of 1938, and Cara had refused to become a member, saying that it was not because she did not believe in peace but rather because she did believe in the inevitability of a second world war. Sarah Calne, the only girl in the Sixth Form who ever dared oppose Cara with any consistency, had handed her with heavy irony, a huge poster of Sir Oswald Mosley, with 'Your Fascist Hero' written across it. Cara had torn it up in silence with huge disdain. Nobody then spoke to Sarah for 24 hours and when she complained of injustice and illogical punishment, was told, in a deputation headed by Alison Burrows, that she was damaging the Peace Movement's reputation and had furthermore alienated the person who might one day be its prize convert.

Cara was not converted. With one of her much older brothers at Cranwell and the other at Territorial Army Camp near Arundel in Sussex, she seemed to feel that their training and eagerness to hammer Hitler should not be wasted. She had explained, eloquently, in a school debate, that England had always been a strong arm to defend the weak. Leaving out all mention of empire building, she had reduced the entire junior school to tears by her accounts of heroic suffering in the Crimean War and had concluded by saying that if the Slovakian countries should need us now, they should not cry for help in vain. The headmistress had sent for her and found that remonstrating with her was as exasperating a business as it had always been, ever since her first crime of climbing the chapel roof on Midsummer's Night, when she was 11. Why Charlotte Swinton had not been expelled on at least four occasions during her career at St Faith's remained baffling to a degree.

Now Cara said, 'You will be – all of you – thankful for Alex before the year is out.'

'Who else? Are my brothers there?'

Cara turned to look at the speaker with elaborate unconcern. Mary Langley was a tall, thin girl of ferocious intelligence, bent on becoming a doctor like the older brother she so closely resembled. Cara said carelessly,

'Your brother, Alan—'

'Not Stephen? Did you see Stephen?'

'I wasn't,' Cara said, lifting her chin, '*Looking* for Stephen.'

Mary flushed.

'Doctors are just as necessary as soldiers. And pilots. Stephen is the most brilliant man at his hospital for years. Everyone says so. Anyone can fly a plane—'

'*Mary*', Alison said.

Mary dropped her head and her fine thin hair, held back by a steel grip, divided unbecomingly over her ears. Cara held out a hand.

'Don't let's fight. Not on the last day. Not we three Cornishmen—'

The sixth form sighed. Cara had ruled them all with singular wilfulness for seven years, but when it came to dividing and ruling, her tactics had always been the same. Out of the whole class, despite the fact that St Faith's had

341

been founded in Bodmin in 1898, only three had been born west of the Tamar. And those three, Alison Burrows, Mary Langley and Cara herself, all came from a headland of North Cornwall between Padstow and Polzeath, and all of their parents had known each other in their youth. It was an indissoluble and, to the others, maddening bond. For Alison and Mary it was both wonderful in the link it gave them with Cara, and exasperating since it was common knowledge – made so by Cara – that both their fathers had been once in love with Cara's mother, and that she had spurned them in favour of Cara's father.

A bell rang loudly outside the class room. Someone burst into sudden tears.

'I don't want to leave, I don't want to, I don't want there to be a war—'

'I do,' said Cara, 'And I shall join up at once. The sooner it starts, the sooner it's over. Hitler has to be stopped. Those poor Poles, goodness knows what he would do to Prague—'

'We must go down. That was the bell. Here, give June a handkerchief!'

'This *horrible* tunic, look what the pleats do in front—'

'You and Mae West, Alison!'

'Pig! Pig!—'

Cara opened the door and looked back at them all. She smiled.

'Bye,' she said, 'It's been fun, mostly, hasn't it?'

'Cara, don't say goodbye now—'

'I say, come back, we're all supposed to go down together!'

'Cara!' someone shouted.

The School Hall had been designed with a medieval Oxford college in mind. It was huge, lofty and as dark as narrow windows glazed in sombre colours of burgundy and royal blue could make it. The roof was heavily raftered, the walls panelled, both in solid dark red mahogany, massively carved. At one end was a stage, over whose proscenium arch hung the coats of arms of Cornwall and Bodmin and on which was arranged a lectern, a table from which to present prizes and a semicircle of battered wooden chairs so that the Sixth Form might surround the headmistress like some sort of heavenly choir. The floor of the hall, apart from the front 20 feet left empty for the junior school, was entirely covered with orderly rows of chairs. Because the day, despite being July, was dull and overcast, six overhead chandeliers had been switched on, gaunt black iron constructions with unshaded low-watt bulbs.

James Swinton had wheeled his father's chair into an excellent position in the aisle of the Hall. If he hadn't done so, Michael would have complained ferociously that he could not see every move that Cara made and would probably have demanded to be wheeled up to where the little juniors sat in front of all the parents, decorously cross-legged on the floor.

'Satisfied, father?'

'Pretty well,' Michael said, 'Pretty well. Better when I've got the baggage at home for good. Where she should have been all the time but your mother wouldn't hear of it—'

'If Charlotte had stayed at home all her adolescence,' Alexandra said crisply, 'I should have become quite demented.'

Michael looked at her fondly.

'Bad enough having me, I know. But I've missed her, my darling, every waking moment.'

'And told me so, every waking moment.'

Michael leaned sideways out of his chair.

'Am I an impossible old man?'

She kissed his cheek.

'Utterly,' she said lovingly.

James climbed hurriedly past them to sit by his brother who was snorting with laughter into the school magazine, copies of which had been distributed round the Hall to waiting parents.

'Oh God!'

'What's up, James?'

'The parents.'

'Canoodling in public again?'

'Yes.'

Alex craned forward.

'Funny, isn't it. It appals us both and Cara never turns a hair. I suppose it's the age gap and modern infants like our little sis are immune to embarrassment.'

'Not so little. She'll be eighteen in September.'

Alex yawned.

'It's ten years since I was eighteen.'

'Twelve in my case.'

Alex put on his father's voice.

'Should be married, my boy.'

'Shall do. Once the war's over. Same to you in any case.'

'Keep trying, old boy. Nobody'll have me. Except other people's wives of course. Always felt that the recent King and I had something in common, buckets of charm, taste for parties, irresistible allure for mature women—'

'Shut up. There's Cara.'

Michael Swinton had straightened in his chair.

'For a kid sister, you know, she is really pretty something.'

'Even down to her hair,' Alexandra said, 'She is absolutely and precisely like her namesake, my maternal grandmother.'

'So, dear mother, you have frequently told us.'

'Lord, what's that lot?'

'Cara's class. The Sixth Form.'

'What in the name of heaven are they *wearing*?'

'Hush, Michael. They are wearing their uniform. It is exactly the same as Cara's and you have seen it often before.'

'Poor children. They look like freaks. Why does Cara look so different?'

Alexandra put on her spectacles.

344

'Cara looks different because she is wearing her sash at waist level, not hip level, and has belted it tightly. She has also turned up her blouse collar, pushed up her sleeves and is as far as I can see, wearing silk stockings. She is also being eyed with manifest disapproval by the headmistress which will serve as a suitable prelude to the lecture I shall give her on the way home.'

'No, my darling, no, not when she looks so pretty—'

'I am not concerned with prettiness,' Alexandra said, 'Only with naughtiness. Her prettiness, more's the pity, she can't help. Her naughtiness she could if she tried.'

A hush fell on the Hall as the headmistress rose to welcome all the parents to this Leaving Assembly of July 1939. Ranged in their semicircle behind her on the platform, the Sixth Form stood with their hands demurely folded before them and heard themselves described as the group going out into the gravest danger known to the world since 1918, but in whom she, Marjorie Ferrars, had the greatest confidence.

'These girls are the heart of Britain,' Miss Ferrars said, 'The heart that is decent and honest and beats soundly for King and country. I have asked some among them to lead us in our prayers in which I ask you all to join. You will find a prayer sheet in the book racks of your chairs.'

When the rustling and creaking had died down, Cara and three others stepped to the front of the stage. All, except Cara, held pieces of paper from which they read their allotted prayers, heads bent. When it came to Cara's turn, she put her hands behind her back, her legs slightly astride in the stance the junior school recognized adoringly as the one she had adopted for the leading role in 'Saint Joan' the previous summer, and recited, clearly and movingly, from memory:

'O Divine Master, grant
That I may not so much seek
To be consoled, as to console;
To be understood, as to understand;

To be loved, as to love.
For it is in giving that we receive;
It is in pardoning that we are pardoned;
It is in dying that we are born to eternal life.'

There was a gratifying flutter of handkerchiefs among the mothers. Alexandra put a restraining hand upon her husband's arm lest he should be tempted to applaud. The semicircle on the stage exchanged glances. A huge pile of new books was brought to the stage and left on the table to Miss Ferrars' right hand for prize-giving.

'You can relax now,' Alex whispered, 'The kid never won a prize in her life.'

The procession of blushingly gratified prizewinners began to file up the aisle towards the platform. Prizes for Latin and Greek, for History and Mathematics, for progress and for steady achievement, prizes for Physics and Chemistry, for Divinity, junior and senior prizes, prize after prize for Mary Langley. And then at the end—

'And now something a little out of the ordinary,' Miss Ferrars said, 'An unique prize. It may not be awarded again for a long time, perhaps never. It has been presented by the staff as a quite spontaneous and unanimous gesture of their own. It is to be awarded to a girl whose presence here, though not academically distinguished, has had a remarkable effect upon St Faith's. We call it the prize for the girl who has contributed most to the life of the school. Charlotte Swinton.'

The Hall exploded. Alex and James stood up to applaud, gallantly followed by the Langley brothers three rows behind despite the fact that their palms already glowed from tributes to their own sister. Cara took the proffered book, smiled at Miss Ferrars, curtseyed her thanks and then turned to do the same to the audience.

'Little minx,' Alexandra said.

'Brilliant!' Michael shouted into the din, 'Wonderful!'

Half the juniors were crying.

'Poor damned school,' Michael said, 'What on earth will they do without her?'

The Swinton Rover was parked in the courtyard of the school. Since Michael's disabling arthritis had driven him to a wheelchair, his was the only car permitted to park in such a sacred precinct. To the rest of the school, it seemed only right that Cara should leave in such a way, like a queen, so that everyone could see her. She came flying down the steps from the main building, her arms full of tennis racquets and hockey sticks while behind her her two brothers, marvellous in their khaki and grey blue, manhandled her trunk between them. Around them the school stampeded, shouting and weeping, trying to thrust last-minute keepsakes into Cara's arms.

The Sixth Form, using the prerogative of their seniority, formed the final escort across the courtyard to the car itself.

'Write to me, Cara!'

'Just postcards, just a line—'

'I'll send you a copy of the tennis six snapshot, I promise!'

Cara whirled from one to another, brushing their cheeks with her lips.

'Bye! Bye! Bye, Sarah, all is forgiven, n'est-ce pas? See you all in uniform! Alison, Mary, see you at home. Don't blub, Juney, it's all beginning, not ending.'

'Get in, you baggage,' Alex said.

'Coming, coming—'

Mary Langley said, 'Stephen would like to say something to you, Cara.'

'*Would* he, now?'

The Langley brothers stood at the edge of the group, Alan exuberantly handsome as his father, George, had been in his own early twenties, Stephen taller and graver, looking towards Cara without smiling.

'Well *Mr* Langley, what is it that you would say?'

'I merely wanted to congratulate you on saying St Francis' poem so beautifully. I never heard the meaning brought out so stirringly. It was splendid.'

Cara laughed and threw her head back.

'That's only a fraction of what I can do!'

Alan Langley said, laughing back, 'Is that a challenge?'

Cara snapped her fingers.

'You can take it as such if you will!'

'Get in the car!' James roared from the driver's seat.

Stephen Langley said to his brother, 'You shouldn't encourage her. Her head is absolutely turned as it is.'

'Then why did you congratulate her?'

'That was different. I didn't know she could be as she was when she said that prayer. I suppose it just shows what a good actress she is.'

Inside the car in floods of tears, Cara was storming.

'Beastly Stephen Langley! Pompous, horrible prig! I hate him, I hate him! Prim, mealy-mouthed medical nincompoop!'

Hands were beating on the windows as the car drove slowly towards the school gates, lips pressed to the glass mouthing farewells.

'Look, look, Cara's crying! She's actually crying! Old Ferrars would give her eye teeth to have proof Cara really cares about St Faith's after all!'

'Stop crying,' Alexandra said, 'A few home truths are long overdue, if you ask me. Now come on, James, put your foot down. I've a new dairyman to interview at five and I want to pick up the black-out material from Waltons on the way—'

'Black-out?' Cara said, raising her face from her father's handkerchief.

Alex said elaborately, 'There is going to be a war, dear.'

'I bought twenty six yards,' Alexandra said, 'And it was only enough for the drawing-room and half the dining-room. It's fiendish to sew. It will give you something to do, Cara. Two and sixpence a yard and they say it will be up by more than a shilling soon.'

'Is that government orders?' Cara said.

'Yes. A very specific broadcast. Low-watt electric bulbs and heavily shaded lamps. Complete black-out after dark. James and Alex have made the dining room quite gas proof. Your mask is in your room and the instructions are with it which you really have to read, Cara, like it or not.'

Cara looked at her parents, at Alex in his Air Force uniform beside her, at the breadth of James' khaki shoulders at the wheel in front.

'Then — then, there really *is* going to be a war.'

CHAPTER TWO

'Of course you can have my bedroom for evacuees,' Cara said, 'I shan't be here. I shan't mind who uses it. I'm to go the moment war breaks out.'

She had gone to join up as soon as she could and her calling up papers had come that morning and were lying in a pool of August sunlight on the breakfast table.

'Why not the Land Army,' Michael had pleaded, 'Then you could stay here and help us.'

'I'll take what I get. The brothers say you can't ask for special treatment unless there is a really urgent reason and I am afraid, darling Pa, that you are not a sufficiently urgent anything.'

'I get more urgent by the hour, you heartless minx. It's an affliction of old age. Don't you think my decrepitude could be put forward to the authorities as a reason for leaving me the solace of my only daughter?'

Cara patted her papers affectionately.

'Your only daughter wants to go and help slug the Hun.'

'What horrible language you use,' Alexandra said from behind the 'Farmer and Stockbreeder'.

'But expressive, don't you think?'

'I want you to help Lyddy clear the boys' rooms today. I gather we shall be packed out with evacuees from Plymouth and Exeter and heaven knows where.'

'James said we were only a neutral area—'

'We are. Exeter and Plymouth are not.'

'Do I have to, this morning?'

Alexandra lowered her paper.

'Yes. You do. Why not?'

'I have an attractive alternative plan.'

'Such as?'

'Being taught to drive Alan Langley's MG.'

'No!'

'Pa!' Cara said pleadingly, 'Mayn't I?'

'Why not, my darling?'

'Because it is time she was of some use around Bishopstow. She has been home from school almost six weeks and despite the fact that a world war will break out any moment she has done not a mortal thing towards providing for it beyond sewing a black-out curtain for that minute window in the downstairs cloakroom so badly that Lyddy had to remake it. The rest of the time she has played tennis and gossipped on the telephone. The evacuation warden – that dreadful woman with buck teeth from Wadebridge – says we may have a houseful any moment. The boys have gone and we must put their rooms to good use.'

'Alan Langley is going on the same Small Arms Course as James,' Cara said, 'He goes on Friday, that only gives me three more MG days. Think how useful it's going to be, being able to drive. Suppose I'm required to drive a tank.'

'Let her,' Michael said, 'Just this once. I'll explain to Lyddy.'

Alexandra stood up and gathered her newspaper and letters.

'You don't need to. Lyddy is as absurdly indulgent as the rest of you and I am too busy to fight you all. Drive Alan's MG, Cara, but Lyddy must leave the wardrobes for you to turn out this afternoon.' She stooped and kissed her husband, 'I shall be in my office. I'm going to do the quarterly accounts early this year for obvious reasons. Don't break your neck, Cara.'

When the door closed, Cara said.

'Thank you, Pa.'

'Why do I spoil you so, I wonder, you child of my dotage?'

'Is seventy five dotage?'

'Definitely. So was fifty seven, which is what I was when you were born.'

'And which Ma is nearly now.'

'Though she doesn't look it, wonderful woman.'

Cara got up and went to examine her teeth in the looking-glass over the fireplace.

'So odd, Pa. All the women in our family have their daughters so late. Ma, Ma's mother, even great-grandmother Charlotte. I wonder if I will?'

'Just have her in wedlock, my poppet, and we will all turn a blind and relieved eye to your age.'

'What exceptionally even teeth I have to be sure, Pa. American girls have theirs all wrenched straight I'm told. Do you realize that on September 3rd next, dear parent, I shall be eighteen?'

'Could I ever forget it?'

She came back to the table and released the brake on his wheelchair.

'Whither, O Papa? The studio?'

'No. I'm stuck fast in a sketch which gave me great hopes by beginning wonderfully and now it has gone dead on me and it depresses me to look at. No, park me on the tennis lawn and I will watch you drive Master Langley's MG into the hedge.'

Cara shifted her feet.

'I don't want you to watch.'

'I can guess why too, you wanton. Then take me into the drawing-room and I shall write to my sons. Do you suppose—' he stopped and looked up at Cara, plucking at the sleeve of her cotton frock, 'Do you suppose that we have said goodbye to them – for good?'

She stooped and kissed him.

'No,' she said, 'Of course not. We haven't even declared war yet.'

'When we do, no-one in the forces will be allowed leave for six months. That will include you, my darling daughter.'

'Yes,' Cara said with satisfaction, wheeling him through the doorway to the hall, 'That will include me.'

Alan Langley said 'No, not like that, don't wrench it. Look I'll show you.'

He put a square suntanned hand over hers on the gear lever.

'Now depress the clutch. Right, now ease her in, gently, feel your way to the left and up. Terrific. Do it again.'

'Will I be driving by Friday?'

'Why Friday?'

'You go on Friday. You said so. To that Small Arms Course in Kent, the one James is going on.'

Alan laughed.

'Good Lord, no. Anyway, you have to take a test.'

'I'd pass it. I always pass tests.'

'Not if you don't concentrate, you won't.'

'I am concentrating.'

'You aren't, my girl. You are looking at me in a way that makes a chap quite mistake eleven in the morning for eleven at night.'

'Well, take your hand off mine then.'

'I get nervous hearing you crash the gears.'

'I shan't crash them.'

'Put her in bottom.'

Cara slid the gear in perfectly.

'Out and in again. Good girl. Much better.'

'How is Mary?'

Alan lit a cigarette, crinkling his eyes as he did so in a way Cara could only admire.

'Calling up papers came this morning.'

'So did mine.'

'She has to report to Exeter.'

'Me too.'

He looked at her gravely.

'I don't want the war to involve you little lot.'

'Little! And how old are you might one ask?'

'Twenty-one.'

'*Grandfather*—'

'I was going into the Army anyhow. I'm to be a Regular. Have to be. Langley brains quite missed me out.'

'I've got an idea.'

He leaned towards her, smiling.

'Have you now.'

'Listen. If you sit in the driving seat and change gear and accelerate, I'll sit on your knee and steer! We could do it down the lane to the village, it's terribly quiet. No-one would mind—'

'Done!' Alan said.

She slid out of the driver's seat while he levered himself over the brake into it.

'There,' he said, 'Tailor made grey flannel lap, madam. Would your revered mother be watching?'

'No. Not a chance. She's doing farm accounts. She might stop if war breaks out this minute, but not before. Ouch. You're bonier than you look. Why are men so uncomfortable to sit on?'

'Vast experience, I suppose?'

'Oh yes,' she said, 'Vast. Let's go.'

He took one arm away and released the brake.

'Ready?'

'Aye, aye, skipper.'

He turned the ignition and put the car into gear.

'Right!'

Squealing, they screamed out of the drive, narrowly missing a gatepost with its grey stone pineapple. Before them the lane to Bishopstow village ran deep between high fields to the church tower and the blue slate roofs of the cottages, sunk in dense August trees. Alan pressed his cheek to Cara's back through the blue cotton of her frock.

'Can't see a thing!' he yelled.

'Don't have to!' she screamed, 'I'm doing the seeing! Faster!'

He began to laugh, his face against her spine, the heavy August sunlight slipping over them through the trees.

'It's wonderful!' she shouted, 'It's like flying! I wish *we* had an open car! Hey! Hey – Alan, stop, slower, slower, slower, *slower*—'

He took his foot up abruptly as she wrenched the wheel sideways and the car buried its bonnet in a bank of bracken. From the lane a knot of children, one leading a yellow-eyed goat on a string, watched them impassively.

'Why didn't you *move*?' Cara shouted at them, 'Why did you just stand there? You saw us coming! Jim Foster, Susie, I'd expect you to have more sense—'

'You was comin' that fast—'

'We never saw it was you.'

'Of course not,' Cara snapped.

They shook their heads. Cara took hold of the dashboard and pulled herself up so that she could step over the door on to the running board. Alan scrambled hastily after her and went to inspect the bonnet of the car.

'Where are you all going?'

'Mis' Swinton said we could graze Nan in the orchard.'

Cara stepped forward, flapping her hands as if shooing a flock of geese.

'Go on then.'

From behind her, Alan said, 'Will they say anything? About the way we were driving?'

'No,' she said scornfully, 'Not them. Is the car all right?'

'Fine, not even a scratch. I think I ought to apologize. I shouldn't have done that.'

'It was my idea.'

'Then I shouldn't have let you.'

'Try stopping me!'

He grinned at her. She came round the car and climbed into the passenger seat.

'Cigarette?'

'Please.'

'Unprincipled young woman. Mary never does! Has some theory, imbibed from brother Stephen, that it causes lung cancer.'

'She wouldn't join my club at school. We used to smoke in the headmistress's garden.'

'Why on earth there?'

'It was the most dangerous place I could think of. Never caught in five years.'

Alan grinned and swung himself back into the driving seat.

'From what Mary says you were too busy being caught for other things.'

Cara put her head on the back of the seat and squinted up through the trees.

'It seems an age away already.'

'That's because of everything else.'

'War?'

'War. This hanging about's no good to anyone. Makes us all behave like lunatics.'

'Are you excited?'

He turned his head to look at her.

'Yes,' he said, 'I am.'

'So am I.'

'Stephen isn't.'

'Don't say he supports the Americans!'

'Being neutral? No, not that. Not that at all. He's the most fiercely patriotic fellow I ever met. But he is a pacifist. He thinks power politics are horribly cynical. He joined something called the Peace Pledge Union while he was at Oxford.'

Cara said with scorn, 'I suppose he gets out of being called up then.'

'Heavens no. You don't know Stephen. From what I've seen of him and his pacifist friends, they will be in the thick of anything that's going, but doctoring rather than fighting.'

Cara sat up.

'I don't want to talk about Stephen.'

Alan laughed and ruffled her hair.

'He didn't mean to upset you. He didn't know you'd overheard him that day.'

'I'm not upset.'

'No?'

'Beast,' she said and put out her tongue.

Alan said with mock gravity, 'And you did read that prayer quite beautifully you know.'

'Let's go home.'

'Me driving. Alone.'

'All right.'

He reversed the car into the lane and swung it towards Bishopstow House.

'I wish you weren't going away,' Cara said, 'I shall die of boredom.'

'There's Mary. And little Alison at the Manor—'

'Tennis threes are no fun.'

'Help your redoubtable mother then.'

'The farm is a bore. Always has been. Ma is obsessed by it. Always has been too. No, I want to be called up and get going.'

'You shouldn't talk like that. It's wishing millions of lives away. Stephen says so—'

'Oh, *Stephen*—'

'Sorry, sore subject. Hang on to your seat, my girl, we are simply going to rip the last half mile.'

Doctor Sharpe's car was in the drive outside the front door. Cara was out of the MG almost before Alan had stopped.

'Pa—!'

He followed her, running, stumbling, over the deep gravel. The front door was open, at the foot of the stairs her father sat in his wheelchair gazing upwards. He turned as they came panting in, his face, under his wild shock of grey hair, as white as paper.

'Your mother—'

'Ma! Ma!—'

Cara fell to her knees beside him, clutching his hands in hers.

'What, what, tell me—'

'She fell,' Michael said, 'She was helping Lyddy with a trunk, helping her to lift it into the loft, and she slipped and fell and struck her head hard, or her back, Lyddy couldn't tell, said it was like a gunshot – Sharpe's with her now. He's sent for an ambulance.'

'Why was she helping Lyddy?' Cara wailed, 'She was doing her accounts, she said so—'

'She went out to answer the door to the evacuation woman and saw Lyddy struggling on the landing. It was the newel post she hit, Lyddy said, it caught her absolutely as she fell. The evacuation woman is still here, she's done most of the telephoning.'

'I'll go up,' Cara said, 'I must go up and see.'

'I'll stay with you, sir,' Alan Langley said, 'I'm most awfully sorry, sir.'

'She can't bear being ill,' Michael said, 'Can't bear it. Gets in a fiendish temper. I suppose it's being so active—'

Diagonally across the huge white bed she and Michael Swinton had shared for over thirty years, Alexandra lay still and utterly blanched. Against the absolute pallor of her face, her hair glowed like amber – it was the only colour anywhere for her mouth was as pale as her skin. The bodice of her flowered summer frock was open and Doctor Sharpe was bent over her, listening intently to his stethoscope. Lyddy knelt beside the bed, tears coursing down her face and behind her stood Mrs Gower, the evacuation warden from Wadebridge, a notebook poised in her hand like a secretary ready for dictation.

Cara knelt beside Lyddy and put her hand in hers. Lyddy's had been the hands she had held all her life because Alexandra's had usually been too busy. Lyddy had been Alexandra's maid since she first came to Cornwall as a raw Scots girl of 21, even before she inherited Bishopstow and became one of the most prosperous small farmers in the county. Lyddy was more to Cara than any nanny could ever have been.

'My fault,' Lyddy whispered brokenly.

'No, Lyd. Mine. *I* should have helped you.'

'Too late now, dear.'

'Doctor Sharpe?' Cara said timidly.

He unhooked the stethoscope from his ears.

'Badly concussed. Maybe that's all it is. But I can't tell without X-rays where she struck herself.'

'Pa says you've called an ambulance.'

'Yes, I did. We'll take her into Bodmin and have a look.'

'Can I come? Can I come with her?'

Doctor Sharpe shook his head.

'No, my dear, you're more needed here. With your father. I'll get word to you as soon as I know anything. She's wonderfully strong you know. In fact I can't remember her ever needing me for anything but you three.'

Cara nodded against a rising flood of tears. Lyddy said, 'Don't cry, dear. It'll only distress your father. Give her a kiss and come away down. I'll find the brandy, not called water of life for nothing, brandy isn't.'

Cara stooped and kissed the pale cold forehead. Close to, there were white hairs among the amber ones, and a tissue of fine lines around the closed eyes.

'Sorry, Ma, oh sorry, so sorry—'

'Come, dear. Come on down. What about your poor father?'

Wheels sounded on the gravel in the drive below. Mrs Gower went at once to the window.

'The ambulance,' she said and made a note in her notebook.

'I can't go down to Pa. I *can't*. It's my fault, all my fault—'

Lyddy stood up and shook her apron away from her knees.

'And has he ever blamed you for anything all your life and would he now? All he needs is comfort and comfort, my lamb, is what you are going to give him.'

There were two ambulance men on the stairs with a canvas stretcher slung on polished poles. They had a jolly, businesslike air Cara could not bear. She pushed past them hurriedly and ran down the stairs to where her father waited in the hall, Alan Langley to attention behind him like a footman.

'Is there anything I can do?' Alan said, 'You know, fetch and carry, telephone, anything—'

'Doctor Sharpe says he will telephone the moment they have the X-ray results or there is any news. He says she is frightfully strong. Oh, Pa—'

Michael said, 'Wheel me into the drawing-room. I can't see her carried down.'

Alan opened the door. The room was full of sunlight, the heavy golden sunlight of late summer falling on all the comfortable shabby possessions, possessions left almost untouched since Alexandra had inherited the house from her Aunt Emily, over a quarter of a century before. Aunt Emily had arranged the house with the crowded, overstuffed comfort common to late Victorian households and no-one had troubled to change more than the details. The walls and woodwork were now all painted cream, the rooms lit by electricity, but apart from that, the furniture remained as Emily Talbot had first decided and the pictures hung as she had directed them in their heavy gilt frames.

Only one picture had been added to the drawing-room, hung there by Michael Swinton himself with the help of the old coachman, Murphy, on the day he had become engaged to Alexandra. It was the painting that had launched him upon the second – and most successful – phase of his career, a painting that had been the sensation of the Royal Academy's Summer Exhibition in 1906. It was of Alexandra herself, young and a little troubled-looking and seated barefoot on a rock, her arms wrapped about her knees, with the sea lapping at the falling folds of her brown serge skirt. A little gilded plaque at the foot of the frame announced it to be called 'A. in Reverie'. Cara knew that for both of her parents the picture was a kind of talisman, a symbol of their love affair, a love affair hardly diminished as time went on and changed Michael from a vigorous black-haired man to a grey-haired man in a wheelchair and Alexandra from a doubting and inexperienced girl into a woman of impressive capability and practicality.

'The picture, Pa—'

'That is why I asked you to wheel me in here. I want to look at it. I want you to stay with me while I look at it. Hold my hand.'

Cara turned to look at Alan. He was standing in the doorway, his face sombre with respectfulness.

She said, 'Thanks awfully, Alan. I'll let you know if there's anything you can do. But I expect we'll manage. I expect – I expect she'll be home right away. Good luck for Friday.'

'Thanks,' he said, 'And – and I'm awfully sorry. Really I am. Goodbye, Cara. Goodbye, sir.'

Michael raised his free hand but did not turn towards

the doorway. When the door had closed behind Alan Langley, he said looking at the painting but holding Cara's hand tightly in his,

'She proposed to me, you know. It was the most miraculous thing you can imagine. Of course, I was enough in love for a thousand men, but I was afraid I was too old for her, afraid I alarmed her—'

A procession of feet came stumbling down the stairs. Michael fell silent. The feet crossed the hall, some-one said, 'Mind that step' and Lyddy's voice could be heard, indistinct but steady. The doorhandle rattled. Cara leaped to her feet. It opened and Doctor Sharpe put his head in.

'I'll telephone as soon as there is anything to tell. Anything at all. Mrs Gower has sent telegrams to your boys.'

Cara went scarlet.

'I should have done that, I should have thought—'

'Doesn't matter, makes no difference.'

'It does, it does. They'll think it so strange, telegrams not signed by me!'

'Too late,' Doctor Sharpe said briefly, 'Try not to worry.'

'Oh,' Michael said savagely, '*That!*'

Doctor Sharpe put a bottle of white pills on a small table by the door.

'For tonight,' he said, 'If sleep is a problem.'

She nodded.

'Thank you. Thank you very much.'

The door closed behind him.

'She came down to the beach to find me. The beach below Trelorne, the house where I lived – pulled down now of course, and no loss to anyone, gloomy old barracks. I was scraping my boat. I can see them now, little feathery curls of old varnish floating down on to the pebbles. At first I thought she had come to tell me she was going to marry George Langley – handsome oaf but no more brains than that boy of his who took you out this morning – and I can remember having to turn away, to compose myself. And when she flung herself into my arms, quite literally, and said was it very improper to ask me to marry her—' he put his free hand over his eyes for a moment. 'Oh my Cara, if you could only be as lucky as I have been!'

'And still are!' Cara cried, 'Still are!'

'Perhaps,' he cried, 'Perhaps, but this war, the boys, now Alexandra and you will go. You said so.'

'I must,' she said, 'You have to see that. I simply must.'

He took his hand out of hers and propelled his chair backwards a little.

'You are like your great-grandmother if tales of her are to be believed. Nothing stands in the way of what you want to do. Open the door for me, would you? If you want me, I shall be in the studio.'

CHAPTER THREE

I shan't ever forget today, Cara thought. Not ever. I am 18 today and we are at war with Germany and my mother, though conscious, has been told she may not walk again. It is Sunday – Sunday, 3 September 1939 and the sun is shining and out of the hospital window I can see convalescent patients creeping along the paths in the sunshine and there are butterflies on the michaelmas daisy clumps. It is nearly midday and three quarters of an hour ago, Mr Chamberlain announced we are at war again and all the time I stand here and look at the hospital garden and the square rosebeds and hear the gentle Sunday noises, Nazi soldiers are goosestepping towards Warsaw. I can hear church clocks striking the hour all over Bodmin, like echoes of each other and when they last struck the hour, we were not at war, only 60 minutes ago. Now we are and it is my birthday, my eighteenth birthday, and tomorrow I shall be leaving home, leaving childhood, to enlist at Exeter—

From the bed behind her Alexandra said, 'How many evacuees are we expecting? Did Mrs Gower say?'

Cara did not turn. Two weeks ago, Alexandra had opened her eyes and demanded to see Michael. She had been unconscious for three days. X-rays had revealed that her spine had received a severe blow at its base, so violent a blow indeed, against the sharply carved top newel post of the bannisters at Bishopstow House, that it had at first seemed that her spinal cord had been almost severed. It had not, however, but had been savagely crushed. She had at present no sensation of any kind below her waist.

What she thought of the situation, she did not divulge to Cara. If she spoke of her feelings to her sons during the brief interviews they were allowed, or to Michael in the hours he spent at her bedside, no-one knew. She lay in bed, her torso raised on a mound of pillows and seemed to Cara the same indomitable and inflexible personality she had always been on two active feet. Cara had been with her within an hour of her regaining consciousness and after a brief caress and a mention of her care of her father, Alexandra had only asked about the farm.

Now, Cara said, 'We haven't any evacuee children, they are in the village. I told you. We have two extraordinarily dreary women teachers who came with their rations which consist, as far as I can see, of Ideal milk and chocolate and sweet biscuits from Woolworths. You can imagine what an ornament they are to the dinner table.'

'You are not to eat any corned beef,' Alexandra said firmly, 'Not until we are ordered to and certainly not while we have any home-killed meat around. Come here.'

Cara turned slowly from the window and came to the bedside. There was a wooden chair, like a school chair, for visitors, but apart from that and the high wheeled bed and a small cupboard the room was a featureless cell, painted eau-de-nil and floored in grey linoleum.

'Did you think we had forgotten your birthday?'

'A bit.'

Alexandra smiled at her.

'The Germans and Mr Chamberlain evidently have. It's a strange coincidence but I know two people now, with birthdays the day war broke out. George Langley – Alan's father – was thirty on 4 August 1914. Open the drawer in that cupboard. There's a packet in tissue paper inside. It's for you. From me. Just me.'

The paper parcel felt heavy and flexible. Cara laid it on her knee and folded back the layers of tissue. Inside lay a heavy coil of big pinkish pearls.

'Aunt Emily's pearls,' Alexandra said, 'I wore them to the first dinner party I went to here. I behaved abominably because I didn't know any better. We never saw any society at Bewick.'

Bewick was Alexandra's birthplace, a castle-like house on the shore of a Scottish loch. Alexandra could never bear to return, so for years it had simply stood there, inhabited only by the farm manager, among the sheep-covered hillsides, the mountains with their deer and grouse, the river and its salmon, all waiting there for James when he decided that he wanted it.

'They're lovely,' Cara said, 'Beautiful. But they're yours, I mean, won't you want them?'

'No,' Alexandra said briefly.

Cara leaned forward and kissed her mother.

'Thank you very much.'

'There's something else,' Alexandra said, 'Not a present. Something I want to say. I had thought of postponing it a day or so until after your birthday, but Hitler has decided against that for me.'

Cara began to wind the long strand of pearls around her throat.

'Just as well. If you leave it even a day or so, I shouldn't be here. I'm to report to Exeter at once—'

'That is what I wish to speak about. I'm afraid you can't go.'

Cara left the pearls hanging.

'You mean you'd like me to stay until you are settled back at Bishopstow? Well, I don't suppose a week or so matters. Mr Price said he didn't see why you had to be here once all the test results are through and he was satisfied—'

'I do not mean that.'

'Then what?' Cara's voice was sharp with alarm.

'The authorities have been enormously understanding. Your father wrote the moment I regained consciousness and we received a letter yesterday granting you exemption from serving in the regular forces but allowing you, by joining the Land Army, to remain at home.'

'But I don't want to be a Land Girl! I don't want to stay at home! What did you say, why did you do it—'

Alexandra reached out and took her hand. Cara snatched it away.

'We explained that we are both now disabled and in need of a considerable amount of nursing. Also that being in possession of a farm, it is very necessary in the event of war, that our production levels are as high as they possibly can be. We pointed out that we have two sons to serve the country abroad and that the country's interests are best attended to by permitting *you* to remain at home both helping to run the farm and to prevent us becoming a drain on public resources which will be stretched to the full in wartime. I am thankful to say that we have had the kindest letter of agreement.'

Cara burst into wild tears.

'You can't make me stay! You can't, you can't! Every-one is going, everyone I know, everyone my age, you can't force me to stay behind! How can you do such a thing! What sort of life will it be, just children and pregnant women and disabled people, just the ones who can't fight—'

Alexandra rolled her head away from her daughter. She said,

'In wartime, Cara, you can't think of what is best for you, what is most pleasant. You must regard this as an order, one that you must conform to, one that is absolutely necessary for your country.'

Cara stood up.

'It isn't for my country!' she said furiously, 'It's for you! It's for you and Pa! You are simply forcing me to do what you want, *preventing* me from serving my country!' She put her hand to the neck of her frock and pulled the pearls out roughly. 'You can keep me here, having got the authorities on your side but you can't make me do anything, not anything at all. And you can keep these!' She flung the necklace on the bed.

Alexandra did not move. Her face had gone very white. She looked quite drained with fatigue. She said in a low voice,

'Please don't think I don't understand what a bitter disappointment this is to you. Or that I don't know how excited you were. Do you think anyone wants war? Do you think Pa and I really want to take any decision that goes against your desires? With the boys gone and – and—'

Cara moved to the door.

'I must go, Ma. I've kept Bassett waiting long enough. One thing is clear and that is that you should have let me learn to drive and then I wouldn't keep wasting Bassett's time driving me in and out.'

'Won't you take your pearls?'

'What will I want those for?' Cara said, opening the door, 'Mucking out the beastly pigs?'

By the time she reached home, her fury had somewhat abated. This was not so much the effect of an hour's reflection in the front seat of the Rover beside Bassett who preferred to do one thing only at a time and therefore, if driving, did not talk, but rather the growing realization that she had always been able to talk her father into or out of anything. Apart from his rather startling brief coolness to her in the drawing-room on the day of her mother's accident, she could not remember any occasion throughout her life when it had not been his desire to give her whatever she wanted. She climbed out of the Rover, thanked Bassett with a cheerfulness which even he found strange after the thunderous expression with which she had slammed her way into the car outside the hospital, and ran indoors.

Her father was in his studio wearing the huge canvas smock that was one of her earliest memories, a smock so encrusted with paint that it was like armour plating.

'Wonderfully timed, my darling! I have just signed your birthday present.'

'Let me see! Oh, let me see!'

On the low easel before him was a painting of Bishopstow House, painted from the seaward side, Cara's favourite side. On the lawn outside the drawing room windows, tea was laid on a table beneath the tulip tree and all the family was grouped around it, her mother in the gardening hat that was a family joke, her father in the painting smock, her brothers and herself dressed for tennis.

'Oh Pa! I love it, I love it! What a heavenly present.'

'And are you wearing the other? Your mother's pearls?'

Cara smiled at him confidently.

'Not at this minute actually.'

'Why not? I was looking forward to seeing them on you. Round your mother's neck they once had a devastating effect on me, one memorable Christmas. Come on, put them on.'

'I can't. They're at the hospital.'

'Darling child, I know we are now at war, but it is still safe to drive through Cornish lanes wearing a string of pearls.'

Cara began to fiddle with the tubes of paint that lay in an open case at her father's side.

'To tell the truth, Pa, we had a bit of a misunderstanding.'

'About the pearls?'

'No. About the war.'

'Tell me. Stop fiddling with my paints. Come on.'

Cara burst into tears for the second time that morning.

'She said I had to stay! That I can't join-up tomorrow! She says you have permission for me to stay at home and – and look after everything here! But *you* know how I want to go, how I *must* go. You can't make me stay here when James and Alex have gone! You'll explain that I can't stay, that it wouldn't be right in fact, dreadfully—'

'I shall do no such thing,' Michael said.

She gaped at him, pink-eyed.

'I know you want to serve your country – at least, that you believe you do. Remember that I have wanted to twice and twice been too old. But you haven't used your imagination, you haven't thought how best England or Cornwall or Bishopstow could use your service. So Ma and I have used our imaginations for you. England has to live through this war quite as much as she has to fight in it. She'll need food. No country can fight without the backing of the people left behind.'

Cara said 'I thought you would see, I promised myself you would understand! How can you! How can you only see things as you want to see them! How can you be so *selfish*?'

Michael drew a sharp breath.

368

'Send for Bassett, would you? No, don't help me with my smock, he can do that for me, quite well. I shall go into Bodmin rather earlier than I had planned. Cara—'

'Yes?' she said. Her tone was more defiant than she felt.

'Dear child. I don't want to see you again until the morning. I want you to go for a long walk until sunset and to reflect very, very carefully on everything that Ma and I have said to you. And tonight, you are in charge of putting up the blackout. In good time, mind you. Regard it as your first duty.'

She did not put up the blackout. She wandered down to the beach in the afternoon and waded in the blue, uncaring sea and cried and cried at the injustice and frustration of her position. She returned to the house well before sunset, observed that Bassett had put the car away and therefore that her father was home and went upstairs to her bedroom and locked herself in. When one of the two billeted school teachers, a Miss Barnes, tapped on the door to say she had just made a fresh pot of tea in the kitchen should Cara care to join them for a cup, Cara refused to reply. At eight o'clock, driven downstairs by hunger, she found that Lyddy had put up all the blackout and that, despite this being the first day of a new war, a very merry party was going on in the stifling kitchen, of which her father appeared to be the life and soul. She stalked through to the larder, found a piece of apple pie and stalked back again. Nobody paid her the slightest heed. She lay on her bed in her dark bedroom – all her light bulbs had been removed since she had refused to have a blackout curtain, saying she couldn't breathe at night if she did – and ate and cried, and the tears ran down her cheeks into her ears and hair. It seemed to her that nobody's eighteenth birthday could ever have been so blighted with such unbearable disappointment.

*

Three days later, James appeared, to say goodbye. He had been ordered into the concentration area at Swindon and had come home to collect everything he might need for the next six months.

'Overseas?' Michael said, pushing unwanted bacon round his breakfast plate.

'Before Christmas, I think.'

Michael nodded. He said, 'Leave plenty of time for getting to Bodmin. The main road is solid with truckloads of troops and aeroplane carriers.'

'Trains, too,' James said, 'I pity poor civilians trying to get anywhere. Learned to drive yet, little one?'

'No,' Cara said stonily.

'You must. You can't rely on Bassett.'

'I wish,' Cara said, 'That people would stop telling me what I must do. It's all very well for you, you're doing what you want to do.'

'Do you really believe that?' James said.

'Yes. You're doing what you want to do and what *I* want to do.'

Michael and James exchanged glances.

'I must be off. Could I have a word with you, Cara mia?'

She shrugged.

'All right.'

'Lead on, MacDuff. Try the drawing-room.'

She strode across the hall and into the drawing-room, banging the doors open.

'Well?'

'Look, Cara, I know it's hard for you. Really I do. But you'll be doing just as great a job, probably greater, as if you were in the forces. If you don't look after the parents, some nurse, who should be nursing soldiers, will have to. And if the farm isn't kept up, food supplies will suffer. Stop thinking it isn't important. It's not so much important as vital.'

'But I don't want to do it!' Cara wailed.

James put his arm round her shoulders.

'And I don't much want to go off and leave Bishop-stow. And Alex, though he loves his planes, doesn't much want to drop bombs on the German equivalent of Bishopstow.'

She wrenched herself free.

'You don't understand! Nobody does. Nobody can imagine how I feel.'

James shrugged.

'I don't know what to say to you. But I mean everything I've already said, really I do. Look after the parents, little one. And write to me. I'll write to you. I'd better be off now because I want some time to spend with Mother. It's marvellous she can be back here in a few weeks.'

'Yes,' Cara said dully, 'Marvellous.'

For a month, she drooped about the house. She did nothing that was of any use to anyone, but lay mooning in her room or on the lawn or drifted down to the sea-shore. The only thing about which she displayed any energy was in having driving lessons from Bassett, but Alexandra soon sent sharp messages to the effect that scarce petrol was not to be wasted on playing about in the lanes. If Cara wished to learn to drive, she must do so on purposeful journeys only. Cara sulked and stopped driving at once. Between them Lyddy and Cook and the two teachers kept the house, looked after Michael, put up and took down the blackout and struggled with the administration of the farm. At the end of the month Mrs Gower arrived to say that a great many children had returned to their cities after the first alarm, the two teachers must follow their charges and Cook, who as both single and under 45 – though not so much under 45 as she had led Bassett to believe – had volunteered for the services and received her call-up papers. Two days after her departure, Mr Price, the consultant at the hospital in Bodmin, announced that what with wartime regulations and Alexandra's really having made an astounding recovery, she should be allowed home within the week.

Neither Lyddy nor her father said anything to Cara about the consequences of all these changes and she affected not to see that there would be any.

One day, early in October, returning from one of her aimless ambles by the shore, Lyddy met her in the back hall to say that there was someone waiting for her in the drawing-room. She went straight through, in stockinged feet, having removed her boots, her shoes in her hand. Stephen Langley was standing in the window bay, in khaki uniform, his hands in his pockets and his back to her. She dropped her shoes to attract his attention and stuffed her feet into them. He turned.

'Cara. I hope you haven't been summoned home on account of me.'

'No. I was coming anyway.'

There was a pause. She stayed where she was in the doorway, fiddling with the buttons on her cardigan. He came forward into the room, quite close to her and stood looking down at her for a moment in silence.

'Are you still angry with me?'

'No. Why should I be?'

'Because I was tactless. At St Faith's Leaving Assembly.'

'Have you come to tell me that next time you want to be rude you will remember to keep your voice down?'

'Not at all.'

'What then?'

'I am extremely sorry for distressing you. And I am even sorrier about your mother. I only heard yesterday. I came home to say goodbye and saw James by chance on the way. How is she?'

Cara moved round him and went to perch on the arm of a chair. He followed her and sat opposite, his elbows on his knees, still regarding her steadily.

'She's much better, thank you. I mean, she can't walk or anything but the rest of her is fine, really.'

'Is it?'

Cara looked up, a little startled.

'Of course! I mean, there's nothing the matter with

372

her brain or her appetite or anything. She's very well. Mr Price said so.'

Stephen cupped his chin in his hands. He had extremely clear hazel eyes and their glance was not, if subjected to it for a long time at least, a particularly comfortable one.

'I saw James,' he said again.

'Oh?'

'Changing trains. At Exeter. He told me – about you. About your change of plan.'

Cara slumped sideways into the armchair, swinging her legs over the arm.

'No doubt you have come to tell me how lucky I am and what a wonderful chance I have.'

'Broadly speaking.'

'Well, don't,' she said with energy, 'Don't bother. Everyone else has. Nobody has the faintest conception of what it feels like to be stuck here while all your friends and contemporaries go off. Mary went almost at once, as you know – as I should have done – and Alison went off to some naval base in Scotland last week. It's *awful*, being left behind, awful beyond anything. And what will people think of me, staying at home and perfectly able-bodied?'

'I don't think,' Stephen said, 'That you have considered other people's states of awfulness at all.'

She swung herself upright.

'I most certainly have! And I think you are all, *all*, indescribably lucky in having a job to go to, work to do, a duty to fulfil.'

'That's not what I meant at all.'

'Well then?'

'I meant your mother. And your father.'

She said crossly, 'What do you mean?'

He said, his eyes never leaving her face, 'I mean that you haven't thought what it is like for their energetic and powerful characters to be confined to wheelchairs. You haven't thought what it is like first, for someone of your mother's temperament to suffer such a physical blow and second, for her to know there is a war going on about which she can do so little. And she is a person who would and could do so much. Your father has the terrible pain of arthritis to contend with, in addition to the paralysing fright of your mother's accident as well as seeing two sons go off. They have, Cara, far, *far* more to bear than you have.'

She jumped up.

'Just what are you trying to say? That I am selfish and spoiled?'

He stood up too.

'I wouldn't put it so extremely. You are used to being in the limelight so no-one's pretending it's easy doing without it. I just don't think it has occurred to you what your parents might be suffering.'

Her eyes were brilliant with fury.

'What precisely did James say to you?'

'He didn't want to hurt your feelings—'

'So he sent you off here to give me a dressing down, did he?'

Stephen put his hands on her shoulders. She tried to shake them off but wasn't strong enough.

'He was simply worried. About you and your parents and everyone here. Lyddy looks exhausted.'

A flash of concern lit Cara's face for a moment.

'Does she?'

'Yes. She does.'

'Even if she does, I don't see what business it is of yours.'

'In your present mood I can't possibly give you my reasons. I did rather hope to reconcile you to your lot.'

She jerked herself backwards and freed herself from his grasp. 'Well, you haven't. And I wish you would go.'

'I know you do,' he said, and smiled. His smiles were so rare that when they did appear they illumined his whole face as if a spotlight had been turned on it. 'May I say one more thing to you?'

She felt close to tears and furious though she could not precisely tell why, with both herself and him.

'I suppose so,' she said gruffly, 'Though I can't think why you bother. You think I'm tiresome and indulged—'

'I told you, I can't tell you why now. Though I do promise you that there are excellent reasons, some of the best I've had for doing anything. Cara, try and imagine what war is going to be like for a lot of those soldiers. People keep saying it will be over in a few weeks, but I don't think so. I think it will be years. And throughout all those years, thousands of men, not brave, aggressive, idealistic men, but normal, ordinary, cowardly men who have been conscripted into the army, will be enduring all kinds of discomfort and fear and pain. And one of the main things that will make their suffering bearable will be their image of England. They'll be dreaming of coming back to England when it's all over. And if people like you don't keep it going in their absence there'll be no England to come back to and all their effort will be for nothing. Staying here, Cara, you are more vital than you could ever be abroad. Vital to your remarkable parents, to the farm and to the image, the essence of England. For God's sake,' he shouted suddenly, 'What else do you think the whole blasted catastrophe is about?'

Cara said looking down, 'Alan said you were a pacifist.'

'I am. But I'm not a conscientious objector if that's what you are implying. Regard my pips, ma'am. Lieutenant Langley, for what it's worth.'

'But you're a doctor.'

'And will continue to be. I'm much more use, doing in war conditions what I am trained to do anyway, than rushing off to volunteer for another job I know nothing about.'

'Do – do you know about – about my mother's sort of affliction?'

'Only enough to know that the psychological effects far outweigh the physical ones.'

'You said you were going away.'

'I am. Next week. Alan has gone already.'

Her head jerked up.

'He never told me! He never said goodbye!'

Stephen said, 'I'm sorry about that. He hardly said goodbye to us, if that's any consolation.'

'He was teaching me to drive!'

'Were you an apt pupil?'

She smiled faintly. He stooped a little to look into her face. 'Am I forgiven now?'

Her smile vanished.

'If you expect me to thank you for another lecture you must be mad.'

'I only wanted to—'

'And don't tell me it's all for my own good. Good, indeed! I can't think of anything good in my present situation at all!'

Stephen said, 'Perhaps I could see your father for a moment.'

Cara shrugged.

'If you want to. I expect he is in the studio.'

In the doorway, Stephen paused, his hand on the door handle.

'Could you bring yourself to say goodbye to me? And perhaps even to wish me luck?'

She did not look up but went on tracing a pattern in the hearthrug with the toe of her shoe.

'Goodbye,' she said sullenly.

'Thank you,' Stephen said with sudden fury, 'For bloody nothing,' and then he went out, slamming the door so violently that the pictures slapped against the walls.

When he had gone Cara collapsed into a chair again. She put her head in her hands and began to rock back and forth, her eyes shut against her misery. Alex gone, James gone, Mary and Alison gone, beastly Stephen going and

Alan gone already, gone – and without even a word of goodbye. For the hundredth time since her birthday, Cara began to cry.

CHAPTER FOUR

On the first day of November, Alexandra came home to a bedroom made by Lyddy and Bassett out of her groundfloor office. By that time, there were very few people at Bishopstow left to come home to with James in France, Alex night flying over Germany dropping millions of propaganda leaflets and the majority of the work force of the farm, apart from Bassett's 15-year-old nephew, and the two old Higgins brothers, gone to serve King and country. They had gone, as they were accustomed to do everything else in the last 20 years, virtually on Alexandra's orders. It was she who had insisted, throughout the thirties, that any man she employed should be a member of the Territorial Army. As she was a generous employer in every way and provided cottages far superior in the matters of bathrooms, warmth and electric light to any others in the neighbourhood, she had never been short of labour. As Territorials, they knew they would be called up in the early days of the war but as Alexandra's employees, they knew that the wives and families they left behind would be well taken care of.

An air raid shelter had been dug in the bank beside the tennis court but there had as yet been no air raids. In order to save fuel, Michael and Lyddy had decided to shut up the drawing-room and the studio, leaving only his bedroom, once his study, and the dining-room habitable on the ground floor. Lyddy and Bassett had pulled armchairs into the dining-room and arranged the wireless in pride of place on the sideboard. Here each evening, they all foregathered for the News, family and staff alike.

Cara had been a little roused from her sulky apathy by Stephen's reference to Lyddy's tiredness. She had offered to take over the poultry yard and was making half-hearted attempts to help in the house. She washed up badly however, dreaming over the sink and making twice as much work in the long run and Old Higgins – so called because at 70 he was two years older than his brother – complained with reason, that she wasted almost as much grain as the hens ate by scattering it casually in inaccessible places. The district nurse, a stout capable woman who had known Cara since childhood, came in to show how to blanket bath her mother. Cara followed her instructions to the letter, but without smiling, leaving Alexandra silent with indignant humiliation. She brought the farm account books to her mother's bedside as instructed and sat listening but not speaking while the annual calendar of farm events was explained to her and the new government circulars as to farm management assimilated. With her father she was smiling but, as Alexandra said wrathfully once to Lyddy, only to exploit him.

'We must dig up some of the grazing,' Alexandra said, 'We only have half the crop output the government says we should have for our acreage. You must get Young Higgins to show you how to handle a tractor. It's extremely easy, I learned in no time.'

Cara learned dutifully but without enthusiasm. It was, Young Higgins said after her first attempt at ploughing, a mercy her poor mother could not see what she had done. Still, there was time for her to improve before the spring drilling, though what he was going to do about the winter wheat he couldn't imagine—

November dragged into December. News came of the battle of the River Plate, of a Russian attack on Finland, of German atrocities in Poland. Food rationing was threatened, petrol grew scarcer than ever and with blackouts and winter nights, it seemed to be perpetually dark and cold. Cara, shivering in her bedroom at night, often wondered what had happened to the person she knew, the person she used to be, the person who had received, only five months before, a prize for having 'Contributed most to the life of St Faith's'. She could hardly remember how it felt to be that person now. What had happened to the buoyancy, the gaiety that had seemed to carry her effortlessly through every day then? What had happened – and that loss was even more painful – to that glorious sense of how lovely it was to be her, Cara Swinton, and nobody else? Mary Langley was far cleverer and Sarah Calne more versatile and Alison Burrows a natural athlete, but none of them had had that indefinable quality that had set her apart, that ability to draw people to her, to set a situation alight, to make anywhere where she was the most desirable place to be. How could you have such a quality all your life and lose it in a few months? Not even a few months, if she was truthful, but a few hours, minutes even, on the morning of her birthday when all her dearest hopes were dashed.

She did not cry any more now. She merely lay and fought against a dull despair. The only thing that could rouse her still was anxiety over her brothers, particularly for Alex who did not have the kind of temperament that liked to avoid risks. For them alone she joined the nightly wireless circle, with her father in his chair, her mother on her wheeled bed, Lyddy and Bassett at a respectful distance and Ted, Bassett's nephew, crouched on the floor by the door as if ready for a swift escape. Both Higgins though invited, declined to come. For them, war was still Vimy Ridge, which they had slogged muddily through together and from which they had astonishingly returned to the cottage where their spinster sister looked after them with the affectionate brusqueness of a dog breeder. They didn't want to know more about war they said; just let them know when that bleeder Hitler was dead—.

Two days after Christmas – a quiet, cold day only enlivened by a telephone call from Alex – two girls from the Land Army arrived to replace – in some measure – the farmhands Alexandra had lost to the war. It was a bitterly cold day, and the snow that was to blanket England for the next six weeks was beginning to drift out of a leaden sky. Cara came in from the poultry yard blowing on her raw fingers – Lyddy had made her some mittens for outdoor work but she perversely refused to wear them – and found the pair standing in the unheated hall, a khaki haversack and kit bag apiece, thick dark green woollen knee socks visible below their greatcoats, and identical green banded felt hats in their hands, gazing blankly at the closed doors that surrounded them. The taller of the two, a coarsely pretty redhead with round blue eyes and a wide mouth, turned at the sound of Cara stamping frozen mud off her boots in the porch.

'Bishopstow House?' the girl said.

'Yes—'

'I'm Ruth Carver.'

The other girl, slight and fair with a grave, narrow face turned also and said, 'I'm June. June Reeves. We're from the Land Army.'

'We're expecting you,' Cara said.

Ruth said, 'It's ever so cold.'

'What do you expect?' Cara said, 'In wartime and in winter?'

Ruth glanced at her companion.

'Where are you from?'

'I'm from Plymouth,' June said, 'I'd just started my nurse's training, but I'd only been at it a month. My uncle has a farm. I've spent every summer there. In Devon.'

'And you?'

'Bristol,' Ruth said shortly, 'And I've never seen a cow outside of a picture in my life. I couldn't say that I much want to either.'

June said, pushing her straight cropped hair behind her ears, 'Your mother's ill, isn't she? Had some sort of accident. That is, if you are who I suppose you are.'

380

'Yes,' Cara said, 'Yes, she has. She is paralysed below the waist—'

'Jesus—' Ruth said in horror.

June said matter-of-factly, 'Well, at least I can help there a bit. I expect that's why I was sent out here.'

'But—' Cara said doubtfully, looking at her narrow shoulders and general air of frailty.

'Oh, I'm as tough as anything. You'll see. Lifting a patient's a matter of technique, not strength in any case. I'm quite nippy with a tractor too. Hadn't you better tell your mother that we're here?'

Standing before Alexandra divested of their great-coats and mufflers, there was even more of a physical discrepancy between the two than had at first appeared. June reminded Cara forcibly of Hans Christian Andersen's 'Little Match Girl', such a fragile little waif did she appear, while Ruth resembled no-one so much as the barmaid at the Mariner's Arms in Rock, with her elaborately arranged red curls and her magnificent bosom. Cara stood behind them both and shuffled her feet while Alexandra spoke to them. What her relationship with them was going to be, she could not possibly imagine. June's undoubted competence, whatever her physical appearance indicated to the contrary, was going to make it difficult for her, Cara, to adopt the natural supremacy that had been hers so easily at school.

'My sons' bedrooms,' Alexandra was saying, 'Sort out which between the two of you. Cara will show you where they are and will introduce you to Bassett. He was our chauffeur-gardener in peace time, but of course now things are different. He works almost entirely on the farm, helped by his nephew, two men and by you girls. You *three*,' she said with emphasis.

Ruth turned her head.

'You a Land Girl?'

'Technically.'

'Them awful breeches—'

Cara flung her head up.

'I don't wear mine.'

'You'll learn to,' Alexandra said crisply.

'Pretty name, Cara,' Ruth said as they jostled their way up the cold staircase, 'Christened Cara, were you?'

'No,' Cara said, 'Charlotte. After my great-grandmother, who was something of a Victorian heroine. My father called me Cara, as a pet name when I was little. It's Italian, for beloved—'

'Where's your father, then?'

'In the dining room. He is very arthritic. He doesn't move about much.'

'Jesus,' Ruth said again, 'All these invalids—'

June stopped on the top stair.

'That's why you stayed at home, then.'

Cara blushed and looked down.

'Yes.'

'What a blessing you could.'

Ruth said, 'I didn't want to stop in England. I wanted to go off with the boys. But was I asked? Not a please or thank you, but it's the Land Army for you, my girl.'

She stopped and looked at Cara. 'Is the work hard?'

'Can't you tell?' Cara said, 'Just by looking at me?'

June said, 'You'll get used to it. It's only a question of getting accustomed to using your body.'

Ruth nudged her.

''Tisn't what I like to use mine for—'

Cara opened Alex's bedroom door. Lyddy had taken down all his treasured model aeroplanes that used to fly from the ceiling on wires and packed all his books and photographs and sporting trophies away in boxes. The room looked as neat and clean and featureless as a school dormitory, even the striped Welsh blanket that covered his bed replaced by a bedspread of green and beige linen.

'It doesn't look awfully welcoming,' Cara said, suddenly conscious of both the bleakness and the absence of Alex's personality, 'But the view is lovely. You can see the estuary and Padstow, there, look, over to the left.'

Ruth shivered.

'Is the other one warmer?'

'A bit. It's over the kitchen. But the view isn't so good—'

'Bother the view.'

'I like this room,' June said.

'You got two brothers then?'

'Yes.'

'Got any snapshots?'

Cara nodded.

'Can I see?'

Cara felt suddenly unwilling to show anything so personal to Ruth.

'Sometime,' she said.

'Do they look like you? How old are they?'

'They are quite a lot older than me. And not so dark.'

'Your hair'd be pretty if you'd grow it a bit. Why don't you put it up, like mine? I noticed your eyes the minute I saw you. Irish eyes, they are, aren't they, so light with those black lashes?'

'I wouldn't know,' Cara said, 'I have no Irish blood at all.'

'Let's see the other room then.'

James' room had been his since he was small. His motoring trophies and tennis cups had, like all Alex's possessions, been packed away, but a birthday card which Cara had drawn for him when she was four and he had framed himself, still hung from a nail above his bed.

'Mind if I take that down?' Ruth said at once. 'I've got all my film stars to put up. I'd like Bette Davis there. Can I bang in some more nails?' She paused and looked round. 'Isn't there a mirror?'

'In the bathroom. You and June can share—'

'The bathroom? What about my make-up?'

'Make-up?'

'Yes, dear. You know. Powder and lipstick and all that stuff.'

Cara thought briefly of her pearls.

'I'm sure the cows will appreciate it terrifically.'

'How old's Bassett then?'

'Sixty,' Cara said witheringly, 'If he's a day.'

'Oh well. Beggars can't be choosers—'

'I'll leave you to unpack. Lunch is at one.'

On the landing, June was waiting.

'Don't worry about her,' she said, 'She'll soon get the hang of things. Shall I come down and give you a hand with your mother?'

Snow fell remorselessly until the middle of February, lying in huge heaps and wind-blown whirls along the lane that led to the village and across all the home fields. The lane itself had to be dug out and kept reasonably clear for the milk lorry to lumber its way up to Bishopstow House and collect the churns set waiting at the farmyard gate. The cattle, a herd of some three hundred, two hundred Friesian for their plentiful yield and a hundred Jerseys for the richness of their milk, were brought into the barns Alexandra had built twenty years before, and fed on hay and chopped root vegetables. Cara, always exhausted and discouraged, did what June and Bassett directed her, winding the handle of the huge awkward mangle slicing machine, ceaselessly mucking out and washing down the concrete floors, going through the twice daily process of milking almost as if in a dream. Her fingers and toes, raw and red from the cold and inevitable contact with cold water, developed chilblains as irritating as wasps' stings, her lips were chapped and her back seemed to ache all the time. Some nights, drooping over the bowls of thick soup with which Lyddy started every evening meal, she felt herself too tired to do anything but hope to die.

Without June, the house and farm would have foundered. With Lyddy, she nursed Alexandra, with Bassett she did more than it was possible to suppose that a girl of twenty weighing barely eight stones could possibly do. She was up in the inky, icy dawns for the first milking, rousing Ruth to help her, and never seemed to go to bed until the last saucepan was washed and Alexandra and Michael both made comfortable for the night. She was also the only person who could deal with Ruth, goading and cajoling her through the wearisome round of heavy, dirty chores involved in a farm in winter. Ruth complained all the time, about the cold, the state of her hands, the muck on the farm, the absence of social life, the solid country food, the Land Army uniform, the general dullness and repetitiveness of each day, and above all of the crippling fatigue. If June had not been there, her antipathy to everything at Bishopstow and her fear of Alexandra and Michael, whose disability and powerful personalities terrified her, would have driven her away within weeks.

The nightly ritual with the news could hardly cheer anyone's spirits either. The Finns were suffering terribly under ceaseless Russian onslaught and the Swedes had decided not to send soldiers to help them. Cara listened dully, thinking only of James and Alex – and Alan. James wrote regularly from Belgium, where he was undergoing much the same sort of training with the British Expeditionary Force as he had had in England, and where he was billeted with a woman whose cooking he claimed would leave him far too fat to fight. The only duty Cara enjoyed was the doing up of weekly parcels to him, socks and cakes and books and letters which she laboured over for hours at night, finding nothing to say which could do anything but discourage him. From Alex there were telephone calls, not regular ones because he said they would only worry should there be a break in the regularity, but usually every ten days or so. He could not say what he was doing, only that he was well and busy. Once he said to Cara,

'So what with Bassett and Ted and Old Higgins and those two Land Girls, you've quite a work force to run! More responsibility than you'd have had abroad, I can tell you.'

Cara, mumbling, said she supposed so.

'Pretty tired, eh?'

'There's a lot to do—'

'Absolutely. Everyone has. Food all right?'

'Oh yes. There's no rationing until March—'

'You won't notice it at Bishopstow! You don't know you're born, lucky little creature.'

'We shall!' Cara said with indignation, 'Ma is going to be a dragon about it. We're hardly left with enough milk as it is.'

'Think of the Finns—'

'I do. And you, and James.' And Alan Langley she added to herself, who never said goodbye and who hasn't written so much as a postcard.

'Cara—'

'Yes?'

'It's rotten, this war happening to you. Just when you'd left school, when you should be having fun—'

'That's all right,' she said awkwardly, 'I can't really remember how I felt before September. Not any more. It doesn't matter now.'

There was a brief pause.

'Are you all right?'

'Yes,' she said, 'Fine.'

'It'll be spring soon, Cara. Primroses and catkins in those copses on the way to Wadebridge, daffodils in the garden. War doesn't stop that sort of thing and you are in a nice, safe spot, thank God.'

'Oh Alex,' she said, beginning to cry, 'I don't want to be, you know I don't. Not while you are doing such dangerous things. Who cares about primroses?'

'I do,' he said, 'In a manner of speaking that's what we're fighting for, and so are the Finns and the Norwegians and, I expect, a whole lot of poor, ordinary, wretched Germans bullied and brutalized into accepting that devil's regime.'

'You don't know what it's like to feel so useless.'

'What do you mean, useless? I should have thought organizing your work force—'

'I don't,' she said in a rush, 'I don't. June does it. She's wonderful. She's everything I'm not.'

'Don't believe a word of it!' he said heartily, 'I'll bet you're splendid. Listen, I'll try and telephone next week sometime. Is Mother all right? She sounded better, in better spirits.'

'Yes,' Cara said, 'She's fine.'

'Take care, little one.'

'And you, Alex! And you!'

The following day brought a letter from Mary Langley. It was postmarked London and bore Mary's ATS number at the top and was written in the hand so familiar to Cara from numerous pieces of Latin prose with no red ink upon them at all bar the alpha at the bottom.

'Dear Cara,

I meant to write weeks ago, but even though this strange war seems to refuse to develop, I am wonderfully busy. I say wonderfully because you know how very poor I am at idleness! I'm working at the War Office and it's fascinating beyond anything – I wish I could tell you more in a letter but I can't so you will have to take my word for it. I'm living with three other WRAC's in a flat in Chelsea – it is unbelievably antiquated, but full of character and I am awfully glad I had dormitory training to teach me how to enjoy living with other girls. It seems immoral to say what fun it all is, but that's the truth!

I saw Alex the other night – I expect he told you. We went to a Deanna Durbin film called "First Love" that I expected to loathe and of course enjoyed awfully. So kind of him, considering all the girls in London he might have taken out. Alan seems to be having a fine time in Belgium – he has just moved billets and had a house-warming sherry party, not to mention his first night between proper sheets for some weeks! Stephen seems all right – his letters don't so

387

much give news as views and the last one had "Base Camp Censor" stamped over half of it in black. Most frustrating.

I do hope you are all as well as can be expected. Please give my love to your parents. I envy you a Cornish spring. Do write.

> With love,
> Mary.'

As if by mysterious communication, the first visitors to struggle to Bishopstow through the snow after Mary's letter were her parents, chugging up the lane in the milk lorry's tracks in the convertible Bentley in which George Langley had taken his wife to Cap Ferrat every early summer of the 'thirties. George Langley had changed little from the buoyant young man who had proposed to Alexandra over thirty years before, except in girth and prosperity, having succeeded to his uncle's ship-building business and shown enormous aptitude for it. Denied Alexandra, he had proposed with characteristic impulsiveness to the sweet-faced, serious daughter of his uncle's doctor and been accepted at once. It seemed to him, then and ever since, that she was the girl he had always wanted to marry. They had a wedding in Bodmin Cathedral in the summer of 1915 and Stephen was born the following year. In 1916, George had gone off to France, managing to escape all major conflicts and returning home with a septic foot as a result of treading bootless on a rusty nail, a year later. Cara had always adored him, regarding him as more relation than friend and indulged by him, as by everyone else, since babyhood.

Seeing the familiar grey Bentley in the drive sent her bolting from a half-done chore in the dairy across the lawn that divided the farmyard from the house. Both Langleys were in Alexandra's room, Mrs Langley arranging a vase of freesias from the conservatory at

Langley Dene beside her. George turned as Cara came flying in and held out his arms.

'Dear child! How's my Cara then!'

'Fine, Uncle George—'

'Heard from Mary, then?'

'Well, yes, I have actually—'

George swung back to Alexandra.

'Doing so well! Can't tell us what it is. Hush hush and all that.' He put an arm around his wife, 'Her mother's brains you know.'

'You have perfectly good brains yourself, George,' Alexandra said firmly.

'All right for business, dear girl. Not much use for thinking. And little Alison Burrows. Heard about her?'

'No,' Cara said in a small voice.

'They've got her sign-writing in the WRENS! All our submarines and warships are going out personally named by Alison. We saw her mother. Tickled pink. Says her letters are so happy.'

Mrs Langley caught a glimpse of Cara's face.

'George—'

'My dear?'

'You exaggerate a bit. The WRENS have hundreds of sign-writers. And there is a war on. It isn't really supposed to be fun—'

'Come on!' George said, 'Must get what fun we can out of things. Eh, Cara? I'll bet you're having fun, tucked up safely here, ruling the roost!'

Cara and Alexandra avoided each other's eyes.

'I'm – learning a lot,' Cara said.

'More than you ever did at that institution in Bodmin, I'll be bound!'

Mrs Langley put a hand on Cara's arm.

'I hear you are doing wonderfully.'

Cara stared at her, her eyes filling with angry tears.

'Oh no, I'm not! I don't know who told you that! I'm so tired I could cry and feel absolutely left out, left behind, different to everyone else when I don't want to

be. If you want to know, I'm doing just as badly as I
told Ma I should!'

And then, wheeling round, she rushed from the room.

CHAPTER FIVE

July 1940

Ruth put her head round the dairy door.

'Someone to see you.'

Cara said sharply, 'Who?'

Ruth sniggered.

'That'll be telling. All I can say is, hope there's some
more like him on the way.'

Cara put a pile of cream pans in a slate trough of
cold water. Something in Ruth's tone made her bristle,
just as it had the morning nearly two months ago, when
she had rushed into the farmyard for the dawn milking,
with the breathless announcement that Hitler had invaded
Holland and Belgium and that the Allies were going to
help. Ruth had simply said,

'That means your brothers won't be home on leave then.'

Cara, excited by the news and tense at the knowledge
that James would be among the mechanized troops
crossing the Belgian border had shouted,

'Don't you *ever* think about anything but men?'

Ruth regarded her with her round, blank blue eyes.

'Not much. Do you good if you thought about them
a bit more.'

'I'm going off for a bit. On my bike. To think, away
from here—'

Ruth had shrugged and then, as Cara had pedalled out
of the yard had shouted,

'If you meet a man under eighty on the way, bring him
back here. Could just fancy one for my dinner!'

She had worn then the look she was wearing now, a sidelong, knowing look that Cara detested.

'Where is my visitor?'

'In the kitchen. Flirting with Lyddy. I should go quick if I were you or she'll have seduced him with veg soup—'

Alan Langley, in civilian clothes, was sitting on the edge of the kitchen table, telling Lyddy a story. She was making pastry and saying, 'Oh, Mr Alan!' and giggling. There were floury marks on her cheeks where she had put her hand to her mouth.

Cara said, her heart racing, 'Hello.'

'Well, well,' Alan said, turning slowly, 'Look at you.'

'I always look like this. Nowadays.'

He swung himself off the table.

'I remember a girl in a blue cotton dress attempting to ruin my gear box.'

'I can drive now. Cars *and* tractors.'

'Pass your test, then.'

'I will. When the war is over.'

He came and stood close to her. He was brown and fit looking, just as he had been almost a year ago, the day Alexandra had slipped from the loft ladder.

'Come on,' he said, 'I'll take you out for a spin. Just a quick one.'

She felt a surge of the old gaiety, a feeling that had deserted her entirely for the last twelve months.

'Oh Alan—'

'Don't Oh Alan me. Just come. It's perfectly above board. I've two weeks leave. A little recuperation after Dunkirk.'

Cara turned.

'Lyddy—?'

'I don't want to be a wet blanket, dear, but you know how it is in the daytime. Shorthanded's putting it mildly.'

'He said just a short—'

Alan took Cara's arm.

'Look. I'll come back tonight. It's a lark driving

without lights. It's low tide too, we might even have a whirl round Daymer Bay.'

'Oh, I'd love it!'

'Cara.'

'Yes?'

'I'm awfully sorry about James.'

Cara drew away, the light in her eyes quite quenched.

'Well, he's alive still. I – I can't tell you what it was like before the War Office phoned the telegram to say he was a prisoner of war.'

'It must have been awful.'

'It was. He was caught in a farmhouse on the Belgian border with forty or so other men. They couldn't escape because of machine gun fire.'

'Where is he?'

'Stalag thirty something.'

Alan shook his head.

'And your mother?'

'The day the telegram came, she thought she had a tingling sensation somewhere in her left leg. But she hasn't had it again.'

'Cara dear—' Lyddy said.

Cara said crossly, 'I know, I know.'

Alan took her arm again.

'I'll frogmarch you back to your pig pens and then I'll march myself off until this evening. When does the factory whistle blow?'

'I'll be free around six.'

'Long day you noble girls work!'

Ruth was standing in the yard when they emerged from the kitchen door.

'Found each other then.'

'We did. Thank you for finding Cara for me.'

'Don't mention it. Any time.'

Ruth watched him cross the lawn to the drive where the MG waited.

'If I could drive, I could take myself into Bodmin and find myself a chap on leave. Fat chance here.'

'Why don't you get yourself a transfer, then? If you hate it so.'

'Oh, I will. Don't you worry, I will. Six months stuck out here is my war effort and no mistake. I'm not going to waste the best years of my life covered in muck and tired out, war or no war. I'm not having another winter here, not on your life. I've got plans to be off, you bet I have. When I've given myself a little treat, that is.'

June came round the corner of the yard, towing a bull calf on the end of a rope.

'Do you know where Bassett is? I want to do this chap's horns.'

Cara said, 'I'll help you.'

'That's all right,' June said, 'Don't bother. Bassett can help me. We've done all the calves this year so we're used to it.'

'Of course,' Cara said, 'I'll find him.'

It was all a repetition of that morning. Her mother had called out for help and Cara, stacking breakfast dishes with Lyddy, had rushed at once to see what she wanted. Alexandra had looked up from her letters.

'Ma? Can I help? Do you want your bath?'

Alexandra had waved her hand.

'No hurry, Cara. But send June to me when she has a moment.'

'Ma, I can—'

'I told you not to worry about when. Any time before lunch.'

'Yes,' Cara had said, 'All right then. I'll tell her.'

As she had looked for June, she now went to look for Bassett. He was with the pigs, as he loved best to be and they were jostling and grunting round his gaitered legs as he poured slops from a bucket into their trough.

'Bassett, June says the newest calf needs its horns cutting. I could hold it easily but June says—'

'I'll come,' Bassett said, shaking the bucket, 'Calf'd no doubt pull you over. Don't hurt them but they don't like it.'

'Bassett, I've been helping with the cows for almost a year—'

'Tell you what,' Bassett said opening the gate of the pig pens, 'It's more that June and me's a team when it comes to this sort of thing. Accustomed to each other's ways.'

'I see. So that leaves Ruth and me.'

'Flighty bit of nonsense, she is, if you ask me. I'll be off, then. Watch and see them little 'uns gets a morsel.'

Cara leaned on the gate and surveyed the heaving mass of pig below her. The huge old sow was fed separately, so were the bacon pigs destined for the abattoir in Bodmin. The wood of the gate was warm under her folded arms, the sun hot in the small of her back through the drill of her shirt. It came to her, leaning there in the sun, while the pigs jostled for chunks of cabbage stalk and coils of potato peeling, that she was, for the first time in – oh, months and months, happy and not only happy but with a recollection of that pleasurable sense of being special, being Cara, that she had so relied upon all her life. Even the two rebuffs of the morning – and they, after all, were no more than came her way every day – seemed to have glanced off her without scarring, without leaving her with the sense of grievance and discouragement that had made the days drag so terribly for almost a year. At this moment, drowsing on the warm wood in the sunshine, the summer air thick with the smell of pig, everything seemed suddenly bearable – her own life, James being a prisoner, her mother's remoteness, Ruth, June's competence—. She picked up a straw and began to scratch the nearest pinkish, mud-smeared back.

'Six o'clock, pigs. Only until six o'clock. Only seven hours to wait—'

'Wish I could drive her onto the beach,' Alan said, 'But I daren't. She'd stick fast in the soft sand at the edge. Come on, shoes off. I'll race you to the water.'

The bay, grown vast at low tide, stretched smooth and blonde to the dwindling ribbon of sea that ran in the mouth of the estuary. The sky was clear, soft in the setting sun, and apricot lights danced in the water. Ahead of them green fields, their smooth slopes broken only by a row of grey cottages curving down to the opposite beach, clothed the further shore of the estuary; to the left, the sea flowed to meet the River Camel, to the right it went dancing out in the rosy sunlight to America.

Cara climbed out of the MG and sat on the running board to take off her sandals. She felt strange and light dressed in a cotton frock for the first time in weeks, being usually too tired to change and the weariness which was commonly unbearable by this time of day, seemed to have deserted her entirely. She stood up, laughing.

'Do look. I'm like a chocolate and vanilla ice cream! Brown face, brown arms, awful white legs and feet—'

'I think,' Alan said, surveying her, 'That it is a pretty devastating mixture. Come on, last one with wet feet's a chicken!'

She could hardly run for laughing. It was like some remembered joy, this racing over the smooth firm sand with the soft summer evening making everything so lovely and Alan ahead of her, shouting and teasing, imitating her. He danced in front of her in the first lazy shallow waves.

'Chicken! Chicken! Hopeless! Why can't women run?'

She stood panting in the water, breathless as much from laughing as running.

'Some can! Not – not this one, though.'

He scooped up a handful of water and showered her.

'Beast! Beast! Just you wait—'

'Catch me then!'

'I will! I will! I can go twice as fast when my blood is up!'

He began to splash her, leaping along the beach in the shallows. By the time she had caught him up, she was drenched, her dark red curls glistening with water, her dress clinging to her thighs.

'Now look at me!'

'Gladly, ma'am.'

'Alan, I am wet right through—'

'It's all part of a plan. Now, to dry off, you will have to walk all the way with me to Rock, where I will buy you a drink at the Mariner's Arms and then we will walk back by moonlight.'

'Terrific!' she said.

He put out his hand.

'Give me your hand. Are you cold?'

'Not in the least.'

'I'll go back for your sandals.'

'I don't need them. It's a relief to be barefoot.'

'All the way to Rock and back?'

'All the way to Wadebridge and back.'

'Game girl.'

Still holding her hand, he began to lead her along the beach, choosing the sand to walk upon that was still damp enough to hold them firmly.

'Have there been any air raids here?'

Cara shook her head.

'Hardly at all. You can hear them droning in off the south coast, that funny uneven beat their engines have, but we have only had to use what Pa calls the Bunkhole once. He's drawn a picture of us all in it, a cartoon. It wasn't really very funny because of getting him and Ma in. Ma didn't want to come so of course he didn't without her, and we had to wheel them in objecting all the way. But the drawing is funny.'

'So odd,' Alan said, 'It's so incredible here. To think Dunkirk happened only a month ago, five weeks—'

She looked across at him.

'Was it awful?'

'Not particularly,' he said carelessly, 'At least, not for me. Worse for Stephen, poor old man, but then he can't even look at the sea without feeling sick. I got away with amazingly little trouble. The boat two behind us got hit but we came across absolutely untouched in a few hours. Stephen was in a fishing boat for over forty eight hours sick as a dog all the way even though the sea was like a millpond. Just as well he was because if there'd been room for him on the ship he'd got all his men onto, he'd have been bombed quarter of a mile out of Dunkirk. He got leave straight away of course and was spoiled rotten by Mother for ten days. He's being sent to the Far East, he thinks eventually—'

'The Far East!'

'Hong Kong is being evacuated of women and children. Japan's a worry. Must keep them sweet.'

Cara said, 'But Hitler's just suggested peace—'

'Come on!' Alan said vigorously, 'What do you think that's worth?'

'I don't know,' she said, 'It's so difficult here knowing anything.'

'You don't know how lucky you are. Anyway, it's absolutely right that you young ones shouldn't be in the thick of things. Mother is stiff with fright for Mary but you couldn't drag her away from London for all the tea in China. They have to rush down to the cellar almost every night, you know, because of the raids but she seems to thrive on it.'

'Yes,' Cara said rigidly, 'I expect she does.'

'Hey,' he said, 'Enough war talk. Tell me about life on the farm.'

The squat grey pub on the quay in Rock was crowded with fishermen and farm labourers. A space had been cleared in front of the darts board, but the rest of the little bar, low and painted the colour of Indian tea, was jammed with bodies and thick with the smell of beer and Woodbines.

Cara said, 'I'll sit on the sea wall. It's still light enough to see what I'm drinking.'

'And what will that be? Gin and tonic?'

'Yes, please.'

He hesitated a moment.

'Shall be,' he said.

Cara swung her legs over the wall so that she could sit facing the estuary. The boats that usually ducked and bobbed on the water were stranded at low tide on the ribbed, weed strewn sand. The sky was deepening now, dusky purple, Padstow no more than a clump of darkness on the further shore.

Alan put her drink on the wall beside her.

'Do you come here a lot?'

'No. Who would I come with?'

'The redhead?'

'Ruth? You must be joking. I have as much in common with her as I should with a Hottentot. Probably less.'

'Good looker, though. Cigarette?'

He lit it for her, holding out a match in cupped hands.

'I've thought about you a lot, you know, Cara.'

She affected to inhale.

'Makes a change from thinking about the Germans, I suppose.'

'No. Be serious. I mean it.'

'Well, thank you then.'

'I gather I was in your bad books.'

'Oh?' she said, turning to him. His face was fast vanishing in the gloom.

'I never came to say goodbye in September. Stephen asked me why I didn't—'

'Oh, *Stephen*,' she said with irritation, 'what business is it of his?'

'He thought I'd been rude. That's all. I think I was rather. I'm awfully sorry. Things just happened in a bit of a rush and being a Regular I was first in so to speak. Funny business, really. I didn't see Stephen from the time I left last autumn until after Dunkirk and then all he did was lecture me.'

'He needn't have bothered,' she said, 'I didn't care.'

'Didn't you?'

She took a swallow of her drink. He said, 'I'd have liked you to. Well, to have noticed I'd gone anyway.'

'I noticed all right. I noticed – oh Alan, you can't think how I noticed when everyone had gone. It's so empty, so awful—'

He took her hand in the darkness.

'Drink up. I should be escorting you home. You're shivering.'

'It's colder now the sun's down. I'll be fine.'

'Have this,' he said, peeling off his jersey.

'But you'll be cold—'

'No, I shan't,' he said, climbing off the wall and picking up their glasses, 'You know what *I've* got to keep me warm.'

He walked her home along the beach under a high midsummer moon, as polished as a silver coin. The tide was creeping up the beach again, dark and shining over the flat, matt sand. He did not hold her hand this time, but walked with his arm around her waist and she matched her stride with his so that they could swing together, hip to hip, bare feet silent on the beach. He talked to her about the army, about Dunkirk, about his views on Churchill, on present military strategy.

'Of course, there'll be a huge air battle any minute. Bound to be. We're bombing Northern France and Germany for all we're worth. Somewhere out over the Channel, we all think.'

'Alex—' she said.

'Don't you worry about him,' he said, 'He'll take care of himself. It's what all his years at Cranwell are for, it's what his life is all about. While we're talking of Alex—' he stopped.

'Well?'

'Not important. Tell you some other time.'

Back at the car, she sat on the running board again and dusted the sand off her feet. Alan came and stood beside her and watched. She stood up.

'Cara.'

'Yes?'

'I've known you all your life and since you were ten, there's something I've awfully wanted to do.' He moved a little closer and put his hands either side of her waist, slipping them up under his jersey to rest warm on the thin fabric of her frock.

'Now,' he said softly, 'Now I'm going to do it,' and he leaned forward still only touching her with his hands and kissed her gently on the mouth. She stayed motionless, her hands by her sides.

He drew away and let his hands fall.

'Right,' he said, 'Your turn.'

She took a step forward and put her arms about his neck. He seized her at once and began to kiss her quite differently – a fierce and hungry business that was at once startling and marvellous. She twisted her face sideways at last, rubbing her bruised mouth on the back of her hand.

'Cara, Cara—'

She bent her head into his shoulder and he began to kiss her hair, the back of her neck.

'I must take you back—'

'No, don't, don't.'

'I must. Or else I'll – In any case you have to be up at dawn. I know. Lyddy said so. Reveille at five.'

'It doesn't matter—'

'It does. And I'll tell you why. If you don't get some sleep, you'll be too tired to see me tomorrow.'

She lifted her head.

'Tomorrow?'

'And the next day. Every day. All this leave.'

'Oh!' she said laughing again, 'Every day?'

'Every one. Come on, now, get in.'

He opened the door and handed her in to the passenger seat, then he went round to the driver's side and vaulted in. He turned to look at her, smiling,

'Glad now you aren't away doing war service?'

'Oh Alan,' she said, 'Of course! Of course! I wouldn't be anywhere but here for the world.'

He leaned across and brushed her mouth with his.

'Tell you something. It's delicious to kiss a girl who doesn't wear lipstick.'

CHAPTER SIX

'Seems to me,' Michael said, 'That young Langley is virtually living here.'

He and Alexandra were side by side on the terrace outside the drawing-room windows.

'Only another week,' she said, 'And then off he goes again.'

'She'll be very low when he goes—'

'Yes,' Alexandra said.

'Out every night, helping her around here every day—'

'He's been a tremendous help,' Alexandra said, 'I never thought we should get all the hay made. I'm going to get rid of that Carver girl, once the harvest is in.'

Michael chuckled.

'You have endured her most patiently, my darling. As you have all else.'

'Michael—'

He put his hand out to her.

'I might live until I'm eighty, ninety. Like this. And a lot of that time without you.'

'My darling—'

'I don't know whether the slight pins and needles I get sometimes are in my mind or my legs. I'm afraid of my mind at the moment, Michael. I suppose I've always been so occupied, so busy with my body, that when I couldn't use it any more, I didn't have any proper mental resources to fall back on. I'm afraid I might panic, Michael, and what should I do if I panicked and you were no longer there to help me?'

He said, 'I think you'll walk again. I can't see you defeated. Nothing has ever defeated you—'

'My mother almost did. Just as I am doing to Cara.'

'Alexandra! It's not you! It's the war.'

'It's both, but it's mostly me. I've had a lot of time to think, especially at night. Too much time. I've neglected Cara and you have spoiled her. Mine has been the greater crime – no, don't interrupt. I repressed her all the time before – this accident, and now I repel her. I have thwarted her ambition and I disgust her. She can't conceal her feelings. You should see her face if she thinks she might have to lift or wash me. Thank God for June. But if I lose you and – and – this is the only time I shall say this, Michael, and perhaps it is better left unsaid but I've gone too far to stop – if I lose the boys too, I am left with Cara. And what is worse, poor child, is that she is left with me. She is potentially the most remarkable of our children and that will be her fate.'

Michael said, still holding her hand, 'I'm glad you think she is remarkable.'

'Perhaps she isn't yet. But I think she will be. When she has grown up a little. I'd rather go into an institution than be a burden to her, a millstone.'

'You can't do that yet,' he said firmly, 'I can't do without you. Not for a moment. And apart from arthritis I am extremely hale. I might live to be ninety two – my father did. That gives you at least seventeen more years of me, getting more bloody-minded every minute, and by that time Cara will be thirty five. Don't cross bridges, my darling.'

'Michael,' she said, 'Oh Michael—'

'I like it when you cry,' he said comfortably, 'It reminds me of the time you put your face down into your bread and butter in the kitchen at Trelorne and cried and cried because you felt yourself a failure. I fell in love as I watched you, like falling into a river.'

'I feel a failure now—'

'Do you, by God? What a greedy creature you are,

Mrs Swinton.' He shook the hand he held, 'Look at this farm, look at our boys – absent I know but never from our thoughts – look at that darling child playing in the hay with Alan Langley, look at *me*, will you, and see a successful painter rescued from obscurity and a man quite transformed by having you as his. Failure, forsooth. I wish, naturally, that there wasn't a war and I wish I wasn't seventy five and arthritic, but all those are natural accidents that have nothing to do with you. Every touch of yours on me has been a golden touch. As a human being, Alexandra Swinton, you are a triumph and don't you ever talk to me of failure again. Not ever. Twenty years ago,' he leaned towards her, smiling, 'I should have spanked you. And enjoyed it.'

She said smiling and sniffing, 'You are wonderful to me, Michael. You always have been. You're quite right – I am a blessed creature and shouldn't forget it for a second. I'll try not to, from now on, truly I will. Oh, if only our children could be even half so lucky!'

In the Dutch barn, Cara and Alan were piling hay bales from a trailer. The air was dim, sweet from the scent of the hay and thick with dust. Cara, poised on the tractor trailer with a pitchfork was tossing the bales on to the floor and Alan was stacking them, column upon greenish-gold column up into the darkness of the curved roof.

'Do you think five minutes off is permissible? I am dying of thirst.'

Cara said with mock seriousness, 'It will mean overtime of course.'

'Of course,' he said, grinning, 'You are my overtime.' He held up his hands so that she could grasp them and leap down to the floor beside him.

'I've only got one cup. The one on my Thermos—'

'A loving cup,' he said.

'Cold tea, Alan? Or cold tea.'

'I think some cold tea—'

403

He pulled her down beside him on a heap of hay in the doorway. Beyond the barn, the gentle fields rolled to the south under an empty blue sky, empty save for a single drift of cloud and, only a speck in the distance, a lonely aeroplane.

'Alan—'

'Mm?'

'That first night, when we were walking back from Rock, you started to say something about Alex. That plane out there reminded me. What about Alex?'

He drained the cup and filled it again.

'Oh that. Nothing much. I just wondered if you knew he was seeing Mary. Quite a lot.'

'Mary!'

He stopped drinking.

'What's so odd about that?'

'Nothing. I mean – well, he has only come home once, since the beginning of the war. He telephones quite a lot, but we haven't seen him except once, at Easter. He must have had leave, lots of leave, even if it's only short, and he's well – well, he's going to London, not here—'

'I think it's quite serious.'

'Him and Mary?'

'Yes. Odd, wouldn't it be, him and Mary, you and me—'

Cara rolled away from him and lay propped on one elbow.

'Of course we don't know where he flies from. We aren't allowed to know. Perhaps it's the other side of London, the wrong side for Cornwall. Actually—', she paused and sat up, 'I did have a letter from Mary, ages ago, in the winter and she said they'd seen a film together. But Alex never says anything on the telephone. We just talk about things here, Ma and Pa and so on. Funny, really, if it's true. Mary isn't his type.'

Alan pulled her round to face him.

'What do you mean?'

'Don't get angry. I only mean that he has never fallen

404

for anyone intelligent before. Or single for that matter. You know Alex's reputation as well as I do. Remember the flap over the dentist's wife in Wadebridge? And poor silly Mrs Whatsername who spent the summer with the Burrows?' She looked at him. 'How do you know about it anyway? You were in France until six weeks ago.'

'Oh,' he said, 'This and that. Hints in letters, the parents, you know the sort of thing.'

Someone was shouting from the field gate. Alan got up and went to the corner of the barn.

'It's Ruth. I'll go down and see what she wants.'

'Don't,' Cara said, 'Make her come up here. Do her good.'

'Why are you so down on her?'

'If you really want to know, I think she is shallow, common, idle and unprincipled.'

He grinned. 'That will do for starters.' Then he went to the corner of the barn again and signalled wildly. 'Come up here, then! Only take a minute!'

'I rather like her,' he said, 'Easy on the eye anyway.'

'Some eye.'

'Jealous?'

'Oh, of course,' she said with heavy sarcasm, 'When I get to regard the Ruth Carvers of the world as competition, I really will be desperate.'

Ruth said, panting up the slope, her shirt unbuttoned lower than June would allow if she noticed, 'They need the tractor. Back in the Ten Acre. Said you was to bring it at once, one of you. And I'm to help stack what's left. Jesus, this heat. I could die.' She looked around her. 'Doesn't look as if much work was going on here. Quite a party. Why didn't you send out invitations?'

Alan held out a hand to pull Cara to her feet.

'Well, old thing? Tractor or hay bales?'

Cara hesitated for a second.

'Tractor.'

'Your wish is my command. One second while I unhitch it for you. Will you come back and get us?'

'Someone will. Or you can walk.'

'Shouldn't mind the walk,' Ruth said.

'Come on, Cara. Come back for us. We'll only be twenty minutes or so. There. Your steed awaits you.'

'Thanks.'

She climbed up into the curved metal seat and put her hand on the key. He swung himself after her so that his face was level with hers.

'Cara. What's the fuss?'

'You know what it is. I don't like her.'

'That's why you are going off on the tractor. So you don't have to endure her.'

'Alan—'

'Yes?'

She looked down and started the engine.

'It doesn't matter,' she shouted above the roar.

'Where tonight?' he shouted back.

'I don't mind—'

'Pentyre Head? To watch the sunset?'

She nodded.

'Back in twenty minutes then!'

He jumped backwards off the tractor and she put it into gear and drove it, shuddering, out of the barn into the sunlight and down the slope to the gate.

'I don't know whether to plead with you or beat you,' Alan said. 'I just wish you'd tell me what's the matter.'

She was sitting beside him in the MG, looking towards the huge fiery ball of the sun which was slipping down the green-blue shell of the sky to the sea.

'All right,' she said, staring woodenly ahead, 'I wonder if you would tell me what happened in the barn this afternoon.'

'Oh!' he said trying to take her hand, 'I'll tell you exactly. We stacked forty seven bales of hay. I counted.'

'And?'

'And nothing.'

'Then why did Ruth sit through supper smirking at

me and go about the place humming, with her eye on me all the time and why were you an hour over forty seven bales?'

'You never came back for us.'

'I didn't want to see anything.'

He said, grinning, teasing her, 'You wouldn't have. We should have heard the tractor coming.'

'Then I'm right!'

'Absolutely. I've never had such an hour in my life. Passion wasn't in it. Come on, Cara, don't be an ass. Ruth and I stacked the bales and had a cigarette and talked about the war and Bristol, where she lives, and then June came roaring up and ticked us off for idling.'

As the sun slipped down, a small breeze came up and began to blow Cara's curls about very softly, patting them against her cheeks. Alan said,

'You're the prettiest thing I ever saw.'

She turned to look at him.

'Really?'

'Cross my heart. You always have been.'

She let him trap her hand and kiss it.

'Alan. In a week you'll be gone. By this time next week, you will have been gone almost a day. Friday morning, you said.'

'I'm afraid so.'

'But you want to get back, really, don't you. I can feel it.'

'I want everything. I want my job and to be here.'

She turned to face him and said teasingly, 'Could it be said that you are, so far, actually enjoying the war?'

He smiled and ruffled her hair.

'It could.'

'But the danger—'

'That just makes some things more precious.'

'Like?'

'Like you.'

She bent her head in silence.

'Cara.'

407

He put his hand under her chin and turned her head so that he could look at her.

'Cara, you are fond of me, aren't you?'

'Fond!'

'Tell me, then.'

'I love you, Alan. I'm in love with you.'

He leaned and kissed her lightly.

'And I'm wild about you. I suppose I always have been, but things like a war sort out one's feelings very clearly. Listen, Cara. It isn't fair, really, what I'm going to ask you. But I – well, I can't help myself. When all this is over, when I come back – I suppose I should say if I come back – would you marry me?'

'Marry you!'

'Yes. Marry me. We needn't wait till after the war – I mean, next leave maybe, why not—'

'Oh Alan, Alan!'

'Will you?'

'Yes, oh yes! Alan, I can't believe it, I'm so happy! Marry you! Oh Alan, kiss me, kiss me—'

A little time later he said,

'Shall you mind not having a ring? I mean, of course, I'll get you one the minute I can but it's a bit difficult. Perhaps you could come up to London and we'll choose one and do a show or something as well.'

'London!'

'You know,' he said earnestly, 'It's on the Thames, capital of England, where the government is—'

'Fool!' she said, laughing, her hand in his.

'My next leave, then.'

'Where will you be till then?'

'I don't know. I don't know what's planned next. No-one does. But we'll keep on training.'

'Here? In England?'

'Oh yes—'

'Then you can telephone!'

'Endlessly.'

'Alan?'

He put his hand round the back of her neck, under her hair.

'Alan – are you going to speak to Pa?'

'Ask his permission, that sort of thing?'

'Yes.'

He took his hand away.

'To be absolutely honest, I'd like it just to be a secret at the moment. Just you and me—'

'I wouldn't tie you down!'

'It isn't that. It's not that at all. I just don't want to spoil what we've got, making it all heavy and official. I want it to stay exciting, free – you know—'

She put her head on his shoulder.

'Of course I know.'

'Look' he said, 'The sun's gone.'

'And the stars have come out.'

'Our stars.'

She said, burrowing her face against his neck, 'Do you know, if it wasn't for thinking of James in a prison camp and always being anxious about what Alex will do, I'd be so happy I wouldn't believe I'm still alive.'

'James will pull through,' Alan said comfortably, 'And Alex isn't a fool.'

'It isn't just Alex. It's enemy pilots.'

Far away to the south, as if on cue, came the faint irregular throbbing of a German aeroplane. They listened in silence, intent upon the distant uneven beat until it faded into the darkening air and silence fell again, broken only by the sea's gentle shushing far below. Alan got out of the car and picked a long-stemmed thrift from a cushion which grew on the cliff's edge. He brought it back to the MG and leaning over the passenger door, wound the stem around Cara's left third finger, leaving the round pink head on the top like a jewel.

'With this ring I thee implore to marry me.'

She looked at him solemnly.

'I will, Alan,' she said.

*

'Is it nasty?' Lyddy said anxiously.

Cara, her mouth full of cake, nodded reluctantly.

'I feared as much. But they promised on the wireless that vinegar made a good lightening and Miss Alexandra's that keen on us sticking to the rules. I'd wanted you and Mr Alan to have something nice to take out with you tonight, being as it's his last night—'

'Lyd, it doesn't matter. Not a bit. We must do what we're told, I just hate to think of your wasted effort.'

'Lord, I don't mind the effort. But I hadn't made a cake in months. I thought we'd have a treat, cheer you up a bit. Don't know how anyone can be cheerful on margarine.'

Cara put the rest of her cake down on the table.

'When Alan goes, Lyd, I won't care what I eat. I'll finish the cake, then, I promise. But really, I'm not hungry now, or tired—'

Lyddy said with sudden sharpness, 'You're not doing anything you shouldn't?'

'No,' Cara said, blushing helplessly, 'No—'

'I remember the last war,' Lyddy said, lowering the failed cake into a tin, 'People were that foolish. My own sister among them. "Ain't you got no shame?" I said to her. "We might all be dead tomorrow," she said to me. Reminds me of that Ruth. I've ironed your frock. The yellow flowered one.'

'*Lyd*. You shouldn't—'

'I know. But I can't help myself. Go and put it on now or he'll be roaring in here shouting for you.'

In the hall, Michael was tapping the barometer.

'Glass is falling.'

'Fast?'

'I don't think you will get rained on tonight, if that's what you mean. No danger of having to bale out the MG. Cara—'

'Pa?'

'I wish I could think of some nice diversion for you for tomorrow.'

She said; 'I'll be all right.'

He held out a letter.

'From James. A blessed relief to hear from him, but he sounds pretty low.'

She backed away.

'I'll – I'll read it tomorrow, Pa. I'll be late—'

Her yellow dress was laid across her bed, the bodice fastened with buttons like daisies. It had been new last summer, Lyddy had made it as a welcome home from school, a welcome to adult life. She had hardly worn it. She had hardly worn anything but shirts and breeches and heavy military jerseys knitted of stiff khaki wool until Alan came one leave. She prided herself that she had worn a different frock every night for him, all the frocks Lyddy had made for her the last two summers. The yellow one with daisies was her grand finale.

It was not only frocks that Lyddy had made. Downstairs in the hall was a picnic hamper, packed by Lyddy for Cara and Alan's last evening together on those westward facing cliffs where they had watched the sun go down into the sea for almost a fortnight now. The failed cake had been intended for the picnic's tour de force, but it would hardly be missed. Cara dressed herself with enormous care, scrubbed her nails, brushed her hair vigorously, hung the gold and coral locket that had been her father's christening present to her around her neck. She looked at herself in the glass, gravely, for a long, long time and then she took up her Bible, her school Bible with her name written on the flyleaf in eleven-year-old handwriting. In the centre at the end of the book of Psalms, she had placed the single stem of thrift, pressing it between sheets of greaseproof paper taken from the kitchen. She looked at it for a while and then stooped and touched the drying flowerhead with her lips before she closed the book and went downstairs.

'That,' Alan said, stretched on the turf, 'Was sensational.'

Cara looked proudly at the chicken carcass, the fruit peels, the empty champagne bottle – donated by her father she supposed, from what was left after Alex's twenty first birthday nearly ten years before.

'Champagne!' he said, 'Think of it—'

'Lyddy meant you to have a cake.'

'Cake! Who needs cake? Come here.'

He had spread a rug between the car and the cliff edge and through the wool she could feel the short turf springing like a mattress. She lay beside him on her stomach so that she could watch him as he gazed at the sky, his cigarette glowing orange in the dim blue dusk.

'Happy?'

'Yes,' she said.

'I'll phone you,' he said, 'Probably in a day or two. Tell you where I am.'

'I rather dread tomorrow.'

He turned to look at her, smiling.

'Hey, hey, I'm only going a matter of miles. I'll phone you, I said so. Cheer up, sweetheart. I'll be back before you know it.'

He sat up and reached out to stub his cigarette on a nearby plate.

'Shouldn't really smoke in the open air. It's against the rules. Jerry got some fellows billetted near Southampton the other night who were smoking outside. Cara—'

'Mm?'

'Turn over. I don't want to kiss the back of your head.'

His mouth tasted of smoke and champagne. She held him against her, her hands cupped behind his head, her fingers in his hair.

'Wild about you,' he said.

'I'd die if you weren't—'

He moved his mouth from her face and began to kiss her chin, then her throat, then the base of her throat where her dress fell away at the neck.

'Cara—'

His cheek lay against the skin above her breasts. She

412

could feel his hand on the daisy buttons down her bodice.

'Our last night, Cara. Let me make love to you.'

She was very excited.

'Alan, oh Alan—'

'Come on, sit up. Help me get this off—'

The moon was rising, silver on her skin.

'Look at you, lovely Cara, lovely, lovely Cara.'

He knelt in front of her, kissing and stroking and she tilted her head back to gaze at the darkening sky, hearing her breath coming in little gasps as if she had been running. He put his hands on her hips and pulled her dress down roughly, tearing the fabric.

'No,' she said sharply.

'Come on, come on, I'll buy you another, it's only cotton—'

'No,' she said suddenly, twisting away from him, 'Stop it, no don't—'

'I won't hurt you, I promise. I'll be awfully gentle, don't be afraid.'

He put his hands on her waist but she slipped from him like a fish, rolling off the rug on to the turf.

'Cara!'

She scrambled to her feet, pulling the torn dress up from her knees.

'I'm not afraid, Alan, but I'm not going to, I don't want to—'

'Cara!'

'I'm not afraid,' she repeated.

'What's the matter?' He knelt up on the rug, his shirt open. 'You never were afraid of anything before! I've never seen you scared—'

'I'm not scared. I'm – just not going to.'

He got to his feet and seized her shoulders.

'Are you mad? This is me, Alan. You are going to marry me. I am not some sex starved stranger. You love me, you said so. Half a minute ago you wanted it as much as I did. What the hell's gone wrong?'

She looked at him clearly.

'I don't know. I can't explain it. I *did* want to, I do still. But I won't. I shouldn't have let you begin. I'm sorry.'

'You bloody little bitch!' he shouted.

She dropped to the grass, tumbling plates and forks and chicken bones back into the basket. Alan bent and caught her arm, twisting her to look at him.

'Some night to remember! Some way to treat a chap who's going off! You're lucky I don't chuck you over the cliff!'

'Chuck me then.'

'Cara, what in hell's name's the matter?'

She sat back on her heels. She had buttoned up her frock haphazardly, and he could see glimpses of skin here and there, breast and ribcage and a long slash of hip through the rent in the skirt.

'Alan, I don't know. I love you as much as ever, I can't tell you how much I love you. But I don't want you to make love to me – yet. I don't *know* why. If I did, I'd tell you. It's something I feel. A sort of sixth sense—'

'About what?'

'I keep telling you. I don't know.'

He sighed and dropped her arm.

'I suppose I forgot how young you are.'

She tried not to sound nettled. 'I'm old enough to know that I've behaved badly, that you shouldn't lead a man on and then – then say no. I'm awfully sorry about that. Really I am.'

He got to his feet slowly.

'I'll get over it.'

She looked up at him.

'Are you angry?'

'A bit. Puzzled, mostly, though. I thought – well, all day I thought we'd – we'd been sort of leading up to this, all these evenings together, you letting me kiss you and touch you—'

'I wanted you to. I still do. I just won't.'

'Who'd know, Cara?'

'I should.'

'It's not *like* you. You don't care about breaking the rules.'

'Well, I seem to about this one.'

'Yes,' he said, sighing, 'You certainly seem to.' He walked to the cliff edge and stood there for a while, buttoning his shirt, silhouetted against the gleaming sea. Then he came back slowly and stood watching her while she strapped the hamper and fumbled in the darkness for her sandals.

'Come on,' he said and his tone was flat, 'I'll get you home.'

It was of no use trying to sleep. It wasn't moonlight that was keeping her awake because ragged black clouds were sweeping in from the west on a strengthening wind and the moon was almost entirely hidden, but far more her own restlessness, her thoughts which hurled her from regret to remorse and back again like a ship in a storm. There was no doubt but that, drowning as she had briefly under Alan's mouth and hands, she could not, in the smallest degree, have disobeyed the impulse that had forced her away from him. She regretted the impulse bitterly, resented it even, but had recognized it as all-powerful. Confused and beaten by it, she had longed for some small sign of consolation from Alan on the way home even though she had seen it was hardly reasonable to expect one – but he had driven stony-faced and silent, and when they reached Bishopstow, he did not even turn off the engine but leaned across her to open her door, kissing her briefly on the cheek.

'Can't we talk?'

'There's nothing much to say.'

'You are the last person I want to hurt, even to annoy—' she said.

'It looks like it.'

'Are you just leaving like that? Going away, leaving things so – so—'

He switched the engine off then and sighed.

'I might go down to Daymer and walk on the beach a bit. Think it out.'

'May I come?'

'I'm best alone.'

She got out of the car and stood looking at him.

'Is this goodbye?'

'No,' he said, 'I'll come by in the morning. I'll feel better then. Is it all right if I leave the car in the yard for an hour?'

''Course,' she said.

It was more than an hour since then. Perhaps she had dozed and had missed the MG's going, though she hardly thought it likely, its engine being so familiar to her now. She sat up and looked out at the night sky. Through the open window she smelled rain on the wind, Alan, wandering down there on the beach, was going to be soaked and the MG, coverless in the yard, would be awash. She swung her legs over the edge of the bed and stood up. The least she could do, after behaving in so utterly feminine and unpredictable a fashion, was to cover his car.

The house was as black as pitch. All the interior doors were shut and the only window which gave light on to the stairs and landing was shrouded in its blackout curtain. Running her hand along the bannister rail, Cara stepped softly down the stairs to the hall. The kitchen, on the way to the yard, would at least be lighter since they ate supper so early in summer in there that it was not necessary to black it out.

She opened the kitchen door as quietly as possible. The room was filled with a dim greyish light and had a frozen air as if some sudden activity had just been suspended there. Cara took a step forward towards the opposite door that led through the sculleries to the yard. Quite close to her, startlingly close, someone laughed, a low, secret woman's laugh. She turned abruptly and saw Alan framed in the huge grey oblong of the window, and

416

in his arms a woman, a woman with her blouse pulled off her shoulders and a tumble of thick red curls.

Alan stood in the barn doorway, backed by the teeming rain, and regarded her.

'*Please*, Cara. You know why it was. I was just out of my mind with wanting you. I only kissed her.'

Cara went on hosing down the concrete, letting the water swish angrily among the litter of dung and straw.

'Ruth,' she said, 'Of all people. How *could* you?'

He took a step forward.

'I told you. I wanted you. I was terribly worked up. Ruth was just around—'

'She watched you.'

'Perhaps,' he said, shrugging.

'Can you imagine how I felt? How I feel?'

'And can you imagine how *I* felt? Last night?'

She put her finger on the hose end so that it shot out in a heavy jet.

He strode over to where a brass tap head protruded from the wall and turned off the hose.

'Listen to me!'

She stood, holding the dripping hose, her head turned away.

'Listen, Cara. You shouldn't have egged me on and then gone cold on me. I shouldn't have kissed Ruth. We're quits. Neither event matters so forgive and forget.'

'How can you,' she said slowly, 'Love me – and do that to her? She was half-naked—'

'Don't exaggerate. Love doesn't come into it with a girl like Ruth.' He leaned forward and twitched the hose out of her hand. 'Make me happy, Cara. Send me away happy.'

In his arms she said, 'When will you telephone?'

He smiled down at her.

'Soon.'

She put her face against him.

'I wish none of it had happened.'

417

'What! You and me?'

'No. Last night.'

'Amen to that. But we'll go on as if it hadn't. Clean slate starts now.'

'You should go.'

'Only if it's with your blessing.'

'It is.'

He bent his head and kissed her.

'You look tired.'

'I didn't sleep,' she said.

'You will tonight.'

'Perhaps.'

'Cara—'

'Yes?'

'About — about last night. Does anyone know?'

She drew back a little.

'Of course not. I have *some* pride. Ruth is packing but then Ma wanted her gone anyway. They know we've had a row — Ruth and me, I mean — but not about what. It doesn't matter anyway since we weren't exactly on the best of terms.'

'You're a brick. The prettiest brick I ever saw.'

He crossed to the wall and turned the tap on again, then stooped to pick up the spurting hose and handed it to Cara.

'On with the great work, sweetheart.'

She smiled at him. He put an arm around her shoulder and kissed her cheek.

'Think of me,' he said.

CHAPTER SEVEN

In late September, Alex came home, in order to prove, as he said himself, that he had survived the Battle of Britain. He sat at the head of the table in the dining-room and told them about it, how the Germans had lost four times as many planes as we had, how exciting and how terrible it was, all at once, how many friends he had lost. Then he said,

'It's very likely we shall be invaded.'

'I know,' Alexandra said calmly, 'And have more and worse raids. Eggs are up to three and sixpence, we are not allowed cream any more and two nights ago the sky was so bright with parachute flares that I thought we were being invaded then.'

'Mother,' Alex said, 'You are wonderful.'

She smiled at him.

'Wonderfulness is a condition of war. Look at the King and Queen. A direct hit on Buckingham Palace and the first thing they do is go off to console the homeless in the East End.'

June said, 'You'd have done much the same.'

Cara said nothing. She had been listening to Alex, her chin cupped in her hands and she stayed like that, her eyes fixed upon a bowl of huge bronze chrysanthemums which Lyddy had put on the table, all of ten days before, to celebrate her nineteenth birthday. It had been so quiet, that birthday, that it was difficult to distinguish it from any ordinary day. She had risen at dawn to show the new land girl, Barbara, the milking routine, then spent the morning picking runner beans to be taken into Wadebridge and the afternoon milking again and cleaning up while June and Bassett dealt with the last acres of the harvest. Indeed the fact of 3 September's being a birthday was quite obliterated by its being the first anniversary of the war and would probably never have arisen at all but for Lyddy, the bronze chrysanthemums and a cake which reminded her so powerfully of Alan's last evening that she averted her eyes from it.

'Saved up the butter,' Lyddy said, 'Kept back a few extra eggs – braved Miss Alexandra for that. I hope the flour is decent – seems there's a government regulation to put calcium in it while the war's on. I only hope it doesn't make the poor thing heavy as lead.'

Michael had painted her a caricature of herself as a land girl, Alexandra had given her a five pound note. There was somewhat naturally, no news from James. Nor was there anything from Alan. He had left at the end of July and in the pocket of her breeches she carried his only two letters. He had telephoned three times, affectionate and busy, from a training camp in Bedfordshire. If he had had leave, he did not say so and Cara would not ask him.

Alex was at home a week. He looked suddenly much older to Cara, his face hollower, with a sort of bruised and exhausted look to the skin around his eyes. He spent a day with Michael and Alexandra, gentle and solicitous, and then he came out into the yard on the second morning to work alongside his sister.

'You needn't,' she said.

'I want to.'

'Are you afraid I cut corners?'

'Do you?'

She said, 'It isn't getting any easier.'

'It isn't for anyone, old thing.'

'I know,' she said, 'But I do rather dread the winter. It's so cold and we're bound to be hungrier.'

'What are you doing this morning?'

'More blasted beans to pick.'

Alex was very thin, she noticed, as he stooped to pick up the stack of bushel baskets to take out to the field. The bones of his spine thrust knobbily through his shirt. He had had a debonair and stylish air about him but now, although his smile was the same, he looked more serious, less carefree.

'Things aren't improving, are they,' he said, 'Between Mother and you.'

Cara said, 'She has June.'

'June isn't her daughter.'

'She's better than I could be. She's more efficient, she knows what she is doing.'

'Suppose,' Alex said, watching her as she stripped the plants with a kind of ferocious skilfulness, 'suppose Mother would rather have the affection than the skill?'

'She wouldn't. She's always asking for June.'

'Because she feels you don't want to do it?'

Cara, face hidden among the leaves, did not reply.

'Don't you want to?'

'I – I daren't.'

'*Dare* not?'

'I don't want to be rebuffed. And I'd be clumsy. She – almost despises me.'

Alex said, 'You couldn't be more wrong.'

'You don't *live* here! You've only seen it for two days! You don't know what it's like here, so monotonous, so shut-in, nobody coming, nowhere to go—'

Alex said angrily, 'So you'd rather be in London, would you? Bombed every night, always short of sleep, wading to work through ankle-deep broken glass? That would be better than a little petty boredom?'

Cara took a deep breath and stripped the plant before her in silence before she answered. He could hear nothing but the pattering of beans into the basket at her feet.

'I am sure London is horrible. Frightening and exhausting. But at least it is where things are happening, one is *living* the war. We're so isolated here, so cut off – so frustrated. For all the broken glass, I'd rather be Mary Langley.'

He broke through the bean rows to face her.

'Why bring up Mary?'

'You know why.'

'Who told you?'

'Alan.'

'Oh,' he said, 'Of course.'

'Does it have to be a secret?'

'No,' he said, 'Of course not. I just don't want it – spoiled.'

She stared at him.

'Alex, are you in love with her?'

'Awfully.'

'But – but she isn't anything like anyone you have ever been interested in before—' She thought of Mary's tall angularity, her thin, flat brown hair, her endlessly long bony feet which had meant she could never borrow anyone else's tennis shoes at school.

'All that means,' Alex said, 'Is that I probably was never in love before. She's teaching me Greek.'

'Heavens,' Cara said, '*Heavens*. What for?'

'I want to know some of the things she knows.'

'At school I thought she was a swot.'

Alex laughed.

'She says she was herself. She always will be, in a way. I get insanely jealous when she's concentrating on some book.'

Cara stooped to pull an empty basket towards her.

'She's only my age.'

'I'm not exactly senile, myself.' He reached up and began to tear the young beans from the top of the poles. 'It's all Stephen's doing, really. I saw him briefly in London, just before he went to France a year ago, and he said would I look Mary up if I had a moment as she was new to London and might be finding it plus a war a bit difficult. So I did, purely as a duty. I took her to the cinema – I was a bit anxious, the whole thing was a bit lightweight for her, but she loved it. And – and I loved it. Taking her, I mean, not the film.'

Cara said, without looking at him, 'Are you going to marry her?'

'If she'll have me.'

'Of course she'll have you!'

'I can't be too sure. She's very independent. And she's writing a novel. She does it in any old corner, mostly in air raid shelters and cellars as far as I can see, and a publisher who has seen the first three chapters is very excited and is clamouring for more.'

'Better than picking beans.'

'Oh Cara,' he said in weary exasperation, 'Why must you insist the grass is always greener over the fence?'

She felt tears standing in her eyes.

'I know whatever I say makes me sound like a spoiled child. But you *must* see, Alex, that there's a gulf growing up between me and my own generation. I can't share what you all know about, I haven't seen what you have seen. I'm a sort of prisoner. And it's worse because you all suppose my life is some kind of idyll.'

'It must have good moments—'

'It's had one good fortnight in a year.'

'When Alan Langley was on leave?'

'When Alan Langley was on leave.'

He glanced down at the ground.

'You pick twice as fast as I do.'

'Plenty of practice,' she said shortly.

'Cara—'

'Yes?'

'Are you engaged to Alan?'

'Did Ma ask you to ask me?'

'Sort of.'

'Yes, I am. No ring or anything, but I've said yes. So I am.'

He said nothing. She watched him for a while and then she said aggressively,

'What's wrong with that?'

'Why – why couldn't you do it properly? Why didn't he ask Father – or you tell him and Mother for that matter—'

'He – we didn't want to. We like it as it is.'

'You mean *he* does.'

'What other arrangement,' she said crossly, 'Would you suggest in the middle of a war?'

He came and put his arm around her shoulders.

'Don't snap, old thing. I'm not criticizing you. We all think too much about love at the moment. I suppose it's a natural reaction to war, a sort of human insurance policy.'

'What do you suppose James thinks about?'

They regarded each other for a moment, solemnly.

'Here, I should think,' Alex said.

'I only hope so,' Cara said, 'It's my only consolation. It's so dreary, having to write to him in a sort of code and his letters back are no better. He can't write about how he's feeling and, being him, I don't suppose he would if he could, just so as not to upset Ma and Pa. Alex—'

'Yes.'

'He won't be – hungry will he?'

'No.'

'Can you imagine what he does? Do you know what prisoners of war do all day?'

Alex said slowly, 'I think his daily life probably seems to him very much as you think yours seems to you. But in his case, he has reason.'

'Cara!' Michael called from the hall, 'Telephone!'

She appeared on the landing in her bath towel, having leapt from one of the three baths Alexandra permitted the girls each week since the ancient boiler devoured coal insatiably and coal was something the nation needed more than the Swintons did.

'Put on a dressing gown. It's arctic down here.'

She wouldn't let herself ask if it were Alan. Struggling into the dressing gown that still bore her St Faith's nametape and house number, she flew down the stairs. Michael held out the receiver.

'It isn't Alan,' he said softly.

Her chin went up.

'I didn't expect it to be.'

'Of course not.'

She put the receiver to her ear. Michael spun the wheels of his chair and moved slowly across the hall to the dining room.

'Cara? Cara – it's Alison! I'm on leave. Can I come over and see you?'

'Alison—'

'How are you? You must have had a gorgeous summer, all this sun. I've been stuck in Scotland and it's poured and poured, not that I'm really complaining. I've played masses of tennis, in fact I'm in the WRNS first six—'

'Good for you.'

'Does it matter when I come?'

'No, of course not. Come for supper. I'll tell Lyddy.'

'Lovely. I say, Cara—'

'Yes?'

'I'm awfully sorry about your mother.'

'That's all right—'

'See you later then. About seven? Mum says I can borrow her Morris and they've been saving petrol for my leave, bless them. We could go to Bodmin for a day perhaps. Visit St Faith's—'

'Yes,' said Cara, 'Yes. See you this evening.'

She put the receiver back and went into the dining room. Michael was by the window, staring out into the wild October weather. The estuary was steel grey and choppy with foam and the leaden sky had drained all the colour from the fields, leaving them dun and dead.

He said, 'Mr Price has ordered a wheelchair for Ma. It's coming tomorrow.'

'A wheelchair! Then – then—'

'She has had some distinct sensation in her left thigh and foot. He wants her to be more upright.'

'But, Pa, that's wonderful! That's marvellous news!' She paused. 'But why didn't you tell me before?'

He held out his hand. The back of it was freckled now, but it had the same warm suppleness of grasp it had always had.

'She wanted to be sure there was an improvement before she said anything.'

Cara knelt beside him.

'Did June know?'

Michael looked at her steadily.

'Oh yes. June has been massaging her for three months, every morning. Mr Price says it may well have helped.'

Cara took her hand away from his and stared stonily out of the window.

'I see.'

'Do you?'

'I must go,' she got up, pulling the belt of her dressing gown round her, 'There's those calves to do.'

'Confidence works two ways,' Michael said, 'You didn't choose to tell us about Alan Langley. We had to hear it from Alex.'

'Why did you need to know?'

'It's a part of love, my beloved and exasperating child. Above all else in the world, we want you three to be safe and happy. But I confess to being very perplexed as to how to help you achieve the latter state.'

'I *was* happy. When Alan was here.'

'Only then?'

She glanced at him.

'I think so.'

'Perhaps you could start with another objective, such as making someone else happy. Ma, for instance.'

'She doesn't want me.'

Michael spun his wheels backwards so that he could see her face.

'Go away!' he said furiously, 'Go away and don't come back until you have grown up a little!'

If there was an atmosphere at supper, Alison Burrows did not appear to notice it. She arrived punctually at seven in her mother's Morris, wearing a new-looking coat and skirt of pale blue wool, with a blouse of coffee-coloured crêpe de chine tied in a bow at the neck. Her hair, which had been allowed to grow since its days at St Faith's, was rolled up neatly at the back and she wore shoes that had Cara gaping with envy made of brown and white calfskin. She looked trim, competent and at least twenty five, and the bosom which had objected so to a school tunic seemed entirely at home in adult clothes.

Cara, in a grey wool frock which Lyddy had tried to cheer up with scarlet buttons, felt dismally ill-kempt and provincial beside her.

Alison was not only well turned-out but well-informed. She had lists of German boats torpedoed, numbers of civilians killed during the bombing which had flattened Coventry Cathedral the week before, precise details, it seemed, of Hitler's plans to inveigle Spain into joining him. Lyddy had made an effort with supper, frying sausages to the crispness Cara had always liked as a child, stewing pears from the old tree on the house wall – almost the only fruit Alexandra did not insist be sent, with all the farm produce, to Wadebridge and Bodmin for distribution. Alison ate and talked animatedly, the guest of honour, the centre of attention. They all sat, or in Alexandra's case, lay, in a circle around her, Michael, Alexandra, Cara, June and Barbara, a slow and silent girl from Devonshire who rarely spoke unless it were absolutely essential that she did so.

'Oh, and Cara, have you heard from Sarah?'

'Sarah?'

'Sarah Calne. You know. I hear she has a fascinating job. She got into the Red Cross, through her mother, I think who's been a patron for years, and she's working for the branch that deals with the repatriation of prisoners of war. The ones with mental breakdowns and so on. It sounds so interesting. She's been to Germany twice already on some investigation team.'

'I bless the Red Cross,' Alexandra said. 'It's the only way we can send anything to James.'

'You can send three pounds a month now, to each prisoner,' Alison said, 'It's a new regulation. And of course, Mary's doing awfully well. I heard she's been taking minutes at some of Churchill's meetings. You wouldn't think anyone like Mary could learn shorthand and things would you, but how wrong can you be. Can't you just imagine her shut up in those cellar offices at the War Office with Churchill and all the generals,

427

scribbling away for dear life just as if it were French dictation—'

'More pears?' Cara said, a spoon raised over the dish.

'Simply couldn't. It was delicious. I always remember nursery tea here as the best. Gosh, it's lovely to be back, you can't think how I miss it. I mean, the Navy is absolutely fascinating and I'm transferring from signwriting to signals, which I shall love, but I do envy you being here. It's so peaceful isn't it. I mean, you'd hardly know, living here, that there's a war on.'

Michael said gently, 'On very still nights, we can hear the planes, you know. And a couple of bombs did fall on St Ives, much to its astonishment—'

'Goodness,' Alison said, 'Is that the time? I promised I'd be home by nine. At least you don't need to worry about the All Clears here – sorry, I should say, Raiders Passed, shouldn't I. All Clear was after gas attacks and of course there aren't any of those. I must fly. Mum and Dad are in an absolute funk about my driving in the dark but my eyes are so good at night now—'

'There's a moon,' Cara said, 'Not much of a one, but a moon.'

In the porch, Alison paused before bustling across to her car.

'What about a game of tennis sometime, Cara? On a fine day. I'm at home for another week.'

Cara said, 'I'll try but I'm really busy. We work a twelve, sometimes fourteen, hour day here.'

'Do you?'

'Oh yes. I didn't spend the summer making sandcastles on Daymer.'

'Cara, I didn't mean to imply—'

'You'd better go or your parents will worry. I'll telephone them and say you're on your way.'

'Look, if I see Sarah or Mary, I'll give them your love, shall I? I must say, I do sometimes think old Ferrars must be pretty pleased with us all. Taken to the war effort like ducks to water.'

In the drawing-room at the Manor House – the drawing-room which had seen Alexandra's entrance upon the first dinner party of her life over thirty years before – Harry Burrows replaced the receiver.

'She's on her way. That was Cara. Nice of her to ring.'

Lettice Burrows, scrabbling fretfully in her workbox for exactly the colour of tapestry wool she sought, said, 'Such a tragedy, poor Alexandra. But so lucky Cara could stay, so lucky they don't have to worry about her. I don't have a quiet moment with Alison gone, I can tell you, and I shan't be happy tonight until I hear her back.'

'It only takes ten minutes—'

'Only ten days' leave. It does seem hard. After all, we aren't sending anyone abroad for the moment, so I don't see why Alison has to be in Scotland. Why can't she do her signals at Plymouth or somewhere? So lucky for Alexandra to have Cara at home!'

'Topping girl, Alexandra was,' Harry said, stroking his moustache, 'Awfully sporting. Splendid seat on a horse, but would not hunt. Can't think why, but simply wouldn't.'

'Well, she can't now. Though I suppose you can run a farm perfectly well from one's bed and she's got Cara, after all, to do any little thing she wants. I miss Alison to do little things for me all the time. I can never find what I want without her. Hush! Is that her?'

Alison, coming into the drawing-room some minutes later, thought how different it all looked to Bishopstow. War had made very little difference to the Manor House beyond causing the servant situation to be an endlessly pleasurable source of complaint to Lettice Burrows. A fire blazed recklessly in a comfortable room still filled with flowers, her father had a tumbler of whisky and her mother had dressed for dinner as usual. It all contrasted acutely with what she had left at Bishopstow – the dining-room crammed with ill-assorted furniture, the invalids, the single-bar electric fire, the forty-watt light bulb hanging limply over the centre of the table, the icy hall and passages, Cara—

'How was Cara then, dear?'

'Awfully changed, actually. I'd hardly have known her. I mean, she looks the same, but she's terribly quiet and hardly ever smiles. It does seem odd, she was such a leader—' She paused and looked down at her neat and expensive clothes. 'You know, I never would have believed this could happen, but I actually felt sorry for her. *Sorry* – for Cara!'

CHAPTER EIGHT

April 1942

In January of 1942, Alan was posted to North Africa with the First Armoured Division. Before he left, he was given four days' leave, and Cara was permitted, for once, to use sufficient precious petrol to get her to Bodmin Road Station to meet him. It was a bitter January day, heavy and dark with a slicing wind, and even wrapped up in Alexandra's ancient musquash Cara could feel the cold creeping in to her skin.

In the interval between Alan's proposal in the summer of 1940 and this farewell meeting, they had only met twice. It had seemed to Cara that eighteen months training must surely allow soldiers regular leave if they were training at home, but she was not going to beg Alan for any information, nor for a moment of his time that he would not offer voluntarily; so she accepted his absence as she accepted the infrequency of his letters and telephone calls.

Waiting, it seemed to her, was what the war was all about. Waiting to hear from Alan, waiting to be reassured that Alex – now involved in the horrible obliteration raids over German cities – was still safe, waiting to hear from James, who had been moved to another camp and who had spent twelve hours a day throughout the last three months of 1941, manacled, along with five fellow officers. In addition to all that, she seemed to be waiting too to hear of Mary's and Alison's promotions, both happening with a steadiness which depressed her terribly, waiting to see if that tiny step forward Alexandra had taken eighteen months before would come to anything, waiting, above all, to see where the war would spread next, engulfing as it now did all Europe, America, Australia, Russia, the Far East, India, North Africa, even the islands of the Pacific.

She was afraid, driving to meet Alan, that the strain showed on her face. She had peered at it long and anxiously that morning, but found she could not now remember what she was comparing it with, how she had once looked. That she was changed, there was no doubt and Alan's first glance reflected the change, though all he said was,

'Hey, don't go and grow up altogether before I get my hands on you.'

She had not driven him back to Bishopstow, but to Langley Dene, the square solid Edwardian house where George Langley had grown up and which he eventually inherited from his uncle. They were very welcoming to her, Alan's parents, very solicitous, very anxious – too anxious – to ask her about Bishopstow, but she felt that they must want Alan alone and so she made some excuse and left them after only twenty minutes. Alan came to Bishopstow the next day, in the MG, and drove her to Bodmin and they sat in the cinema watching 'Gone with the Wind' and holding hands and at the very end, when Rhett said to Scarlett, 'Frankly my dear, I don't give a damn,' Alan laughed and squeezed her hand,

'Wonderful! Of course women love a bastard—'

There had been a dance the next night in the Village Institute in Bishopstow and Alan had insisted that they go. Cara had wanted to dance with him and had nothing to wear, had felt herself weighed down by months of mud and boots and physical labour. But she had made an effort for him and then, of course, she had loved it, the moving bodies, the warmth, the brief forgetfulness, Alan singing love songs in her ear. When he took her home, walking her up the frosty lane from the village to the house, he had stopped her in every field gateway to kiss her and then he had said, holding her against him, both bulky in their overcoats.

'Do you still have that stalk of thrift?'

'Of course.'

'It's rotten of me – not to have given you something better. When the war's over—'

'*When.*'

He began to sing softly in her ear again.

'If you were the only girl in the world—'

She said, 'Alan. Oh, Alan!'

'Won't be long, sweetheart. Just a few months to blast Rommel out of North Africa and that'll be a turning point. You'll see.'

He slid his arm through hers and marched her ceremoniously up to the house.

'Arrivaderci, signorina, bellissima signorina mia.'

'Take – care, Alan.'

'Will do.' He leaned forward and kissed her, pushing his tongue gently against her mouth. 'Don't forget me, sweetheart.'

Since then, since January, one letter only, posted in Cairo, cheerful and breezily affectionate. And since then, little else of any kind to cheer one. Rationing was made more severe and baths were officially restricted to a depth of five inches – Alexandra instructed Cara to paint a red line around both the bathtubs at Bishopstow to make sure that no-one cheated. The news was grim, Cara grew to dread those nightly sessions around the wireless listening to Japanese victories in the Pacific, the slaughter going on between Russia and Germany, the fall of Singapore in February. The days plodded on the same, digging and ploughing and sowing and feeding, the only variations being visits to the village for scarce soap powder and lavatory paper, visits to old Mrs Chamberlin, widow of the late Rector, who talked incessantly a rambling flood of anecdotes and reflections, but whom Alexandra insisted she should visit.

'She was so kind to me, when I first came. I always visited her when I could. Now I should like you to do it for me.'

June taught both Cara and Barbara to knit. They were neither of them very apt, but the thought of James kept Cara faithful to her nightly ritual of needles and khaki wool, sock after sock whose heels June always had to turn for her. They would knit round the dining-room table after supper while Alexandra did her accounts, going over and over them as if the outcome or the war depended solely upon her profitability, and Michael nodded in his wheelchair or watched his wife and daughter with his powerful, hooded gaze.

The daffodils were late that year. It wasn't until the first week of April that the customary sheets of yellow spread in their full glory across the lawns to the east and south of the house, blowing in drifts down the grassy terraces, brilliant and heartening. Cara went out to pick some, great jolly armfuls of yellow King Alfreds, bunches of pale scented narcissi, laying them carefully in the battered withy trug that had been as much part of Alexandra as the gardening hat, hanging unworn now in the scullery for almost three years. She stooped low among the flowers, stepping as carefully as she could in her boots, inhaling the faint, damp scent of them, brushing her tired rough hands through their petals. Stephen Langley, coming out of the house to find her as directed, stood for a moment and watched her khaki figure moving softly through the waving yellow, her dark red head close to the flower heads. She straightened before he had to call to her and turned and saw him, almost as if she had sensed he was there.

He waited for her to wade towards him through the daffodils.

'Stephen!'

He took her hands, peering down into her face.

'I haven't seen you since September '39.'

'Would you like to come inside?'

He looked round at the soft pale April day.

'Much rather not. I spend my life in an operating theatre as it is. The air is a relief.'

'What are you doing here? I thought you were at St Bartolph's, your parents said so—'

'I am. I've been there for nearly two years – ever since Dunkirk. But I think the Middle East looms—'

'Like Alan.'

'Yes,' he said.

She glanced up at him. He looked tired, with that kind of relentless tiredness that was beginning to mark everyone's faces, which had marked Alex's long ago – as long ago as September 1940.

'Shall we go down to the sea?'

'Of – course!' she said, in surprise.

'Can you spare half an hour?'

'I think so.'

He opened the garden gate for her. Before them the fields sloped to the pale sand that ribboned the edge of the estuary. He took her elbow as they walked, and she let him hold it, moving very slightly ahead of him towards the sea, in silence.

'Here,' Stephen said.

He waved his arm sideways and indicated a grassy mound to their right.

'Sit below that. Then we can look at the sea.'

'Stephen,' she said, 'What is all this?'

He folded himself up on the turf and held out a hand to her.

'Please come and sit down. I won't keep you long.'

She stayed on her feet, staring down at him.

'Cara, I know you don't want to hear anything from me, about me, anything to do with me but please, please bear with me for five minutes—'

She knelt in the rough grass then a little distance from him.

'What is it?'

'Cara – I'm not on leave. Well, I am, but not officially. I've two days, today and tomorrow, courtesy of my immensely understanding senior officer. I came down on the night train to Bodmin, I go back tomorrow. I came to see you.'

'What about—'

'Alan,' he said.

She flung herself forward.

'He's not – not – you haven't heard he's been—'

'No,' Stephen said, 'He isn't hurt. He's alive. It isn't that at all.'

He reached out and gripped the only hand of hers he could reach.

'Cara, I can't wrap it up for you. Alan is married. He was married at Christmas in London. He didn't tell any of us, nobody—'

She was staring at him, chalk-faced.

'No,' she said.

'Yes, Cara. I'd give anything for it not to be the case. Anything. But he is married. To a girl whose father is making a fortune out of armaments. She's called Tessa, Tessa Beard. She told her parents about Alan – after all, she wasn't to know there was any suggestion that he might – might not be free to marry her. It's because she told them that I know. Her father came to find me at St Bartolph's, ostensibly to introduce himself, but really I think to check up on us as a family. Tessa is obviously the apple of his eye, he couldn't refuse her

435

anything but he didn't like the marriage happening so quickly. I think it made him uneasy and I was easier to find than mother and father, so he came to me, to reassure himself that Tessa hadn't made some awful mistake—.'

'In January,' Cara said in a cool, remote voice, 'Alan came down here to see me. Before he went to Egypt. He – he talked of our future then. And he was married.'

'Yes,' Stephen said, 'He was.'

She ducked her head and began to tear at the tawny clumps of grass.

'That's why he hardly ever rang up. Or wrote. Is that why he wouldn't give me a ring?'

Her voice caught. She put an arm up across her face and Stephen knelt up, holding his hands out to her.

He said with some diffidence,

'Would you like to cry?'

She said nothing, merely looked at him over her upflung arm.

'I know I am hardly your favourite human, Cara, but if I can be of any comfort to you at all—'

She shuffled forward on her knees and put her hands out to him. He said,

'I don't know what to say to you about Alan. It's the most appalling behaviour I ever heard of. Father is absolutely stricken by it – he had such hopes for you both, he was so pleased. How anyone could act so – and to *you*—'

She had begun to shake, long shuddering movements that made her teeth rattle.

'What – what is T-Tessa like?'

'You couldn't hate her,' Stephen said, dropping her hands, reaching out to put his arms round her, 'She doesn't know about you. I suppose she's about your age, very rich, very protected, very much in love with Alan—'

436

'Oh!' Cara said in anguish.

'Say what you like. You couldn't say anything worse than the things I have already thought. Be angry—'

'I can't. I don't feel angry. I might later. I just feel – desolated.'

'Yes,' he said, holding her and rocking her a little.

'So you came – all the way, all night – to break this to me?'

'Mary wanted to. But I bullied her into letting me. She's distraught—'

She said unexpectedly, looking up at him,

'How kind you are.'

He shook his head.

'No.'

'It *is* kind,' she said politely, 'To take so much trouble.'

'He is my brother. I feel responsible for his bad behaviour even if I am as horrified and amazed at it as you – more so, probably, than you. I mean, think how you might have found out.'

'Did you say anything to – to Tessa, about me?'

'No,' he said.

She shut her eyes tightly.

'Quite right,' she said with an effort.

'I think so.'

Cara withdrew herself gently from his arms and got unsteadily to her feet.

'I suppose he thought he could have his cake and eat it—'

'I hope,' Stephen said, looking up at her, 'that he didn't even think. Stupid, blind impetuosity is one thing, calculated selfish cruelty quite another.'

She said slowly, 'I've pinned too many hopes on him. He was going to be the knight in shining armour who carried me away from all this, who took me to a place where there wasn't this tension, this drudgery—'

'I can't believe how well you're taking it.'

'It's – it's you,' she said stumblingly, 'You're being so – I can't explain it—'

He stood up too, laughing a little forcedly.

'Don't be nice to me, Cara, or I'll lose my head completely.'

'Look,' she said, 'Look at the sun on the sea. Just a shining stripe of it.'

'I wanted to say something else to you. But perhaps now you'd rather be alone. Maybe you've had enough talking—'

'I'd rather talk than think.'

'Let's go down to the beach.'

The sand above the high water mark was pale and crumbling, dimpled with recent rain, with tufts of coarse grass thrusting up through it, spiny and dark. There were little dunes before the beach began, mounds and hollows and deep twisting paths where children ran in the summer. Someone had left a broken wooden spade, bleached silver by a winter in the air. Stephen went before her down the dunes, turning and holding out his hand to her when the path became briefly vertical but saying nothing until they were on the beach, crunching over a band of scattered pebbles streaked with weed.

'It's been on my mind,' he said abruptly, 'The way I spoke to you when we last met. I lectured you, if I remember rightly, about your duty to stay here, keeping England going, looking after your parents, being grateful and thankful to be living in one of the safest places in England. Did I? Did I speak to you like that?'

'It didn't matter,' she said tiredly, 'You were only one among many. Everyone has talked to me like that for nearly three years. I'm almost hardened to it.' She kicked at a pebble and sent it skimming over the ribbed sand at the water's edge. 'I expect everyone's right, by now. I was – am – spoiled, I did take my anger out on everyone else, I suppose, I still do—'

'I want to take back what I said.'

She stopped to look at him.

'You what?'

'I shouldn't have said it. I didn't know what I was talking about. I mean, it is true about keeping England going as a place to come back to after the war, about being a moral support, but I had no idea what civilian life here would become like, no idea at all until after Dunkirk, until I went back to London and saw what a struggle it was, what an exhausting, relentless struggle to keep going, keep cheerful. I suppose I was in France for eight months before Dunkirk and that – even Dunkirk itself – was easier, I think, easier to live through because one had a job, life was extraordinary so that the deprivations were part of the peculiarity, part of a pattern. But here, civilians have to battle to be ordinary, to keep the show going, on less and less, on terrible uncertainty, imprisoned in small areas because transport and petrol are so difficult, separated from their children in many cases – Cara. Oh Cara, don't cry, I didn't mean to make you cry—'

She said unevenly, smearing her tears with the back of her hand, 'It just shows how spoiled I am doesn't it, a bit of sympathy from someone and I am awash with self-pity—'

'I don't believe it's self-pity,' he said, holding out a khaki handkerchief.

'I'd like to think,' she said, sniffing, taking it, 'It was relief, but I daren't. You're the first person, the first person since war began who's had an idea of what it felt like. I was furiously angry at not being allowed to join up, I really was, at the beginning. But now I'm not. I just feel all the things you described just now and on top of that, so desperately far away down here, so cut off—' She blew her nose hard. 'I read something in the paper the other day about how callous and complacent people in Cornwall were, how much more concerned people were in this part of Cornwall when a stick of bombs fell ten miles away than when they heard the whole of the centre of Plymouth had been flattened. The writer said there was a huge spiritual gulf widening between smug people like us safely down here and the exhausted inhabitants of London and Birmingham and Southampton – If she only knew—' She looked up at him, pink-eyed, screwing up her handkerchief. 'Do you understand me?'

'Yes,' he said.

'And James too. His last letter made reference to using his hands so I suppose they've stopped tying him up all day—. And he's asked for some books on mechanical engineering, he wants to work for some examination or other. I wish I knew where Oflag V was. Or where Alex was at the moment, I mean, every night might be his last night—' She stopped. 'Sorry,' she said, 'I didn't mean to abuse your kindness.'

'You aren't.'

She sighed.

'I must go back. I'll – I'll wash this and get it back to you somehow.'

'It doesn't matter.'

'Stephen—'

He waited.

'Stephen, I suppose Alan wasn't really in love with me. He just liked flirting. I – I suppose I ought to hope that – that he's in love now—'

'I don't think you should try to be heroic,' he said, smiling a little.

'Me, heroic! Don't make me laugh. Ask my parents about my heroic capabilities—'

'Will you tell them?'

'About Alan? I shouldn't think so. It will just be more proof to them of my general incompetence. I'm not capable of nursing my mother, now I'm unable even to hold a man – just as well I didn't join up because I'd probably have failed at that too—'

'Stop it,' he said.

She shrugged and began to walk away from him and the sea, up the beach towards the house. He ran to catch up with her, seizing her arm.

'*Don't* run yourself down. You're wonderful, you know you are. It's just that you're not in the right sort of atmosphere at the moment—'

'What do you suggest then?'

'I daren't – suggest anything just now—'

She was silent.

He said, 'I wish I didn't irritate you so.'

'I irritate myself,' She gave herself a violent shake, like a dog after a bath. 'Stephen, when you get home, will you tell your parents that I really am – fine, and that I'll come over and see them, I promise, I really will, very soon, just as soon as I can, well, bring myself to. And – and give my love to Mary and anyone else I know in London—'

'I see quite a lot of Sarah Calne,' he said, 'She has a tremendous job – I mean, it's tremendous for her.'

'I must go,' Cara said, 'June will be wondering where on earth I am. I was supposed to feed all the pigs when I'd picked the daffodils. Stephen—' She held out her hand to him. 'I'll be all right, really I will. And – and thank you for coming.'

'I'd come over tomorrow, but what with going off to North Africa and the parents being in a bit of a turmoil—'

'Don't think of it. It doesn't matter, we're always so busy—'

'Goodbye, then, Cara.'

She tried to smile at him.

'Goodbye,' she said, 'And good luck.'

Usually she was so tired that sleep hit her like a hammer blow the moment she let herself relax into her pillow. She was used to the heavy, drugged tide of it sweeping irresistibly over her but now she lay and waited for it, fretful and restless, and it wouldn't come. She felt her limbs and back leaden with fatigue, limp between the sheets, but behind her closed eyes her mind raced like an engine, tired too so that she couldn't think properly but refusing to be quietened.

She had gone back a hundred times that day over everything she could remember Alan saying to her, all the endearments and promises she had saved up to remember as a luxury in his absence. There was nothing she could recall, standing with him in the porch at Bishopstow that January night, that indicated him to have anything on his mind, to be any less blithe and carefree than he usually was. But even as he had kissed her then, telling her not to forget him, Tessa — Tessa Langley — had been somewhere else, sitting reading in bed, perhaps *their* bed, wearing his wedding ring on her finger, presumably trusting him—

She sat up in bed and put her arms around her knees. If she had agreed, that July night on Pentyre Head, to let him make love to her, would she now be Cara Langley? Is that what Tessa had done? And if he could kiss her, Cara, when only a month married, what kind of a future did Tessa have, for all her money and her love for him — Did she want him still? Was this aching feeling jealousy and anger or the bitter solitariness of having to face the future without him? Were her own ideas of fidelity, based upon her parents' relationship, old-fashioned and impractical? How — she put her face down on to her knees in an attempt to press the tears back out of her eyes — how could Alan do this to her, how could he consider her so little?

With a sudden movement, she flung back the blankets and stood up. Her bible, squat and black, lay where it always lay, on her dressing table. She picked it up, balanced the spine on her left hand and let it fall open at will. It fell open where it always did, at the blank page between the end of the Book of Psalms and the beginning of Proverbs. With the forefinger and thumb of her right hand, she picked out the stiff, papery stalk of thrift, the round head flattened now to a pinkish-yellow disk. Then she went to the window and opened it and reaching out let the thrift blow away from her into the night.

CHAPTER NINE

'I've – something to tell you,' Cara said.

Alexandra was in her wheelchair by the drawing-room window, the inevitable account books on a table beside her, the newest government circular on the most productive system of crop rotation on her knee. She brandished it at Cara.

'It makes me simply furious. I'm doing all I can to cudgel every last root and grain out of the earth and what do they do but nag and object. I've been farming for over thirty years and I am perfectly convinced that most of the Agriculture Ministry men have never even got their shoes muddy. What do you want?'

'I wanted to tell you something—'

'Cara – could it wait? I want to get through this beastly thing and it's written in such awful governmentese that I'm afraid I'll lose the thread if I stop. Tell June—'

'No,' Cara said.

It was two weeks now since Stephen's visit, two weeks of enduring the grinding pain of knowing that Alan was no longer hers to think about, that there wasn't even the sunlight of another leave to look forward to. Jealousy, she had decided, battling with it as she fed the cows and pigs and trudged behind Bassett clearing the choking spring ditches around the farm, was the most crippling emotion. She did not know Tessa at all, she had no *real* reason to hate her – even less, she had to admit, since Tessa herself had not known of her own existence and therefore could not possibly be accused of taking Alan from her deliberately – and yet the thought of Tessa was agony to her, she detested her. She knew that was illogical,

443

that it was Alan she should hate – but that was jealousy for you, perverting and twisting things, turning you into quite another kind of person, an obsessed and vengeful being who could love something merely because that was what it wanted, not because there was anything good in the love object at all. And, by the same token, jealousy made you hate someone merely because they – however unconsciously – stood in the path of your desire.

The struggle with her feelings was the first battle of her life that she had made any attempt to fight alone. The household had always rung to Cara's emotions, joyous or furious – she was not accustomed to endure, not self-schooled enough to restrain herself from casting, usually at Michael, a tempest of emotion, imploring sympathy. Now it seemed different. Part of the difference, she knew, was that she had, to put it baldly, failed over Alan and she was accustomed to success. Alan had chosen another, there was someone in the world he found preferable. It was a painful humiliation, only to be endured at first alone, in silence. It was followed by anger and resentment, but it did not seem to be the kind of resentment Cara was used to, the kind she had known at the beginning of the war when she was utterly convinced of the injustice done to her. This time she was not so sure – indeed, not convinced at all that she was unjustly wronged. Perhaps there were, after all, reasons why a man might tire of her—

But in all these anxious wanderings in her mind, there was one small crumb of comfort. It didn't amount to very much and yet it was curiously consoling for Cara to remember Stephen saying that he understood how it felt to live her life, that he would never again underestimate the effort it cost civilians to keep going in wartime. Every time she recalled what he had said, she was a little soothed. It was, after all, a great step forward to have someone, even Stephen Langley, sympathetic to her point of view and her difficulties.

Cara closed the drawing-room door now and leaned against it.

444

'It's nothing to do with June. It's to do with me. Something has happened that I want to tell you about.'

Alexandra put down her papers and looked up at last. She said, with an edge of uncertainty,

'But you never want to tell me anything. Pa's in the studio, if you want him.'

'Ma!' Cara said pleadingly.

'Come here, then.'

Cara walked slowly across the room and knelt beside her mother's chair.

'Damn. Look, I've put muck on the carpet—'

'It doesn't matter. Cara, what is it?'

She knelt back on her heels and put her hands in her breeches' pockets.

'It's rather a long story really but I expect you guessed the beginning. At the end of his leave, Alan asked me to marry him. And – and I said yes. He said he couldn't give me a ring just yet, but I didn't think anything of that, what with the war and leave being so short—' she looked up at Alexandra. 'Did you guess?'

'That you were engaged? I suppose – I suppose we thought you must have discussed it, all those evenings together. Cara – why didn't you tell us? Why didn't Alan speak to Pa?'

'He didn't want to.'

'Just that?'

'Yes. And – and I'm afraid – then – that I didn't see a need for it either. I wish I had told you then, I wish – oh, I wish a lot of things, but I wish I had been older, wiser, known how precarious everything would be—'

Alexandra said, 'You have never talked to me like this before.'

'I can't get near you. June—'

'It isn't June. Wasn't June, either, before the war.'

'Well, the farm—'

'Perhaps. Plus our temperaments.'

'Yes,' Cara said, 'Mostly those.'

'Go on, then.'

445

'After that leave, in the summer of 'forty, you know I've hardly seen him, hardly heard from him. It made me miserable, because I longed to be with him, but I didn't – doubt him. Didn't know enough to doubt him, either about life or myself I suppose. And then – well, Stephen came two weeks ago, you remember, and he came to tell me that Alan has been married since Christmas, even when he was here in January, and took me to that dance at the Institute, he was married then. To a girl who's the daughter of an armaments manufacturer, Tessa somebody, very rich Stephen said, about my age—'

Alexandra's hand descended on her shoulder.

'Two weeks ago? You have known this and been this unhappy for two weeks without saying anything?'

'Yes.'

'I could murder that young man,' Alexandra said furiously. 'How could he be such a monster.'

'I shouldn't have believed him. I've known him, on and off, all my life and I should have known his charm wasn't to be relied on. I believed him, because I wanted to. He took my mind off – other things—'

'Cara, you don't even sound angry while I am seething.'

'Of course I'm angry,' Cara shouted, 'I'm angry and jealous and lonely and terribly unhappy! I'm only trying to suppress it a bit so that you don't say Oh here come more fireworks, more same old Cara. Ma, I could cry all day and night, but I won't. And I'll tell you why. Alan Langley is never going to know how much I mind. He cast me off like an old shirt and he's going to think I did the same to him. I'm going over to Langley Dene to show Uncle George how heartwhole I am, so that the news will trickle back to Alan that I couldn't care less. And I'll tell you something else—'

'You will?' Alexandra said, smiling.

'I'm going to look after you now. June's been terrific I know, but I want to do it now.'

'No,' Alexandra said.

'You don't want me to!'

'No. No, I don't. Not because I don't love you but because I do. Looking after me is a horrible job, a disgusting endless ritual of hard work and bedpans and washing. It humiliates me beyond anything to be like this – I can get used to being immobile but I can't get used to the indignity of being almost as helpless as a baby – and I couldn't bear to revolt you, as I surely would. June is very kind but she's remote, too. It makes it easier for me, I don't have to imagine what she is thinking because I know. She is simply thinking in cool practical terms of what she is doing.'

'Listen,' Cara said, 'I want to be necessary.'

'Oh, you are.'

'No. I just do what June and Bassett say. I have for three years. I'm like Barbara, or the old Higgins.'

Alexandra looked wistfully at the account books.

'Do you want me to teach you those? It would leave me with precious little—'

'No. I want to do things. I want to nurse you.'

'I'm so afraid of repelling you.'

Cara knelt up and took Alexandra's hand.

'Alan Langley's behaviour is more repellent than your poor body could ever be.'

'Perhaps. Can we start slowly, for my sake?'

'All right,' Cara said, unwillingly.

'It – it was kind of Stephen to come. To tell you in person. He was always very kind as a child I remember, very imaginative of other people. Do you remember him bringing you his bicycle every time he went off to a new term at prep school? You couldn't ride but you admired it tremendously, so he brought it faithfully for – oh – three or four years. I expect he's a marvellous surgeon. George was telling me that he's been doing quite incredible work on people's hands, all those poor hands damaged by bomb blasts. He's off to Libya, he said, I suppose he will be there by now. Can you imagine being shut up in a tank in desert heat? And the dust!'

447

Cara got to her feet, flexing her knees a little.

'Will you tell Pa?'

'He'd like you to—'

'No, thank you. I don't want anyone being sorry for me or I'll dissolve myself.'

Alexandra smiled up at her.

'So you came to me.'

'Yes.'

'My mother was sorry for herself all her life. It's a terrible affliction. Everyone else gets so absolutely sick of you.'

'Yes,' Cara said, 'I realized that.'

'Bend down,' Alexandra said, 'So that I can reach you. Even though you do smell powerfully of pig, I want to give you a hug.'

A few days later, a letter came from Mary Langley. It enclosed a brief note from Stephen, written the night before he left for North Africa which said little more than that he would be thinking of her. She put it in her pocket and took Mary's letter to the dairy to read.

'Dear Cara,

Whatever you so bravely said to our parents, I don't underestimate what you feel for a moment. I shan't of course reveal that to anyone, but I didn't want you to think I didn't know or care. I don't know what to say to you about Alan either – I haven't heard from him and I won't write to him. I'm afraid this is all rather incoherent but we are all a bit short of sleep and there seems to be no time for writing letters at the leisure they deserve.

I awfully wanted to come down to Bishopstow myself, as I expect Stephen told you. I think he was probably right. I should only have burst into tears and made you feel worse than ever. I do miss not having Stephen in London and so, I think, does St B's where he was being such a success. He's got to work at some burns unit in Benghazi, men burned in tanks mostly, I can't bear to think of it.

Sarah Calne was here earlier this evening. She saw a lot of Stephen but of course he's awfully interested in her job and they have a lot in common. She sent you her love and said she's coming down to talk to St Faith's about the Red Cross soon and will get in touch.

Write if you can. It would reassure me to think you haven't washed your hands of the whole Langley family.

With love,
Mary'

It seemed so curious to be turning the Rover in to the courtyard at St Faith's, parking it alongside the red brick wall of the chapel just as her mother had always done, bringing Michael to Speech Days and Christmas concerts, ends of terms and summer plays performed in the garden – weather permitting – around an ancient mulberry tree whose fruit made wasps a menace to the audience. And now here she was, driving herself, arriving at St Faith's almost three years after she had left it in a flurry of good wishes and a glow of success. She stood for a moment and looked about her at the familiar walls and roofs, the red and blue patterns of brick like a Fair Isle jersey, and heard the equally familiar summer term sounds – distant tennis balls, someone practising a fiddle, the hum of traffic from Bodmin, the clear and unmistakable tones of Mademoiselle Dubois leading some luckless form in a vocabulary chant.

Miss Ferrars had asked her to spend the night. Of course, she had written, Cara must come and hear Sarah speak and naturally she must not think of trying to make her way home in the dark. A sick room could be made into a temporary guest room since Sarah would be occupying the official one. They all so looked forward to seeing her and hearing all her news – it was so difficult in wartime to keep up with old girls—

As to the present girls, those who would know her now would have been thirteen or fourteen when she left. She would be embalmed for them in the photograph hanging in the Long Corridor – an interminable passage lined with school photographs, mostly teams of distinction or dramatic productions which had earned particular applause – in which she stood in tunic and cloak as the Maid of Orleans. She determined, walking across the courtyard, carrying her small suitcase, that she would not look at that photograph – could not perhaps—

The school secretary, unchanged in every aspect, even down to the same brown wool skirt and fawn rayon blouse fastened at the neck with a brooch of sea shells which Cara remembered staring at during her first interview at the school, ushered her to her room.

'Seems so silly, I'm sure you know your way about, should have said Little Sick Bay, shouldn't I then you would have known where you were, wouldn't you? So lucky, a bomb two nights ago only a few hundred yards away and the walls on the netball courts shielded us completely but we haven't had a night without a warning this summer but I expect you are just the same, aren't you, always dodging under the beds. Miss Ferrars said it really would be easier to sleep in the cellars but then of course she has such wonderful spirit and I'm sure it's never occurred to her to be afraid of spiders. Well, here we are and don't forget the blackout, Miss Ferrars likes it up by six in the summer whatever the weather and when you've settled in she's expecting you and Sarah for tea—'

Cara had had chicken pox in Little Sick Bay when she was thirteen. She hadn't been very ill, only very bored, lying itching and picking at her spots and keeping the under-matrons in stitches of laughter. Nothing had been done to the room since then. It had the same cream woodwork, the same limp cretonne curtain across the front of a hanging cupboard too shallow to accommodate a coathanger. Even the bed was the same, cream-painted iron, chipped and showing black through, and covered with the linen bedspreads that were uniform throughout the dormitories, green with a tan border and the school badge embroidered in the centre.

Cara sat down on the edge of the bed. The room even smelt the same, faintly antiseptic, faintly of pencil shavings and ink. It seemed so odd that this, the first night she had spent away from home in three years, should be here, back at St Faith's, almost as if she had marked time since she left and was being sucked back, inexorably. She opened her case and took out her brush and comb, threw her nightgown and a book on the bed, put her toothbrush on the square white basin with its bar of yellow school soap and tracery of grey cracks – but the room remained just as characterless, just as firmly Little Sick Bay, as if it had been empty.

Miss Ferrar's study was equally unaltered. Its furniture remained precisely where Cara remembered it, heavy red mahogany pieces on a Turkey carpet, the walls still bore gloomy reproductions of Holman Hunt, even the castor oil plants which had obscured most of the light from the windows with their thick, dusty leaves appeared hardly to have grown, so familiar in shape were they. On a low table by the fireplace lay the tea Cara had known as an occasional and doubtful privilege in the Sixth Form – bread and butter (though now it would be margarine), rock buns and a yellow seed cake so dry as to be almost unswallowable. And Miss Ferrars herself, like the school secretary, seemed to have remained transfixed in time, her hair still in earphones, small gold-rimmed spectacles on her nose, the same grey flannel coat and skirt, lisle stockings—

The only thing that was different was Sarah Calne. She was sitting in one of the massive armchairs facing what light there was, with such an air of comfortable competence and self-assurance about her that Cara was almost

451

daunted. She wore uniform, impeccable uniform, and a Red Cross badge in her lapel and the heavy brown hair that had been jabbed back from her brow with hairgrips at school was rolled smoothly above her collar.

'Charlotte!' Miss Ferrars said, 'I am so glad to see you. Sarah has come down from London, you see.'

'Hello,' Sarah said.

'You represent, I think,' Miss Ferrars said, ringing for the teapot, 'Two of the three aspects of life in wartime, the civilian and the medical auxiliary. Were we to have Alison Burrows this afternoon, we should have a representative of the fighting forces.'

'How is your mother?' Sarah said.

'No distinct improvement but at least she is in a chair.'

'And I am told,' Miss Ferrars said, 'That you have a land girl of considerable nursing talents which must be a boon in such a tragic situation.'

Cara said, 'I look after her mostly. I like it.'

Sarah said, 'I shouldn't have thought it was your cup of tea at all.'

'Nor me, particularly. I never knew how fascinated I was going to be, in how a body works and how bits of it keep working, even compensate, when other parts stop functioning.'

Miss Ferrars was pouring dark Indian tea into thick white cups.

'Of course Mary Langley should make a name for herself in the medical world when the war is over. I believe her brother already has.'

'Yes,' Sarah said, 'He has. He's done amazing work on the repair of hands particularly, even when the nerves seem hopelessly shattered.'

Miss Ferrars turned to Cara, holding out the plate of bread triangles.

'And your own brothers, Charlotte?'

'James is a prisoner in Germany. Alex is a night fighter.'

'You should see those cities,' Sarah said, 'I went to Cologne last month. We have flattened it, absolutely flattened it. There was a case of severe melancholia, one of our prisoners there, he kept trying to commit suicide. I'm glad to say it was a question of repatriation.'

'I think the girls will be so deeply interested by your experience,' Miss Ferrars said, 'I fear too many of them see the Red Cross simply as an organisation of stretcher bearers.'

After tea, while Miss Ferrars went, as she had done all their time at St Faith's, to read the Greek testament with the Classical Sixth, Cara and Sarah went into her garden, a small enclosure surrounded by such high walls that the sun only had a fleeting chance of entry at midday. All the rosebeds had been dug up and were planted with orderly rows of lettuce and carrots, but the laurel and rhododendron bushes remained exactly as they had been when Cara and anyone else she could seduce into joining her, had smoked illicitly in their sooty depths.

'Good of you to come,' Sarah said.

'Mary told me you were speaking here. It isn't far, anyway.'

'I suppose you get fairly marooned out there, though it must be lovely to be able to sleep. When was your brother taken prisoner?'

'Right at the beginning, before Dunkirk even. We had a letter yesterday which was a rare treat.' She paused and looked at Sarah beside her, so trim and composed, in her navy blue and white. 'He said they saw a woman pass the camp and they all rushed to the wire like animals. It was the first woman they had seen in eight months.'

'And do you hear from Alan Langley?'

'No,' Cara said, 'Why should I?'

'He used to admire you. When you were here. We envied you because he was so good looking.'

Cara said carelessly, 'He's married.'

'I know. I wondered if you did. I see a lot of the Langleys but you never know how news gets about.'

'And Mary?'

'She's fine,' Sarah said, 'Doing awfully well. I think Churchill has taken a fancy to her because she's always taking the minutes at those 3 a.m. meetings at the War Office. Stephen's gone to Libya.'

Cara said, 'Do you feel odd, being back here?'

Sarah looked at her.

'I feel almost as if I never was here. After all the people I've met, the places I've been to, the things I've seen. It's as if so much has happened in the last three years that I am not the same person. I don't suppose you feel like that, you seem to have got a bit stuck—'

Cara waited, looking steadily at her.

'I suppose I won't put this very well, but – well, you were such a star at school and we imagined you out there as the first woman to win a DSO and – it sort of hasn't worked out like that – has it?'

Cara said slowly, 'I know you never liked me much at school, but I didn't know quite how powerfully you disliked me.'

Sarah coloured a little.

'I didn't say that!'

'No. You didn't say it. But you implied it in your smug comparison between your war and mine. Being able to recognize a sheep with staggers may not be in the same league as recognizing that some poor prisoner of war has schizophrenia, but it's all part of the same thing, the same effort to keep going until this is all over. I didn't – choose my war, Sarah, and I'm surprised that you are so blatantly sure that yours is better. Of course it's more exciting, more ⌐ glamorous if you like. That's just your luck. And then for you to crow with triumph over me for mine—'

'Oh, I didn't mean to imply that at all. I only meant how – how funny it is, the way things turn out. I'm sure your life is very satisfying, it must be wonderful to be so needed especially with things being a little difficult between you and your mother—'

454

Cara glared.

'What do you mean?'

'Cara, come on. You were always telling us stories of the rows between you and then there was something Alex said recently—'

'Alex! How do you know anything about Alex?'

'I see quite a lot of Mary and you can't see Mary without seeing Alex whenever he can get away.'

Cara turned to face Sarah.

'And what precisely did Alex say?'

Sarah's chin went up and she regarded Cara with the determined courage she had faced her with all their adolescence.

'He wasn't particularly specific, he simply said he wished things between you could be easier.'

'How excessively good of you to tell me.'

'Cara, don't be silly—'

'Silly!'

'Yes, silly. It's childish to resent perfectly accurate criticism.'

'Sarah, you know nothing about it. Nothing about me, my life, my parents, *nothing*—'

Sarah said, 'You're jealous.'

'I'm *what*?'

'Jealous,' Sarah said coolly, 'Of me. Of my life and my job and my friends. I could see it in your face when you came into Miss Ferrars' study, I could see you looking at my uniform and comparing it to that cotton frock of yours. I don't blame you, in fact I'm sorry for you. It must be awful having to stay outside everything that's happening, getting no travel. Especially when you expected so much.'

Cara waited until the blind surge of rage in her throat and behind her eyes had abated a little, though to begin with Sarah's calm, oval face swam before her through scalding tears.

'I've only got two things to say to you, Sarah. The first is that I now know how extremely pleased with myself

I was at school and I know it because I think I am at last growing out of it. And as I have such a keen eye for the symptoms, I recognize the disease most acutely in you. A pity, don't you think, to grow into it rather than out of it? And the second is that I am not going to be the prize exhibit in front of the school for you to triumph over tonight. I'm going home and you can tell old Ferrars what fib you like. I could stay and fight you but you aren't worth it.'

Sarah said, 'Oh, don't take everything to heart so—'

Cara turned her head as she moved away.

'How lucky that your mother could get you into the Red Cross. My poor mother has to be content with merely getting me into adulthood—'

And then she crossed the grass and opened the door in the wall into the courtyard, letting it fall to behind her with a shattering slam.

George Langley was alone when Cara came, pedalling up the drive in her Land Girl's uniform, her regulation felt hat on the back of her head like a bookmaker's.

'My dear! Vera's out – she'll be so disappointed at missing you. It's a Red Cross bandage session today. Did you hear about Essen? We sent more than a thousand aircraft over—'

'It's all right,' Cara said, propping her bicycle against the balustrade at the foot of the porch, 'Alex wasn't on that raid. He telephoned yesterday.'

George took her arm.

'You must be pretty thankful at least to know where James is, even if he isn't in the lap of luxury. Libya must be an inferno, absolute oven. Jerry's brought in a huge quantity of anti-tank artillery to cover the gaps he made in our minefields. I say, Cara, we're so – sorry.'

She turned to face him.

'That's really what I've come for, Uncle George.'

His face twisted in misery. He said in a broken voice quite unlike his usual heartiness,

'I don't know what to say to you, my dear. Quite frankly I wish Vera was here. I'm at a loss, an absolute loss—'

'Show me the garden,' she said.

He looked at her doubtfully.

'Well – if you'd like it. I put in a bed of dahlias at the weekend and a whole acre of french marigolds. Vera hates them but I think they jolly the place up a bit. Heaven knows—'

'Uncle George—'

'Yes, my dear.'

'I – I just came to say that you weren't to worry.'

He stopped on the edge of the lawn and held his hands out to her. She tried not to think how like Alan's his face was.

'You always were a plucky little thing. Remember that pony we had that only you could ride?'

'Uncle George, what I came to say was that I don't need to be plucky. There's nothing to be plucky about.'

''Fraid I don't quite follow you—'

'I mean that there was nothing much beyond a flirtation between Alan and me anyway. We always had great fun together, you know that. But that's all.'

He looked at her a little doubtfully.

'Stephen seemed to think—'

'Oh!' she said, beginning to walk away, 'Stephen! Always so serious! Of course there wasn't anything! We were like brother and sister, it suited us both being a bit daredevil. Honestly, Uncle George. Look at me!'

He followed her and peered into her face. His own lightened at once.

'My dear – I can't tell you – Vera will be overwhelmed – we've been so worried—. Silly boy, Alan, so impulsive you know. But good-hearted, always good-hearted.' He began to gather confidence, 'Of course, I did feel Stephen might be making a bit of a meal of it, you know. And if you and Alan were just having a bit of fun, then there's no harm in his marrying this little girl, though I think he might have told us. Upset Vera a bit, I can tell you. But she'll be a new woman when she hears your side of it. Cara – promise?'

She looked squarely at him, smiling.

'I promise. There's nothing to worry about. There was nothing serious between us at all.'

He put his arm round her.

'There's my girl! Taken years off my age! I say, stay for half an hour and then you can see Vera. She'd love to see you herself. It's Cook's day off, or I'd do something about some tea for you—'

'No thank you, Uncle George. And I won't stay, I really ought to get back.'

He wheeled her bicycle into the drive for her.

'Vera got all the handlebars taken off the children's bicycles in case a German parachutist landed and helped himself to one! Where could he have gone, I wonder – Land's End? Actually,' he leaned forward confidentially, one hand on the saddle, 'That's a pretty creature Alan's married. Very. He sent us a snapshot. Like to see it?'

'Another day, Uncle George,' Cara said, wheeling the bicycle clear of him. She stepped across it and put her right foot on the pedal. 'If – if you're writing to Alan, Uncle George, would you give him a message? Would you say congratulations and good luck – from me?'

CHAPTER TEN

March 1943

'What a dreadful night,' Lyddy said, 'Look at us all!'

They were gathered round the breakfast table in the kitchen, hollow-eyed and crumpled, after the third successive night in the air raid shelter to avoid the German reprisal raids – reprisal for the bombing of Cologne and Munster, Frankfurt and Lubeck, Rostock, Essen, Bremen. For three nights now planes had droned in from the south-west coast for seven, eight hours on end, so regularly that there had been no point at all in even attempting to go to bed in the house. Nothing would induce the Old Higgins' to come into the shelter, however – they had spent the night as usual in the little damp bedrooms of their cottage where mice scuttered between the rafters and the slates – but everyone else crammed in, Michael, Alexandra, Cara, Bassett, June, Lyddy and slow obedient Barbara rubbing the sleep from her eyes. All the deckchairs that used to live in the summerhouse by the tennis court had been carried in, and piles of rugs, and Lyddy had brought the picnic spirit stove and the kettle and tea things and a box of biscuits. But all the same it was cramped and cold, even wrapped in rugs, and because of the planes and the strain of listening, counting, listening again, sleep was impossible.

'Do we look awful?' Alexandra said.

'In my youth,' Michael said, his hands, trembling with cold round a mug of tea, 'I cared very much how I looked. I now only care how I feel. I feel terrible.'

Cara got up to fetch the electric fire from the dining room. The damp raw chill of the dugout only made Michael's arthritis worse, you could see the pain marking his face as clearly as if it had drawn lines on it. And his pills were so little help.

'Ma, I'm going to disobey you and put two bars on. Otherwise Pa will never thaw.'

'I wouldn't dream of objecting.'

'Oo,' Barbara said, 'Porridge—'

Michael said, 'Do you know what I'd like? I'd like a vast, boiling hot bath, and a shave with steam towels and breakfast in front of an obscene, *huge* fire – ham and eggs, kippers, muffins, pounds of butter, coffee, cream—'

Lyddy looked at him worriedly.

'There's eggs. But no more bacon until ration day—'

'Lyd, I'm dreaming.'

'I'll scramble you an egg,' Cara said, 'Have mine. Porridge is fine for me.'

'No, my darling. I'm not really hungry. Just greedy – greedy for a little comfort again.'

'Have you seen Ma's toenails?'

'*Toenails?*'

Alexandra laughed and said, 'Absurd child. She would paint them yesterday after she had bathed me. Extraordinary colour, like black cherries. I've never had a painted nail in my life. And of course I couldn't move a muscle to stop her.'

'I'll take it off for you,' June said quickly.

'Oh no thank you. They make me laugh. I thought of them all night, being there inside my gumboots, ridiculous things.'

'I'll cut your hair next,' Cara said, 'And your eyelashes—'

Lyddy said from the sink, 'Someone's just gone up to the front door. Saw him through the hedge. Drat this cat – I'll break my neck over it one day and—'

June said, 'I'll go—'

Cara got up.

'It's all right, June. 'It'll be Jim Foster with the toothbrushes.'

'Toothbrushes?'

'Yes. He's got a cousin who could get us some on the black market—'

'I don't approve of buying anything on the black market,' Alexandra said.

'I know you don't, Ma, but I have to sneak in under your principles sometimes to get us what we need. Your toothbrush has a dozen bristles, Pa's is quite bald and mine has lain down quite flat like a cornfield after a storm. The chemist in Wadebridge hasn't had a toothbrush in since November, only four million miles of horrible Bronco. So I said yes please, gratefully, to Jim Foster's cousin.'

'Cara—'

'Don't you object,' said Cara, dropping a kiss on her mother's head, 'To a girl who built a new hen house in three days single handed, not to mention scrounging an extra bar of chocolate out of old Mrs Miller in Wadebridge when we'd run out of coupons. Wait till you can polish up your gnashers with a toothbrush that brushes teeth.'

It was not Jim Foster in the porch but a telegraph boy, buttoned up in leather against the cold. Cara, suddenly sick, stared at him.

'They tried to phone you from Wadebridge, miss, but the line don't seem too good.'

'No,' she said, 'No. It was the gale – a week ago—'

He held the envelope out to her.

'Best of luck, miss. Hope it ain't bad news.'

She watched him stamp away to the motorbike he had left leaning against a gatepost. Then she looked down at the envelope in her hand, small, oblong, yellowish buff. It was addressed to her father. She put her thumb under the flap and tore it open. It was handwritten – written, no doubt by Mr Burleigh, Postmaster at Wadebridge.

By hand delivery:

> M. Swinton, Esq.,
> Bishopstow House,
> Bishopstow,
> Near Rock.

Regret to inform you that Flying Officer A. J. Swinton of -th Squadron—

Cara stopped and closed her eyes tightly. Not dead, not Alex – she looked again. He regretted, said the Under Secretary of State for War, that Alex had not returned, after the raid on Berlin and that he was presumed dead. Further details, he added helpfully, would be forwarded as soon as received. Cara leaned her forehead against the cold cream-painted door jamb, the telegram crumpled in her fingers. This then was what one lived in dread of, the finish, the utter desolation, the unbearable knowledge that someone was gone, finally, utterly gone, and gone doing something he was ordered to do, dropping bombs on German families sitting at meals just as everyone was round the kitchen table now, victims—

She would never see Alex again. He was no longer there to see. He had fallen out of her life, ripping a jagged hole in the fabric of it, the brother she had had *all* her life, all her consciousness. She looked down and saw that the telegram was darkly blotched with tears, her hands slippery with them. The pain inside her was terrible and it was going to get worse with every bitter moment of realizing that Alex was dead. Dead. Not coming back. Not *ever*.

And now she had to create a pain as horrible as her own. She had to cross the hall and open the kitchen door and see them turn towards her, porridge spoons raised and she had to say to them, 'Alex is dead'. Every moment she delayed they were safe in happy ignorance, yet every moment she delayed she was only postponing the anguish, not dispelling it.

She folded the damp telegram and pushed it into her breeches' pocket. Then she ran her fingers through her hair, rubbed her eyes on her sleeve and crossed the hall resolutely. She could hear them all talking, hear June say to Barbara, 'Take it out to the pigs then, don't stand there!' and Michael telling Alexandra some story and her low laugh and the rattle of spoons and plates, Vera Lynn still singing away on June's wireless, and the farmyard cat pleading for milk – she opened the door.

'– so there you are,' Michael was saying, 'The wages of sin. Which in Cara's case, if you let the black market stand for sin, are toothbrushes. Are they khaki?'

'It – it wasn't Jim Foster—'

'Cara—'

June snapped off the wireless. Cara went round the table, collecting a stool as she went and putting it down between her parents' wheelchairs. Then she sat down on it and took a hand of each, holding it tightly in her own.

'It was a telegram from the War Office. Alex did not return from the Berlin raid. He is presumed dead.'

She drew the two hands together to clasp each other and then she held them between hers. An awful silence fell upon the kitchen, a hollow, echoing stillness, only broken by the cat winding itself around Lyddy's legs, and whining on for its milk.

'You go,' June said, 'I like looking after your mother. You know that. It'll be like old times.'

'Is it unfair to them? If I go?'

June picked up a shovel and began to scrape the muck out of the cowpens towards the central drain.

'How do you mean, unfair?'

'I mean, that having lost Alex so recently, is it unfair of me to impose additional worry on them by going off to London?'

'You won't be gone long, will you?'

'Just a few days'

June stopped shovelling and eyed her.

'You aren't going to enjoy yourself, are you?'

'On the contrary. I'm going – I'm going to see the girl Alex wanted to marry.'

June whistled.

'Didn't know he had a sweetheart!'

'I don't think many people did. But he had. Since almost the beginning of the war.'

'Why didn't he marry her then?'

'I don't know. Perhaps she didn't want to marry him. Perhaps he thought life was too uncertain.'

'That's not how war takes most people. Never been so many weddings they say. How're you going to get to London? We haven't much petrol—'

'I know. The coupons aren't nearly enough and the petrol officer won't give us another spoonful though I've begged and begged. We need all we've got for the tractors. I'll thumb lifts to Bodmin and get a train.'

'Your ma won't like that. You haven't done anything like that before—'

'All the more reason for starting now.'

'I'm not against you going,' June said, 'I just don't see why. I mean, I should think she'd know already.'

'I'm sure she does. It isn't the knowing. Suppose she had agreed to marry him—' Cara looked away. 'You need some comfort then, losing a man.'

'I wouldn't know,' June said, 'I'm not much interested in men myself. Take them or leave them, it's all the same to me.'

'You're very lucky then.'

'Do you miss them, then, having them about?'

Cara said, 'I've almost forgotten what one looks like—'

'Come on—'

'Can you and Bassett manage then? Just for a few days?'

'If you could leave a list, maybe. We'll be fine.'

'I wouldn't go if we were lambing—'

'Go,' said June, 'Go on, go. I can see it will be on your mind until you do.'

'I don't see why,' Michael said stubbornly, 'If you want a jaunt to London, come out and say so. Anyway, I never knew anything about Alex and Mary Langley, nobody told me—'

'Alex didn't tell anyone. Well, hardly anyone. But he really loved her and – and I think she loved him—'

'But what could you do in London? Sit and cry together over him? While Ma and I get frantic down here worrying about you in London. Write to her, say you're sorry that way.'

'Pa, it isn't *enough*—'

'I should have thought it was more than enough for any Langley, after the way that bounder treated you.'

Cara said, 'There are Langleys and Langleys.'

Alexandra had been sitting a little way off, apparently immersed in the paper. Now she looked up and spun her chair a little nearer.

'Michael, don't you remember?'

'Remember what?'

'When Alan jilted Cara, Stephen made a special journey down here to break the news to her gently. Mary is much more like Stephen than Alan. It's perfectly understandable that Cara should feel—'

'Cara always feels what Cara *wants* to feel.'

'No,' Alexandra said firmly, 'She does not,'

'Anything to get away from here, to have fun, to amuse herself—'

'Do you really suppose that crawling along in a blacked out train for seven or eight hours is fun? And when did she last leave Bishopstow except to go to Wadebridge? Last summer for an abortive night at her old school. You're behaving like a selfish old man.'

'With Alex gone—'

'You still have me,' Cara said, 'And James. I shall go tomorrow and come back at the weekend.'

'James!' Alexandra said, 'Just think of him for a while! No sheets, no tablecloths, no knives and forks, just a bowl and a spoon. And poor Stephen Langley in hospital in Cairo with hepatitis—'

Michael waved a hand at Cara.

'Get going, baggage, go on, begone.'

Cara paused at the door and looked back at them. Alexandra raised her head and for a fleeting second caught Cara's eye, then she lowered it to the newspaper again and said to Michael.

'Now, here's a really jolly piece of news for you. Two hundred people suffocated to death in an East End air raid shelter.'

'What are you trying to do?' he said indignantly, 'Kill me with gloom?'

'No,' Alexandra said, 'Just make you count your blessings—'

The station at Bodmin Road was as depressing a place as Cara had ever been. It wasn't simply the grey and gusty weather, or the sharp wind which blew grit in little whirls over the platform, but the total absence of anything pleasant to look at. It had been rather a cheerful station before the war, the brown and cream livery of the Great Western Railway enlivened by tubs of very scarlet geraniums and very blue lobelias, and a family of tortoiseshell cats whom the station master claimed were salaried mousers. The tubs had all now gone, there wasn't a cat in sight, only crates and boxes piled on the edge of the platform, stencilled with numbers, and across the line a raw and ugly crater where a bomb had fallen, missing the rails by fifty feet.

There was no-one else on the platform beyond a woman and a man with two crying children, all looking cold and wretched. Even Cara, in wool trousers and boots and a thick khaki overcoat which Jim Foster's cousin had insisted was army surplus, had to stamp and tramp to keep her circulation going. She had had an easy time so far since the milk lorry had taken her as far as Bodmin itself and then a laundry van, conveniently delivering clean overalls at the dairy, had needed to collect a new roller iron from the station. Both vehicles had been bitterly cold, but it was exciting all the same, an adventure, something different. She had packed all she could need in an old rucksack of James' for easy carrying and Lyddy had crammed her pockets with sandwiches and biscuits, a flask of tea, two cold chicken wings wrapped in greaseproof paper, a few toffees.

'Try and find some soap,' Lyddy had begged.

'Or an orange—'

'See what people in London are wearing.'

'Don't sleep on the top floor of anywhere, even the Ritz—'

'Particularly the Ritz!'

'Give Mary our love.'

'If you passed a shop with any burnt umber in it – or rose madder – or chrome yellow. Paint is one thing you don't need coupons for.'

The train was late. It came creeping in from the south-west with a hang-dog air and hissed to a halt. It wasn't very full and Cara, climbing on, saw the crying children clinging to the shivering man who was trying to get on board, to detach himself. The woman was attempting feebly to pull the children off, crying herself now.

'That's war for you,' a woman in Cara's carriage said, 'Busts up families. Wicked it is. 'Spect he's got a job in London and the kiddies have to stay down here. Got a light?'

At Exeter, more people got in, two of them soldiers with long khaki canvas kitbags and a pale, thin man who began to cough, steady and relentless as a metronome, the moment he was seated. There was mist swirling over the city, Cara could hardly see out, but everyone told her what she would have seen.

'Black it is. Great holes everywhere. My grandad had a shop, a men's outfitters, dated from the sixteen hundreds the building did and it took us two days to put the fire out. Fine way to spend leave, I can tell you.'

When she pulled out Lyddy's sandwiches, they fell upon her.

'Hey, that's never powdered egg!'

'No – of course not. We live on a farm—'

'You don't know you're born, dear. I haven't tasted a fresh egg in three years—'

'Have a sandwich,' Cara said.

'Your own chickens?'

'Yes. We have almost five hundred now.'

'Fresh chicken!'

'You don't see biscuits like that in Woolworth's.'

'They're home-made—'

'What's in the other sandwiches? Spam?'

'I'm afraid so,' Cara said, 'My mother insists that living on a farm should make as little difference as possible.'

'But you have fresh milk, don't you?'

'Yes—'

'You don't know you're born. That dried stuff. You can even taste it in custard.'

As the afternoon wore on, the light thickened and died around the train, filling the fleeting fields, the wide high stretches of Salisbury Plain with dimness. The landscape, unenlivened by any faint gleam of light, became as leaden as the sky and the train, thudding slowly on, became colder and colder.

'Here,' one of the soldiers said, 'You sit between us.'

She looked at them, hesitating.

'No funny business,' he said, 'Scouts honour. Not in front of anyone else anyhow. Keep you warmer.'

They smelled of raw, rough khaki wool and boot polish and they nudged her and grinned at each other.

'Where are you going?'

'London.'

'We know that. Whereabouts?'

'Chelsea.'

'Have a drink with us. When we get to London. Send us off right on the boat train—'

'Where are you going?'

'Italy, I shouldn't wonder. Flush out Jerry.'

'Them Italians,' the woman said savagely, 'One glass of wine and they're anybody's. My sister married an Italian in 1930 and nothing but a trouble he's been to her.'

She took a lipstick out of her bag and twisted the greasy red stick out of its black bakelite case, then she began to apply it with elaborate care using the train window as a mirror.

'Have a drink with us' one of the soldiers urged again, 'Just a quick one.'

'All right,' Cara said, 'I'd like to—'

The woman sniffed.

'No shame, girls these days. That's war for you.'

'I'm only having a drink—'

The soldiers guffawed.

'No time for anything else, grandma! We've only a couple of hours between trains.'

'I'm Derek,' one said, 'He's Neville.'

At Salisbury, soldiers crowded into the carriage in hundreds it seemed, standing in the corridors, in the aisle between the seats, piling up their kitbags and sitting on them. It was almost entirely dark by now, but the press of bodies made the air warmer now, if only with a thick stale human warmth. Either Derek or Neville groped in the crush for Cara's hand.

'No—' she said and then she thought, 'Why not, what harm, I'll never see either of them again—'

'All right,' she said, 'A hand each,' and she heard them laughing in the darkness beside her. Someone in the corridor began to sing and several people joined him, some of them breaking down at missed notes and laughing. The train ground on towards Reading, towards London and Cara sat there in the darkness, pressed in on by bodies on all sides, and listened to the singing, smiling to herself and holding hands with two unknown soldiers.

'Got you some port,' Neville said, 'Girls like port.'

It was blue-red in her glass, not at all like the fine Indian red port that Michael decanted so lovingly at Christmas.

'Cheers!'

'And best of luck—'

Derek eyed her over his glass of beer.

'What're you in London for?'

'Oh – something personal.'

'A fella?'

'No.'

'D'you know where you're going?'

'No – I mean I have an address.'

'D'you know where we are?'

'No.'

They doubled up laughing, punching each other.

'How d'you know we're in London?'

'I know *that.*'

'Wish we'd got more than two hours. Don't you, Nev?'

They were in a bar off Piccadilly decorated to resemble someone's fantasy of the Tyrol with heart-shapes cut out of beams, everything made out of rustic wood, edelweiss painted everywhere, strings of cowbells, an alpenhorn slung from the ceiling. There were a lot of people crammed into the smoky red lit room, mostly in uniform but a lot of women in short, narrow skirts, wide-shouldered jackets, their hair falling in heavy bobs turned under at the shoulder.

'I must look the proverbial country cousin.'

'It's your face we look at. Isn't it Derek?'

'Will you write to us?'

'No,' she said smiling, 'There's no point.'

'Have another port.'

'No – really – you shouldn't spend your money on me—'

'What else is there to spend it on? Wine and women—'

She stood up with difficulty, heaving on her ruck-sack.

'I must go and find a taxi.'

'We'll get you one.'

'No,' she said, 'No, thank you. I'll do it for myself.'

'Try Piccadilly—'

'Thanks. I will.'

They stood up.

'What about a goodbye kiss, eh?'

'Of course.'

They leaned forward, grinning, smelling of beer. She kissed them each in turn.

'Good luck,' she said, 'And thank you for the drink.'

'Forget it. Cheerio.'

Outside it was clear and cold. The mists of the countryside had not penetrated the city and moon hung over Piccadilly, bright and solid-looking, a silver disc. The pavements were quite full, even in the semi-darkness and there was, after Cornwall, an air of holiday despite the broken buildings Cara could see all around her and the raw smell in the air, the smell of fires recently put out.

There were taxis cruising along the pavement's edge. Cara let several empty ones go past, content to savour where she was, the freedom, the dangerous crackle to the atmosphere, the people with linked arms moving along the pavements. The taste of the port was still sharp in her mouth, the smell of the bar in her nostrils. She looked up at the sky and breathed deeply, several times. Then, swinging the rucksack on to her shoulder, she stepped forward to the curb and hailed a taxi.

CHAPTER ELEVEN

'Look,' the taxi driver said, 'That pile of rubble. That's all that's left of Chelsea Old Church. Them bastards. Where did you say? Down here?'

'Yes,' Cara said, 'Yes, please.'

'Shouldn't be out after dark. It's my bet it'll be bad tonight with this moon. Of course, raids don't scare you like they used to, do they, I mean, you just says to yourself Oh Gawd, here we go again—'

'Yes. Yes – I suppose we do.'

Chelsea looked awful from the taxi windows. Every street seemed ragged with bombed buildings and beams and bricks lay everywhere, silting up gutters and pavements.

'Here we are then.'

Cara peered up at the tall, flat-fronted house. Without lights, it was impossible to tell if anyone lived there, but it was, without doubt, the address that had been at the top of Mary's letters. The lower windows had been boarded up and there was a pile of broken glass brushed up into a neat cone against the house wall.

When the taxi had gone off towards the Kings Road, Cara climbed the three shallow steps to the panelled front door and pressed the bell. It rang distantly, far away somewhere inside the house. No-one came. Cara rang again, more insistently and this time she heard slow footsteps shuffling towards her behind the door.

The door opened a crack.

'What you want?'

'I'm looking for Mary Langley.'

'Friend, are you?'

'Yes – I've known her all my life—'

The door opened a little wider.

'Thank 'eaven for that. Come in, then.'

It was absolutely black inside after the moonlit glimmer of the streets.

''Ere. Follow the wall. Second door on the right. Mind the step.'

A dull line of light showed around a doorway ahead.

'Is she here? Mary, I mean?'

'Yes. She's 'ere all right. Come in an' see—'

It was a small, shabby back room furnished with cheap furniture from which the veneer was peeling in splintery flakes.

'Glad you come, dear, and that's for sure.'

She was a small, elderly woman in a hairnet with a cigarette stuck to her lower lip, dressed in layers of fancy cardigans.

'I'm the landlady 'ere, dear. Violet Pink. Been looking after them girls since the war started.' She peered at Cara. 'You don't look like a Londoner to me.'

'I'm not. I'm from Cornwall.'

472

"Course. Like Mary.'

Cara said, 'Can I see her? Is she in?'

Mrs Pink kicked off her slippers and began to rummage under a sofa upholstered in brown leather cloth.

'She's in all right, dear. Not fit to go out, if you ask me. I've had the doctor to her and all. There's me shoes! Knew I'd put 'em somewhere.'

'The doctor!'

'Oh yes, dear. She's been right poorly. Ever since she heard about her young man. Took it ever so bad, ever so bad, much worse than my brother's Marlene did over her husband if you ask me. I'm at my wits end to know what to do about her—'

'Mrs Pink, is she ill?'

Mrs Pink straightened up.

'If you ask me, dear, I think she's ill in the head. Look, dear, I've a favour to ask. I wouldn't ask it, 'cept you're a friend of Mary's. I promised I'd go round Flood Street to my friend's, see – her husband's a warden and she gets ever so jumpy on her own. Lives on her nerves, she does. I like to go when I can. But I didn't want to leave Mary, neither. So if you stay with Mary, dear, you'd be doing all of us a favour—'

'Of course I'll stay,' Cara said impatiently, 'Where is Mary?'

'I'll show you, dear. The other girls have been lovely to her – so's all the men in his squadron, in and out of here at all hours, they've been, ever since he went – but they're on duty just now. Follow me, dear. Wait, I'll get a torch. Mind the stairs, there's ever so many holes in the carpet but I ask you, what can you do with a war on?'

By the wavering light of Mrs Pink's torch, Cara climbed the narrow stairs behind her. The house smelled musty and damp and the wallpaper, caught in irregular flashes of light, was speckled with something other than its pattern. They climbed up and up, past two half landings and half a dozen closed doors, to a narrow landing at the top and what was evidently a skylight covered in a sagging

473

hammock of blackout material. The door before them was slightly ajar.

'In 'ere, dear.'

The room was small and cold and scrupulously neat. It contained a cheap wardrobe, a dressing table with an orderly row of books marching across the top, two upright chairs, a round rag rug on the floor and beneath the slope of the ceiling a narrow bed upon which Mary lay, straight and still like a medieval knight on a tomb. The only light was from a small lamp beside the bed on a stool.

'Mary, dear, there's a friend to see you.'

· Mary did not move. Mrs Pink sighed and shook her head.

'It's always like this, dear. Won't speak to anyone. Won't move either. Scares me to death, it does. The doctor wasn't much use, said it was mild shock and she was to be left to herself. But she's not eaten more than soup in a week and not always that.' She looked up at Cara, 'You be all right, dear?'

Cara looked at the still figure.

'I think so. Can we get the room any warmer?'

'There's the gas fire. If you've got something for the meter—'

'And if I want to boil a kettle?'

'There's a ring the girls use on the landing. It's on a meter too. I'll be back at daylight, dear, soon as it's daylight my friend's herself again.'

'Is there any food?'

'I don't know what she's got, dear. Used to be very sensible about food, the only one who didn't run out of things. I'll be off, then, dear, shall I? Leave you together—'

'Yes,' Cara said, 'Yes. You go.'

She closed the door between herself and Mrs Pink's retreating feet then crossed to the gas fire let into the wall and dropped sixpence into the meter. There were matches nearby, lying neatly in the middle of a saucer.

She turned the tap and let the gas hiss out for a moment, then struck a match and lit it.

'Mary,' she said, without turning round, letting her hands thaw in the warmth, 'Mary, it's Cara.'

Mary said nothing.

'I came up from Bodmin today on the train. I've come to see you. You are the reason why I have come.' She turned her head. 'I should think you are starving. I'm going to open the cupboards and see what you've got. I've brought some dried milk and cocoa from home and Lyddy has sent you some biscuits and a cake which we had to make secretly and not tell Ma because it's a fruit cake and we aren't suppose to have any dried fruit but I have a useful little contact on the black market. You can't imagine what it was like, trying to keep Ma away from the smell of fruit cake baking – I had to wheel her all the way to Bishopstow and she was really difficult all the way, demanding to be taken back—'

She turned her head. Mary was still staring at the ceiling. Cara got up and crossed the narrow space between them. She stooped to touch Mary's hand.

'You're freezing. That can't be good for you for a start. Where's a hot water bottle?'

Mary's lips opened.

'Don't bother! I'll find one. Goodness, aren't they precious – ever since the fall of Singapore there's been no rubber for anything. Think of all those poor people with babies and no teats for their bottles.'

'Here,' Mary said.

Cara tried to sound as ordinary as possible.

'Where?'

Mary patted a small mound under the bedclothes. Cara put her hand down the bed and felt how chill the sheets were, cold with dampness—

'It's stone cold! How long have you lain with it like this? Why didn't that old hag give you another? Come on, Mary, get up, let's wrap you up by the fire. Just long enough for me to air your bed—'

Mary's mouth was working. Huge tears began to swell up in her eyes, spilling over and sliding down her thin cheeks running into her hair, her ears.

'Cara—'

Cara said, 'Oh don't, or I shall and that's just what Pa said we would do, sit here and howl together—'

'I want to die.'

'Sit up,' Cara said, 'Sit up—'

'I can't—'

'You can. You must. Here,' she slid her hands under Mary's armpits and heaved her upwards and forwards. Mary sagged against her like a rag doll, heavy with despair.

'You're terribly thin, Mary. You shouldn't be so thin. Come on, help me, get out of this, get towards the fire. Anybody'd want to die, if they were as cold as you are.'

'Cara! Oh Cara—'

Mary flung her arms around Cara's neck and burst into violent sobs.

'I want to die! I do, I do! I can't bear it without him, I can't bear anything, I can't think of anything but how terrible it is without him! I don't want to go on living without him, I don't want another day like this, another minute—'

'You're ill,' Cara said, 'You've made yourself ill. You can't possibly cope with anything until you're warm and fed. I'm going to find you some clothes—'

'Don't leave me!' Mary shrieked, 'Don't leave me!'

'I'm only going to cross the room. No further. The furthest I will go is to boil the kettle. Let go, Mary, I'm choking. Let go. I can't look after you if you won't let me move.'

Mary slumped back on the bed. In her long flannel nightgown she looked about fourteen, her thin wrists and ankles protruding awkwardly, her fine straight hair flopping over her high forehead.

'Which drawers?'

Mary said nothing but keeled over and buried her face in the pillow. Cara began to open drawers and cupboards at random, pulling out underclothes and jerseys, socks and trousers.

'How neat everything is! You would gladden Lyddy's heart, everything so folded and foursquare. Mary, come on, sit up. I can help you dress but I'm not going to do it all for you.'

It took ages with Mary alternately cooperating and flopping sideways again, tears bursting out afresh.

'At least,' Cara said, 'The effort has got me warm—'

She left Mary wrapped in a blanket on the rug beside the fire while she went to boil the kettle. Outside on the landing she could hear the planes going over, more than she ever heard at home but with the same uneven engine beat that she had crouched in the shelter by the tennis court and listened to, night after night.

She made cocoa and unwrapped the fruit cake. It was difficult to make Mary drink or eat, more like feeding a sick bird with tiny patient sips and crumbs, but she persevered, holding the mug to her mouth, pushing morsels between her lips. She refilled the hot water bottle and wrapped Mary's nightgown round it, tucking it in under the sheets. The gas meter was voracious, gobbling up coins, but Mary's hands were warmer now, and so was the air of the room, thick with the sweet steam of cocoa.

They sat like that for about an hour, Cara talking and feeding, Mary swallowing and crying, but more quietly now, the sobs less shuddering.

'Are you supposed to be on duty?'

'No. No, I'm not. I was owed a fortnight's leave, I kept not taking it because I wanted to be here in case – in case Alex came, so I suppose I'm having it now—'

'Is there somebody I should tell? Does your senior officer know?'

'Oh yes. She knows. The others told her. She came to see me, it was so kind, but it was very soon after

– it happened, I was so stunned, I just said yes and no and thank you and she told me to take it easy, not to worry—'

A sudden thud shook the room, so close that the windows rattled in their frames. Cara's head went up.

'What's that?'

Mary said, 'A bomb. A high explosive. It doesn't matter—'

'It does! How close was it?'

'I don't know, fifty yards perhaps—'

A second one fell, a little further away and then another and another and the house began to shudder beneath them, trembling in its foundations. Cara leaned forward and turned the gas tap off.

'Come on, down to the cellar—'

'No. No. You go. I don't want to. I don't care.'

'Mary, don't be so stupid! Listen to them, they're absolutely raining down! Come on, come on—'

Mary said, 'No, leave me. I want to die. I'd rather.'

Cara went behind her, putting her hands under her arms again and dragging her backwards resisting and limp towards the door.

'You're coming if I have to throw you downstairs!'

Mary struggled feebly.

'Don't, let go, leave me, don't bully! I don't want to be safe, I don't want to, I want to stay here! That's why I've stayed up there all week, waiting for the nights, waiting for the bombs!'

Cara wrenched the door open and rolled Mary out on to the landing. Behind the blacked out skylight a red glow was dully visible, the glow from fires started by incendiary bombs.

'There is one thing,' Cara said, 'That is very useful about being a land girl. I am extremely strong. And I am by nature extremely determined. So you don't stand a chance.'

Mary rolled herself into a ball against the wall.

'Go away! Go away and leave me!'

478

Cara bent down and pulled Mary's hands away from her face.

'Is this what Alex would want? Is this what he would admire? A piece of stupid self-indulgence that does nothing but bring grief upon your family and friends? He trusted you, you know he did. He trusted you and he believed in you. He told me that you were wonderfully independent, he admired you for that, that was one of the things he loved most. What would he think of you now, snivelling and whining about not wanting to live? He wouldn't recognize you, Mary Langley, he wouldn't know who you were!'

Mary said, 'You can't imagine what life is like without him—'

Another thud, terrifyingly close and then two more and an awful scream, a piercing wild scream and the crash of falling masonry.

'I can!' Cara said furiously, 'Of course I can! He was my brother, remember? And what is more, he was my brother long, long before he ever was your lover. Get up, Mary, or I will kick you up!'

Slowly, Mary uncurled herself and crept to her feet. Then, sliding her shoulder down the wall, she let Cara push her downwards step by step, stumbling in the darkness while the house shivered and trembled and the thuds outside beat down on London.

'You can imagine those pilots up there, can't you,' Cara said, 'Letting the bombs go and saying to themselves "That's for Cologne's museums, and that's for Munster Cathedral, and that's for Monte Cassino." Where's the cellar door? Oh, come on, Mary, don't stop there—'

The cellar stairs smelt of earth and potatoes.

'There's a lamp,' Mary said, 'it should be on the third step. We always leave it there.'

'Got it. Matches?'

'Beside it. Oh my God, listen!'

'Shut the door. Goodness, you've obviously spent half the war down here.'

479

'At least half the nights.'

There were old armchairs in the cellar, a garden seat, several tea chests to serve as tables, books, magazines, a tray with mugs on it, tins of dried milk on a shelf, a kettle.

'We had a gramophone once. One of the boys brought it, one of the Pilot Officers from Alex's squadron. He was awfully keen on Richard Tauber. I can't ever come down here without thinking of that fruity voice singing "We are in love with you, my heart and I, and we are always true, my heart and I"—. Oh heavens, *heavens*, Cara, what am I going to do?'

'I heard Ma say that to Pa, but you'd never know it from her manner otherwise. I suppose – I suppose that each day it's a little more bearable, just a little—'

Mary sat down in an armchair and put her head in her hands.

'I'm behaving appallingly.'

'There – are some things you can't help.'

'It's so marvellous of you to come. I never dreamt of such a thing. And – and, well, with the way you must feel about our family. I used to think you must all wish Alex had chosen anyone in the world but me.'

Cara set the lamp down on a tea chest and began to pile rugs round Mary.

'That was all long ago. Anyway, whatever feelings I had about Alan after he married didn't extend to the rest of you.'

'Didn't they?'

'No. He isn't very like the rest of you in any case, except perhaps your father to look at. Even I – even at my most unreasonable – couldn't blame all of you for him. Anyway, I was awfully grateful to you in a way – you for writing, Stephen for bothering to come. There, is that better? Look, tuck this round your feet. I suppose that's partly why I'm here because – it made

480

all the difference to me, Stephen coming, telling me in person. Heavens! Do they often do that?'

A particularly close and violent shudder had sent a shower of white flakes and fragments of old plaster pattering down from the ceiling.

'It's been bad the last few weeks. But not as bad as last year altogether. Did it really help? Stephen coming, I mean.'

'Yes. But it wasn't just that. It was other things he said, things about understanding how civilians felt, how I felt, stuck out there in Cornwall. I've never forgotten it.'

'He doesn't know I've – cracked up like this. I'm awfully glad he doesn't. Being him, he'd be out of bed and here like a shot, hepatitis or no hepatitis—'

'All the way from Cairo?'

Mary looked up.

'He's not in Cairo. He's here. He's in St Bartolph's. They sent him back, he's been awfully ill, you see. The consultant he used to work under before the war happened to be in Cairo too, and he said he couldn't afford to lose a man like Stephen after all he's done with burns and Cairo was no place for recovery. He was flown home. I've had a letter. He sounds very embarrassed at what he sees as preferential treatment. Cara—'

'Yes?'

'Has there been anyone else since Alan?'

'No.'

'Do – do you think one could ever fall in love twice?'

'Mary, I don't know. I simply don't know. I'm not sure that I *was* properly in love, maybe I was just infatuated.'

'I was in love. Still am—'

'I know.'

'Look,' Mary pointed to a pile of books near her. 'Our Greek books. I was teaching him.'

'He told me. He was jealous of your intellect – well, not

jealous because you were clever but because he wanted to follow your mind wherever it went.'

'Did he say that?'

'Yes.'

'I never could believe that a man like Alex would – could – look twice at a plain skinny bookworm like me. I remember a snowy day – oh, only weeks ago, perhaps the end of January – and a whole crowd of us went into Hyde Park to snowball. And everyone was laughing and fooling around and I kept looking at Alex, so glamorous, so magnificent in his wonderful greatcoat and flying boots and I said to myself over and over, he can't be mine, he *can't*, and he was hurling snowballs about and laughing with the others and shouting – like a schoolboy—'

'He wanted to marry you right from the beginning,' Cara said.

Mary put her hand down the neck of her jersey and pulled out a ring, a half hoop of sapphires and diamonds, suspended on a chain.

'He kept asking me. Over and over again. And I said no and no and no because of what I just told you and the war. He gave me this at Christmas. I couldn't say no any more but I said I'd only put in on my finger at the end of the war. I couldn't believe he would survive and then as the months wore on and back he came, raid after raid, I began to feel he was special, protected somehow.'

Cara said, 'You made him awfully happy. He never was really in love, before you.'

'That's something, isn't it?' Mary said, struggling with tears again, 'I've got that, haven't I? But – but oh! Cara, what now, what's the point—'

'Come back to Cornwall with me.'

'You don't want me—'

'I do. I improved vastly in the care of the needy. Ma and I still fight a bit about how much I should do for her, but she's taught me an awful lot.'

'She won't want to see me. I couldn't – couldn't make Alex go home more often. I suppose I could have, utterly refused to see him, but of course, I didn't. Your mother would be so right to resent that.'

'My mother,' Cara said, looking up as another cascade showered from the ceiling, 'Can be a pain in the neck. But she has no mean feelings, not one. She'd have wanted Alex to do what he liked to do, what relaxed him most, what helped him to do his job better. If that something was you, she would think you an entirely good thing. Anyway she loved him, Pa loved him, you did, I did – we're all in the same boat.'

'My parents—'

'They'd want you?'

'I – I can't go there and explain everything, I can't talk to them about it.'

'You'll have to. In the end. They have as much right to know as anyone.'

'Cara, you're so sensible.'

'Thanks a million. Do you think you could sleep at all?'

'I'd rather talk.'

'I might nod off, bombs and all.'

'Cara—'

'Mm?'

'Would – would you go and see Stephen?'

'Funnily enough, I thought of that, when you mentioned him. He ought to know that you feel a bit frail. Of course I'll go and tell him. Before we go down to Cornwall.'

Mary said, 'He'd be so—' and then something hit the house, with a weight like a mountain falling sideways and a terrible sliding and crashing began to happen above them.

'We've been hit—'

'Quick, get over by the wall. As near to solid earth as you can!'

The cellar door at the top of the steps bulged and

creaked and then burst open and a rubble of bricks and dust cascaded down.

'Let's get out!'

'No – no, don't move. Wait till there's no movement overhead.'

'The noise!'

'Cara – thank heaven you're here!'

'Aren't you glad you aren't in bed now, you dolt? I say, what about old Mother Pink, isn't this her house?'

'No. She's only a caretaker. She went out to play cards tonight, she's absolutely addicted. Cara, don't move till the All Clear sounds.'

It seemed hours until it did, hours in which they crouched together in the dusty cellar while the debris above them shifted and groaned, almost as if the house were alive and in pain. Occasionally a small avalanche of rubble clattered down the steps from the hall above, but the planes overhead grew scarcer and the thud of bombs around them less frequent, farther away.

'Listen,' Cara said, 'It's raining, pouring—'

'That's what stopped the raid then.'

The All Clear sounded, clear and welcome.

'Come on. Let's go and see—'

'Cara, you must be careful. Anything might fall on you, the house will be terribly unsafe—'

They scrambled up the littered staircase to the hall and could immediately get no further. The house which had been hit was not theirs but the one next door, but the walls had been blown in by the blast, blown through the doorways to pile up in broken heaps along the hall and up the stairs. On the top floor the stairs themselves had been blasted out, smashing through the closed bedroom doors of the floors below.

'Oh Lord,' said Cara, 'Look, no roof.'

Above them the moon still hung as it had earlier in the evening, bright and round, but the sky behind it had a reddish glare.

'You said it was raining!'

'I heard rain—'

Slipping and sliding, they clambered over the broken bricks to the front door.

'It won't open!'

'The windows then.'

'They're boarded up!'

Cara turned round.

'Well then. The back of the house.'

Unsteadily, they picked their way back along the rubble, past the ruins of Mrs Pink's sitting room – the mantelpiece lay face down amid the wreckage and the chimney-breast was no more than a gaping hole where next door should have been – and the cellar doorway to a narrow backdoor that led into an area at the back.

'I think it's stuck too—'

'Pull, Mary, *pull*. Hold me round the waist. Now, one, two, three, *pull*—'

The door came away with a jerk flinging them backwards on to the debris.

'Come on!'

'I can't, Cara. My books, my photographs—'

Cara bent down and seized her arm.

'Much better not to have those. They'll only remind you. Now, who do you know around here? Where can we go?'

Mary said, 'There's some girls in my division in Nell Gwynne House. In Sloane Street—'

'Can you walk that far?'

'Yes. Yes, I think so.'

Outside in the little area where the dustbins now lay on their sides, disgorging potato peelings and empty tins and tea leaves, they stood and looked up at the house. The left hand side was entirely gone, leaving rafters poking out into the air like fingers, and the bare ribs of the roof were outlined against the night sky. Odd things were suspended here and there, a sheet, a shoe, a uniform cap, a pillow sagging like a body over a beam.

'Oh God,' Cara said, 'Look—'

From the crater next door, where a house had stood half an hour before, tongues of flame were beginning to flicker upwards.

'An incendiary bomb, then—'

'Quick! We must get through the gap, into the street!'

She took Mary's hand and began to tow her behind her, as obliging and unresisting as a child, picking her way between the crater and the damaged house over a landscape of jagged blocks of shattered masonry.

'Mary! Mary, look! There's my rain!'

Down the centre of the street water was pouring from a broken main.

'At least that will be useful for putting out the fire!'

'I can't walk to Sloane Street. I can't go any further. I want to stay here, Cara, I want my photographs.'

Cara said patiently, 'You have to come. First, to be safe and second, because I don't know where Sloane Street is. Do you think having got you this far that I'll leave you here beside a burning house?'

Mary sank on to the pavement.

'Let me stay. Please let me. You go. There's nothing for me to go for.'

Crouched before her, Cara said, 'Did you hear anything of what I said to you before? Are you going to fail Alex now? Are you going to let me go to Stephen and say, sorry, I tried to help Mary but she was determined to die so I let her? Are you going to let your parents feel they weren't worth living for either? Are you? Are you?'

Mary held up her arms.

'I'm so tired—'

'So am I. And getting jolly cross too.'

'You sound like you used to. At school.'

'Get *up*, Mary.'

They stood together, swaying a little.

'Now, which way?'

'That way. Towards the King's Road.'

Cara put her arm round Mary and felt her sag against her.

'Come on. Right feet first. One, two. One, two. We must look drunk, reeling about like this. One, two. One, two. Head up, Mary. I can't actually carry you.'

Dusty and dishevelled, staggering a little but locked together with their arms round each other's waists, they turned the corner into the King's Road and began their steady but uneven progress towards Sloane Square.

CHAPTER TWELVE

'He's already had a visitor today,' the Sister said, 'He's not supposed to see many people. He's been a very sick man.'

'Please,' Cara said, 'I won't be long. Or excite him. I'm – I've – I've known him all his life. It isn't as if I were a stranger.'

The Sister eyed her.

'Wait here a moment, please.'

The corridors of St Bartolph's were painted shiny dark green halfway up and above that shiny paler green. They were floored in dark linoleum and smelt powerfully of antiseptic and polish. There was nothing pleasant to look at, even the light bulbs were unshaded, hanging nakedly at the end of black flexes, and the only places to sit were little neat rows, every so often, of grey folding metal chairs.

It had been a horrible journey to get there. Cara had left Mary, at last blessedly asleep in the bed of one of the friendly ATS girls at Nell Gwynne House, who had seemed not one whit surprised to be woken at four in the morning by the two of them, exhausted, dishevelled and shrouded in dust. She had made them some tea, and then she and Cara had put Mary to bed in her own bed and had spent the remainder of the night in armchairs, rolled in blankets. Cara had supposed herself tired enough to sleep in any position, but the moment her body was comfortable, her brain sprang awake and hammered in her skull like a headache. The friendly ATS girl snored comfortably almost at once – she had said to Cara that one could always sleep in this block, it was so utterly solid – but Cara had lain awake and listened to Mary crying through the wall, an awful childlike sobbing. Once or twice, she had gone into her, but she had not stopped crying, only clutched Cara's hand and wept over it, and Cara, thinking that perhaps she would cry herself to sleep, had simply sat there and stroked her hair and murmured.

At seven, when the ATS alarm shrilled piercingly, Mary fell at last into a profound slumber. The ATS girl sprang out of her chair with every appearance of having had ten hours' excellent undisturbed sleep and made tea and toast for herself and Cara.

'I'm Alison. Poor old Mary. Alex's going was the most awful blow. I hardly knew him but they were frightfully keen on each other.'

'He was my brother.'

'I say. I'm awfully sorry—'

'That's why I came up to London. I had a feeling she might be wretched. Though I didn't expect this.'

'She'd have been a goner if you hadn't turned up. More toast?'

'Please.'

'Help yourself to marg. Look, Linda will be back soon, she's been working nights, she lives here. If you drop off, just leave her a note to say Mary's in my bed. Stay as long as you like. We're used to it, we've been sixteen here before now, bodies wall to wall!'

'Do you think I could have a bath?'

'Go ahead, help yourself.'

Alison stood up and brushed crumbs from her uniform skirt.

'Must fly. Would you be a brick and wash these things up? Have to muck in round here!'

'Of course I will. You've been awfully kind. I say — how do I get to St Bartolph's from here?'

'The hospital? It's in the City. I should get a bus. From Knightsbridge. There's a timetable in the living room, under the 'phone.'

'And may I telephone my parents?'

'Sure,' Alison said, 'Telephone Hitler if you want to, as long as you put money in the box.'

'That's the other thing,' Cara said, blushingly. 'I haven't got a penny. I mean, I did have, but it was all in my rucksack last night, at the top of the house.'

Alison whistled.

'Poor you. What an infernal bore. Would a couple of quid do for now? I'd let you have more but—'

'No, no, that's fine. It's so kind of you. I'm so sorry to be such a nuisance.'

'You aren't a nuisance. You can't help it. That's what wartime's all about. I say, when you have a bath, don't on pain of death use the pink soap. Linda was sent it from America and she goes mad if anyone touches it.'

Linda turned out to be a tall and elegant blonde, as equally unsurprised to find Cara in her bath and Mary in Alison's bed as Alison had been to see them both in the middle of the night.

'Poor kid. Did it scare you?'

'Only in retrospect,' Cara said, towelling her hair, 'I wasn't frightened at the time.'

'On leave?'

'No. Land Army in Cornwall.'

'Good Lord.'

'I came up to see Mary. Alex was my brother, you see.'

Linda said seriously, 'He was absolutely first rate. It's a wonderful squadron that, but he was the tops.'

'Yes,' Cara said.

'You look all in. Why don't you doss down in my bed? I'm perfectly used to an armchair.'

'No, I couldn't do that. It's so kind of you. I want to go and see Mary's brother, he doesn't know how shaken she is. I feel someone in the family ought to know and her parents – well, they're so cut off, down there in Cornwall, that I feel they'd only panic, be too alarmed.'

'The doctor brother?' Linda said, lighting a cigarette.

'Yes.'

'Another winner, that one. I always have liked rather serious types. He's had jaundice or something.'

'If I went to see him, would you be here in case Mary wakes?'

'Absolutely. I shall be out for the count at least until tea time. Leave her a note to tell her I'm around and she can squeak if she needs me.'

'Do you mind?'

'Don't be daft. We've all been helping each other out for four years now.'

Cara went softly into Alison's bedroom and stooped over Mary. She was lying on her side, her cheek pillowed in her hand. She stirred for a moment and said with great distinctness, her eyes still closed,

'Mosquito and Lancaster, Wellington and Lysander, Spitfire, Anson—'

Behind her, Linda laughed softly.

'Poor old thing. RAF on the brain. Come on out or she'll be muttering about wizard prangs and duff gen. I'll keep an eye, don't you worry. Off you go.'

She had had to wait twenty minutes for a bus in the raw cold. There had been a long queue with her, standing mutely on the slope leading to Hyde Park Corner, all gazing blankly at nothing in particular. The air of excitement that had so delighted her the night before on the crowded pavements of Piccadilly seemed to have vanished with the grey dawn, everything looked tired and beaten and lifeless, the people, the buildings, even Hyde Park where a few daffodils had come up bravely among the guns.

The bus was crammed. It smelt of old cigarettes and humanity and Cara was forced to travel standing, wedged between two men in mackintoshes, one of whom held an attaché case which dug painfully into her legs. Then in Piccadilly the bus broke down and they were all turned out into the street, where it had begun to rain, a thin, cold slanting rain, and where evidence of last night's raids had not yet been entirely cleared away. Outside a tailor's shop a broken bowler hat tottered on its stand and an elegant grey kid glove on a wooden hand lay in a pool of water, outstretched as if pleading for help. The water in the gutters was thick with wood and glass splinters and the bitter smell of burning hung in the air.

The relief bus was forty minutes in coming. Cara was too dazed by London and lack of sleep now to think of going on eastwards by any alternative method, so she stood and leaned against the bus stop and watched rescue workers in a building opposite going in with stretchers and coming out with burdens on those stretchers, lumped in grey blankets. Smoke was still rising from the direction of St James', thick yellowish smoke which vanished into the wet air as it climbed upwards.

When the bus did come, it took almost another half hour to get to the City, crawling along the Strand and Fleet Street past more scenes of devastation, more bombed holes in streets, more blackened buildings, more dispirited people in utility clothing. A man across the aisle of the bus stared at Cara all the way, a wet-lipped, beady-eyed unpleasant man and even when she looked directly away from him, out of the window at the passing buildings, she could feel his stare, unsettling and intimate.

Then there was too much dazed wandering around Smithfield Market, shouted at by the meat porters, looking for the hospital and when she found it, too much asking of the same question, too many corridors, too many wrong turnings and then the Sister, impeccable in white and blue stripes, saying no, she couldn't see Stephen, he was too tired.

Cara slumped into one of the metal chairs and put her head back against the green and glossy painted wall, closing her eyes. Feet went past her continually, rubber soles squeaking on the linoleum, but they began to sound faint and far away to her, part of a dreamlike drowsiness that was stealing over her. A rattling trolley sound like distant bells, voices became a murmur like the sea—

'You may see Major Langley,' Sister said sharply, 'If you stay no longer than fifteen minutes.'

Cara's eyes snapped open.

'Thank you, of course, I'll—'

'Third door on the left. The bed at the far end on the right. The one with screens.'

'Screens!'

'He needed a private room but we hadn't one. It's the best we could do.'

The ward, men's medical, was painted like the corridors, lined with a double row of white covered beds. Cara hesitated on the threshold. Every head had turned to look at her and she wished suddenly that she hadn't been so obedient to Alexandra and Lyddy in sensibly wearing trousers but had brought a frock to London, even a pair of precious nylons and her only pretty shoes. What a dreary sight she must seem to them, dark trousers and sweater, khaki coat, no makeup—

'Who's the lucky man, luv?' the man in the nearest bed asked.

She smiled at him and pointed.

'That one up there. Behind the screens.'

''E's been proper poorly—'

She began to walk down the ward, past the beds and the temperature charts, the symmetrically arranged lockers and chairs, the rows of following eyes. The screens covered in pleated green cloth had been wheeled into

492

a neat oblong at the end of the ward, enclosing the last bed against the angle of the far wall.

'Stephen?'

There was a pause.

'Stephen? Stephen, it's Cara. May I—'

He said rapidly, 'Oh come in, do please, I'd no idea it was you when Sister said I had a visitor.'

He was lying almost flat in bed, his head turned towards her. On the locker beside him was a pile of books and a huge vase of daffodils, illuminating the little cell with their colour.

'Cara. Cara, I can't believe it—'

He held his hand out to her.

'Poor Cara. I must alarm you. I'm sorry to look so terrible.'

She took his hand in both hers and looked down at him.

'You can't help that. Anyway what does it matter if you don't *feel* too terrible.'

He smiled.

'I did. I'm so much better, I just am infernally tired all the time. I got jaundice on top of everything. That's why I'm this attractive colour. I can't offer you anywhere very comfortable I'm afraid – those chairs are the best I can do. What on earth are you doing here?'

She sat down and looked across him at the daffodils.

'I haven't brought you anything. I am sorry. The primroses were just out at home but of course, I didn't know I was going to see you, I didn't know you were home again.'

He said softly, 'That primrose wood outside Liskeard—'

'Yes.'

'I – suppose Mary told you I was here? You went to see Mary?'

'That's why I came to London. Because of Mary – after Alex—'

'You angel,' he said.

She looked down at him.

'Oh no! I was only copying you.'

'Copying me?'

'You took so much trouble over me – about Alan. It made so much difference to me.'

He rolled his head away from her so that she could only see his profile, the high forehead and straight nose, the thin cheek and fringe of thick lashes, the shadowed chin. He said awkwardly, as if interpreting her gaze,

'I'm so sorry, I need a shave.'

'Oh, Stephen, don't be so stupid! What does it matter—'

He turned his head back.

'You're terribly tired, Cara.'

'I didn't get much sleep last night.'

'Where were you?'

'With Mary—'

He said very gently, 'Is that what you have come about? Mary? To tell me something about Mary?'

'It seems so unkind,' she said in a rush, 'So – unfair to burden you when you aren't well, but someone ought to know, someone in your family. She was all alone in the house when I got there, except for an old slut in slippers and she'd been in bed for almost a week it seems, not speaking, not moving, hardly eating or drinking, sort of frozen in her grief. I tried to get her warm and feed her but when the raids began she said she wanted to stay up there at the top of the house and be bombed, that she wanted to die. I got her down to the cellar eventually but she was awfully weak and confused and we stayed down there, oh, two or three hours and then the house next door was hit and the ceiling was blown off Mary's room and the staircase went too – Stephen, it's all right, don't look like that, we weren't hurt, I wouldn't be telling you otherwise—'

He had seized her hand again. He said hoarsely, 'You might have been killed—'

She tried to smile, 'That's what I'm here for. To tell you that Mary is perfectly safe. I've telephoned Bishopstow and Ma, being Ma, was absolutely calm and sensible and was going to telephone your parents. Mary is asleep in the bed of someone called Alison, a friend of hers. We walked there in the middle of the night.'

'You saved her life—'

Cara said, 'I don't want to talk about that. I want you to tell me who I ought to get in touch with about Mary, a doctor, I mean. She is really badly, deeply shocked about Alex, helpless and – and like a child, not knowing what to do. I thought of taking her back with me to Cornwall, I don't think she ought to stay here, not until she is more herself. What do you think?'

He said slowly, 'I think – you are absolutely wonderful.'

There were sudden tears in Cara's eyes. She put her free hand up to her face and rubbed it.

'Don't exaggerate. Think of all the people you have saved, probably hundreds of them—'

'That's my job. Here. Have my handkerchief.'

She blew her nose violently.

'Should I tell Uncle George?'

'Not yet,' Stephen said, 'It would frighten them so.'

'That's what I thought.'

'They didn't really know how involved with each other Mary and Alex were. They came up to see me ten days ago and I know they saw Mary then, but that was before Alex was killed. Would you pass me that pad and pencil?'

She leaned across the bed and picked them off the top of the pile of books.

'Thanks. Look, I'm writing down the name of a friend of mine here, at St Bartolph's. He's called Dick Swift. He's met Mary even though he doesn't know her well and he's been dealing with psychological cases since '39, shell shock and so forth. If he can't help us directly, he will know someone who can.' He wrote slowly for a moment, holding the pad in the air above his head, then he held it out to her. 'Cara, I can't thank you enough. What would have become of poor Mary if you hadn't turned up with all your sweetness and sense and courage?'

Cara coloured.

'I've discovered I rather like looking after people. Maybe after the war—' she looked round smiling a little at the green walls and screens, 'I'll come here and learn to nurse.'

'Lucky hospital,' he said, 'Lucky patients.'

She looked at her watch.

'Don't go.'

'A very fierce Sister said I wasn't to be more than fifteen minutes.'

'I shall threaten her with a relapse if you don't stay a little longer. Tell me more about last night, everything, all the details—'

'No,' Cara said, 'Not now. When you're stronger and I'm not so tired.'

'You'll come back then? Soon?'

'Of course. The minute I know anything more about Mary.'

His eyes darkened for a moment with an expression very like disappointment. Then he said, 'God, I hate being in bed! If I hadn't this confounded thing, Mary would never have had to endure all that time alone! Why didn't those wretched girls she lives with do something? Why does it have to be you, toiling all the way up from Cornwall, a stranger in London—'

'Perhaps it's better it was me.'

Stephen said sharply, 'Because you know what that sort of loss feels like?'

Cara's chin went up.

'Only partly, if I'm honest. You didn't need to say

that. You know perfectly well that whatever I felt for Alan wasn't in the same league as Mary's love for Alex.'

'I'm so sorry,' he said, turning his head away, 'So terribly sorry. I'm driven by a demon, Cara—'

The screens rattled.

'Time your visitor left, Major Langley.'

'Two minutes, sister.'

'Two minutes *only*.'

Cara stood up.

'Go back to Mary and get some rest yourself,' Stephen said, 'I'd give anything to be fit enough to look after you – both, myself. You can't imagine how frustrated I feel.'

'I can. I know all about frustration.'

He smiled.

'Yes,' he said, 'So you do. Now I must copy you.'

She said slowly, 'Do you think it's very wrong if I tell you that I – almost enjoyed last night? That – that there was a satisfaction in using my instincts, in being responsible? I have a rather legendary great-grandmother who was only happy when she was doing something, particularly in a crisis. I feel rather a sympathy for her, when I think about last night.'

'I told you,' he said, 'I think you're wonderful. Why should it be wrong to take pleasure in being so resourceful and cool and competent? I wish—' he said and stopped. 'I wish you weren't going.'

'I'll come again soon. I said so. And I'll try to find you some primroses. Those daffodils are lovely.'

'Sarah brought them.'

'Sarah!'

'Sarah Calne. She came earlier this morning. She's been tremendously kind, in and out all the time, whenever she has a spare hour, bringing me books and things. She's very good at diverting me, stopping me lying here and feeling sorry for myself.'

'Of course.'

'Give my love to Mary. Poor little Mary—'

Outside the screens, Sister said, 'Major Langley! Your visitor!'

'Stephen, just one more thing—'

'Yes,' he said, 'Anything.'

'Stephen, all my money was in Mary's room when it was hit. I borrowed two pounds from Alison—'

He turned and pulled open the door of his locker, extracting a battered wallet which he held out to her.

'Help yourself.'

'Oh, no. Just a few pounds. To tide me over until I know what's going to happen—'

He sighed and opened the wallet on his chest, pulling out two white five pound notes.

'If I don't give you too much, it will at least make you come back to get more. Is ten enough, for food and taxis and so on?'

'Too much! I only need five. And anyway I go by bus.'

He held the notes out, closing his eyes.

'Don't argue. Take it. It's the only thing I can do for you both at the moment.'

She stooped and kissed his rough cheek lightly.

'Try not to worry, Stephen. I'll go and find Dick Swift now and maybe he can come and tell you what he thinks while I go back to Mary.'

'You'll like him.'

'I'll like anyone who can help.'

Stephen said with sudden savagery, 'I don't stand a blasted chance, do I, flat on my back, yellow eye-balls—'

The screens opened.

'Major Langley, I absolutely insist that you are left to rest. Otherwise visitors will be entirely forbidden.'

Cara touched his hand.

'Goodbye, Stephen,' she said, but he did not reply, only rolled his head away from her and closed his eyes.

'Come along, young lady.'

'Coming,' Cara said, 'Coming.'

CHAPTER THIRTEEN

Dick Swift said, 'It's quite a severe emotional breakdown. The stubbornness, the clinging to you, the defeatism, the childish dependency – they all point to it. She's a single-minded sort of girl, I should imagine, and as single-minded emotionally as she is academically.'

'Is it serious? I mean, do people recover?'

Dick smiled.

'Oh yes. Most certainly they do. Especially given the right circumstances for their particular needs. Complete recovery may take years – for instance, in Mary's case she may not be able to fall in love again easily for a while but at – what is she? Twenty two? – that isn't the end of the world.'

'And what are Mary's particular needs?'

'At the moment, I would say a friend like you.'

'So she doesn't need hospital?'

Dick held out a packet of cigarettes to Cara. She shook her head.

'Sensible girl. Do you mind if I do? No, I don't think she needs to be hospitalized but she ought to have a professional eye kept on her at frequent and regular intervals for the time being. And she may have trouble with sleep for a while.'

Cara got up and went to the window, standing looking down into Sloane Street.

'Would you say then, that if I took her home with me, I could look after her there, maybe give her even a few little easy untiring jobs to do around the place? I mean, if a doctor saw her regularly? It seems a bit mad, with her parents only a few miles away. Maybe she'll want to go home to them when she sees them.'

'Maybe. Maybe not. In her present acute stage, I doubt it. She mustn't go anywhere at the moment under compulsion and she will go anywhere you go. Can you manage at home though? Your parents, I mean—'

Cara came back to her chair.

'Yes. We can manage. There's two other land girls and one of them is a tower of strength.'

'I think it would be the answer for Mary.'

She looked at him.

'Dick – I would so like to think so.'

'In fact I think you look the answer to all sorts of poor problems I can think of. Come on. Let me buy you a drink. You've had a hell of a couple of days. I'll take you to the Ritz.'

'The Ritz! Like this! I couldn't possibly! And I couldn't leave Mary.'

'Damn,' he said, 'I forgot Mary. What about when Alison comes back?'

'I don't know. She was so terribly upset when I went out to get some food this morning. I really don't want to risk it. I know she's asleep now but suppose she should wake and panic?'

'It's pretty strong, the dope I gave her.'

Cara said, 'I'd love to go to the Ritz. It's the best offer I've had in years. But I wouldn't be happy—'

'You're pretty fond of Mary, then?'

Cara coloured a little.

'I've known her all my life. We were at school together. I suppose I feel – I'm taking care of her for – for her family.'

Dick stood up.

'I'll go find something to drink and bring it here. D'you drink gin?'

'I haven't for ages—'

'Time you did again, then. I'll be back in a jiffy.'

When he had gone, Cara emptied his ashtray and hit all the cushions back to plumpness, conscious that, but for Alison and Linda's easy kindness, they would be homeless and also, that to have four people in a tiny flat was inconvenient at the best of times. Then she went through to Alison's cupboard of a bedroom and looked down at Mary, lying as she always lay with her cheek on her hand. She was a pale as paper, her skin almost translucent, the hand clutching the sheet to her chin unbearably thin. She had eaten a very little that day and cried a good deal, watching Cara all the time and reaching out for her now and then like a child in need of comfort. 'Stay as long as you need to,' Linda had said, but Cara didn't want to.

'I feel I want to get her out of London,' she had said to Dick at their first meeting yesterday, 'Away from all the memories. I know she knew Alex in Cornwall but there are no associations with their love affair down there, not like there are here.'

Today, he had said she might do that, in fact he had virtually said it would be the best thing. It wouldn't be easy, hampered in all she did by Mary's dependency upon her, feeling awkward, to say the least, in trying to explain to Uncle George and Aunt Vera that Mary wanted, preferred, to be with her, for the time being anyway. But for all that, she wanted to do it, she wanted to look after Mary, to restore her to spirits, to make her laugh again as she had made Alexandra laugh. She wanted to do all this – for Mary, for Stephen, lying helpless and longing to help. Was it maybe a desire to repay him for his kindness to her? She stooped over Mary and pulled the blankets up around her thin shoulders. It was curious, really, what a comfort there was in thinking of Stephen.

Dick came back with half a bottle of gin, some angostura bitters and a carton of orange juice.

'Only Food Office, I'm afraid. The juice I mean. I tried at least to find some lime juice.'

'It doesn't matter. I couldn't feel less fussy. Those don't look very generous glasses but I couldn't find bigger ones.'

'Little and often, then.'

'It's so good of you,' Cara said, 'Giving up your free time like this.'

Dick shrugged.

'It's nothing. You wait till you see how Alex's Squadron will rally round, the RAF is quite remarkable when it comes to looking after the girls of lost airmen. For my part,' he held up his glass to Cara, 'This isn't business at all. This is pleasure.'

Alison came home while they were drinking, accompanied by two men from Alex's squadron.

'Good-oh!' she said, 'A party! Just what I need.'

One of the airmen pulled a bottle out of his greatcoat pocket.

'I brought it for Mary. Maybe it's the last thing she wants. I didn't like to bring her flowers because Alex was always giving them to her, I thought it would only upset her—'

'It upsets *me*,' Cara said, 'You all being so kind. I can't get over it.'

'You've been wizard,' the airman said, 'Absolutely first rate. We went to see Stephen. He couldn't stop talking about you.'

Alison said, 'Look, more glasses. What did you bring, Pete? More gin? Goody, goody. What's that, Simon, *cider*? Cider and gin? We'll be as tight as ticks. Cara, do wake Linda, she hates to miss any fun.'

Simon said to Dick, 'I hope the diagnosis isn't too bad.'

Dick nodded at Cara and grinned.

'Ask her. She's in charge.'

Simon raised his glass.

'Like brother like sister, then. We thought the world of Alex.'

Dick came to put his arm round Cara's shoulders.

She said, 'I wish I didn't keep wanting to cry.'

'Don't tell me you aren't used to praise.'

502

'Not this sort. Not from people who are so praise-worthy themselves.'

'I suppose,' Dick said, 'There's no chance of seeing you before you go back to Cornwall? Taking you out, I mean.'

'I don't know. I'm coming to the hospital tomorrow, I thought I'd take Mary if she's at all up to it. Would it be all right, if I take her in a taxi?'

'Yes. Yes, I should think so. But you haven't answered my question. Can I see you? Alone, I mean, not to talk about Mary, just to talk to each other.'

She said, 'I'd like to but—'

He took his arm away and sighed.

'I know, I know. It's difficult for you. Perhaps I could engineer myself a breakdown and insist that you are the only therapy that's any use.'

'Come to Cornwall some time. When you get away.'

'Mean that?'

'Of course. There's us and the Langleys after all. You'd better come and check up on Mary's progress.'

He smiled at her.

'I'll take you up on that. And it's a promise.'

The telephone jerked Cara out of a drugging sleep the next morning. She stumbled across to it in a tangle of blankets before it should wake Mary and Linda, snatching up the receiver with her eyes still shut and hearing Dick say,

'Cara? Is that Cara?'

'Mm—,' she said.

'Did I wake you?'

She opened her eyes with difficulty.

'You did a bit.'

'I'm sorry. Really I am. I'm ringing to say I can't wait until Cornwall to see you. I want to see you today.'

'Oh Dick—'

'Please.'

'I'm taking Mary to see Stephen—'

503

'I know. But not until after lunch. Let me give you lunch.'

'I don't think so. I'd be away too long—'

'A drink before lunch then. Ask Linda to stay with Mary. I'm sure she will. Cara, you're yawning, I can hear you. Am I that boring?'

'No, no, it's just that I'm not really awake—'

'Then I can bend you to my will. I'll be round to collect you at twelve, then I can have a look at Mary at the same time. I just want one hour of your time.'

'All right,' Cara said, 'I'll ask Linda. And – and Dick, thank you. Thank you very much.'

'You go,' Linda said later. ''Course I'll stay. I don't have to be anywhere until two and you'll be back long before then. He's a nice bloke.'

Mary said, 'How long? How long will you be?'

'An hour.'

'An hour!'

'Only an hour. You stay in bed till I get back. I'll get you some lunch then. The time will go very fast, you'll see.'

Dick was early. He spent ten minutes with Mary who cried again when she saw him.

'Why does Cara have to go?'

'Because she needs a change of scene. She'll be back before you know it. You look better today, you know.'

Mary put her face into her pillow. Linda sat down on the end of her bed and tweaked her foot through the blanket.

'I'm coming in here to write a love letter, Mary, and you can help me with the spelling. Never could spell, even when I was a kid. What's the Latin for love, brainbox?'

Dick grinned and stood up.

'You're a brick. I'll return Cara prompt at one.'

Dick's Austin was filled with books and papers and games paraphernalia.

'I never play anything, no time really. I just like to feel I've got the kit on hand should the chance come up.'

'I love tennis,' Cara said, 'but Ma made us dig up the lawn for vegetables. The croquet lawn too. It was all beetroot last year, and it's all parsnips this.'

'I detest parsnips.'

She smiled at him.

'Me too. Where are we going?'

'The Ritz. Like I said.'

'But – but look at me!'

'I'd love to. Nothing I'd like better in fact, but Hyde Park Corner takes all my concentration.'

'I look the original country cousin,' Cara wailed.

'Nothing nicer. Look, there it is. Monument to absolute comfort *and* I'm told, the best ladies lavatory in London.'

'I'll go and vet it.'

'That you won't. And waste our precious hour? Look, a parking space almost outside. What a bit of luck.'

There were sandbags piled under all the windows, but the plate glass of the swing doors glittered invitingly giving glimpses of carpets and chandeliers beyond, opulently removed from all the discomforts of wartime. Once inside Cara stood and took deep breaths.

'Oh, smell it!'

Dick sniffed.

'Money, mostly. With overtones of musquash and Chanel Number Five. The bar is this way. Don't you think some champagne would be a good idea?'

Cara was appalled.

'You *can't*! It's wickedly extravagant! Champagne is for celebrations and birthdays, not just for drinks before lunch!'

'I feel like it and I am paying for it. You can sit and watch me drink it if you feel that strongly.'

Cara grinned at him.

'Perhaps not that strongly—'

He chose a table in the corner and left Cara there in an armchair while he went to order the champagne. There weren't many people in the bar, just a few men in formal dark suits and a pair of thin and elegant middle-aged women in beautifully cut suits with fur stoles thrown over the backs of their chairs. Cara thrust her trousered legs out of sight under the table. There was, she noticed, hay on her jersey. How could there possibly still be Cornish hay on her jersey after three days in London?

Dick returned, followed by a waiter bearing an ice bucket on a stand and another with glasses and a dish of olives and little biscuits spread with pâté. He settled himself beside her while the ceremony of the cork was performed.

'I have a very grand aunt,' he said, 'who was here, having tea, the day the Jarrow marchers got to London. She said it was the most poignant thing that she ever saw. She and several friends were sitting there, having tea and gossiping, and suddenly the swing doors began to revolve and into the Ritz poured a stream of shabby, exhausted, emaciated men. My aunt of course stopped eating watercress sandwiches, and so did everyone round her, and a complete silence fell upon the Ritz. She said it was quite transfixing, all these rich, well-dressed Society people gazing in absolute silence at the poor weary Jarrow marchers who stared back, equally silent, as if they were looking at creatures from another planet. And then, without a word, they turned and stumbled back out into Piccadilly.'

'What an unnerving story.'

'It unnerved my aunt. She cried for hours and never wept in her life otherwise, before or since. Now, pick up your glass and let's think of a suitable toast.'

'Like the war ending.'

'You can if you like. I don't feel particularly noble or patriotic today. I shall drink to you.'

Cara blushed. He raised his glass.

'To you, Cara. To the prettiest, most resourceful and delightful girl in the Land Army. And probably in England. I wish you weren't going back to Cornwall.'

'In some ways, so do I.'

'War is a nuisance. We can none of us please ourselves, we have to keep thinking of duty. What I should like to do – and I hope you would like me to – is to carry you off into the country for the day. But I can't. You have Mary and Stephen, I have a clinic. Why is it that my clinic is my duty and you are not?'

She laughed.

'You obviously aren't a man who likes hair shirts.'

'Oh I do. As a normal rule. Just not today. Do you like this champagne?'

'Enormously.'

'Keep drinking then. We've a bottle to finish in forty minutes. How altruistic of Stephen to introduce you to me, but then he is a very generous fellow. Have you known him all your life?'

'Yes.'

'And thus, I hope and pray, regard him in the light of a brother?'

She said, laughing, 'I suppose so—'

Dick leaned across the took her hand.

'Would you write to me?'

'I'll try—'

'Cara – is there someone, anyone you are in love with?'

'No,' she said.

'Because you know what is happening to me? I am falling rapidly into a state of mind in which I do not want you to be in love with anyone.'

Cara took too large a swallow of champagne and choked. She said with difficulty,

'Don't do that, Dick. Please don't. I'm not in love with anyone but I recently was rather and I don't think I'm ready to be again. I really don't know. I feel – oh, sort of—'

He said, smiling at her broadly, 'That you would like me to decide for you?'

'No,' she said firmly.

'Pity.'

'You are so nice to me and so charming, but I really do not want to think about love at the moment.'

'Rubbish.'

She shook her head.

'Not really.'

'Poor me, then.'

She smiled at him.

'I suspect you are very easily consoled.'

'Certainly not. And not at all easily deflected, I warn you. I shall enlist Stephen's help in getting myself invited to Cornwall.'

'Poor Stephen.'

'Why do you say that?'

She shrugged a little.

'He so hates being ill and tied to a bed. And jaundice must be so demoralising.'

'It is. But he's through the worst.'

She drained her glass and put it down.

'We ought to go, I'm afraid.'

'I hope,' Dick said, standing up, 'that the Langleys are suitably aware of the treasure they have in you.'

Cara said crossly, 'Don't talk like that.'

'Sorry. Very sorry. Can I really come to Cornwall?'

She put her hand out to him.

'Of course you can. It would be lovely. And thank you so awfully much for the champagne. It was simply delicious and made me feel I can face anything.'

'Even the Sister on·Men's Medical at St B's.'

'Oh yes,' she said. 'Even her.'

Stephen was sitting up in bed this time, propped up against a high mound of pillows. He held out his arms to Mary but she was gripping Cara's hand like a vice and only stared at him, her mouth trembling.

'Mary, dear Mary—'

Cara said, 'Come on, Mary. Go to him. Show him you're all right.'

'Don't go,' Mary said, 'Don't leave me. Stay right here, don't move—'

'I promise,' Cara said, 'Right here.'

She led Mary forward to Stephen's bedside, pushing her down to sit on the edge.

'I'm so glad to see you,' Stephen said gently to his sister, 'You can't think how glad.'

He put his hands on Mary's shoulders and she bent forward onto his chest, still holding Cara's hand with one of hers, shaking with sobs. Over her head Stephen looked up at Cara.

'You are distinctly less yellow today,' she said to him. He smiled.

'I think it's just there being twice as many daffodils. The contrast—'

'Sarah again?'

'Sarah again. Little Mary, don't cry so, don't. You'll be back home soon.'

Mary said, her voice muffled against his pyjama jacket, 'Not home. Not there. With Cara.'

'Wherever you want,' Stephen said, 'You know that.' He looked up at Cara again. 'You have enslaved Dick, he can't talk about anything else.'

'He's been wonderfully kind. He's even telephoned Bodmin General and got some friend of a friend to take—' she glanced at Mary, quieter now but still crying softly, '– an interest. A frequent one.'

'I rang home,' Stephen said, 'I persuaded Sister to let me totter to the telephone. I think they understand pretty well.'

'Oh, Stephen, I'm so relieved! I was dreading that—'

'When will you go back?'

'In the morning.'

'So – I shan't see you again—'

'Won't you be home to convalesce?'

'I hope so. Heavily escorted by Doctor Swift. He says you have invited him to Cornwall and that I shall make a fine excuse—'

The screens clattered behind them.

'I've a message from Sister,' Sarah Calne said, 'It's doctor's rounds any minute and I'm to turn you out.'

Cara turned round with elaborate slowness.

'Good morning, Sarah.'

Sarah nodded. Then she went quickly over to Stephen's bed.

'Mary, how are you?'

'I shouldn't touch her—'

Mary shrank against Stephen, away from Sarah, still gripping Cara's hand.

Sarah said quietly, 'It can't be as serious as all that. Girls are losing their fiancés every day and they don't all crack up like this.'

'I'm sure you know best,' Cara said.

Sarah said to Stephen, 'You aren't supposed to be tired you know. And this sort of thing—'

'She's my sister,' he said gently.

Cara stooped down to Mary.

'Come on, Mary. We must go. So that the doctors can talk to Stephen.'

Mary rose, trembling a little, to her feet.

'Do what Cara says,' Stephen said, 'won't you. Everything Cara says.'

Mary nodded.

'Have you had any experience of this sort of thing?' Sarah said across the bed, 'Do you have any kind of idea of what you are doing?'

'None at all,' Cara said, 'Not the faintest. You know that I don't know about anything except pigs.'

Sarah said nothing but bent to rearrange Stephen's pillows and smooth the bedclothes that Mary had disarranged. While she did so, Stephen looked away from them all with an expression Cara could not fathom and Mary stood still and obedient, holding Cara's hand.

Cara said, 'We ought to go or dragon Sister will be upon us. I'll send you a cheque, Stephen—'

'You'll do no such thing.'

She smiled.

'Thank you, then.'

'Cara—'

'Yes?'

'Thank *you*. Thank you from the bottom of my heart.'

'You need some more books,' Sarah said to him, 'You must have read all these. I'll get some more. And you'll be pleased to hear that the man who feigned madness to get out of Colditz is safely home. We now just have to hope he can readjust again. I'm to visit him later this week—'

'Goodbye,' Cara said.

Mary stooped suddenly and kissed her brother.

'I'm all right,' she said, 'I'm so sorry – all this – such a nuisance—'

Cara said, 'If you apologize, I lose my temper. Remember?'

'Heavens,' Sarah said, 'You don't change—'

'Goodbye, Stephen,' Mary said.

'Goodbye, little one. Take care.'

'And you—'

'I'll see to that,' Sarah said.

A sudden surge of irritation caught at Cara's throat and much more roughly than she intended to, she pulled Mary out from the shelter of the screens and towed her, stumbling a little, down the ward.

'Of course she must stay,' Alexandra said, 'She looks better already after only one night in the sea air.'

'I ought to go over to Langley Dene. To explain. They must think it so odd. And me so interfering.'

'I've telephoned them,' Alexandra said, 'They're coming over later. You can explain later. Vera did sound in a bit of a state.'

'She needn't be. There's nothing seriously the matter, it's just a question of time. I'll tell Aunt Vera exactly what happened—'

'You're getting exactly like your mother,' Michael said,

'Just as bossy. How am I supposed to live with the pair of you?'

Cara kissed him.

'You love it, Pa.'

'Don't be so sure.'

'It's awfully kind of you both, not being startled about Mary or saying we can't, that it'll distract me from all I ought to be doing. Which it will—'

'Only for a little while, then she can help you. We wouldn't think of turning her out. I'm only so thankful you found her.'

Michael said, 'You are not to go to London again. That's an order. I can't take it.'

'He was terrible,' Alexandra said, 'Fidgetting and nagging and wheeling himself about restlessly. A real menace in the dark.'

'I ought to go,' Cara said, 'I left Mary with Lyd, supposedly peeling vegetables. But she doesn't really, she just dawdles and dreams and asks where I am. Lyd's marvellous but it drives her round the bend.'

'It's progress that she will even stay ten minutes with Lyddy. And so soon.'

'Yes,' Cara said, 'Yes, it is.'

The journey back to Cornwall had seemed interminable. Mary had talked from London to Reading without pausing once for breath and then had fallen utterly silent and sat beside Cara with her eyes wide open and occasionally, when Cara looked to see if she had fallen asleep, allowing slow, silent tears to slide down her face. Cara had felt a strange reluctance to leave London – strange because she could not account for it, being thankful to leave the damage and noise and discouragement – and this had made her impatient with Mary and angry at herself, for her impatience. She had wanted to leave Alison and Linda a present, but all the coupons she possessed – notably the clothes coupons with which she might have bought them some precious stockings – had been in that shattered house in Chelsea, so all she could leave was the money she owed them and a grateful letter. She determined to send them something from Cornwall.

Bassett had been at Bodmin Road with the Rover. Mary was green-white with fatigue when they reached Cornwall, having steadfastly refused all sustenance but a few sips of tea the entire length of the journey.

'Stephen said you were to do what I said,' Cara said, 'And I say you are to eat this sandwich.'

'When we're there, later, when we're home—'

Bassett had brought rugs and a flask of coffee and some pieces of Lyddy's gingerbread, unfamiliarly pale now that black treacle was so hard to come by. He and Cara rolled Mary in blankets in the back of the car and then Cara, not intending to, had gone to sleep beside him, quite suddenly, as if coming back to Cornwall meant that she could relax, come off her guard.

There had been no sleep since then for Mary, refusing a sleeping pill, had had a wakeful and wretched night. Despite this, the grey transparency of her face was much improved this morning and although she had watched Cara with some degree of anxiety, she had not clung to her physically. She was sitting at the kitchen table when Cara went in, with a mound of swedes and carrots before her, only gazing at them, not peeling them, though she held a knife slackly in her hands.

'I've got something to read to you,' Cara said, 'A letter from James. Ma is thrilled to bits. He's got awfully keen on growing things. Listen to this. "We started digging last autumn and we shall dig on until we are told we can go home. I'm planting onions and tomatoes and beetroot and runner beans. It's the most extraordinarily satisfying business – I wish I'd started three years ago. I wonder why I never thought of it at home? Mad, really, with all that cultivation on my doorstep." Ma is simply glowing, you can imagine.'

Mary said, 'Does he inherit the farm?'

'Yes. And over fifteen thousand acres in Scotland. It would be wonderful if he took to it.'

'Don't you want it?'

'I don't think so.'

Mary said, 'Alex – wouldn't have, either.'

'No. He wouldn't. Mary, your parents are coming later today.'

'I needn't go, need I? I mean, I don't want to hurt them but I don't want to – I can't—'

'I'll tell them. I've got Dick Swift's letter. And they've spoken to Doctor Marsh in Bodmin. You're not making much progress with those.'

'No.'

'Come outside then. I'm going to help June with the cowpens. We'll wrap you up well and you can watch.'

'I don't understand it,' George Langley said, shaking his head over Dick's letter, 'But I accept it. Got to really, haven't I—'

Vera said, 'I understand, I think. I just wish I'd known about Alex and Mary. It makes me feel so callous.'

'How could you know?' Alexandra said, 'How could you possibly know? You only know what they choose to tell you. We didn't know how serious Alex and Mary were either. It was only Cara who knew. That's why she went.'

'Thank God she did—'

'She's being wonderful.'

Michael said, 'She is also having an uncharacteristic fit of self-doubt and hopes you don't think her interfering.'

'Absolutely not,' Vera said.

George waved Dick's letter.

'Doctor's orders—'

'It seems such an extra burden on you. You have enough to deal with here.'

'Nonsense,' Alexandra said.

514

'We've got some news to cheer little Mary up, anyway, haven't we, dear? Stephen's coming home to convalesce. He phoned this morning. That might make her change her mind.'

Vera Langley said a little nervously, 'You mustn't bully her, George, not in the smallest degree.'

Michael smiled.

'Cara does.'

'It's good news for Cara too, Stephen coming home. Tell you why. He's being brought down by an old school friend of theirs – what's her name?'

'Sarah. Sarah Calne—'

'Good of her, don't you think? Seems some medic friend was all set to do the journey and then Sarah offered, insisted according to Stephen. Amazing what a war makes people do for each other, isn't it. There's this young woman with, by all accounts an extremely responsible job with the Red Cross, and she's using precious leave to escort an old school friend's brother home to Cornwall. I call it pretty handsome, don't you? What's more, Stephen says she has dealt with all those old biddies in the ATS for Mary, explained the whole business, got her sick leave. And telephoned all her friends so nobody thinks she's dead. I'm most impressed—'

'Sarah Calne,' Michael said, 'That's the one Cara went off to hear speak last summer at St Faith's and never stayed to hear?'

Alexandra said, 'They never got on very well at a school. I don't think time has improved things much.'

George laughed.

'Well, they've got something in common now, haven't they? Assisting Langleys in need—'

'Could we see Mary?' Vera said almost timidly.

Alexandra propelled herself briskly towards the bell by the fireplace.

'Of course,' she said, 'Lyddy will fetch them. Cara took Mary to watch the afternoon milking.'

'Are you asleep?'

'No,' Cara said.

'I shouldn't be with you. I keep you awake.'

'You did last night. You aren't now. I'm keeping myself awake.'

'I'll take a pill. It isn't fair—'

'You aren't to take them for my sake.'

Mary raised herself on one elbow so that Cara could see the smooth outline of her head against the uncurtained window.

'You were wonderful with Mother and Father today—'

'Shut up.'

'Cara – what's the matter?'

'Nothing's the matter.'

'It is. It is, I'm wearing you out—'

'I want you to get better, Mary. I *want* to look after you. It isn't you.'

Mary lay down again. After a while she said.

'I'm glad about that,' and then she paused a little while and added, 'Are you, in your heart of hearts, disappointed that Dick isn't coming with Stephen?'

Cara sound surprised.

'I don't think so—'

'I think you are. In the first place you don't like Sarah much, do you? And then I think you must have been looking forward to seeing Dick again, mustn't you?'

'Perhaps,' Cara said and her voice was still puzzled, 'Perhaps I was looking forward to it more than I thought. I don't know—'

She lay and considered this for a while, gazing into the blackness and then Mary said.

'I wondered, listening to the news tonight and the victories at El Hamma and Gabes and the Eighth Army doing so well at the Mareth Line – I wondered, does it ever make you think of Alan?'

'No,' Cara said shortly.

'I can't help wondering if I will ever be like that, if I will ever be able to think of anything but Alex—'

'Of course you will. You even have today for quite some minutes together. It's only a question of time.'

'And you really don't think of Alan? Ever?'

'No. I can promise you that. I never think of Alan.'

'It must give you such contentment, Cara. It must be a wonderful state of mind. It – it should make you so reconciled to everything else.'

'Yes,' Cara said slowly, 'I suppose it should. Shouldn't it—'

CHAPTER FOURTEEN

April 1945

'I don't believe it!' Alexandra said, crying and laughing, rocking herself back and forth in her chair, 'I don't, I can't, oh it's a miracle, a miracle—'

Michael was holding the paper in front of him but his hands were shaking so that the print was only blur.

'Read it again, Pa, read it—'

'I can't, my darling, I can hardly even hold the thing—'

'Mary, take it from him. Go on. Take it and read it, it *can't* be true!'

Mary, smiling broadly, took the paper from Michael.

'It *is* true. It is! It says "War Office Message" at the top and then underneath it says that all prisoners from Oflag V have been freed and are being marched to Munich.'

'James!' Alexandra said, 'Oh James—'

Lyddy was crying uncontrollably, her apron thrown over her head. Even June, for all her phlegmatic calm, was smiling and sniffing, her eyes fixed upon Alexandra. Only Barbara – whose conversation throughout the last four years, as Michael had pointed out, would occupy the surface of a sixpence if written down – continued to chew solidly, spooning in her porridge with almost mechanical regularity.

'And look at this!' Mary said excitedly, 'Goebbels is supposed to be dead and Hitler is said to have had a cerebral haemorrhage! What a pity one can't believe anything the Germans say. And Mussolini and his mistress have committed suicide – oh no, he hasn't, Italian patriots executed him. Good for them! And Milan has surrendered and Spezia and Vicenza—'

'Stop it,' Alexandra said, 'I can't take any more. I feel – oh Michael—'

Cara said, 'I'm going out to the cows, I'm going to cry all over the cows—'

'I'll come with you,' Mary said.

'What about your Greek?'

'Bully! Today of all days, Herodotus can wait. I've worked so hard, I'm days ahead of schedule.'

Michael, cradling Alexandra's head against him, said, 'I thought you were doing erotic Latin poetry.'

'I was. That was a day off. Oh darling Swintons, you can't imagine how glad I am for you!'

'James,' Alexandra was saying, 'James, James, James!'

'He shouldn't be long,' June said, 'They aren't usually more than a week or two. My cousin was home ten days after the Americans got to his camp.'

Cara pulled at Mary's sleeve.

'Come on. Quick. I can feel the crying coming on quite terribly.'

'It's so stupid, crying and crying when you're so happy you could sing.'

'It's the right kind of crying,' Mary said, 'As right as mine was wrong. Do you realize I haven't cried for a year?'

Cara blew her nose.

'You couldn't help it.'

They were sitting on milk churns at the end of the cowpens in the manure-smelling gloom.

'If the war hadn't still been going on, I'd have loved the last two years. Actually I loved them anyway. It's been marvellous, being here, being with all of you. Being able to talk about Alex until I can do it quite comfortably.'

Cara said, 'I suppose he'll be awfully thin, poor James—'

'I shouldn't think so. Not from a German camp. Not like those poor creatures the Japs have got. Anyway, if he is in poor shape you can do to him what you've done to me.'

'Cornwall's done that. And time.'

'They might have improved my health physically. But they didn't get my brain going again, bullying me into daily hours of work until I was so lost in it I forgot to come to meals. And the Land Army!' She stuck out her legs, encased in the same dark green woollen stockings as Cara's, 'Me, a land girl! What with one thing and other, I've certainly seen most sides of how a war is run!'

'Let's go and plant something—'

'What do you mean?'

Cara jumped up.

'Bother mucking out! Like Herodotus, it can wait. Let's plant something for James. Go and find a little sapling and plant it for him, to celebrate today. And then he can look at it when he's an old man, and remember—'

'Cara, you think of everything!'

'Bossiness, Pa calls it.'

'Rubbish!' Mary said, laughing, following her out across the yard to where the tools were kept, 'A tree for James!'

Cara stopped and turned to her.

'And for Stephen, safe at the end of all this, even when St Bartolph's was bombed. And for Alan, safe after all that fighting in the Western Desert. And for everyone we know who is safe and all the millions we don't. And for Alex.'

'Yes,' Mary said and smiled at her, 'For Alex.'

How to write the letter had posed an impossibly difficult problem. Cara had been entranced with the idea when it first came to her, but had been quite at sea as to what she should do next, how she should proceed. She was reluctant to confide in anyone in case the plan failed and the news of the failure did, even to the smallest degree, reach Mary, and so when she was in Wadebridge one day she had plucked up the courage to telephone Miss Ferrars. Her courage had needed plucking. The last time she had seen Miss Ferrars was when she had bolted from Sarah's talk at St Faith's with no word of excuse or apology. It was therefore hardly surprising that Miss Ferrars should sound guarded.

'Ah, Charlotte.'

'Miss Ferrars, I know it's a little late, to say the least, but I am awfully sorry that I never apologized for leaving so suddenly that day, when someone had made a bed up for me and everything—'

'Is that why you have telephoned?'

'No. It's got nothing to do with it. I just felt I couldn't ask you what I wanted to ask you without mentioning it first.'

'I see.'

'I really am most ashamed of behaving like that, I wish I could explain—'

'Suppose we forget the matter and come to the burden of your call? I have parents to see in ten minutes.'

Cara took a deep breath. A woman had come to the telephone kiosk and was gesturing to Cara to hurry. Cara pulled a face at her and turned her back.

'It's about Mary Langley, Miss Ferrars. I don't know whether the news reached you that she has been living with us since 1943, since my brother was killed, in fact. She was engaged to him and she had some sort of breakdown—'

Miss Ferrars' voice became much warmer.

520

'I did hear that, Charlotte. I was so very sorry. In fact I wrote to Mary's parents. I also heard that you played a large part in Mary's recovery.'

The woman had now come round to the other side of the kiosk and was mouthing crossly at Cara through the glass. Cara was tempted to stick out her tongue, but somehow having Miss Ferrars the other end of the line restrained her.

'Miss Ferrars, do you remember that Mary was going to Cambridge? At least, that there was talk of it and she was going to go for some scholarship or other, staying on in the Sixth Form for a seventh term, and then war broke out?'

'Of course I do. Mary had an outstanding competence in Greek and Latin prose. I sometimes doubted her imaginative capacity for classical verse—'

'Miss Ferrars, could that plan be resurrected?'

'Resurrected?'

'Yes. Could Mary go to Cambridge now, next autumn, now that the war is ending? Could I get hold of the College Principal or whatever she is called? Would you help me?'

There was a pause at the other end during which the woman pulled open the door a crack and said, 'I've to phone me sister.'

'If you annoy me any more, I shall spin this call out as long as I can,' Cara said, her hand over the mouthpiece.

Miss Ferrars said, 'Are you suggesting that Mary should attempt to take up the place she was offered in 1939?'

'Yes.'

'But the reading—'

'She's been reading like mad for a year. Anyway, the universities will be full next winter of returning soldiers who haven't read either. I've thought of that. I was a bit worried because she is twenty four but then I thought, what does it matter, there'll be lots of much older men about, all the ones like her whom the war prevented from taking up their places.'

'You seem to be taking this very seriously, Charlotte.'

'I am.'

'Whom have you discussed it with? What does Mary feel herself?'

'I wouldn't dream of telling her. She is wonderfully better but her confidence isn't very reliable. That's why I don't want a breath of this to get to her until there is at least a reasonable chance. I haven't told anyone at all but you. And I should be awfully grateful if you would keep my confidence. It would transform her to feel that there was Cambridge to look forward to. I know she's worried about the future.'

Miss Ferrars said with the nearest thing to enthusiasm she could muster,

'Charlotte, I think it's an excellent plan.'

'Oh, Miss Ferrars! You will help, then?'

'Certainly. I will write to the Principal myself. I will endeavour to do it today. Perhaps you could send me Mary's reading list? It would not be necessary to include it in a preliminary letter but it might well help matters later on—'

'Oh thank you!' Cara said, 'Thank you!'

'Not at all. You are yourself the prime mover. Between us we may achieve something. And what of your own future, do you have any plans?'

'Plenty,' Cara said, 'But whether I can manage them—'

'Charlotte, forgive me, but my visitors are here.'

'Miss Ferrars, don't telephone home, will you? I will ring you in a week or so – It must be a secret—'

'It shall be,' Miss Ferrars said.

'My sister will be sick with worry,' the woman said to Cara when she came out, 'I always phone eleven dead on, Tuesdays, she'll think I've had an accident. Some people have no thought for others, do they!'

Cara smiled at her.

'No.' she said, 'They don't.'

'It isn't announced,' George Langley said heartily, 'But we think it's only a matter of days. Don't we, dear? And she's a splendid girl.'

They were all in the drawing-room at Bishopstow, around tea on a low table in front of the fire. In view of blackout being lifted and encouraging war news arriving by every bulletin Alexandra had allowed the fire to be fractionally more generous and Lyddy to make the first real cake, full of butter and eggs, since Cara's nineteenth birthday, five years before. It was in anticipation of James' imminent arrival that some celebration had been felt necessary and the Langleys invited to Bishopstow.

Vera Langley said, 'She was so kind to Stephen after he'd had hepatitis. And she's kept such a careful eye on him since.'

'What with our Mary looking quite her old self and Alan and Tessa due here any day, and an engagement in the offing, I'd say we felt pretty pleased with things in general.'

Michael said, 'Not to mention a world war ending.'

Cara shot her father a secret smile. He had never found it easy to tolerate George Langley's amiable insensitivity at the best of times and found his present mood of smug ebullience perfectly intolerable. It amused her sometimes to imagine George proposing to Alexandra, as he had done nearly forty years before in this very drawing-room. Alexandra said that when she refused him he had been downhearted for at least three minutes and then he had bounced up again and asked her to watch him ride in a point-to-point. She tried to think of that now, feeling that she should like to be amused, for some strange reason, but could not divert herself at all. George achieved it by lunging sideways from the sofa and digging her in the ribs.

'You'll be pleased to have Alan back, eh? Your old playfellow?'

'George dear—' Vera said.

Cara smiled broadly at him.

'Most certainly I will. He never finished teaching me to drive. I've probably learnt how all wrong from Bassett so Alan can iron out the biggest mistakes.'

George gave a roar of laughter and held out his cup for more tea.

'Alexandra, why hasn't some young fellow snapped up this girl of yours?'

Alexandra regarded him levelly over the teapot.

'Because a young fellow of sufficient calibre hasn't turned up yet.'

'Touché, George,' Michael said.

Cara stood up.

'Do you mind if I disappear to the yard? I said I'd help June with the sow—'

Mary said, 'She can manage! She said so.'

'I'll just make sure—'

Mary stood up.

'I'll come with you.'

Cara smiled down at George.

'Control her, Uncle G. Make her stay. She works quite hard enough as it is.'

As she passed her father, she stooped to kiss him.

'*I'd* come with you if I could,' he muttered.

'Rubbish,' she said, 'You like Langley baiting.'

'Heartless minx—'

'Look,' June said, 'Litter of ten. Not bad for a little one and a first timer. Fine piglets, too.'

'Yes,' Cara said without looking really, 'Fine.'

'What's up?' June said, 'Had enough drawing-room company?'

'Probably.'

'Full of themselves at Langley Dene, they are. The gardener told Bassett. Waiting for Stephen to announce his engagement now.'

524

'Yes. Yes, they said so.'

June leaned down and scratched behind the sow's pale hairy ear with a stick.

'He's the best of the bunch, I reckon. Always did think so. Mind you, I've more time for Mary than I thought I'd have. Doesn't it make you feel proud, looking down at these little ones?'

Cara said truthfully, 'Not as proud as it makes you.'

June shrugged.

'You'll never really take to farming, will you? Not if you stick at it for a hundred years. And I will say this for you, you have stuck at it. I never thought you would, but you have.' She squinted up at Cara. 'What'll you do when the war's really over?'

Cara sat down on an upturned bucket.

'June – and this is a hypothetical desire because, things being what they are, I can't do what I want – what I should really like to do is something medical. I've loved looking after Ma and Mary, I've been really interested. I don't know if I've got enough School Certs for a teaching hospital or whether I'd better settle for physiotherapy or nursing or something. I really don't know enough about it. But I do know that's what I'd do – if I could.'

'Why couldn't you?' June said.

'June! There's Ma and Pa and the farm – I couldn't leave them!'

June squatted beside her.

'There's me.'

'You! But you'll want to go home—'

'I shan't,' June said, 'This is home. I couldn't leave your Ma. War or no war, I'd rather be here, it suits me.'

'But the farm—'

'James'll be home soon. And the men'll be back on the farm or your Ma will be hiring others.'

Cara said laughing,

'June, I could hug you!'

June edged away.

'Don't you dare. I'd be doing what I want to do anyway. It'd break my heart to leave here.'

'I'd have to take the whole plan awfully slowly. With Ma and Pa, I mean.'

"Course,' June said, 'But even if you were in London you could come back for weekends or any time they needed you.' She looked at Cara. 'Is that what was on your mind? When you came out here? That why you looked so glum?'

'I certainly feel a lot better now.'

'Should have said something before,' June said.

'I – I couldn't. I mean, we've never talked about anything except practical things, have we, in almost six years. I – I often felt you must resent me taking over nursing Ma, but I didn't know how to say anything to you, how to ask you if you minded—'

'I did mind,' June said, 'But not for long. It's right really, a daughter should look after her own mother. Anyway, if you go off to London, I'll have her back to myself, shan't I? And your Pa, too. I've a lot of time for your Pa.'

'So you don't think it's selfish and self-centred of me to go off – that is, if some hospital will have me?'

June stood up.

'No, I don't. You've only got one life. And you can always come back, like I said.'

'Suppose James doesn't want the farm?'

'Suppose fiddlesticks. Really, you're an awful one for crossing your bridges. You'll be leaving home some day in any case, when you marry.'

'Marry!' Cara said. Her stomach gave a curious lurch of misery. 'I don't think – that'll happen—'

"Course it will!'

'Well, not the way I want.'

'Get up,' June said, 'I want that bucket. Marriage doesn't interest me, much, I must say. My parents weren't much of an example, all flying plates and screaming. If you can manage it like your Ma and Pa, that's one thing but they're a couple in millions. I'd rather have pigs.'

'June. June – I'm really terribly grateful. Far more than I can express to you.'

June stared at her, swinging the bucket.

'What for? For pleasing myself? Come on, there's those calves to feed. You going to stand there gawping or are you going to help me?'

The days wore on and no news of James. The wireless spilled out information of the Allied advance, the freeing of towns and camps across Germany and the Low Countries, food being taken in to feed the starving in the occupied zones.

'I'm going to stop waiting for the telephone,' Alexandra said at breakfast at the beginning of May, 'It's wearing me out.' She looked round the table. 'Where's Mary?'

'In her room,' Cara said.'

'No breakfast? Doesn't she want any?'

'She says she will later. She's too happy to eat, she says, so she's having raptures on an empty stomach.'

Michael looked up from the paper.

'Raptures? Mary? What on earth about?'

Cara said carelessly, making patterns with her knife in the marmalade smeared on her plate, 'Miss Ferrars has come up trumps. She has got Mary an interview with the Principal of the Cambridge College she was going up to in '39. It seems there's almost a certainty of a place, especially after all the work Mary has done this year.'

Alexandra said, 'Well done, Marjorie Ferrars.'

Cara smiled.

'Well done, Mary, I say.'

Michael went back to his paper. He said to Alexandra from behind it,

'That will give your erstwhile admirer more fuel for fatuous self-congratulation. Beats me how a brain like Mary's can come from an oaf like George. Or Stephen's for that matter—'

'Vera was quite a clever girl. And her father was brilliant. He could have been top of his profession but he wouldn't leave Wadebridge. I hope he knows how well Stephen is doing, that would please him so.'

Cara said with studied nonchalance, 'And would he be pleased about Stephen's marrying Sarah Calne?'

'I should think so,' Alexandra said, 'Everyone else seems to be.'

'Yes,' Cara said, 'They do, don't they—'

'Of course, I don't think there's been any definite announcement—'

The telephone rang. Cara stood up.

'I'll go.'

'If it's Lettice Burrows,' Alexandra said, 'Tell her I have no intention of ceasing to be President of the W.I. Not until I'm thrown off the committee.'

Cara smiled at her.

'Will do.'

There was a lot of clicking and whirring on the telephone line. Cara said, 'Hallo? Hallo? Who's speaking?'

At the other end, someone said hesitantly, 'Is that – is that Wadebridge 42?'

'Yes – yes, it is. Who's that?'

'Cara?' the voice said, 'Cara?'

A flood of tears rushed down her face.

'Cara? Is that you? Cara?'

'James!' she said, crying and clutching the receiver, 'Oh James, Oh James, Oh James—'

CHAPTER FIFTEEN

'Now, tell me again,' James said, 'How many pigs?'

'Four sows. Two bacon pigs. Three litters of – well, the total is twenty seven.'

'And cows?'

'Three hundred.'

'And hens?'

'Don't know. Lost count. James, you are to eat this. Ma says you are to eat every two hours until you don't look like a toastrack any more.'

'Of course, when everything's back to normal we shan't need to have all these acres of root vegetables. And I'd like to build up the herd a bit, especially the Jerseys. They do so well down here and I'm sure one could do something commercially with clotted cream. After all, it would last in the post for at least a week.'

'James!'

'Yes,' he said, scribbling.

'Please eat your sandwich.'

He looked at it in surprise.

'I don't want a sandwich.'

'You *must*. Ma insists. Little and often.'

He looked up at Cara.

'Are you sure you don't mind? If I take over here?'

'I *told* you—'

'I know you did. I just want to make sure.'

'I am perfectly sure. And so is Ma. Pa will need a little more winning round to my plans but I think Ma is working on him. And St Bartolph's will at least see me. I don't know what that means but I do know that I want to go off and get myself properly trained.'

'I ought to do that,' James said, 'I ought to go to Cirencester—'

'Sandwich!'

'What's in it?'

'Ham.'

'Our pigs?'

'Of course.'

He picked it up and bit into it.

'Why didn't you say so before? It's delicious.'

Cara sighed. The door from the hall opened and Alexandra propelled herself into the kitchen.

'James, I hope you are eating.'

'Voraciously, mother.'

'That was Vera Langley on the telephone. She sounded full of suppressed excitement and wants you two to go over this afternoon for tennis. Alan is home with his wife, and Stephen and Sarah—'

'James can,' Cara said quickly, 'But I'll stay here I think. I said I'd help Mary finish that dress for the Cambridge interview.'

Alexandra said, very gently, 'Alan?'

'No, Ma,' Cara said vigorously, 'Not Alan at all. Just a surfeit of Langleys recently. Anyway, if James goes over on his own they can all croon over him to their hearts' content.'

James said, 'I'd rather you came, Cara.'

'It's awfully nice of you but—'

'I think you should anyway. I mean, you've known Stephen from the nursery, it seems a bit much not to congratulate him in person.'

'I do rather agree with James,' Alexandra said.

Cara took a deep breath.

'All right then. I'll go and tell Mary. We'll do her dress tonight.'

'I suppose,' James said, 'You wouldn't think of cleaning my tennis shoes, sister mine?'

'Certainly not. You mustn't exploit the returned-prisoner-of-war role too far.'

'Never mind,' James said comfortably, 'Couldn't matter less. I'll get June to do them. Wonderful girl, June. I say, is there any more of this ham?'

There was nobody in the hall at Langley Dene when they reached the house, although the front door stood open to the gentle May sunshine.

'I wish Mary had come,' Cara said, 'But she wouldn't until she'd done the buttonholes and I bet she forgot that her bicycle has a puncture—'

'Let's go through to the garden,' James said, 'They'll be playing already.'

'No,' Cara said, 'Stop a minute, listen—'

From behind one of the closed doors, the one that led to George's study, the sound of crying was coming, muffled but unmistakeable.

'Oh Lord. What do we do—'

'Let's cut and run,' Cara said, 'I'll play you at home.'

'No. We can't. They're expecting us.'

Cara reached out to pull his sleeve and dropped her tennis racket. It clattered noisily to the polished floorboards.

'Oh heavens, what have I done?'

The door of George's study opened and George came out looking bothered, quite without his usual buoyancy.

'So sorry – bit of an upset – don't quite know what's going on—'

Behind him Vera was visible in his huge swivel chair, mopping at herself with a handkerchief. Cara went forward at once.

'Aunt Vera!'

George looked relieved.

'That's it, all girls together. Much the best bet. You come on out when you're better, dear. We might have a men's four—'

'You can't!' Vera wailed, 'Stephen's gone!'

'Gone!'

'Yes!' Vera said turning to Cara, 'Just walked off! And there's poor Sarah gone off to the station in tears! And Stephen wouldn't say what had happened and Sarah crying as if her heart would break. She wouldn't tell me anything either, she said she was too upset to discuss it.'

'Perhaps it's just a brief quarrel – it'll blow over.'

Vera blew her nose and stood up.

'It's not what it looked like to me.'

'Did – did Stephen look angry?'

'No. Not exactly angry. More thoroughly mortified about something. Oh dear, Cara, and when everything seemed to be going so well!'

Cara said, 'Are you very fond of Sarah?'

'I like her. I like her very much. And of course one tries to love the people your children choose. Cara – I do hope that – that Alan and Tessa—'

'I want to meet them,' she said smiling.

Vera patted her arm.

'You're a splendid girl, my dear. I'm so sorry, crying like this. It's ridiculous as well as extremely unbecoming at my age. But Stephen can be – so alarming somehow and then George was cross and seemed to think it all my fault—'

'How could it be?'

'I'm the nearest and therefore easiest to blame. Come along. You have done me a lot of good. We'll see what they are all doing and then we'll decide whether or not to go and look for Stephen.'

Alan Langley said, 'Well, well. Cara.'

'You look fine,' she said.

'I am. Had a great war. Cara, this is Tessa.'

Tessa was slight and pale with the face of a pretty child and blonde hair tied away from her face for tennis with a ribbon. She held out her hand to Cara.

'It's lovely to meet you. Alan has told me all about you. He told me how you rescued Mary. He says you are awfully—'

'Sh,' Cara said laughing.

George was balancing two rackets, one across the other, to assess the height of the tennis net.

532

'Will somebody come and wind?'

Alan said heartily, 'Great news about Mary, isn't it? Cambridge and all that.'

'Mary is awfully clever,' Tessa said, 'Isn't she, Alan? I hardly know her but Alan told me she was. I can hardly spell myself, Alan's always correcting me, aren't you, Alan?'

'Please!' George shouted, 'Won't take a moment!'

'Go on, Tess.'

'What do I have to do?'

'Wind the net up for Father.'

'I'm hopeless at tennis,' Tessa said, 'Ask Alan. Daddy used to say I was the most useless creature he ever saw so it's a good thing he made me rich and God made me decorative!'

'Tess—'

'Going!'

'I suppose,' Alan said to Cara when she had shipped off, 'That – well, you don't think too well of me.'

She met his eye easily.

'Why should that be?'

'Come on, Cara, don't make things worse, don't play games.'

'If you want it absolutely squarely, Alan, I thought of you for a few months five years ago and now I don't think of you at all.'

He seemed a little chagrined. He said, 'Hey, steady on, don't overdo the anti—'

'I'm not anti, just indifferent.'

'I suppose there's some other fellow.'

She hesitated for a second.

'No.'

'Then I don't believe you.'

'You mean your vanity doesn't want to.'

He looked at her for a moment in silence.

'You're a tremendous looker, Cara.'

'So is your wife.'

'I – hear great things of your war effort—'

'Oh,' she said, smiling, 'I shouldn't pay too much attention to what you hear.'

'Cara—'

'Yes?'

'Doesn't – doesn't it mean anything to you, seeing me again?'

'Yes,' she said.

He leaned towards her a little.

'Well then?'

'I am very pleased to see you. You look fit and well and I'm sure you will be a general one day and your wife is very pretty.'

'And?'

'And I'm going to play tennis.'

From behind them Vera said, 'I wish you could but George insists on a men's four. He had planned on mixed doubles but now of course, Sarah isn't here and Tessa really isn't up to much of a standard. Cara dear, would you be an angel and see if you can find Stephen? If he is in a mood, he won't be in it with you and you stand much the best chance of persuading him to come back.'

She hesitated.

'I – I don't think he'd be pleased to see me at all—'

James shouted from the court where he had been practising his service.

'Oh go on, Cara, do! He can't eat you.'

Alan said, 'I'll come with you.'

'No, you won't,' his mother said, 'Where are your manners? You will stay and play with James until Cara gets back. And I will talk to Tessa. And George, I imagine, will drive us all demented.'

'Where did Stephen go?'

Vera Langley pointed.

'Down there. Through that gate into the field. He may even have gone to the hollow tree on the edge of the Ten Acre. He always used to when he was small.'

'Maybe he doesn't want to be disturbed.'

534

'Disturbing him is the lesser of two evils. George, frustrated, is much the greater.'

Cara put her racket down on the garden seat.

'All right,' she said, 'I'll go.'

Stephen was not in the hollow tree. Nor, for that matter was he in the copse where she and Mary had played hide and seek as children nor in the pigeon loft or the orchard or the stables or any other childhood haunt. After half an hour of hunting Cara decided to give him up and return to the tennis court and admit defeat. She came back from the stables – empty now save for George's massive old hunter and the ancient pony who, long ago had pulled the lawn mower – across the lawn in front of the house and found Stephen lying on his back under the walnut tree.

'I've been watching you,' he said.

'Watching me?'

'Yes. I thought you might be sent to look for me. So I watched you until I thought you'd given me up and then I flung myself in your path.'

He looked at her with his clear hazel glance.

'They sent you to look for me?'

For some reason she couldn't look back at him. She knelt on the grass some distance from him.

'Yes.'

'Which you did to be polite.'

'No.'

He rolled over suddenly onto his face and said, his voice a little muffled by the grass.

'I haven't seen you for two years.'

'Is it that long?'

'Since I was in hospital. I should know. I've counted.'

'You did see me! You came back to tea at Bishopstow, to see Mary—'

'That didn't count. I couldn't talk to you.'

'Stephen—'

'Yes,' he said, not turning over.

'What's happening? Everything is rather Alice in Wonderlandish here this afternoon, everyone seems either enigmatic or confused.'

He rolled over then and sat up.

'You really want to know?'

'Yes. I mean, if you want to tell me.'

'Of course I want to tell you! You are the only person I do want to tell. But I don't think you really care, one way or the other.'

Her hands were suddenly shaking so much she thought he must notice. She put them behind her back.

'Please tell me.'

Stephen said with a sort of angry precision, 'I made the most terrible mistake over Sarah. Because I was so absolutely not in love with her, I failed to see that she was falling in love with me. I thought she was one of those kindly, supercompetent people like the best sort of nurse, the kind that flirts with a patient simply to improve his morale. This afternoon, over coffee after lunch which we happened to be having alone together – I see the hand of contrivance in it now – she proposed to me. And I refused her. Flat. So she summoned a taxi and fled. I feel perfectly terrible that I could have let her get so far and sick with relief it's all over. At least that – that part is.'

It wasn't only Cara's hands that were shaking now. In a voice she seemed to have little control over she said,

'P-poor Sarah—'

He said, 'Why should you say that? She's not poor to you. You don't want me, you couldn't understand some lunatic who did—'

'Stephen—'

He went on angrily, 'It's all because of you. You see? I'll never be able to fall in love with anyone. I've been in love with you as long as I can remember, certainly all my adolescence and all my feelings do as time goes on, is get stronger and stronger. I know you don't give twopence for me, I know you never have. I think you

536

were sorry for me in hospital and I was so grateful for the crumbs of your pity that I used to lie there, grinning like an idiot, savouring the memory of every look, every word. But that's the warmest you've ever felt, isn't it? You don't care for me, do you, Cara, not one whit—'

'I love you,' she said.

'Even though I love you enough for both of us and then some,' he said, rushing on, not listening to her, 'You wouldn't want me even on those terms, would you? You just don't want me at all, under any circumstances. I've thought over and over again, that I've just got to live with knowing that, but it's unbearable, Cara, quite unbearable. I was so jealous of Alan I could have killed him – brother or no brother – and I ordered, yes ordered, Dick Swift not to come down here because I couldn't have borne to see you fall for him. How could I behave like that? He is one of my closest friends. He was marvellous about it. It's pathetic, isn't it, when I have no hope at all?'

'Stephen.'

'Yes,' he said.

'Would you do something for me?'

'You know I would. You know I'd do anything for you.'

'Well – it's two things actually. But you will have to come a little closer for one of them.'

He moved to kneel beside her.

'That's not really fair. You know I couldn't disobey and you're so lovely, so unutterably lovely—'

'Stephen. Shut up. That's the first thing. Shut up, just for a little while. And this is the second thing. Will you kiss me?'

'Kiss you,' he said flatly, staring.

'Yes. Kiss me—'

'But – but—'

'Heavens,' Cara said, laughing and beginning to cry, 'I shall have to do it for you – Oh Stephen, darling Stephen—'

When she took her mouth away from his, he said,

'You're shaking—'

She said unsteadily, 'I think it's love. And relief.'

'*Love?*'

She tried to disengage herself a little but he pulled her back against him, holding her hard.

'Yes. Love. I told you just now but you were in mid oratory. I love you. I've loved you – oh I suppose it might even have begun all that time ago when you came to tell me about Alan—'

'You love me? You, Cara Swinton, love *me*?'

'Yes.'

'But – Alan—'

'Oh!' she said impatiently, 'That! That was a severe case of infatuation. I think even I suspected it at the time but I knew it for certain when Alex died, when I saw the difference between losing someone you really loved and someone you merely had a crush on.'

Stephen stood up, pulling Cara with him.

'Say it again. That you love me.'

'I love you.'

'And again.'

'I love you. I love you. I love you.'

'Enough to marry me?'

'Oh yes. More than, I think.'

His smile seemed to radiate out all over him as if he were illumined from within. He bent his head and kissed her, holding her face gently between his hands, then he flung his arms around her and pulled her against him, pressing his cheek to her hair.

'I can't believe it. I simply can't. That I can hold you, kiss you—'

'I wish you would again.'

'I could eat you,' he said a little later.

She looked up at him.

'Your eyeballs are pure white again.'

'I must have looked disgusting.'

'You didn't. Only rather sad. And how I hated Sarah! Oh Stephen, you can't imagine how I did!'

He smiled.

'It's absolutely luxury for me, thinking of you being jealous of Sarah.'

'But poor Sarah, really poor Sarah.'

'Come off it,' he said, gently teasing, 'You detest her.'

She nodded, laughing. He began to kiss her lightly, her nose, and cheeks and forehead and ears.

'I've got an interview at St Bartolph's,' she said.

He stopped kissing.

'You haven't!'

'Yes, I have. I don't know if they'll have me—'

'Of course they will! So – so you meant it. What you said to me in hospital.'

'That was the beginning.'

He picked up her left hand and kissed the third finger.

'And this is ours.'

'Yes,' she said.

'This,' he said, 'This moment. It's beyond the wildest fantasising—'

'There'll be more.'

He put his arms around her again and held her there in silence.

'Stephen.'

'Mm—'

'You are supposed to be playing tennis. A men's four. To please your father. We ought to go back.'

'No.'

'Yes. Come on. We've got all our lives after tennis. Anyway—' she stopped and coloured a little, 'You ought to tell them that they're right after all.'

'Right?' he said, 'About what?'

Cara took a step away from him and held out her hand.

'Come on, Stephen! Come and tell them that it's just as they thought it was! That you *are* engaged to be married!'

Then she began to laugh and to run away from him, and he followed her across the lawn, catching her up with easy strides, towards the gate in a stone wall that led to the tennis court.

THE END

A SECOND LEGACY
by Caroline Harvey

Behind Alexia Langley stood the legacy of three remarkable and indomitable women. There was Charlotte who had survived the Afghan war in Victorian times – Alexandra who had bravely carved a life for herself on a Cornish farm – and Cara, who was Alexia's mother and who was tough and resourceful and a terrific worker on all kinds of committees.

The trouble was that Alexia, with the example of three wonderful women behind her, wasn't brave or extraordinary at all. She was nervous and shy and wasn't particularly good at anything except cooking. She was totally unsuited for the free-wheeling world of the 60s, and when Martin Angus made a bee-line for her she let herself fall wildly and gratefully in love. At last someone really liked her, in spite of what she was.

It took just over a year for her to discover his betrayal – for her to realise that from now on she had to fight, for herself, her future, and the future of her child. With a legacy of her own, a crumbling castle in Scotland, she began to build a new life, shared at first only with little Carly, then at last with someone she could trust.

It was Carly, her small daughter, who was to bring the legacy of love full circle – back to Afghanistan – where the story had begun so many years before . . .

Caroline Harvey is the pseudonym of the award-winning writer Joanna Trollope.

0 552 13917 3

PARSON HARDING'S DAUGHTER
by Caroline Harvey

The Reverend Henry Harding, parson to the excellent living of Stoke Abbas, was a handsome and prepossessing man. Unfortunately fate had seen fit to bless him with a family of extremely plain and unprepossessing children. Caroline was the least offensively plain according to Lady Lennox, but the entire Lennox family also admitted that Caroline was the most insignificant person in the county of Dorset.

Caroline, already twenty-six, was bullied by her elder sister, was nervous in company, and had no prospects at all. She had one golden memory, of an admirer when she was eighteen, but John Gates, nephew to the Lennox family, had gone to India and forgotten her. Or so she thought.

When Lady Lennox summoned her and said that Johnny Gates had sent a proposal of marriage, Caroline at first declined. She suspected that somehow Lady Lennox – for reasons of her own – had contrived and pressured her erstwhile suitor into proposing. But within a few short weeks tragedy had overtaken Caroline. The little contentment and security she had known vanished from her life and left her no option but to accept Lady Lennox's offer.

In the October of 1776, Caroline Harding set sail for India, to a new life, and a man she had not seen for eight years.

Caroline Harvey is the pseudonym of the award-winning writer Joanna Trollope.

0 552 14299 9

THE STEPS OF THE SUN
by Caroline Harvey

1899 – As the rumblings of dissent and racial resentment began to erupt into a savage war between Boer and Briton, so three young men found their lives drawn together.

Matthew Paget, son of an archdeacon, was turbulent, rebellious, and longing for excitement. Throwing away all the privileges that could have been his, he enlisted as a trooper – only to find himself loving the beautiful, war-torn country of Africa and finally falling in love with a girl on the enemy side.

Will Marriott, his cousin, was an officer who believed in England's greatness and the glory of battle. But as his comrades were maimed and killed, as he himself was wounded, and then betrayed by a one-time friend, so his values began to change. The one thing that never changed was his love for Frances, Matthew Paget's sister.

Hendon Bashford was an upstart social climber, a swindler and a cheat. Half English, half Boer, he owed allegiance to no one while creating havoc in the lives of more honourable men.

As the passage of war unfolded, so the lives of these three young men, and the women they loved, moved towards a tumultuous climax.

Caroline Harvey is the pseudonym of the award-winning writer Joanna Trollope.

0 552 14407 X

A SELECTED LIST OF FINE NOVELS
AVAILABLE FROM CORGI AND BLACK SWAN

THE PRICES SHOWN BELOW WERE CORRECT AT THE TIME OF GOING
TO PRESS. HOWEVER TRANSWORLD PUBLISHERS RESERVE THE RIGHT
TO SHOW NEW RETAIL PRICES ON COVERS WHICH MAY DIFFER FROM
THOSE PREVIOUSLY ADVERTISED IN THE TEXT OR ELSEWHERE.

☐	13313 2	CATCH THE WIND	Frances Donnelly	£5.99
☐	14442 8	JUST LIKE A WOMAN	Jill Gascoine	£5.99
☐	14096 1	THE WILD SEED	Iris Gower	£5.99
☐	14537 8	APPLE BLOSSOM TIME	Kathryn Haig	£5.99
☐	14566 1	THE DREAM SELLERS	Ruth Hamilton	£5.99
☐	13917 3	A SECOND LEGACY	Caroline Harvey	£5.99
☐	14299 9	PARSON HARDING'S DAUGHTER	Caroline Harvey	£5.99
☐	14407 X	THE STEPS OF THE SUN	Caroline Harvey	£5.99
☐	14529 7	LEAVES FROM THE VALLEY	Caroline Harvey	£5.99
☐	14553 X	THE BRASS DOLPHIN	Caroline Harvey	£5.99
☐	99694 7	DROWNING IN HONEY	Kate Hatfield	£6.99
☐	14535 1	THE HELMINGHAM ROSE	Joan Hessayon	£5.99
☐	14333 2	SOME OLD LOVER'S GHOST	Judith Lennox	£5.99
☐	14320 0	MARGUERITE	Elisabeth Luard	£5.99
☐	13910 6	BLUEBIRDS	Margaret Pemberton	£5.99
☐	14499 1	THESE FOOLISH THINGS	Imogen Parker	£5.99
☐	13904 1	VOICES OF SUMMER	Diane Pearson	£4.99
☐	14124 0	MAGNOLIA SQUARE	Margaret Pemberton	£4.99
☐	14577 7	PORTRAIT OF CHLOE	Elvi Rhodes	£5.99
☐	14549 1	CHOICES	Susan Sallis	£5.99
☐	14554 8	THE FAMILY AT WAR	Mary Jane Staples	£5.99
☐	99494 4	THE CHOIR	Joanna Trollope	£6.99
☐	99410 3	A VILLAGE AFFAIR	Joanna Trollope	£6.99
☐	99442 1	A PASSIONATE MAN	Joanna Trollope	£6.99
☐	99470 7	THE RECTOR'S WIFE	Joanna Trollope	£6.99
☐	99492 8	THE MEN AND THE GIRLS	Joanna Trollope	£6.99
☐	99549 5	A SPANISH LOVER	Joanna Trollope	£6.99
☐	99643 2	THE BEST OF FRIENDS	Joanna Trollope	£6.99
☐	99700 5	NEXT OF KIN	Joanna Trollope	£6.99
☐	14118 6	THE HUNGRY TIDE	Valerie Wood	£5.99

All Transworld titles are available by post from:

Book Service By Post, P.O. Box 29, Douglas, Isle of Man IM99 1BQ

Credit cards accepted. Please telephone 01624 675137,
fax 01624 670923, Internet http://www.bookpost.co.uk or
e-mail: bookshop@enterprise.net for details.

Free postage and packing in the UK. Overseas customers allow
£1 per book (paperbacks) and £3 per book (hardbacks).